Books by Anna Bradley

LADY ELEANOR'S SEVENTH SUITOR
LADY CHARLOTTE'S FIRST LOVE
TWELFTH NIGHT WITH THE EARL
MORE OR LESS A MARCHIONESS
MORE OR LESS A COUNTESS
MORE OR LESS A TEMPTRESS
THE WAYWARD BRIDE
TO WED A WILD SCOT
FOR THE SAKE OF A SCOTTISH RAKE
THE VIRGIN WHO RUINED LORD GRAY
THE VIRGIN WHO VINDICATED LORD DARLINGTON

Published by Kensington Publishing Corp.

The Virgin Who Vindicated Lord Darlington

Anna Bradley

LYRICAL PRESS
Kensington Publishing Corp.
www.kensingtonbooks.com

LYRICAL PRESS BOOKS are published by
Kensington Publishing Corp.
119 West 40th Street
New York, NY 10018

All Kensington titles, imprints, and distributed lines are available at special quantity discounts for bulk purchases for sales promotion, premiums, fund-raising, educational, or institutional use.

Special book excerpts or customized printings can also be created to fit specific needs. For details, write or phone the office of the Kensington Sales Manager: Kensington Publishing Corp., 119 West 40th Street, New York, NY 10018. Attn. Sales Department. Phone: 1-800-221-2647.

Lyrical Press and Lyrical Press logo Reg. U.S. Pat. & TM Off.

First Electronic Edition: February 2021
ISBN-13: 978-1-5161-1038-4 (ebook)
ISBN-10: 1-5161-1038-2 (ebook)

First Print Edition: February 2021
ISBN-13: 978-1-5161-1042-1
ISBN-10: 1-5161-1042-0

Printed in the United States of America

"We're all ghosts. We all carry, inside us, people who came before us." –Liam Callanan

Prologue

White Friars Dock, London
April, 1779

Cecilia Gilchrist was the second.

Lady Amanda Clifford could no longer recall what had brought her to the docks that day. It was, she would later reflect, one of those peculiar cases where fate, generally content to let one stumble blindly along, had deigned, for good or for ill, to put her directly in the way of her destiny.

Face to face, as it were.

At the time, she'd been of the mind fate had done Cecilia Gilchrist a good turn, throwing the child into Lady Amanda's path as she'd done. It wasn't until later she came to understand it had been quite the other way around.

Cecilia Gilchrist, who'd been mudlarking in the Thames that day, had had the great good luck to find a guinea buried in the filth. For a grimy little waif like Cecilia Gilchrist it was a fortune, the gold coin clutched in her fist the difference between starvation and salvation.

But fortunes were as fickle a business as fate, both being apt to turn catastrophic in the blink of an eye, or the flip of a golden guinea.

Thus it was with Cecilia Gilchrist. No sooner had she wrapped her thin fingers around her salvation than her luck turned. When Lady Amanda came upon the child, she'd been set upon by a horde of rioting street urchins, a veritable mob of diminutive rabble-rousers, all of them pleased to pummel her into a bloody pulp in order to snatch the guinea from her fist.

Lady Clifford's servant, Daniel Brixton, a man indifferent to fate and fortune alike, made quick work of deciding both. He tossed aside a half-dozen of the miniature ruffians, seized the scrawny, mud-streaked waif at the center of the melee, and deposited her on the gray velvet seat of Lady Amanda's carriage.

Lady Amanda could no more recall what she'd said to the child that day than she could recall what errand had taken her to the docks—likely something about the tediousness of the masses, the capriciousness of fate, or the wickedness of children—but she recalled with perfect clarity Cecilia Gilchrist's response.

She said, "They're hungry."

Not a trace of resentment in that childish voice. No bitterness. No judgment. *They're hungry.* That was all.

Lady Amanda Clifford would still hear the echo of that sweet voice decades later, a reminder of how easy it was—how unforgivably, criminally easy—to overlook a precious flicker of gold hidden in an ocean of mud.

Chapter One

Edenbridge, Kent
February, 1795

If the day had been a less pleasant one, or the Marquess of Darlington a less striking gentleman, Cecilia Gilchrist might have concluded at once that he was a murderer.

As it happened, the first time she laid eyes on Lord Darlington was one of those mild, sunny days, so rare in February, and his lordship showed to great advantage in his smart blue coat and flawlessly polished Hessians. To be fair, he'd been quite a distance away from her that day, and she'd been safely concealed behind one of Hyde Park's more extravagant shrubs at the time.

But proximity to a man suspected of murdering his wife being, alas, what it was, Cecilia came to quite a different conclusion upon her second meeting with Lord Darlington.

That day began auspiciously enough. The stagecoach made good time from London, and Edenbridge, home to Darlington Castle, seemed the last place a villain might be tempted to commit a murder. It was as lovely a little village as Kent could boast, with its row of squat timber-framed buildings with cheerful flower boxes in every window. The boxes were empty now, it being wintertime, but the prospect of cheerful flowers was enough to reassure Cecilia.

Surely there could be no question of a marquess committing a heinous crime like murder in a village with such an abundance of flower boxes?

A pretty country hamlet, then, with its own sweet little river to the southeast, nestled in its own sweet little valley, and boasting a rather distinguished-looking church with its own stained-glass window. Cecilia's companion on the stagecoach, a young lady named Molly who was about her age and who'd grown up in Edenbridge, told her the church was called St. Peter's and St. Paul's.

Two saints. Surely there could be no question of a marquess committing a heinous crime like murder in a village with two saints?

Edenbridge was a mere twenty-five miles from London, too, a half-day's journey from Cecilia's home at the Clifford School, and thus within easy reach of Daniel Brixton, Lady Clifford's most trusted servant, and the biggest man Cecilia had ever seen.

Should anything go wrong, Daniel could be at her side in a matter of hours. Nothing *would* go wrong, of course, yet it comforted her nonetheless he should be so near, and so reassuringly large.

Why, half a day was nothing, a pittance, an instant, a snap of the fingers—

"Beg pardon, Cecilia. Did ye say something?"

Cecilia turned to find her new acquaintance regarding her with a puzzled look. Molly was her one and only friend in Edenbridge, and it wouldn't do to frighten her away by muttering to herself like a Bedlamite. "No, I…I was just saying it's taking ages for our driver to hand down our baggage."

Molly's broad face split into a grin. "Anxious to get on, are ye? Ye never did say what brings ye to Kent. Do ye have a sweetheart here?"

Cecilia smothered a snort. The closest she'd ever come to having a sweetheart was an infatuation with Valancourt, the hero of Mrs. Radcliffe's *The Mysteries of Udolpho.* "No, no, nothing like that. I've come to take up a post as a housemaid."

Housemaid, investigator, spy—weren't they all just varying degrees of the same thing?

Molly gave Cecilia a doubtful look. "Ye look a bit dainty to be a housemaid, but no matter." She nodded at their stagecoach driver, who'd climbed onto the roof and was handing the baggage down. They hurried to retrieve their things, then stepped aside as the other passengers pressed forward. "My father's coming here to fetch me. Mayhap he can take ye where yer going, to save ye the walk."

"Oh, that's kind of you. I'm going to Darlington Castle."

A gasp arose from the small knot of travelers nearby. The coachman froze, a trunk tumbling from his hands and landing with a thump in the frozen dirt below. Cecilia glanced behind her at the scuffle of shuffling feet, and found her fellow travelers had backed away from her, as if she were tainted.

Molly stared at her, aghast. "Darlington Castle? Ye mean ye're going to serve as housemaid for *Lord Darlington*?"

Cecilia gulped as her gaze shifted from one horrified face to the next. "Er, yes. I—"

"But he's a murderer!" Molly patted her chest, as if the very mention of Lord Darlington was giving her palpitations. "Did away with his wife, didn't he?"

"There's no proof he—"

The lady beside her silenced her with a hiss. "Don't be daft, girl. Everyone in England knows he did away with his wife."

A murmur of assent rose from the crowd, and a craggy-faced man stepped forward and shook his finger in Cecilia's face. "Sent her off to an early grave. Make no mistake about it, miss. He's the Murderous Marquess, sure as I'm standing here."

Cecilia pressed her lips together. They called him the Murderous Marquess here in Edenbridge, as well? She'd thought the nickname an invention of the *ton*, but it seemed folks here were quite as capable of being horrible as those in London were.

Perhaps Lord Darlington *was* a murderer, and perhaps he wasn't. Lady Clifford had tasked Cecilia with unraveling that particular mystery while his lordship was in London with his betrothed, Miss Fanny Honeywell. Cecilia had seen him there herself just yesterday, walking in Hyde Park with Miss Honeywell on his arm.

For her part, Cecilia didn't think he looked much like a murderer. Given the gossip about him, she'd been expecting a sinister, monster of a man, but if Lord Darlington had committed the wicked deeds he was rumored to have done, his sins didn't show on his face.

Even her friend Georgiana, who knew a great deal more about sins and murder than Cecilia did, had admitted that if Lord Darlington *was* a murderer, he was an exceedingly elegant one. Of course, Georgiana had also pointed out a handsome gentleman in a fine silk waistcoat was as likely to murder his wife as any other. More so, really, as people were quicker to condemn a plain face than a pretty one.

But it wasn't his handsome face that inclined Cecilia in his favor. No, it was the protectiveness with which he held Miss Honeywell's arm, his head bent graciously toward hers as he guided her over the uneven pathway. He was a large man, far larger than Fanny Honeywell, who was a petite, fair-haired creature, and he handled her with great care, as if she were a delicate china figurine on the verge of shattering.

Try as she might, Cecilia couldn't imagine so civilized a gentleman would murder his wife, not even when Georgiana reminded her the notorious highwayman John Rann was thought to be quite charming and elegant, and his neck had still been fitted for a noose.

Cecilia hadn't argued the point with Georgiana. She knew herself to be too soft-hearted by half, and too apt to think the best of everyone, including the murderous—that is, including Lord Darlington—But there was no proof he was a murderer. Just ugly gossip, never in short supply in London.

Lady Clifford might have been content enough to leave him alone to molder away in his castle if his betrothed, Miss Honeywell, hadn't been niece to Mrs. Abernathy, and Mrs. Abernathy a generous benefactor of the Clifford School. But poor Mrs. Abernathy had fallen into a hysterical fit when the betrothal was announced, and Lady Clifford had been obliged to promise she wouldn't allow Miss Honeywell to toddle off to her doom without lifting a finger on her behalf.

"Some say as he smothered her with a pillow." Molly drew closer to Cecilia and lowered her voice to a horrified whisper. "Others say he poisoned her and hid her poor murdered bones in the castle walls, but I think he drowned her in his moat."

Cecilia shuddered. "Heavens, how vile!"

"I don't know for sure he done that, mind, but he's done something with her, and I don't see why he'd bother digging about the castle walls when he has a moat. I can't speak to that for sure, but I can tell ye this much—there's not a soul in Edenbridge who saw the poor lady put proper-like into her grave."

"Aye, he's a murderer, all right," said the man with the waggling finger. "But the good Lord sees our sins, and Darlington won't get away with his wicked deeds. The marchioness is back again, come to take her revenge."

"Back?" How could the Marchioness of Darlington be *back*? There were plenty of rumors about Lady Darlington's death flying about, but no one seemed to doubt she *was*, in fact, dead. So, how could she come back to take her revenge?

Unless...

A chill rushed over Cecilia's skin. "You can't mean—"

"That the poor marchioness as was is now a lonely, wandering spirit? Aye, miss. That's what I mean. Half a dozen people in the village have seen her ghost drifting through the woods behind Darlington Castle. They call her the White Lady, on account of her white gown and hair, and a face paler than death itself."

Cecilia's mouth dropped open. No wife wished to be consigned to the murky depths of her husband's moat, but at least then she could rest peacefully. It struck Cecilia as dreadfully unfair a murdered wife should be put to the trouble of haunting the husband who'd murdered her.

"A ghastly sight she is, floating in the air, with only the toes of her white slippers dragging over the ground. Old Mrs. Crocker saw her t'other night, and she's been in a hysterical fit ever since."

"A hysterical fit?"

"I've never known Mrs. Crocker to be silent a day in her life, but not a word has crossed her lips since she saw that ghost. She sits and stares, her mouth frozen open in horror."

"Ye don't have to go there, Miss Cecilia." Molly clutched at Cecilia's arm. "Ye can go back to London right now, and never spare Darlington Castle another glance."

Cecilia cast a longing look at the stagecoach driver. She could be back in London in a matter of hours, back at the Clifford School where her friends would welcome her with smothering kisses and squeals of delight, and she'd be petted and soothed until she forgot the cowardice that made her break her word to Lady Clifford.

She might have done it—she might have let her misgivings get the better of her, despite her best efforts. Indeed, she'd actually taken a step toward the stagecoach when it occurred to her that nothing material had changed since she'd boarded the stagecoach in London.

Moats, and skeletons hidden in the castle walls, ghosts and hauntings—it was just more gossip, much the same as the gossip she'd heard in London. More lurid, yes, but still gossip, nonetheless.

Ghostly rumors or not, her task was to discover the truth about the marchioness's death, and Lady Darlington was, alas, as dead as she'd ever been.

Or undead, if the villagers had the right of it, but Darlington Castle might be stuffed to the rafters with frightening ghouls, and Lord Darlington the fiend all of England supposed him to be, but she *would* keep her promise, even if it meant she ended her days floating face-down in the Murderous Marquess's moat.

"No, that won't do, Molly." Cecilia bent to grasp the handle of her case, then straightened and met Molly's eyes. "I've already accepted the post. Mrs. Briggs, Lord Darlington's housekeeper, is expecting me."

It was too late to turn back now. Lady Clifford had gone to a good deal of trouble to see this thing arranged, and in any case, Cecilia's business was with Lord Darlington's servants. If his lordship had any secrets to hide, his servants would know them. Her task was to shake those secrets loose, then return to London without ever crossing paths with Lord Darlington at all.

Molly didn't look convinced, but she didn't argue. "All right, then. My father won't set foot on Darlington Castle's grounds, but we'll take ye as far as we can in the wagon."

"Thank you." Cecilia reached for Molly's hand and gave it a grateful squeeze.

Molly shook her head. "I hope ye don't live to regret it, Miss Cecilia." *What an unfortunate choice of words.*

Cecilia hoped she *did* live to regret it, but she didn't give voice to the insidious whisper inside her head. Instead she followed Molly across the street toward the knot of wagons and carts, dragging her case along behind her.

* * * *

Dusk came upon them quickly, as it tended to do during wintertime in England, but there was enough light for Cecilia to make out Darlington Castle in all its distressing, blood-curdling glory.

God in Heaven. She didn't believe in ghosts, but if any stray phantoms or wraiths *did* happen to be floating about in the February mists, *this* was the castle they'd choose to haunt.

"Grim old pile, innit it?" Molly, who was seated on the far side of the wagon, leaned across Cecilia to get a better look.

"Grim enough. The portcullis looks as if it might eat one alive." Cecilia gaped at the monstrosity sprawled out before her, and a shiver darted down her spine. She wished with all her heart she was exaggerating, but that portcullis looked like nothing so much as a set of gaping jaws, the pointed iron teeth lined up in a row across the bottom of the latticed grill. If looked as if it were just waiting to snap closed on anyone foolish enough to venture beneath it.

If the first portcullis didn't sever limb from body, the second one surely would, because if the blackened stone and shadowy courtyard beyond that gaping maw weren't sinister enough, Darlington Castle had a *double* portcullis.

A double moat, as well.

The Marquess of Darlington was not, it seemed, the trusting sort, but then if the rumors about him were true, he had a great deal to hide.

"How deep is the moat, do you suppose?" Cecilia fought to suppress another shudder as her gaze fell on the dark, sluggish water under the drawbridge. God only knew what nightmares were lurking in those dreary depths.

Deep enough to hide a body? The Marchioness of Darlington's body, for instance?

"Not more than a fathom," said Mr. Hinshaw, Molly's father.

Only a fathom? That wasn't so very deep. Certainly not deep enough to hide a—

"Darlington Lake is said to be much deeper," he added, before Cecilia had a chance to breathe a sigh of relief. "But I couldn't tell ye how deep."

There was a lake, as well? How many bodies of water did one marquess need?

One for every wife he murders.

Cecilia swallowed, cursing her penchant for gothic horror novels, which had been all very well until she'd stumbled into one.

Molly covered Cecilia's hand with hers. "It's not too late to change yer mind."

Cecilia cast one last fearful look at the wide, yawning jaws guarding the cavernous courtyard beyond, straightened her shoulders, and, with a bravado she was far from feeling, stuck her chin in the air. "No, no. I've given my word, and I won't turn coward now."

Mr. Hinshaw and Molly glanced at each other, but Mr. Hinshaw came down from his seat, retrieved Cecilia's case from the back of the wagon, and reached up to help her down. "We'll wait until you're inside. If ye do change your mind beforehand—"

"That's kind of you, Mr. Hinshaw, but please don't wait on my account." Cecilia could see the man wished himself and his daughter far away from here, and in any case, she might lose her nerve and flee Darlington Castle if she knew she had such a ready escape.

She took the hand Mr. Hinshaw offered before she could change her mind, leaving the safety of the wagon behind, and paused at the long stone bridge leading onto Lord Darlington's property.

Mr. Hinshaw handed over her case. "We won't go until you're past the portcullis, leastways."

"To make certain it doesn't devour me?" Cecilia attempted a smile as her nerveless fingers wrapped around the handle of her case. "Well, then I'd best get on with it, hadn't I?" She waved to Molly and Mr. Hinshaw, then stepped forward. The heel of her boot struck the wooden boards of the bridge with a hollow thump.

It didn't feel like a single step so much as a leap into the unknown, but Cecilia continued to put one foot in front of the other until she was standing at the edge of a second bridge—this one the narrow footbridge that led to the portcullis.

She allowed herself one glance over her shoulder, but the wagon was hidden behind the tall, thick hedge that surrounded the castle grounds. After a single wary glance at the iron teeth above, Cecilia stepped onto the drawbridge. She took one step, another, looking neither to the right or left, her gaze focused on the tips of her boots.

Don't look at the moat.

Another step, another, until she passed through the darkened courtyard and into another world.

Chapter Two

The frozen leaves crunched under Gideon's feet as he broke through the tree line and strode onto the formal castle grounds.

Dusk was descending, throwing gloomy shadows across the gardens and the rose walk, but it wasn't yet dark. The dying glimmers of a pale winter sun caught at the rippling surface of Darlington Lake. Beside it he could just make out the gray stones of the courtyard. Darlington Castle itself loomed over the scene like a hulking beast, casting everything it touched into darkness.

It looks like a nightmare.

He hadn't always thought so. There'd been a time not long ago he'd thought of the castle as his home, but one nightmare had toppled into another this past year, like a row of cursed dominoes, and Darlington Castle had somehow tipped over into the chasm.

This time, the nightmare was ghosts. And why not? Once a lady's tragic death became a murder and her husband a murderer, a vengeful ghost made sense, the inevitable next step from one nightmare into the next. He'd say this much for the villagers of Edenbridge—they kept their rumors in the proper order.

Gideon didn't believe in ghosts...or, no. It was more truthful to say he hadn't given ghosts any thought at all, other than to consider phantoms, specters, and disembodied spirits figments of fevered imaginations only, an invention of harassed nursemaids and exhausted governesses, meant to frighten children into obedience.

Now, well...he still didn't believe in ghosts. Even if he *had* given the ghostly rumors any credence, he wouldn't have concerned himself much with them. The undead were far less terrifying than the living, and ghosts not the worst of the horrors that could haunt a man.

As for the White Lady, in her flowing white gown, with her pale face and trailing locks of white hair, she was nowhere to be seen tonight. Perhaps she'd chosen another castle to haunt.

Gideon's lips curled in a bitter smile. Not that it would make any difference. The rumors would persist, regardless of whether the ghost ever appeared again. The White Lady was simply too delicious a tale for the villagers to relinquish her easily. There would be more sightings of this terrifying apparition who'd taken up residence in the woods behind Darlington Castle.

She was said to be colorless aside from her lips, which were a ghastly shade of scarlet red. Indeed, she'd been described in excruciating detail, even by those who claimed to have been struck senseless with terror upon seeing her. With such vivid detail, even the good citizens of Edenbridge who were inclined to doubt the existence of ghosts were convinced Gideon's dead wife was haunting their village. They said she'd come to take her revenge on him—to make the Murderous Marquess pay for his monstrous crimes.

After all, *someone* had to.

Half the village had reported seeing her—the more fanciful half. Others claimed they'd seen a mysterious light bobbing amongst the trees. Gideon would have dismissed this as another rumor if his housekeeper, Mrs. Briggs, hadn't confessed she'd seen the same strange light herself, as if someone were wandering through the woods behind the castle with a lantern.

Poachers, most likely, or pranksters intent on reviving the worst of the rumors and frightening his betrothed away. It wouldn't work. Gideon had gone to a good deal of trouble to secure a proper mother for his four-year old niece, and he didn't intend to give her up now.

After his prolonged absence from society and the ugly rumors attached to his name, he hadn't expected London's belles would be waiting breathlessly to receive his attentions. He was made to understand by their frigid glares and malicious whispers that most of the *ton* thought him guilty, but he *was* still a wealthy marquess, and there were those who were willing to overlook the rumors in favor of a title and fortune.

In the end, Gideon had secured his bride.

After more than a year of turmoil and grief, Miss Honeywell was like a sip of the finest champagne trickling down a raw, parched throat—light, sweet, and bubbly. If it was difficult to recall the taste once the bubbles had dissolved on his tongue…well, it hardly mattered. He wasn't interested in a grand passion, and he didn't believe in fairy tales, any more than he believed in ghosts.

Miss Honeywell was a beauty. If she'd had a title or a fortune or a less vulgar mother, she might have been considered a diamond of the first water, but he hadn't chosen her for her pretty face. She appealed to him because she wasn't a demanding young lady, or a complicated one. Her disposition was as bright and sunny as her hair, and she had a sweet, guileless smile. She'd be an affectionate mother to his niece Isabella, and that was all Gideon cared about now.

So, at the end of the next fortnight, Miss Honeywell would become the Marchioness of Darlington, much to her mother's delight. Mrs. Honeywell was happy enough to overlook a murder accusation if it meant acquiring a marquess as her son-in-law.

He and Miss Honeywell would wed in the chapel at Darlington Castle, just as every Marquess of Darlington before him had done. But first he had a vengeful ghost to exorcise, unless he wished to bring his new bride home to a haunted castle.

Gideon drew in a deep breath of the frigid air as he passed through the formal gardens and approached the courtyard. The cold was sinking into his bones. The darkness was deep and penetrating, bleak in the way only wintertime in England could be, silent but for the murmur of water washing over the worn stones—

Plop.

What the devil? Gideon paused mid-stride, his eyebrow arching.

Plop.

Had he imagined the sound? He went still, listening.

Plop. Then again, a moment later, louder this time…

Splash.

He caught a movement in the darkness ahead, the arc of an arm, a flash of pale skin. A figure, too slight to be anything other than a woman, was poised at the edge of the stairway leading into the courtyard, tossing something into Darlington Lake.

She wasn't one of his servants. Those who hadn't abandoned him over the murder accusations had fled when a ghost descended on the castle. He'd recognize those who'd remained with him, and he didn't recognize *her.*

This lady was dressed in a plain, dark traveling cloak, not a white gown, and her hair…well, Gideon didn't have the faintest idea about her hair because it was hidden under her hat, but he didn't see any trailing white tresses.

Either he had a second ghost—the Dark Lady, perhaps—or else a strange woman had wandered onto his property to assault his lake. Given the choice, Gideon would have taken the ghost. He didn't care for spirits, but he cared even less for strangers. "Who the devil are *you*?"

She whirled around to face him, a gasp on her lips. She'd been holding something in her hand, but in her fright she let go, and it scattered at her feet. "I-I beg your..." she began, but her words trailed off into a choked whimper when she saw his face.

She wasn't the first woman who'd shrunk from him in horror, but she was standing in front of *his* castle, beside *his* lake, on *his* grounds. Was he not to be allowed any peace at all, even in his own home? "You may beg all you like, but do it somewhere else."

His voice was as icy as the bitter wind blowing off the lake. It wasn't the sort of gentlemanly greeting that befitted a marquess, but he wasn't obliged to be courteous to dim-witted chits sneaking about his property. Given the hostility he'd experienced at the hands of the villagers, the girl was fortunate not to find herself on the other end of his pistol.

Her throat worked for some moments before she managed to produce anything coherent. "But I-I'm Cecilia Gilchrist."

Coherent, yes, but not illuminating. "Very well, Cecilia Gilchrist. Get the hell off my property."

Her eyes went wide, but to his surprise, instead of scurrying off like a frightened rabbit, Cecilia Gilchrist held her ground. "But I...I'm supposed to be here. Mrs. Briggs is expecting me."

He eyed her with suspicion. She wouldn't know Mrs. Briggs's name if his housekeeper wasn't expecting her, but why was she creeping about his courtyard like a thief? "Am I meant to know who you are?"

"Yes. I mean, no. I mean, not if you don't choose to. That is, I suppose you may do whatever you please, being the marquess." She offered him a tentative smile. "Unless of course there happens to be a duke about?"

Gideon didn't smile back. Was she *teasing* him? No one teased him. Not anymore.

He crossed his arms over his chest. "Why? Are you a duchess?"

"Goodness, no. I'm just a housemaid." She laughed, a light, tinkling sound, but then seemed to think better of it, and bit her lip. "Your housekeeper, Mrs. Briggs offered me a position as a housemaid. I've come on the stage from London today to take up the post."

Gideon's gaze moved over her as he considered this. She didn't look much like a housemaid to him. She was taller than he'd first thought, but slight, with narrow shoulders, a long, delicate neck, and enormous dark eyes in a pale oval face. She was young, too. Too young to be teasing a murderous marquess. Didn't the girl have any sense at all?

"If you came to Darlington Castle to take up a post as a housemaid, then why haven't you made your presence known to Mrs. Briggs? I fail to see what you're doing out here in the dark." Gideon frowned as he recalled the splash he'd heard as he approached. "What *are* you doing out here in the dark?"

Color rose in her pale cheeks. "Nothing of any import, my lord."

Gideon's lips tightened. She didn't *sound* much like a housemaid, either, unless they'd become a great deal more impertinent than they used to be. He glanced down, then bent to retrieve the handful of stones she'd dropped when he'd startled her. He rose and opened his hand to show her. "Nothing?"

She blew out a breath. "I was, er...throwing stones into the lake."

Gideon stared at her. "I can't think of a single reason why you'd be doing that, when you must be aware Mrs. Briggs is awaiting your arrival."

"I wanted to see if I could tell how deep it is." She lifted one slender shoulder in a shrug.

"Six fathoms at its deepest point, though I've no idea why it should matter to *you*."

She blinked at his curt tone. "I...it doesn't matter, my lord. I was simply curious."

He closed his fingers around the stones in his fist. "Curiosity isn't a desirable quality in a housemaid."

"No, I suppose not. I didn't think of that." She frowned, considering it, but then her face brightened. "I've got excellent aim. Perhaps that might prove a useful skill?"

Gideon didn't like strangers, or impertinent servants, or surprises, but to his great annoyance, he found himself asking, "For what, precisely?"

"I should think it would come in handy for any number of tasks, like..." She paused, her brow wrinkling. "Wait, I know! For slapping cobwebs from the corners with a broom! This castle looks as if it's dripping in cobwebs."

"You're too slight to be a proper servant." Her thin, white wrists looked as if they'd snap under the weight of a broom. "I doubt you could lift a coal scuttle without toppling over."

Gideon didn't usually concern himself with the sturdiness of his housemaids, nor was he in the habit of questioning Mrs. Briggs's judgment, but he was curious to hear what she'd say in reply, and it had been a long, long time since he'd been curious about anything.

Her smile faded. "I'm stronger than I look, my lord."

Gideon grunted, thinking whatever she lacked in strength she'd likely make up for in ingenuity, but he didn't say so. It sounded too much like a compliment. "Mrs. Briggs didn't say a word to me about a new housemaid arriving today."

He didn't mention he'd hardly exchanged a dozen words with Mrs. Briggs since he'd arrived from London this afternoon. There hadn't been time. He'd been impatient to begin a search of the grounds, and Mrs. Briggs, who hadn't been expecting him to return to Kent until next week, was up to her neck in wedding preparations.

He'd intended to remain in London with Miss Honeywell for another week, but his friend Lord Haslemere, who'd spent most of the winter rusticating at his country estate in Surrey, had heard the rumors about the White Lady and sent Gideon a note, warning him a ghost was prowling about his castle, and calling him back to Kent.

"I assure you, Mrs. Briggs is expecting me today, my lord." Miss Gilchrist's chin hitched up. She was doing her best to brazen it out, but she was beginning to look as if she'd rather plunge into Darlington Lake than spend another moment with *him*.

Gideon couldn't blame her, really. Housemaid or not, no young woman wanted to be trapped alone in the dark between the Murderous Marquess and his enormous, haunted castle.

"Mrs. Briggs is expecting *someone*." He doubted it was this peculiar young woman who didn't look or speak like any servant he'd ever seen, and who'd appeared out of nowhere to throw stones into his lake. Still, she was here, and Mrs. Briggs needed the help. "Very well, Miss Gilchrist." Gideon beckoned her forward with a sigh. "Come with me."

"Yes, my lord." She took up the traveling case at her feet, and followed him through the arched doorway on one side of the courtyard and into the long, narrow entrance hall.

"This way," he said, when she paused to take in the timbered ceiling and carved wood paneling on the walls. He led her down a corridor off the entry hall to his study, which was tucked into a back corner of the castle.

"Sit down." Gideon waved her to a chair near his massive carved mahogany desk, then crossed the room to pull the bell and summon Mrs. Briggs.

He seated himself behind the desk and rested his elbows on the arms of his chair. Neither of them said a word as they waited, each staring at the other until Mrs. Briggs tapped her knuckles against the door. "Yes, Lord Darlington?"

"Mrs. Briggs. Come in, please. Cecilia Gilchrist, the new housemaid, has arrived."

"Yes, of course. With one thing and another, I nearly forgot." Mrs. Briggs hurried across the room and held out her hand to Cecilia. "My goodness, you're a tiny bit of a thing, aren't you? Welcome, welcome. I'm Mrs. Briggs, the housekeeper."

Miss Gilchrist rose and dipped into a hasty curtsy. "How do you do, Mrs. Briggs?"

"Very well, very well indeed. Sit down, child."

Miss Gilchrist sat down.

"I'm relieved you're here at last," Mrs. Briggs went on. "I expected you an hour ago. I thought perhaps you'd changed your mind about accepting the post when..." Mrs. Briggs trailed off, and an awkward silence descended.

There was only one reason Miss Gilchrist would have changed her mind about the post. Mrs. Briggs had told him their last prospective housemaid had arrived in Edenbridge, heard the rumors about the Darlington Castle ghost, and turned right back around, leaving that same day.

"But here you are," Mrs. Briggs went on with a bright smile. "Not a moment too soon, too. We dearly need the help to ready the house for Lord Darlington's bride."

"I'm, ah...pleased to be here, Mrs. Briggs. I've brought my reference from Lady Dunton, as promised." Miss Gilchrist reached into her reticule, withdrew a paper, and handed it to Mrs. Briggs.

"Ah, yes." Mrs. Briggs turned to Gideon. "Miss Gilchrist comes with excellent references from Lady Dunton, my lord. She worked for eleven years as an upstairs maid at Lady Dunton's country estate in Stoneleigh, near Coventry."

"Did she, indeed?" he asked in surprise. Miss Gilchrist had the bearing and speech of a Londoner.

"Oh, yes." Mrs. Briggs beamed at Miss Gilchrist. "I daresay she'll be a great help to us here."

He held out his hand. "May I see the reference?"

"Yes, of course, my lord." Mrs. Briggs handed him the paper.

Gideon read the page over carefully, paying particular attention to the date and Lady Dunton's signature. It looked authentic enough, but he wasn't satisfied. He tossed the letter onto his desk. "Forgive me, Miss Gilchrist, but you look quite young. At what age did you go into service?"

"Twelve, my lord."

"Then you're three and twenty?"

"Yes, my lord. Three and twenty."

Gideon steepled his fingers under his chin, his eyes narrowing on the wash of color rising from her neck to her cheeks. Either Miss Gilchrist didn't like to own her age, which was unlikely for a woman of three and twenty, or she was lying to him, and doing a poor job of it. "You don't look to be older than nineteen or twenty, Miss Gilchrist."

"Um...thank you, my lord?"

Despite himself, Gideon's lips twitched. "Were you raised in Stoneleigh?"

"Yes, my lord."

Another lie, if the deepening red at her throat was any indication.

"Stoneleigh is quite a distance from Kent. Is this the first time you've ventured out of Warwickshire county?" Gideon was toying with a letter opener on his desk, and Miss Gilchrist was following the movement, her gaze fixed on the point as he turned it casually between his fingers.

"Yes, my lord."

Gideon raised an eyebrow. That was her third *yes, my lord* since she'd entered his study. The impertinence he'd noticed in the courtyard had disappeared, replaced by a docility much more appropriate in a servant. Perhaps it should have reassured him, but it felt false, as if he were watching her play-act at being a housemaid.

"Well then, my lord. Shall I take her upstairs and see her settled?" Mrs. Briggs didn't seem to notice anything amiss, but appeared well satisfied with her new housemaid.

Miss Gilchrist half-rose from her seat and hovered there, like a bird balanced on the edge of a branch, ready to take flight at any hint of a nod from him. He took in her clenched fingers and the fluttering pulse at the base of her throat, and shook his head. "No, not just yet, Mrs. Briggs. I'd like to have a bit more conversation with Miss Gilchrist first."

"Of course, my lord."

"Thank you, Mrs. Briggs." Gideon waved a hand toward the door. "You may leave us."

Miss Gilchrist looked as if she were digging her fingernails into her palms to keep herself from clutching at Mrs. Briggs's arm to prevent her leaving.

"Yes, my lord." Mrs. Briggs offered Miss Gilchrist an encouraging smile, then turned and made her way toward the door.

Miss Gilchrist watched her go, swallowing as Mrs. Briggs closed the door behind her.

Gideon tossed the letter opener aside and rapped his knuckles against his desk. "Your attention if you please, Miss Gilchrist."

She jumped, and met his gaze. "Yes, my lord."

Gideon regarded her in silence for far longer than was comfortable for either of them, then he said, "The ribbons on your hat."

She reached for the bonnet perched atop her head. "My ribbons?"

Gideon noticed her hand was shaking, but he ignored the twinge of his conscience. "That shade of blue is the latest fashion in London, and your cloak, which was also almost certainly made in London, is an exceptionally fine one for a Warwickshire housemaid."

Her dark eyes went wide. "I—"

"I don't know what reason you'd have to lie to me, Miss Gilchrist, but—"

"Yes, my lord...I mean, *no* my lord. I mean, I beg your pardon, my lord, but I didn't lie to you."

Gideon held up a hand to silence her. She'd come all this way from... *somewhere*, at Mrs. Briggs's request. He didn't like to send her away again like this, but there was something off about her, and it was more than just her ribbons and cloak. Those could be explained easily enough, but her dainty hands and smooth skin, her voice and bearing, and the way she looked directly into his eyes when she spoke to him...

He didn't trust her, and he couldn't afford to employ people he didn't trust. He simply had too much to lose. "I don't allow liars in my house, Miss Gilchrist. You are dismissed from Darlington Castle."

Chapter Three

"You're dismissing me from your service because my ribbons are blue?"

A thousand tangled thoughts were flying through Cecilia's head at once, and somehow *this* was the one that burst from her lips? Of all the things she might have said or done—deny she'd lied, protested her innocence, burst into a flood of noisy tears—she'd chosen to quibble with him over *blue ribbons*?

But really, how could she be cursed with the ill luck to come across the one lord in London who knew this particular shade of cornflower blue was fashionable this season? She'd never come across such a creature before. Most gentlemen couldn't tell the difference between azure and cerulean.

And here she'd thought Lady Darlington's ghost rising from her grave to haunt Darlington Castle would be the most shocking part of her day.

Lord Darlington glared down his aristocratic nose at her, his eyes colder than the bits of ice floating in Darlington Lake. "You don't appear to understand me, Miss Gilchrist. The color of your ribbons is irrelevant. I'm dismissing you because you're a liar."

She *was* a liar, and not a particularly good one, but that didn't make his accusation any less infuriating. Why, what shameful arrogance, for him to accuse her of dishonesty based on nothing more than the color of a few ribbons. "I beg your pardon, Lord Darlington, but I don't see how the color of my ribbons is irrelevant, given you're using it as an excuse to dismiss me."

"I don't need an excuse to dismiss you, Miss Gilchrist." Those icy blue eyes bored into her as if he could see right through her skin and bones, straight to her wildly beating heart. "Now, allow me to make myself perfectly clear. *You are dismissed.*"

How he managed to inject those three words with such menace Cecilia couldn't say, but that deep voice, rough and clipped at the edges, wrung a shiver from her that made goosebumps rise on her skin. "But that's not..." She began, then trailed off again.

It wasn't what? *Fair?* No, it wasn't, but what was the use in arguing with him over it? He was right. He didn't need any better reason than the color of her ribbons to run her out of his castle. He didn't need any reason at all. He was master here, and might act like a haughty, ill-tempered tyrant if he chose.

Why would she even *want* to argue with him, in any case? If Lady Darlington's ghost wasn't enough of a reason to go scurrying back to London, surely Lord Darlington's unexpected presence here was?

He wasn't *meant* to be here. He was meant to be in London with his betrothed, and *she* was meant to creep about his castle, insinuate herself among his servants, and determine whether he truly was the Murderous Marquess most of England believed him to be.

If Lady Clifford had known she was thrusting Cecilia directly into Lord Darlington's path, she never would have sent her here at all. She would have sent Georgiana, who was as relentless as she was clever, or Emma, who would have charmed Lord Darlington into letting her remain at his castle, liar or no. If anyone could discover the truth about what had happened to Lady Darlington, it was Georgiana or Emma.

But just as Cecilia was about to gather her fancy cloak and fashionable blue ribbons and flee Darlington Castle, she recalled something Daniel Brixton had said to her before she left London.

If Lady Clifford says you're fit for this business, lass, then you're fit.

Lady Clifford had more faith in Cecilia's abilities than was warranted, because she wasn't fit. Not for *this*. There was no reason in the world why she shouldn't do just as his lordship commanded and leave this cursed castle without a backward glance.

Cecilia rose to her feet, drew herself up to her full height, and peered down the length of her nose at Lord Darlington. She'd meant to preserve a dignified silence as she took her leave, but looking down on him must have loosened her tongue, because suddenly she wasn't content to scurry away like a coward without saying a word in her own defense. No, if she was to be sent away from Darlington Castle, she was going to meet her fate as bravely as any of her friends would have done.

He'd already dismissed her, so why not have her say?

"Very well, my lord. I see there's no point in arguing my innocence. The blue ribbons are indeed damning evidence against me." She raised her chin. "But before I go, allow me to say if I'd judged you on your appearance today, as you've done me, I wouldn't have known you were the Marquess of Darlington."

Whatever he'd been expecting her to say, it wasn't *that*. He gaped at her, openmouthed. "Explain yourself, Miss Gilchrist."

"I don't mean any insult. It's just that you don't look terribly…" She waved a hand at him. "Lordly."

Privately Cecilia knew she would have known him as a nobleman no matter what. All gentlemen of rank had a certain haughtiness, and Lord Darlington more than most, even dressed for the country as he was now, in a dark coat, dark breeches, and a long, flowing cloak swirling around a pair of tall, tight-fitting boots.

He was still an impressive figure of a man, but he wasn't the graceful aristocrat on the strut in the fashionable buff-colored breeches and navy coat he'd worn that day she'd spied on him in Hyde Park. She'd thought him quite elegant then, whereas now…

His clothing, his hair, his perfectly fitted leather gloves, his expression—all were black. Only the edge of a snowy white shirt peeking from his open cloak and a pair of startlingly blue eyes interrupted this unrelenting sea of gloom. He looked like a fury ascended straight from the netherworlds, and that was *before* she added the haunted castle into the equation.

But as angry and humiliated as Cecilia was, she wouldn't say *that*. Indeed, if she could judge by the temper now kindling in his eyes and the wash of red creeping up his neck, she'd already said quite enough.

"Lordly," he repeated flatly.

"Elegant, I mean. Lords wear fashionable embroidered silk waistcoats, and their behavior is so *gentlemanlike*." Cecilia couldn't resist putting an emphasis on that last word.

"So, your measure of a gentleman is an embroidered silk waistcoat? That's ridiculous."

"Yes, it is rather ridiculous, isn't it?" Cecilia touched her fingers to the ribbons of her hat to make certain he took her meaning, then offered him a polite curtsy. "Thank you for taking the time to see me today, Lord Darlington. Goodbye."

She turned on her heel and marched toward the door, but she hadn't taken more than a few steps before Lord Darlington stopped her. "Wait, Miss Gilchrist."

Now she'd said her piece, Cecilia's limbs were twitching with the urge to flee this place, but there was an unexpected note of grudging admiration in his voice that made her pause and turn to face him. "Yes, my lord?"

He nodded toward the chair she'd just left. "Sit down, please."

Cecilia didn't want to sit down. She'd already decided it was one thing to peek at Lord Darlington from behind the safety of a thicket of shrubs in Hyde Park, and quite another to be trapped alone with him in a dimly lit study inside a haunted castle.

The first was vastly preferable to the second.

Even from a distance she'd noticed he was a large gentleman, but now, with only a desk between them, Cecilia could see Lord Darlington was as close to rivaling Daniel Brixton in height and sheer, muscular bulk as any man she'd ever seen.

The wisest course was for her to seize the excuse he'd given her to leave Darlington Castle and abandon him to his fate, but she'd made a promise to Lady Clifford, and she found she couldn't give it up for lost quite yet. So, she sat, her hands folded in her lap, and waited.

Lord Darlington was scowling, as if he already regretted calling her back. "If there's something you wish to say to me, you may do so now."

Cecilia blinked. "You mean about silk waistcoats, and you not looking like a marquess?"

He pinched the bridge of his nose between his fingers. "*No*, Miss Gilchrist. You said earlier you weren't lying to me. If you care to explain what you mean, I'll listen to you."

"That's, ah…very good of you, Lord Darlington." What a pity she'd been so busy denying his accusations she hadn't thought of any convincing lies.

But the next thing she knew her traitorous lips opened, and a half dozen lies spewed forth. "I didn't lie to you before, my lord. My cloak is a gift from Lady Dunton's daughter. She made a present of it to me when I left Stoneleigh."

"A present," Lord Darlington repeated.

"Yes, my lord." That much at least was true. The cloak *had* been a gift. From Lady Clifford, not Lady Dunton's daughter, but it was as close as she could get to the truth. Georgiana always warned her to stay as faithful to the truth as possible when telling an enormous lie, and the lies one *was* compelled to tell should be simple ones, and thus easier to remember.

"How generous of Lady Dunton's daughter." He didn't bother to hide his skepticism. "I suppose the blue ribbons were a gift, as well?"

"No, my lord. I have a great-aunt who lives in London. She sent me the ribbons."

Alas, one lie seemed to be her limit, because this second one didn't leave her lips quite as smoothly as the first one had. He noticed it, and his gaze sharpened on her face. Much to her dismay, Lord Darlington appeared to be the sort of man who noticed *everything*.

"Your aunt's name, Miss Gilchrist?"

Cecilia nearly groaned aloud. Oh, *why* had she mentioned a great aunt? She might have just said she'd purchased the bonnet in London, but she'd had to throw a great aunt into it, and complicate things. If Georgiana were here, she'd be appalled.

"She's, ah…Mrs. Bell, my lord." There, let the blasted man do a search through the hundred or so Mrs. Bells living in London.

"Her direction?" Lord Darlington snatched up the quill from his desk, dipped it, and hovered it over a scrap of paper.

Cecilia's satisfaction faded. "Lambeth Road, my lord." Surely, there must be at least one Mrs. Bell in Lambeth Road?

He scrawled the direction on the paper, then tossed the quill aside and leaned back in his chair, his hands over his wide chest, his hard, blue eyes fixed on her face. "You did say you were born in Stoneleigh, didn't you, Miss Gilchrist?"

Cecilia resisted the urge to squirm. "Yes, my lord." Again, it wasn't a lie, precisely. She'd been born in Stoneleigh, and had spent her infancy there, but it was so long ago it might have been in another lifetime. After her grandmother died her parents had moved to London, and Cecilia had been there ever since.

But if Lord Darlington knew she hailed from London, he might connect her to the Clifford School. Lady Clifford made it a point not to call attention to their activities, but the school and its proprietress were infamous among certain people in London. Lord Darlington would find out who she was eventually, of course, but Cecilia intended to be gone from Darlington Castle long before then.

He didn't speak for some time, but leaned back in his chair, his arctic blue eyes moving over her face. His posture bespoke casual ease, but Cecilia wasn't fooled. There was nothing easy about the rigidity of his spine, the tightness of his lips, the clench of his fingers.

She crossed her ankles under cover of her skirts, then recrossed them. She twiddled her thumbs, avoiding his gaze, but the silence stretched on for so long a bead of sweat gathered in the tightly bound hair at her nape and slid down the back of her neck. Finally, she glanced up at him, unable to bear the quiet another moment, and found him staring at her from the other side of his desk.

Cecilia returned the stare, cocking her head. It was a great pity his eyes were such a cold blue, because with those long, dark lashes they were quite stunning.

She blinked, surprised at herself.

"This glowing reference from Lady Dunton." Lord Darlington drew the page toward him across the desk, his gaze once again flicking over the signature. "If I were to contact her ladyship regarding your service, she'd verify every word written here. Is that right, Miss Gilchrist?"

Lady Dunton was one of the Clifford School's aristocratic, silent patrons. Not one word of the reference she'd written for Cecilia was true, but her ladyship would swear to Lord Darlington it was. So, Cecilia opened her mouth, and pushed another lie between her lips. "Of course, my lord."

Once again, he didn't reply right away, just gazed at her with narrowed, suspicious eyes. Cecilia was losing heart, her faith in her ability to convince him waning with every moment, but just as she'd given it up for lost, Lord Darlington spoke.

"I don't like liars, and I care even less for gossip and strangers prying into my private affairs. My servants are loyal to me, and they know better than to gossip. If I find you've carried any tales outside my home, I will dismiss you instantly, without references. Is that understood?"

"Yes, my lord." Cecilia gulped, both relief and dread pooling in her stomach. He was going to let her stay on as housemaid, but being his housemaid meant living at Darlington Castle under the cold, watchful eye of Lord Darlington, who seemed to have taken an immediate dislike to her.

He looked hard at her, then gave a short nod. "It won't be an easy post. I've lived in retirement for the past year, and the castle has been closed to guests. We're short on staff, and a great deal of work is yet to be done before my betrothed arrives in Kent in a fortnight. You'll be treated fairly, but you'll be expected to work hard."

Cecilia had never been afraid of hard work. That is, she'd never worked as a housemaid before, but it couldn't be any more difficult than mudlarking in the Thames, and she'd survived that for more than two years. "Yes, my lord."

"I suppose we'll find out how sturdy you are, won't we, Miss Gilchrist?"

Heat rose in Cecilia's cheeks, but instead of snapping that she was far sturdier than he'd ever imagine, she wisely kept her mouth closed.

That dark eyebrow quirked once again at her silence. "Just one more thing, Miss Gilchrist. You are not, under any circumstances, to enter my late wife's bedchamber. It's kept locked at all times, so as not to tempt the curious, but it's crucial all of my servants understand no one enters that room without my explicit permission."

Well, that was strange. Cecilia couldn't help but wonder what Lord Darlington intended to do with the future Marchioness of Darlington if she wasn't meant to take up residence in the marchioness's apartments, but it didn't seem a good idea to ask.

"If you disobey me in this, you will be dismissed and sent from the castle immediately. Is that clear?" Lord Darlington leaned across the desk, pinning her with his gaze.

"Yes, my lord." They were the only three words Cecilia was still capable of uttering in his presence, it seemed.

"Very well." Lord Darlington rose from his chair—and rose, and rose, and rose, his long body seeming to take ages to unfold—and pulled the bell once again. Cecilia stumbled to her feet as well, and the two of them stared at each other in silence as they waited for Mrs. Briggs to answer the summons.

Fortunately, she bustled into the study again in a matter of moments. "All right then, Lord Darlington? Come with me, Cecilia. We'll drop off your case upstairs, then have a cup of tea in the kitchens and get to know one another, shall we?"

For the first time since she'd entered Darlington Castle, Cecilia was able to draw a deep, calming breath. If Mrs. Briggs had been half as alarming as Lord Darlington, Cecilia likely would have taken to her heels and fled all the way back to Edenbridge, but the housekeeper was a matronly creature, with deep laugh lines fanning out from her kind brown eyes.

"Yes, ma'am. Thank you, my lord." Cecilia offered Lord Darlington an awkward curtsy. His only response was a brief nod of his head, but those frigid blue eyes were enough to pucker the skin on the back of her neck.

Mrs. Briggs prattled cheerfully as she led Cecilia down the hallway. "Lord Darlington ordered the upper floor of the castle closed, there not being enough servants left to tend to it, so you'll have a bedchamber on the second floor."

"Yes, ma'am." Cecilia hurried after Mrs. Briggs, her traveling case bumping against her knees with every step.

"It's not a large room," Mrs. Briggs went on. "It was intended for the marchioness's lady's maid, but you'll have it all to yourself. Won't that be nice?"

It was unheard of for a mere housemaid to have a room to herself, so Cecilia took care to make all the appropriate appreciative noises, but as they made their way down the hallway, her attention was caught by the portraits hanging on the wall. One dour Darlington ancestor after another glared down at her from their ornate gilt frames. They were a grim-looking lot, not a smile amongst them, and the current Marquess of Darlington seemed to take after his forbears. He certainly looked a good deal like them, with his guarded blue eyes and severe mouth.

Cecilia's heart sank at the thought.

Between Lord Darlington's harsh demeanor and the row of his forbidding ancestors hanging on the wall, she couldn't shake the feeling she'd just accepted a post from Bluebeard himself.

Chapter Four

Gideon awoke the next morning to a thundering crash so powerful his bed—an enormous, solid mahogany affair with a towering canopy and enough heavy silk drapery to drown Darlington Castle—jumped half a foot across the floor.

"What the *devil*?" He shot upright so quickly a pillow tumbled to the floor, wide awake in an instant. The noise had exploded in the quiet room with such an ear-splitting bang the thick, stone walls of the castle actually vibrated. Had the heavens run out of patience with him at last and struck his castle with a lightning bolt, or had the roof of Darlington Castle collapsed?

"Oh, dear." The voice was small in the sudden silence.

Gideon dragged a hand through his rumpled hair, setting the dark locks on end. Not a lightning bolt, then. No, an entirely different force of nature was the cause of the deafening din.

Cecilia Gilchrist.

"For God's sake, Cecilia, you've just aged me ten years in a single instant. What happened?" It was a foolish question really, given she was kneeling on the floor in front of the fireplace, her hands already black with soot from her frantic attempts to retrieve the scattered pieces of coal she'd dropped. The scuttle was beside her, tipped over on its side with the few remaining lumps of coal falling out of it.

Her hand froze at the sound of his voice. She remained still for a moment, much like a fox when it realizes it's been cornered, but then her chest heaved in a caught breath, and she raised her face to his. "I-I beg your pardon, Lord Darlington. I don't know…" She trailed off, biting her lower lip as she took in the spilled coal in despair. "I don't know what happened. It just s-slipped out of my hand."

"Slipped out of your hand." A sarcastic comment threatened—something about her hands being too dainty for a housemaid—but Gideon held his tongue, if only because he couldn't quite excuse his own part in this mess. He'd goaded her yesterday about being too frail to carry the coal scuttle. Human nature being what it was, he'd as good as guaranteed she'd drop it this morning.

"Yes, my lord." There was a sound of scuffling feet, then the clink of coal being thrown piece by piece into the wooden bin.

"It was an accident," Gideon allowed, somewhat grudgingly. "Not the sort of accident one would expect from a housemaid who's served eleven years with Lady Dunton, but an accident just the same."

A brief silence followed this ill-tempered observation, then she said meekly, "Yes, my lord."

Gideon stared up at the canopy above him with a frown. He never slept well these days, but last night had been a particularly fitful one. He'd lain awake for hours before dropping off at last. Being woken so early, and with such violence, didn't put him in the best humor, but something about her timid response made his teeth clench. "What's happened to your sharp tongue this morning, Cecilia?"

The clink of the coal against the bin paused. Gideon waited, but then it resumed again without her answering.

He peered around the edge of the pillow he'd pulled over his face. Cecilia was crawling around the floor on her knees, gathering up the spilled coal. The blue ribbons and expensive cloak were gone, and in their place was the plain gray dress, white apron, and ridiculous white caps his housemaids wore. Her hair had been scraped back and stuffed underneath it, but a few thick strands peeked out the edges.

It was dark, like her eyes.

She looked so different he wouldn't have recognized her as the same woman who'd been tossing stones into Darlington Lake yesterday. He thought of the wide sweep of her arm, the flash of white skin where the sleeve of her cloak had pulled away from her wrist, the hesitant half-smile on her lips when she'd turned to face him...

I've got excellent aim. Perhaps that might prove useful?

There was no reason she should have made such an impression on him, but when he'd fallen asleep last night, it hadn't been to blissful dreams of his betrothed. No, instead he'd found himself pondering Cecilia Gilchrist, with her fashionable blue ribbons and fine woolen cloak.

Perhaps it was simply the surprise of finding her there in the courtyard, in the last place he'd expected to find movement, or sound, or anything so…alive. His first instinct had been to chase her away, to banish her from Darlington Castle before it smothered all the life out of her.

But Mrs. Briggs had hired the girl, and she'd come to Kent in good faith to take up the position. His housekeeper appeared satisfied with her, and so the least he could do was give her a chance. God knew he had enough to worry him without quibbling over his servants' ribbons and traveling cloaks.

He needed a housemaid, and Cecilia was *here*. He had misgivings about her, yes. Despite the innocent widening of those enormous dark eyes, he knew she hadn't been truthful with him yesterday. He wasn't persuaded she came from Stoneleigh, or that she'd ever worked for Lady Dunton, and the accident this morning confirmed his suspicions. No housemaid who'd served in a country estate for eleven years dropped the bloody coal scuttle.

But he'd allowed her to remain in his employ, and so he was obliged to be as patient with her as he was with all his servants. There'd been a time not so long ago he'd been a considerate gentleman, and a kind employer. He didn't like to think the bitterness and grief of the past months had bled all the decency from him.

"No need to take all day about it, Cecilia." Gideon threw his coverlet aside with an irritable sigh, padded across the room in his bare feet, and joined Cecilia in front of the fireplace. He began tossing errant lumps of coal into the scuttle, but paused when he felt her gaze on him. When he looked up, she was sitting back on her heels, staring at him, her eyes wide. "What's the matter *now*?"

Her gaze darted between him and his empty bed, the coverlet trailing on the floor. "I…nothing, my lord."

No doubt she was stunned he'd left his bed to help her gather up the spilled coal. "There's no need to look so shocked. I'd do the same for any of my servants." That is, he assumed he would. He'd never known Amy, his other housemaid, to drop so much as a single piece of coal, never mind the whole scuttle.

Gideon tossed the last piece into the bin and rose to his feet. He was dusting off his hands when he realized Cecilia had gone still. He glanced down at her, and found her staring up at him, her cheeks flaming. "What is it?"

"You're, ah…" She made a vague gesture toward him. "Your…"

Gideon looked down at himself. He was dressed in the same breeches he'd been wearing when he came upon her in the courtyard yesterday, but before he'd fallen into his bed, he'd shed his boots, stripped off his coat and loosened the buttons at his neck. His white linen shirt gaped open from his throat to his mid-chest.

It was his bare skin that had flustered her. At least, Gideon thought it must be that, because she couldn't seem to look away from it. Even as her cheeks went scarlet with embarrassment, her avid gaze slid from the notch in his throat to the long lengths of his collarbones, then down, down, down, her pink lips parting on an indrawn breath as she took in the smattering of dark hair on his chest.

As her dark eyes moved over him like a caress, touching skin so long neglected Gideon had nearly forgotten it was there, he became uncomfortably aware he'd also loosened the buttons at the waistband of his breeches before he'd climbed into his bed last night. Thankfully, the long tail of his shirt covered him to mid-thigh, otherwise Cecilia would have been witness to some unexpected, unwelcome, and ungentlemanly...

Twitching.

It wasn't anything to do with her, specifically. Nothing at all. He was *betrothed*, and to an undisputed beauty. It was just that it had been so long since he'd had a woman in his bedchamber, and longer still since a woman had looked at him with anything other than suspicion or horror. His body was confused. It would have reacted the same way to any woman.

But that didn't stop heat from sweeping over him, blazing across every inch of his skin. He must have made a sound—a sigh, perhaps, or a choked gasp, but *not* a groan, certainly not *that*—because her gaze shot from his chest to his face and lingered there. Their breaths quickened as moment after moment unfurled, and neither of them was able to look away—

"I...please, my lord, there's no need for you to, to..." Cecilia made a frantic dive for the scuttle, and stumbled to her feet. She dragged an arm across her forehead, leaving a black smear on her pale skin.

Gideon frowned at it, his fingers twitching with an odd urge to rub it away. "Wait, Cecilia, you have a mark on your—"

"I apologize for my clumsiness, Lord Darlington. It won't happen again." Then she was gone in a whirl of skirts and coal dust, before Gideon could utter a single word.

* * * *

Cecilia flew down the corridor as fast as a lady could fly with a full coal scuttle tripping up her every step. She didn't stop until she rounded the corner, then she dropped the scuttle—*again*—and fell against the wall at her back.

That...hadn't gone well.

The sick plummeting of her stomach when she realized the bucket was slipping from her fingers—that she was, in fact going to drop it, just as he'd predicted she would—then the deafening crash when the overflowing bucket hit the floor, and the shocked look on Lord Darlington's face...

Each torturous moment of it had felt like a waking nightmare.

It hadn't occurred to her until that deafening crash Lord Darlington might be right—that she *did* lack the physical strength to make a proper housemaid. Cecilia had never been a lady of leisure, but teaching children their numbers and letters was far less taxing than hauling buckets of water and coal up dozens of stairs.

She hadn't been prepared for him to rise from his bed and cross the room to help her pick up the coal. Even now, she couldn't make sense of it. He hadn't hidden the fact he wasn't delighted by her presence in his house, and God knew waking the lord of the manor with such a clumsy accident was reason enough for him to dismiss her.

His ears were probably still ringing.

Why had he helped her? She'd braced herself for an outraged shout, and perhaps some gloating, but the next thing she knew his bare chest had appeared, and—

No. Not Lord Darlington's *chest*, for pity's sake. That is, his chest *had* appeared, but it was attached to Lord Darlington himself. She'd glanced up and found him on his knees beside her, his breeches pulled tight against his thighs and those fascinating dark hairs peeking from the opening of his shirt, and then she'd commenced that awful staring...

Her cheeks burst into flames just thinking about it. How was she ever meant to look at him again without seeing that intriguing chest hair in her mind's eye? She'd never seen a gentleman in a state of undress before, but instinct told her it would have been far better if her first glimpse had been of a man with less impressive musculature than Lord Darlington.

Perhaps then she wouldn't have made such an utter fool of herself.

Then again, it likely wouldn't matter, would it? He was sure to send her away now, and she'd have to return to London and admit to Lady Clifford that Lord Darlington had dismissed her not because she'd uncovered all his secrets with her brilliant sleuthing, but because she'd been caught gawking at his naked chest.

But there was nothing for her to do but go downstairs and confess to Mrs. Briggs she'd made a mess of the first task she'd been given, and was likely to be dismissed by Lord Darlington before the morning was over.

Cecilia reached down for the coal scuttle, but as she hauled the heavy bucket up by the handle, the most dreadful thought occurred to her, and she gazed down at it in dawning horror.

The bucket was *full*.

Oh, no. *No*.

She slapped her hand over her eyes, overcome with mortification. She'd scurried out of Lord Darlington's bedchamber with such haste, she'd neglected to light a fire for him!

She'd have to go back. He'd freeze if she didn't, especially in that drafty shirt.

But...she couldn't go back! There was no way she could face him *now*, much less build a fire, what with the way her hands were shaking. She'd be sure to set his bed hangings ablaze.

Cecilia squeezed her eyes closed and bumped her head rhythmically against the wall behind her. Oh, *how* had she managed to get herself into such a dreadful tangle? She hadn't even been at Darlington Castle a single day yet, and already she'd made an irretrievable mess of things.

What in the world had ever made Lady Clifford think *she* could manage this task? Sophia, Georgiana, Emma—any one of her friends would have made quick work of this business, but not Cecilia. Now poor Fanny Honeywell would end up married to a murderous marquess, and it would be all Cecilia's fault—

She jumped as a sudden, despairing shriek pierced the silence, her eyes opening wide. Dear God, that hadn't been *her* who'd shrieked, had it?

Cecilia just had time to mutter a fervent prayer she hadn't given voice to her despair when a door she hadn't noticed beside her flew open, and a ginger-haired girl with a smattering of freckles across her nose stuck her head out into the hallway. "Oh, thank goodness you're here! It's Cecilia, isn't it? I'm Amy Wells. Did Mrs. Briggs send you?"

Cecilia stared at her. "I—"

That was as far as she got before the girl seized her by the wrist and dragged her over the threshold. "She's woken in a foul temper this morning, she has. She'll have me at my wit's end soon enough, I don't mind telling you."

"Who will?" Cecilia asked, completely baffled.

"*Who?* Why, Lady Isabella, of course!" The girl—Amy—pointed a dramatic finger toward the corner of the room, where a child's bed with pink silk hangings had been arranged against the back wall. "Don't say Mrs. Briggs didn't tell you about Isabella?"

"No. I'm afraid she didn't." Cecilia and Mrs. Briggs had just sat down to their tea yesterday when the housekeeper had been called away. Cecilia had waited for her in the kitchen until she'd received a note from Mrs. Briggs explaining she'd be busy for some time, and Cecilia might retire for the rest of the evening.

She hadn't said a word about there being a child at Darlington Castle.

Cecilia drew closer to the bed. The hangings were drawn, but she could hear sniffles coming from the other side of the draping. "I daresay Mrs. Briggs would have said something, but she only had time to outline my duties before our meeting was interrupted."

"Well then, Cecilia, allow me to present Lady Isabella Olivia Cornelia Rhys." Amy swept the draperies aside, and there, huddled in the middle of the bed, was the prettiest child Cecilia had ever seen. Or she would have been if her face hadn't been red from shrieking, and her cheeks stained with tears.

"Oh, dear." Cecilia tutted. "Why so many tears?"

She had some experience with children. Lady Clifford had put her in charge of the Clifford School's youngest pupils, declaring Cecilia to be the only one of her four teachers who was gifted with a naturally patient, affectionate temper.

This child appeared to be about four years old, which was old enough for her to think herself very grown-up indeed, and to demand to have her own way in every particular, while in truth she was still very much a child.

"Lady Isabella is Lord Darlington's daughter?" Cecilia hadn't heard a thing about his having a child, but then she hadn't heard a thing about Darlington Castle having a ghost before she arrived, either.

"No, no. Lady Isabella is Lord Darlington's niece, daughter of his late elder brother and the previous marchioness."

"Is the child's mother——"

Amy put a finger to her lips, glanced at Isabella, and shook her head.

Cecilia wasn't certain whether that meant Isabella's mother was simply not present, or dead, or undead, for that matter, but Amy was right—one didn't talk about such things in front of a child. So, Cecilia said no more. Instead she turned back to the bed to find Lady Isabella peeking up at them with wary interest.

The child's hair was tangled, her night dress soiled with what looked like spilled porridge, and her mouth marred by a sulky twist. Taking into account she was the only child in a wealthy household, and a very beautiful child at that, Cecilia guessed she'd been too much petted and coddled.

"How do you do, Lady Isabella?" Cecilia sank into a solemn curtsy. "My name is Miss Cecilia. Will you come out of there, please, and greet me as a proper young lady is meant to do?"

The child regarded her with a pair of wide eyes. Cecilia couldn't say whether they were brown, gray, or green, but they were remarkable—quite the prettiest eyes ever to grace a child's face.

She blinked uncertainly at Cecilia, as if not quite sure what to do.

"Come now, miss." Cecilia held out a hand to the girl, her voice kind but firm. "I'm certain you must have very pretty manners. Come out and show them to me."

For the first time that morning, she'd said precisely the right thing. The little girl scrambled down from the bed, eager to show herself off to advantage. The soiled night dress rather spoiled the effect, but she plucked up the folds in her little fists and offered Cecilia a proper curtsy. "See?"

Cecilia smiled. "I do. Very nice, indeed, just as I thought."

"Well, I'll be," Amy murmured, watching the little girl preen over Cecilia's praise. "It took me more than an hour to get her to come out of there yesterday."

Cecilia turned to Amy, tapping her finger against her lips. She had a perfectly brilliant if somewhat cowardly idea. "I, ah, I had a bit of trouble lighting Lord Darlington's fire this morning."

Amy's lips twitched as she took in the black smudges staining Cecilia's apron. "Did you, now? I thought I heard a crash."

Cecilia nodded, her lips quirking in an answering grin. "You did. Indeed, I had so much trouble, his lordship's fire remains as yet unlit. I'd rather not venture into his bedchamber again this morning, after causing such trouble. Perhaps we could—"

"I'd be pleased to attend to Lord Darlington's fire and whatever else his lordship might require, if you'll see to it her little ladyship is dressed and served her breakfast."

Cecilia let out a breath, her shoulders sagging with relief. It wouldn't do her much good in the end—if Lord Darlington didn't dismiss her, she'd be obliged to attend him again—but at least she wouldn't have to face him quite yet. "I will, with pleasure."

Amy gave her a cheeky wink, snatched up the coal scuttle as if it were a bucket of feathers, and hurried from the room. A few moments later Cecilia heard a knock, then Amy's cheerful voice bidding Lord Darlington a good morning.

Indeed, she could hear Amy quite clearly as she bustled about in the next room. Cecilia's brows drew together as she noticed a door in the wall opposite Lady Isabella's bed, and realized this room was connected to Lord Darlington's apartments.

How odd. Surely Darlington Castle had a nursery? Or was it on the third floor? Mrs. Briggs had mentioned that floor was closed, but even if the nursery was unavailable, why would Lord Darlington's niece sleep in a room connected to his apartments? A room that wasn't, Cecilia now noticed, intended as a bedchamber at all. It looked more like a sitting room.

It was a strange arrangement, but she didn't have time to ponder it just now. She turned back to the little girl, who was still waiting by her bed, one little foot resting on top of the other. "Now then, Lady Isabella, do you have a favorite frock?"

The child nodded eagerly. "Yes, I do! It's a pink one."

Despite her worries, Cecilia felt a smile curve her lips. The child really was exceptionally pretty, especially when she smiled. "Pink? How curious. That happens to be my favorite color."

Chapter Five

Gideon didn't approve of gentlemen who debauched their housemaids. *He'd* never done such a thing, and he didn't intend to start with Cecilia Gilchrist.

He didn't know what had possessed him to leap half-dressed from his bed this morning, but he cringed when he recalled her shocked gasp at the sight of his bare chest. He'd never seen anyone's cheeks go a deeper shade of red than hers.

Before he descended the stairs to the breakfast parlor, he'd taken care to make certain there wasn't a glimpse of bare skin to be seen on his entire person. Breeches and boots, shirt, cravat, waistcoat, and coat—every inch of him was safely hidden under several layers of fabric.

By then, he'd persuaded himself there'd been nothing at all unusual about his encounter with Cecilia in his bedchamber. Still, perhaps it was for the best Amy had appeared in her place to light the fire. He and Amy were easy with each other, and there was no sense in tempting fate by having Cecilia—

That is, he wasn't *tempted* by Cecilia Gilchrist. Not in the least. It was entirely the wrong word to use, because there'd been nothing at all tempting about the incident. No, what he meant, of course, was she'd been so flustered he'd been afraid she'd bumble into another mishap, and he'd rather his bedchamber remained intact.

She'd never seen a man in a state of undress before, that much was certain. He would have thought a woman of three-and-twenty might have caught a glimpse of *something* by now, but if she'd spent the past eleven years shut up at Lady Dunton's remote country house as she claimed, she would have led a more sheltered life than one of London's most closely guarded virgin debutantes.

No doubt she was shy of gentlemen, wary of them, even—

"...wretched old pile of stones, but I daresay you'll become fonder of Darlington Castle than you'd ever think possible."

Gideon paused in the doorway to the breakfast parlor. His friend Benedict Harcourt, Lord Haslemere was lounging in a chair at the table, grinning flirtatiously, and beside him, not looking at all shy or wary stood Cecilia Gilchrist, a teapot in her hand and an answering smile on her lips.

"Where did you come from, Haslemere?" Gideon stalked across the room in a sudden and inexplicable cloud of irritation.

Haslemere and Cecilia both looked up at the sound of his voice. Haslemere's grin widened, but Cecilia quickly looked away from him, down at the teapot in her hand.

"From Surrey, same as ever," Haslemere drawled.

"Don't you have some debauching to do in London?"

Haslemere shrugged. "The debauching has been rather dull of late. I thought chasing ghosts might be more entertaining."

"Some tea, Cecilia, but take care, if you please." Gideon yanked out a chair and dropped into it. "I don't want another mishap. A burst eardrum is enough misery for one morning. I don't fancy scalding tea in my lap."

Haslemere frowned at Gideon's sharp tone, and Cecilia's face flooded with color. "Yes, my lord."

Gideon blew out a breath, regretting his ill temper at once, but Cecilia poured his tea and hurried from the breakfast parlor before he could say another word.

"A trifle irritable this morning, are we, Darlington?" Haslemere raised an eyebrow at him. "Didn't you sleep well?"

"Well enough." He hadn't, but Gideon didn't mention it, nor did he tell Haslemere he'd been woken with an ear-splitting crash, and had gone on to inadvertently expose himself to his housemaid.

Haslemere sipped from his teacup, eyeing Gideon over the rim. "I see you've found another housemaid at last. Hails from London, does she?"

"No, from Stoneleigh. She has a letter of reference from Lady Dunton. She's been with her since she went into service." Or so she claimed. Gideon still wasn't convinced.

"Odd. I would have sworn I'd seen her face in London before, though I can't recall where. What's her name? You chased her away before I could ask."

Gideon gave him a sour look. "You're curious this morning, Haslemere."

Haslemere smirked. "Curiosity is a characteristic of an active mind, Darlington."

"A prying one, too, but if you must know, her name is Cecilia Gilchrist."

"Cecilia Gilchrist! But she's one of—" Haslemere broke off, leaving the unfinished sentence hanging between them.

Gideon's gaze narrowed on his friend's face, his suspicions about Cecilia Gilchrist rushing to the surface. "She's one of *what*? Do you know her, Haslemere?"

"No, er…no." Haslemere ruffled a hand through his hair until the dark red strands stood on end. "How should I know her?"

"I've no idea, but it appears as if you do."

"Her name sounds familiar, that's all, but I suppose there's more than one Gilchrist in England. She seems an agreeable young woman, in any case."

"Agreeable enough." Gideon glared down at his perfectly poured cup of tea. "Not suited to be a housemaid, though."

Haslemere helped himself to more cream. "Oh? Why is that?"

"She's too pretty to be a serv—" Gideon broke off, blinking. What the devil? That wasn't what he'd meant to say at all. But it was true enough, and it wasn't as if it were a secret. Haslemere had eyes, and he wasn't one to overlook a pretty face.

"It would be the height of contrariness for you to start chasing housemaids *now*, Darlington, when you're a fortnight away from marrying one of London's darlings. Cecilia *is* pretty, but I'll wager she doesn't compare to Miss Honeywell."

Gideon wasn't about to discuss the varying degrees of beauty between his betrothed and his housemaid with Haslemere, but if it was up to him, his friend would lose that wager. There was no question Miss Honeywell had the sort of pale, fair beauty the *ton* admired. She caught one's attention, with her golden hair and blue eyes.

Cecilia was beautiful in a different way—in the same way Cassandra had been. It was a rarer, subtler beauty that had more to do with a woman's expression than her features…not that he'd paid Cecilia much notice, of course, Gideon reminded himself, clearing his throat. He'd hardly spared her a second glance.

"What news of our ghost? Any sightings of the old girl?" Haslemere asked, when Gideon remained silent on the question of Cecilia's beauty.

"No, none." Gideon drew in a breath, relieved at the change of topic. He didn't want to discuss Cecilia Gilchrist. He'd do well to put the girl out of his mind entirely. "The villagers claim she haunts the woods, but I didn't see any sign of her yesterday."

"What, nothing? Not a glimpse of a white gown, or a single lock of white hair fluttering on the end of a branch?"

"Not even a single strand."

"No footprints?"

"Ghosts don't leave footprints, Haslemere. Anyway, the ground's frozen."

Haslemere drummed his fingers on the table. "Yet the rumors persist. I stopped at the Three Crowns in Lingfield on my way here—they do an excellent meat pie—and at least a half dozen of the grizzled old fellows there claimed they'd seen your ghost with their own eyes."

Gideon snorted. "Half of Kent's claimed to have seen her, too. She seems to appear readily enough to those who are either ancient or too deep in their cups to tell what they're looking at. She's elusive enough, otherwise. Mrs. Briggs did say she's seen lantern light in the woods at night. Poachers, most likely."

"Dashed unpleasant business. Not to worry, Darlington. I won't leave you to chase your ghost alone. Between the two of us, we'll get to the bottom of this business."

"I hope so." Gideon gave his friend a grateful smile. "It's good of you to come, Haslemere. Once darkness falls, we'll scour the grounds, and see if we can't catch the elusive White Lady."

* * * *

Isabella Olivia Cornelia Rhys, treasured niece of the Marquess of Darlington, had a trickle of drool running down her chin. Her sleepy gaze fixed on Cecilia's face as Cecilia began another ballad, this one about a beautiful but proud young lady who is called to her death too soon.

It wasn't at all a proper subject for a child, but Cecilia had been singing for the better part of an hour and had exhausted her supply of sweet lullabies. If Isabella minded the shift from lambs frolicking in meadows to grief and graveyards, she kept it to herself. Her big, hazel eyes followed the movement of Cecilia's mouth, a smile on her pretty lips.

Shall I, who am a lady, stoop or bow
To such a pale-faced visage? Who art thou?
Do you not know me? I will tell you then...

Cecilia's voice trailed off as she tried to recall the rest of the verse. "It's something about conquering the sons of men, and...oh, yes. I have it. '*No pitch of honor from my dart is free, my name is Death! Have you not heard of me?*'"

"Me!" Isabella repeated, with a drowsy giggle.

Cecilia hummed the tune, her brow wrinkling. The music echoed as clearly in her head as if she'd last heard it only moments ago, but she could only recall the words in brief snatches, sung in a soft voice by a mother whose face she could no longer remember.

"I don't like to spoil the ending for you, but death scorns the proud lady's offer of bags of gold, inflicts the fatal wound, and hurries her off to her grave. It's not a pleasant bedtime story, I'm afraid. I hope it doesn't give you nightmares, Bella."

It was rather presumptuous of her, really, to address the daughter of the house so familiarly, but she couldn't bring herself to call the child Lady Isabella, much less her full name. It was a ridiculous number of syllables for such a tiny young lady.

Isabella, for her part, had accepted her new nickname cheerfully enough. The pettishness Cecilia had noticed this morning didn't seem to be a natural feature of her temperament. She was a touch shy, and anxious from too much turmoil in her young life, but Cecilia saw signs of a sweet, even-tempered child underneath the fussiness. She seemed more apt to smile than frown, to laugh than cry, and she had a sunny, lopsided grin so charming it could melt the coldest of hearts.

The child's eyes, though, were her most outstanding feature. Such an unusual hazel color, so bright and distinctive there was no overlooking them. They made Cecilia think of Lord Darlington's eyes. Not the color, as his were blue, but the brightness of them, the way they dominated his every other feature.

The similarity ended there, though. Where Isabella's eyes sparkled with life, Lord Darlington's eyes were burdened with shadows and secrets.

Cecilia glanced down into Isabella's sweet face. The big, hazel eyes had grown heavy as she hummed. "Ah, nearly asleep at last, and not a moment too soon." A wry smile curved her lips. "The only other ballad I can remember is about a fairy that steals a child away while his mother is picking berries. Not at all the thing, I'm afraid."

She continued to rock back and forth, Isabella's warm body limp in her arms. She stroked her soft, golden-brown curls, watching her heavy, black eyelashes until they fluttered closed against her plump cheeks.

Once Isabella was asleep, Cecilia's gaze wandered over to the cot that had been arranged against the wall on the other side of the fireplace. Amy slept there, on orders of the Marquess of Darlington, who insisted his niece never be left alone.

It was a strange arrangement, but it wasn't the only strange thing about Darlington Castle. Perhaps whatever secrets Lord Darlington was hiding had addled his brain. A guilty conscience was a burdensome thing, wasn't it?

What precisely he was guilty of, however, she still couldn't say. Her subtle attempts to prod the servants for information had come to precisely naught. Lord Darlington had told her his servants didn't tell tales outside the castle, but Cecilia had assumed they must tell tales to each other.

They didn't. She'd never seen servants more loyal to their master. None of them had a bad word to say about the Marquess of Darlington. But no one could escape their sins forever, not even a marquess. They were part of him now, the secrets he hid woven into the very stone of these castle walls.

It was simply a matter of uncovering them.

Cecilia snuggled Isabella more securely against her and watched the firelight dance in the grate, the shadows flickering against the stone walls. Soon her eyelids began to grow heavy. She was just drifting off to sleep when the sound of the door opening made her eyes pop open. "Amy?"

The shadowy figure paused in the doorway. "Try again."

Cecilia jerked upright, her heart quickening into a frantic rhythm under her breastbone. There was only one person at Darlington Castle who had such a deep voice and such broad shoulders, and it wasn't Amy. "Lord Darlington?"

"What are you doing in my niece's bedchamber, Cecilia?" Lord Darlington closed the door behind him, shutting the two of them alone together in the dim room. "Where's Amy?"

Cecilia leapt to her feet with Isabella clutched in her arms. "I beg your—"

"No, don't beg my pardon," Lord Darlington grumbled. "You've already begged my pardon a half dozen times today. I'm weary of it."

"Yes, my—"

"No more *yes, my lords*, or *no, my lords* either."

"Very well, my—" Cecilia began, then broke off with a soft gasp. He'd taken a step closer, and he was moving closer yet.

Closer, and closer...

God in heaven, the man was enormous.

She backed up a step, and he paused again. "There's nowhere for you to go, unless you intend to leap out the window. Do I make you nervous, Cecilia?"

"No, my—"

He raised an eyebrow, and she caught herself just in time. "I, ah...very well. The truth is, you do make me a trifle nervous."

"The truth. How refreshing." A grim smile drifted over his lips. "You don't need to be afraid of me. Not while you're holding my niece, at least."

His pitiful attempt at a smile tugged at a raw place in Cecilia's chest, and in the next breath she found herself rushing to reassure him. "I never said I was *afraid*. Nothing so drastic as that. Just a little unnerved. I daresay I'll become used to you soon enough."

Another grim smile. "I doubt it. Not to worry, though. You won't be the only woman in Kent who's alarmed by my presence." He didn't give her a chance to respond, but held out his arms for Isabella. "I've only come to say goodnight to my niece."

Cecilia hesitated, but she could hardly refuse to turn Isabella over to her uncle. "She fretted for a bit, but now she's nearly asleep." She settled Isabella into Lord Darlington's arms.

Lord Darlington squeezed into the rocking chair, despite being far too tall for it, and sat with his legs sprawled out before him, Isabella gathered against his chest. He cupped the back of her head with one big hand and waved the other at the chair opposite the one Cecilia had just vacated. "If you've decided not to go out the window after all, you may as well sit down."

Cecilia, whose legs were like jelly from the number of times she'd run up and down the stairs today, and *not* from Lord Darlington's sudden appearance, sank gratefully into the chair. But just when she'd drawn a relieved breath, he turned to her expectantly. "Let's have a lullaby, then."

"A lullaby?" Cecilia's mouth fell open. "I don't know any lullabies, my lord."

"I heard you singing to Isabella earlier. I assume you were singing her a lullaby?"

"Well, yes…I mean, no, not…" Cecilia bit her lip. "I don't know any proper lullabies."

Lord Darlington shrugged. "Sing an improper one, then."

Cecilia gaped at him. He wanted her to sing an improper song *now*, in front of *him*? "But—"

"You *are* meant to be putting Isabella to bed tonight, are you not?"

"Yes, but—"

"Aren't lullabies a common enough occurrence at bedtime?"

"I suppose so, but—"

"Well, then." He waved an imperious hand at her.

Cecilia wracked her brain, but the few sweet lullabies she knew had fled in a panic the moment he demanded one. The only songs she could recall were the drinking or shanty songs the mudlarking urchins used to sing.

Perhaps "Jack Hall" would do? No, that was about a man hanged for burglary. "The Fair Maid of Islington" was a pretty tune, but wasn't there something in it about a vintner paying a fair maiden five pounds to…

Cecilia's cheeks went hot. Dear God, she couldn't sing *that*.

"The Irish Girl," then. It was proper enough, if she left off the last verse about drinking whiskey and dangling a lassie on one knee.

She drew a deep breath, and with a muttered prayer, began to sing:

I wish my love was a red rose,
And in the garden grew,
And I to be the gardener;
To her I would be true…

Lord Darlington didn't look at her, but he went still when she began to sing.

I wish I was a butterfly,
I'd fly to my love's breast;
I wish I was a linnet,
I'd sing my love to rest.

Cecilia sang through the rest of the verses, leaving off the last one about debauching the lassies. Lord Darlington murmured something to Isabella when the song ended. Isabella stirred, nestled her head against her uncle's chest, and drifted back to sleep.

Lord Darlington continued to rock quietly, but he was studying Cecilia over the top of Isabella's downy head. "Why don't you know any proper lullabies?"

Maybe she had once, but if anyone ever had sung lullabies to her when she was a child, Cecilia didn't remember them. "I can't recall them, I suppose."

Lord Darlington didn't appear satisfied with this reply. He opened his mouth, but Cecilia didn't choose to share anything more, so she rose from the chair before he could speak, and hurried to the window on the other side of the room.

He didn't speak to her again, but she felt the heat of his gaze on her back, and sought out his reflection in the glass. He was caressing Isabella's hair, his big palm stroking gently over the girl's head, the rocking chair squeaking beneath them.

Cecilia kept herself busy on her own side of the room, folding and then refolding Isabella's clothing and blankets and sneaking looks at Lord Darlington's reflection. She turned to face him again when he rose from the rocking chair, and watched as he drew the pink silk hangings aside and lay Isabella in her bed, careful not to wake her. "Sleep well, little one."

He reached for the coverlet and tucked it snugly under Isabella's chin, and brushed the golden-brown curls back from her forehead. Isabella didn't wake, but she hummed contentedly in her sleep and nestled closer to her uncle's stroking hand.

A smile—a real one—curved Lord Darlington's lips at the girl's unconscious affection. He waited until Isabella's breathing became deep and even, then straightened. He looked vaguely surprised when he noticed Cecilia again, as if he'd forgotten she was there. He didn't speak to her, but he gazed at her so long Cecilia's heart began to pound.

She cleared her throat. "Good night, Lord Darlington."

He blinked, then with a little shake of his head he dropped his gaze and strode to the connecting door. "Good night."

Cecilia stared at his closed door for a while after he left, not sure what to make of him, then returned to the rocking chair to wait for Amy. She must have dozed off, because when she woke, Amy was beside her, gently shaking her shoulder. "Wake up, Cecilia. You can go off to your own bedchamber now. You look right worn out, you do, poor thing."

Cecilia gave a great yawn, and stretched her aching arms over her head. "It has been rather a long day." After the debacle in Lord Darlington's bedchamber this morning, she and Mrs. Briggs had spent the day scouring every corner of the drawing room and entry hall.

"Tomorrow will be another long one." Amy drew back a corner of the pink silk hangings Lord Darlington had drawn around Isabella's bed, and peeked inside. "Did she give you any trouble tonight?"

"Not much, no. She's a dear little thing."

"You've got a natural way with her, that's certain." Amy gave her a sly grin. "Not so much with the coal scuttle, though."

"Oh, hush." Cecilia huffed, but her lips were twitching. She'd confessed the details of the debacle in Lord Darlington's bedchamber this morning, and Amy, who was a hearty, high-spirited girl, had nearly laughed herself sick.

All things considered it had been a rather humiliating morning. One good thing had come of it, though. She and Amy had agreed to trade morning and evening tasks. Cecilia would take care of Isabella, and Amy would attend to Lord Darlington. They were both well pleased with the new arrangement.

Amy pulled the coverlet on her cot aside and plumped up her pillow. "It's a shame you can't sleep here. It would save us both a good deal of fuss."

Cecilia hesitated. "It's an…unusual arrangement, your sleeping here with Isabella, isn't it? Why does Lord Darlington insist on it?"

Amy shrugged. "He rests easier if he's near Isabella at night. She's been in this room for a year or more, even before Lord Darlington ordered the third floor closed. The nursery is too far a distance from his own apartments for his liking."

"Well, this room is certainly closer," Cecilia murmured.

Much, much closer. The room was nestled between Lord Darlington's apartments on one side, and the Marchioness of Darlington's on the other. It had previously been a shared sitting room, but Lord Darlington had ordered it be made suitable for Isabella and her nursemaid.

The arrangement was irregular, but not necessarily suspicious, as long as it didn't end with Lord Darlington creeping up to Amy's cot and holding a pillow over her face.

"I came to Darlington Castle after Lady Darlington passed," Amy said, "But Mrs. Briggs said as her ladyship liked having Isabella close by her, as well."

Whatever his servants truly thought of Lord Darlington, they were all in agreement about his late wife. Cassandra, Lady Darlington had, by all accounts, been as lovely and kind a lady as one could hope to find. All the servants, from Mrs. Briggs down to the scullery maid, described her as the sweetest of angels.

An angel called to heaven far too soon.

"To hear Mrs. Briggs tell it," Amy went on, "Lady Darlington doted on Isabella. She couldn't have loved that child more if she'd been her own. Treated her like a daughter, she did."

Cecilia's eyebrows rose. Amy spoke as if Isabella had no mother aside from her aunt, but no one in the castle had said a word about the child being an orphan. "Where is Isabella's mother, Amy?"

Amy shook her head. "She's been gone these six months now. Poor lady said she couldn't bear to stay here after Lady Darlington passed."

"Where has she gone?" Cecilia wasn't willing to let it drop. She didn't like to push too hard, but subtlety had gotten her nowhere so far. It was only a few short weeks until Lord Darlington's wedding to Fanny Honeywell. Those days would pass quickly, and Cecilia needed answers before then.

Amy dropped down onto the edge of her cot with a sigh. "She's in London now, and meant to be marrying the Marquess of Aviemore this spring."

It was the first time anyone had offered any information at all about Isabella's mother, Lady Leanora, other than that she'd been wife to Nathanial Rhys, the current Lord Darlington's elder brother, who'd died three years ago. Cecilia wasn't certain what had happened to him. She'd gathered it was some sort of accident, but no one in the castle spoke much about either him or his absent wife.

"But why would she leave Isabella behind?" It didn't make any sense.

Amy glanced at Isabella, then scooted to the edge of the cot and lowered her voice to a whisper. "Mrs. Briggs said Lady Leanora thought Isabella would be better off here with Lord Darlington until she'd settled. There was some talk of her going to the Continent, you see."

"My goodness," Cecilia murmured. "It's all rather unfortunate, isn't it?"

"Yes, and that's not the whole of it. A few months after Lady Leanora left, Lord Darlington was obliged to dismiss Isabella's nursemaid, Mrs. Vernon. The woman stole a gold crucifix that had belonged to Lady Cassandra that was meant to be saved for Isabella." Amy's mouth tightened. "Stealing from a child! Can you imagine? And you may be sure it's no coincidence those dreadful rumors about the Murderous Marquess started just after she left."

Cecilia gasped. "But that's awful, Amy!"

"It is," Amy agreed with a sigh. "First poor Lady Darlington dies, then Isabella's mother goes away, and then her nursemaid turns out to be a thief. All of them gone, one after the next, just like that." Amy snapped her fingers.

Cecilia glanced at Isabella, tucked so sweetly into her bed, and a tiny fissure opened in her heart. She was no stranger to tragedy, having lost her parents in a fire when she was four. She only remembered them in broken images, or in traces she caught here and there of familiar scents. She did remember the miserable years she'd spent in London at the Foundling Hospital, and later, trying to dig a living from the muddy depths of the Thames.

If it hadn't been for Lady Clifford, she'd likely be dead by now. Cecilia was tremendously grateful to her, but as much as she loved Lady Clifford, there'd always been an ache inside her, a blank space where her memories of her parents should have been. She hated to think Isabella was destined to suffer that same emptiness.

Amy tutted. "You get on to bed now, Cecilia. You look done in."

Cecilia rose unsteadily to her feet. "Yes, all right. Good night, Amy."

Amy patted her arm. "Good night."

Cecilia closed the door quietly behind her and made her way down the hallway toward the other side of Lady Darlington's bedchamber, where her own little room was, her head spinning with a thousand thoughts and questions.

What had happened to Lord Darlington's elder brother, and why did Lord Darlington refuse to let anyone enter his late wife's bedchamber?

Today had brought more questions than answers.

Cecilia let out a weary sigh as she stripped off her clothing, hurried into her night rail and dove under the covers, shivering. She couldn't understand why such a tiny chamber as this should be so unaccountably cold. It was hardly bigger than a closet, but despite her thick coverlet and the blazing fire in the grate, her feet and the tip of her nose were half frozen.

But exhaustion caught up with her despite the cold, and before long her limbs relaxed and her breathing deepened. She was just tumbling off into the oddest dream, where she and Lord Darlington were singing "The Irish Girl" to Isabella, with Cecilia enthroned on Lord Darlington's knee, when a peculiar sound startled her awake.

It sounded like...scratching? Like fingernails on wood. She struggled up onto one elbow and listened, but all she heard was the crackling of the fire. Cecilia waited, her ears perked for the strange noise, but the silence stretched on, and soon enough she settled back against her pillow. Her eyelids grew heavy once again, but just as she was about to drift off...

Scratch, scratch, scratch.

She opened her eyes and turned her head slowly toward the sound, her heart pounding. It was coming from the other side of the connecting door, the one that led from the lady's maid's closet into...

The Marchioness of Darlington's bedchamber.

A bedchamber that had remained locked since the marchioness had met her mysterious and untimely end there. A bedchamber no one had dared enter since her death, on orders of the Marquess of Darlington.

If you disobey me in this, you will be sent away from the castle immediately.

It wasn't a loud noise, only a faint scratching. Cecilia wasn't certain why she'd noticed it at all, unless it was that one didn't expect to hear such a sound from an empty bedchamber. She huddled into a ball, drew her knees up to her chest, and tugged the coverlet over her head. She squeezed her eyes closed, blocked her ears with her fingers, and ordered herself to go to sleep.

It didn't work.

No sooner had she closed her eyes than she was awake again, every muscle in her body pulling tight. That sound—

Yes, there it was again!

There was no mistaking that distinctive scratching, as if something had been locked behind a wooden door, and was clawing feebly to be let out.

Something, or someone.

Chapter Six

It was nothing. Of course, it was nothing, just a figment of her imagination—

Scratch, scratch, scratch

A disturbingly clear, persistent, and distinctive figment, but a figment, nonetheless. She wasn't going to let a figment frighten her off, was she?

Cecilia swallowed, then eased the coverlet aside, and paused by the bed. A shudder rolled over her and goosebumps chased up and down her arms, but she took a breath, rushed across the room, and pressed her ear bravely against the door.

She *didn't* believe in ghosts, no matter if all of Edenbridge swore they'd seen the Marchioness of Darlington's phantom floating through the woods behind Darlington Castle, here to wreak vengeance on the husband who'd sent her to an early grave.

It was a rumor, nothing more.

Cecilia liked the *idea* of ghosts as much as any avid reader of gothic romance, but she was skeptical as to their actual existence. Mrs. Briggs had stoutly declared the ghostly gossip utter nonsense, and dismissed it with a scornful wave of her hand. But now here was this peculiar scratching sound, coming from the marchioness's abandoned bedchamber. If it wasn't a ghost, what was it?

Mrs. Briggs had mentioned poachers were wandering about the castle grounds, but surely they wouldn't dare venture inside the castle? Even if they were bold enough, how would they get into Lady Darlington's bedchamber?

But if they had somehow managed to get inside…

Some say as he smothered her with a pillow…buried her poor bones in the castle walls…he's the Murderous Marquess, sure as I'm standing here.

Cecilia's stomach lurched as she recalled the hateful things the villagers had said about Lord Darlington, that first day she'd arrived in Edenbridge. If one of them *did* manage to sneak into the castle, there was no telling what they might do, or how far they might go to see his lordship punished.

She thought of the pretty pink bed with its silk hangings just two doors down, of Isabella sleeping with her little hand curled under her cheek, and Cecilia's throat closed.

She turned back to the door with her teeth caught in her lower lip. Perhaps she'd just try it, so she could reassure herself it was indeed locked. She grasped the door latch, the wrought iron slick against her damp palms.

It wasn't locked. It gave way under her hand, and opened with a creak almost as if someone had tugged on the latch from the other side, encouraging her to enter. Cecilia hesitated, her knuckles white.

This wasn't like the accident with the coal scuttle this morning. Lord Darlington had chosen to overlook that, but if she entered the marchioness's bedchamber, it wouldn't be an accident. She would be intentionally disobeying his direct order. He'd dismiss her for that, and for good reason.

If he caught her.

He and Lord Haslemere had gone out tonight. A peek inside Lady Darlington's bedchamber was the work of a moment only. She'd be in and out before they returned.

Wasn't this, after all, why Lady Clifford had sent her here? To sneak into locked bedchambers, peer into dark corners, and uncover Lord Darlington's secrets? She wouldn't get another chance like this one. Whatever oversight had led to the door being unlocked would doubtless be corrected by tomorrow.

Cecilia pushed the door wider, wincing as the iron hinges squealed in rusty protest. She took a cautious step into the room, her heart beating madly, Lord Darlington's warning never to enter his late wife's bedchamber echoing in her head.

A blast of freezing cold air sliced through her as she paused on the threshold, and she gathered her night rail closer, shivering. She hadn't thought the bedchamber would be warm—a fire hadn't been laid here in months—but it was much colder than she'd expected. Cold enough she could see her breath freeze in the air as soon as it left her lips.

Had someone inadvertently left a window open? Cecilia peered at the row of windows on the other side of the room, but the heavy silk drapes drawn across them were still, not a breath of fresh air stirring them. The room smelled stale as well, in a way it wouldn't if the windows had been left ajar.

As her eyes adjusted to the gloom, she noticed the room didn't look quite as abandoned as she would have expected. The furniture wasn't draped with dust cloths, for one, and there wasn't the musty, stale scent in the air one would expect from a chamber that had been sealed for so long. It was...strange.

Gooseflesh that had nothing to do with the cold made Cecilia's skin prickle. Her shoulders instinctively jerked up to her ears to protect her neck, because God knew if ever a ghostly, skeletal hand were going to choke the life out of her it would happen here, and now—

Scratch, scratch, scratch...

"Oh!" Cecilia gasped, all thoughts of cold and ghosts and skeletons fleeing her head. That haunting sound was back, much louder this time, and it was coming from an alcove in one corner of the room. It looked like a dressing room. The door was slightly ajar, and she could just make out a massive clothes press situated against one wall. She eyed it warily, her instincts urging her to turn and flee back to the safety of her bed.

Well, how absurd. Was she really so fainthearted as that? No, she wouldn't give into such shameful cowardice. What did she suppose was inside there? A ghost, or a dead marchioness's moldering skeleton? It was a clothes press, for pity's sake, not a crypt.

She steeled her spine, crept forward, and eased the door of the clothes press open a crack with one finger. A little wider, then a little—

"Heaven and earth!" Cecilia stumbled backward, a scream rising to her lips as something darted out the door. It scrambled over her bare feet and vanished into the bedchamber beyond, its claws scrabbling over the floorboards.

"What in the world?" Cecilia patted her chest to calm her frantic breathing. Her first horrified thought was that it had been a rat—

No, that wasn't true. Her *first* thought was it had been a ghost, a very small one with four clawed feet. Her second was it was a rat, but if it *was* a rat, it was a giant one, indeed. That wasn't precisely a comforting thought, giant rats not being the sort of thing she wished to encounter in a dark room, but before she could fall into a panic over it, another thought occurred to her.

She tiptoed back into the bedchamber. There could only be one explanation for scratching claws and a dark, furry, darting thing—

"Ah, ha. Just as I thought. Where did you come from?"

A black cat was sitting right in the center of the thick Aubusson carpet spread across the floor, calmly licking its paw. It looked up when Cecilia spoke, regarded her for a moment with disinterested green eyes, then went back to its grooming, as cool as you please.

Cecilia couldn't recall ever having been so summarily dismissed in her entire life. "I beg your pardon, madam, but if it weren't for me, you'd still be trapped inside that clothes press." Because of course, that's what the noise had been—the cat scratching on the door to escape. "I believe I deserve your gratitude. At the very least, you could introduce yourself."

The cat lowered its paw to the floor, abandoning its toilette to consider Cecilia. This mollified her somewhat, as the cat's sleek, shiny black fur indicated a preoccupation with cleanliness.

"How did you get in here, madam?" Cecilia wasn't certain how she knew the cat was a madam rather than a sir, but she did, perhaps because the cat's regal air reminded her of Lady Clifford.

Cecilia perched on the edge of the bed and stared at the furry creature, at a loss as to how to proceed. "Well? What am I meant to do with you?"

The cat seemed to consider this for a moment, its green eyes gleaming, and then, to Cecilia's surprise, she padded daintily over the carpet, leapt up onto the bed, and settled herself on Cecilia's lap without so much as a by your leave.

"What, you mean to say I'm to pet you?" Cecilia reached out to stroke the cat's silky head, and within seconds it began a loud, contented purring. "Yes, it's all very well for you, isn't it? Lord Darlington isn't going to dismiss *you* for being in here."

But she sighed and gave in, scratching behind the cat's ears, soothed by the rumbling purr vibrating against her legs. She couldn't leave the cat in the marchioness's bedchamber. What if it got trapped in the clothes press and took up that infernal scratching again? It wouldn't do any harm to bring the troublesome little creature into her room tonight, then take her outside tomorrow morning.

Her mind made up, Cecilia tried to gather the cat against her chest, but before she could get her arms around it, it leapt from her lap and prowled to the dressing room door, which was still cracked open.

Cecilia let out a weary sigh. Of course, Darlington Castle would have a haunted cat. "Very well, then. Let's get it over with, shall we? What do you want? You want me to go in there again?"

At this point Cecilia wouldn't have been surprised if the cat answered her, but thankfully it didn't. That is, not in words. It indulged in a lazy stretch, but didn't move from its place by the door. It stared at her expectantly, until at last Cecilia gave in. "Well, if we're meant to be partners in this, I suppose I'd better name you, hadn't I?"

She considered calling the cat Amanda, which was Lady Clifford's given name, but in Cecilia's fond opinion there could only ever be one Amanda, and so she discarded it in favor of an extravagant name worthy of any swooning gothic heroine.

"I'll call you Seraphina. Come along then, Seraphina, and be quick about it, will you? If Lord Darlington catches us in here, he'll have both our heads."

* * * *

"Cold out tonight." Haslemere crossed the study to the fireplace and thrust his hands out toward the blaze. "It would have been much pleasanter if your ghost had appeared in the spring or summer, Darlington."

"Or hadn't appeared at all." Gideon poured a generous measure of port into a tumbler and handed it to Haslemere. "Here, this will warm you more quickly than the fire."

Haslemere took the tumbler and dropped into a chair, his expression thoughtful. "I don't deny Darlington Castle is the first place a ghost would choose to haunt, but I believe we can conclude the White Lady is a figment of Edenbridge's imagination."

"I never suspected otherwise." Gideon's lips twisted into something meant to resemble a smile. "It seems my neighbors aren't pleased with the idea of my marrying again. What better way to chase off my betrothed than with a haunting?"

Haslemere grunted. "Bloody nonsense. Why can't they just leave you in peace?"

"Because they think I'm a murderer." Gideon sipped at his port. "A murderer must be punished, one way or another."

"More bloody nonsense. This is why I detest small villages, Darlington— willful ignorance and malicious gossip. I can't think why you'd stay here at all. Once you're married, you should bring your bride to London."

Gideon stared down into his glass. "Most of London thinks I'm a murderer too, Haslemere. You may be the only person in England who doesn't."

"Miss Honeywell doesn't think so," Haslemere reminded him. "No one with any sense does."

The thought of his betrothed should have cheered Gideon, but the faint spark of hope he'd felt while he remained in London seemed to have been swallowed by the shadows lurking in every corner of Darlington Castle. A marriage wouldn't undo what had happened between these walls. It wouldn't make him forget.

But the alternative was even grimmer. He couldn't remain in this desolate castle alone forever. He owed Isabella better than that, and even putting his niece aside, he had an obligation to his title. He couldn't remain *here*, in this dismal place. "Perhaps you're right, Haslemere. Perhaps we'd be better off in the London townhouse."

"You can't be worse off than you are here. It's something to think about, anyway." Haslemere rose to his feet. "I'm off to bed. We can have another look in the woods tomorrow night, if you like. There's no ghost, but someone else may be out there."

Gideon nodded. "Good night, Haslemere, and thank you."

Gideon remained in his study for a while after Haslemere left, sipping his port and staring out the window at the thickening shadows falling over the grounds. It had become his habit to avoid his bed. Being there only reminded him how elusive sleep had become.

But it was late, and the day had only grown more wearisome after his abrupt awakening this morning. He finished off the last of his port and set the tumbler on the windowsill. He was just turning away from the window when he caught a flicker of movement from the corner of his eye and jerked back around, his heart quickening. "What the devil?"

It was a light near the tree line, faint but unmistakable. He tracked it as it moved steadily closer, toward the rose walk and the castle courtyard. *Mrs. Brigg's mysterious lantern light.*

He watched, breath held, as the light wound around the edge of the wood, flickering as it passed through the trees. Someone was out there, and whoever they were, they were cunning enough to have eluded him and Haslemere.

Gideon followed the movement of the light as far as the rose walk, but as it neared the wall surrounding the kitchen garden, it vanished. He squinted into the darkness, but it was gone as quickly as it had appeared, swallowed by the gloom.

He ran from his study into the entrance hall, then darted through the doorway into the courtyard beyond and found...nothing. The light and whoever had been carrying it were gone, vanished into the air as if they were...

A ghost.

A chill rushed through Gideon, helped along by the biting February wind. He didn't give the wild stories about the White Lady any credit, but what he didn't know was how far one of the villagers might go to make him believe his castle truly was haunted.

He stood in the courtyard, the wind tearing at his cloak as he peered into the black night. By the time he gave up the vigil and went back through the arched doorway and into the long, narrow entrance hall his hands and feet were numb from the cold and his eyes tearing from the relentless assault of the wind.

The house was dark and silent, but Gideon couldn't shake the uneasy feeling gnawing at him as he mounted the stairs to the second floor. He started down the hallway, intending to have a quick look into Isabella's room before he retired, just to reassure himself she was slumbering peacefully, but he hadn't gone two steps before he froze, his heart leaping into his throat.

He'd heard a squeak, like the sound of footsteps creeping across the floorboards, faint but unmistakable, coming from a bedchamber he'd forbidden his servants to enter, one that should be still and shrouded in silence. A locked bedchamber, sealed up as tight as a tomb for more than a year now, with a connecting door into the sitting room where his young niece was now sleeping, vulnerable and defenseless.

Cassandra's bedchamber.

Panic and fury surged through him, weakening his knees for an instant before instinct took over. His heartbeat thundered in his chest and his ragged breaths roared in his ears as he crashed through the door, the force of his attack causing it to shudder in its frame before it flew open, slamming back against the inside wall. The wrought iron lock, weakened from centuries of use, wrenched loose from the stonework and hit the floor with a heavy thud.

Later, he'd recall she'd made a sound, a shocked gasp or a hoarse cry, but at the time he didn't hear it, because the sight that met his eyes as he loomed in the doorway drove every other thought from his head.

She was dressed in a white gown, her face as pale and stark as the villagers claimed it was. If he'd been in a rational state of mind, he might have recalled they also claimed her hair was a ghostly silvery-white, and nothing at all like the dark mahogany locks crowning this apparition's head.

But Gideon was far beyond rational thought, and so, when the apparition turned to flee from him in a whirl of white skirts, he did what any man half crazed with shock and fear *would* do.

He leapt after her.

It wasn't much of a chase. Gideon caught a fold of her gown, jerked her backward against his chest and wrapped an arm around her shoulders to hold her still. "What do you want?" he bit out. "How dare you enter my home and threaten my family?"

She gasped again, her slender body rigid with shock, but she didn't speak. Her back was heaving against his chest, but some moments passed before Gideon realized she was so terrified she was fighting for breath, each lungful tearing in painful rasps from her throat.

If the situation had been different, he might have felt some compassion for her, some softening of his heart, but if the last year had taught him anything, it was that he wasn't the man he'd always believed himself to be. The rumors and gossip and ugliness had turned him into the monster everyone thought him, because he felt nothing but rage.

"I've got you now, and I'll have some answers." He backed her into the stone wall, then seized her chin in merciless fingers and jerked her head up so he could see her face. "Do you understand me? This ends here—"

He broke off, choking on his words. He didn't know what he'd expected to see when he turned her face up to his, but what he found landed like a ferocious blow to his gut.

The eyes gazing back at him were dark, familiar, and the lips opening and closing as she struggled for words were the palest pink, not a ghastly crimson. "I-I b-beg…" she tried, but trailed off with a whimper, her body slumping against the wall as panic caught up to her.

It was enough, though. It didn't take more than those whispered words for Gideon to recognize the same sweet voice that had sung *The Irish Maid* to Isabella tonight.

Cecilia Gilchrist. He'd attacked Cecilia Gilchrist.

Gideon snatched his hands away from her and stumbled back a step, shame, heavy and bitter, lodging in his throat. How had he not known her? God knew he'd spent enough time gawking at her tonight to recognize the wide dark eyes and dark hair, the narrow shoulders and slight frame. That, and the white garment she wore wasn't a gown at all, but a night rail.

"I-I beg your pardon, Lord Darlington," she managed at last, her voice quivering.

She begged *his* pardon?

Gideon stared down at her, stunned. Her chin rose a fraction, and his chest tightened at the little display of courage, but though her eyes remained dry her lower lip wasn't quite steady, and she was trembling like a frightened animal.

Good Lord, he must be losing his mind, to have grabbed a woman in such a threatening way. He'd never been so ashamed of himself in his life. He was about to beg *her* pardon when to his surprise, she spoke again.

"I shouldn't have come in here."

Gideon blew out a breath, some of his anger returning. No, she bloody well shouldn't have gone into Cassandra's bedchamber. He'd forbidden it, and that should have been the first thought to occur to him when he found her here. Somehow, it hadn't been, and that only made it worse. "No, you shouldn't have, so why did you?"

His voice was harsher than he meant it to be, and mortification flooded over him again as she shrank away from him, pressing closer against the wall, and all at once he became aware of the way he towered over her. The top of her head only reached as high as the middle of his chest.

"I thought I heard—" she began, but Gideon interrupted her.

"How did you get in here? The door to this bedchamber is always locked."

Her forehead wrinkled. "No, my lord. It wasn't locked."

Gideon dragged his hands roughly through his hair. "It must have been locked, Cecilia. Every servant in this castle knows they're never to enter this room. I've given explicit instructions to that effect, and ordered the doors be locked at all times."

"Well, someone must have come in, and forgotten to lock it when they left."

"Are you accusing my servants of negligence?" Gideon's voice was cold. "If so, I'll remind you that you're the newcomer here. I'm far less likely to credit your account of the matter than any of theirs."

"I beg your pardon, Lord Darlington. I'm not accusing anyone of anything. I don't like to disagree with you, but the door was most decidedly not locked. If it had been, how do you suppose I got in here? Slid under the crack at the bottom?"

Gideon raised an eyebrow at her tone and the flash of temper in those dark eyes. Ever since their disagreement over the blue ribbons she'd been careful around him, confining herself to *yes, my lords*, and *no, my lords*, but her sharp tongue was back again.

"You haven't answered my question, Cecilia." Gideon fixed a stern gaze on her. "What are you doing in my late wife's bedchamber?"

"I'm trying to tell you, my lord. I heard a strange noise, and came to see what it was."

Gideon's eyes narrowed on her face. Had someone been sneaking about in Cassandra's bedchamber before she came in? "What sort of noise?"

"It was a scratching sound, like fingernails on wood, or so I thought. It turned out to be claws. There was a cat trapped in the clothes press in the dressing room, and it was clawing at the door to get out."

"A *cat*?" How in the world would a cat find its way into a sealed bedchamber? It seemed a flimsy story. "I don't see any cat."

"Well, no, my lord. She's gone now. She fled when you broke down the bedchamber door."

Gideon glanced at the broken lock lying in pieces on the floor. It would have to be repaired at once. He wouldn't have people traipsing about Cassandra's bedchamber.

"It's terribly cold in here." Cecilia wrapped her arms around her waist with a shiver. "I noticed it as soon as I entered. It's much colder than it should be, isn't it?"

Gideon stared at her, becoming uncomfortably aware she was wearing only a thin night rail, and though the bedchamber was dark, he could see the gentle rise and fall of her bosom under the filmy fabric in the muted light from the hallway. Her hair was unbound, tumbling in a thick, dark cascade of waves over her shoulders, and her feet were bare. Her dainty, naked toes looked strangely vulnerable, and the way her night rail swirled around the long, pale line of her legs was oddly riveting.

Sudden warmth pooled in his lower belly and his skin prickled with heat as he realized how near she was, how tempting the smooth, pale skin under the thin covering of her night rail. It was only the impropriety of their situation that made him notice, of course—the lure of the forbidden that heated his blood and stirred long-dormant urges he'd thought gone forever.

He averted his gaze, shifting uneasily. It was scandalously improper for him, a betrothed man who claimed to be a gentleman, to be standing alone in a darkened bedchamber with his housemaid, who was clad in nothing more than a sheer night rail. Gideon took a hasty step away from her, clearing his throat. "I wish to speak to you in my study, Cecilia. Dress yourself, and attend me there at once."

He didn't wait for her to reply, but turned his back on her and passed through the connecting door and into his niece's room. Isabella was tucked safely into her bed, her cheeks flushed with sleep, her thick curls wild around her head.

Gideon's heart clenched with the tenderness he always felt when he gazed at his niece. Isabella didn't resemble his late brother at all, but when Gideon looked at her, he thought only of Nathanial, the brother he'd loved and still missed with the same sharp ache as when he'd died more than three years ago.

But Gideon didn't linger over Isabella this time. He passed into the hallway, closing the door behind him, and made his way back down the stairs to his study, his stomach tight. He had some business with Cecilia, and the sooner it was done, the better.

Chapter Seven

"Dismissed?" Cecilia's thoughts ground to a halt, her mind going blank.

She shouldn't be as shocked as she was, but somehow it wasn't what she'd expected Lord Darlington to say. He had every right to be angry with her, of course. She'd broken the rules of the house by entering the late marchioness's bedchamber. She hadn't expected he'd be pleased about it, but for all his glowering, she hadn't thought he'd *dismiss* her before giving her another chance to explain herself.

But the man who'd been waiting for her on the other side of the study door tonight was not the same calm, forbearing gentleman of this morning. The patience he'd shown over the coal scuttle incident had vanished, leaving the Lord Darlington with the icy blue eyes in his wake.

This was the other Lord Darlington, the one she met the day she arrived. The black-clad avenging fury who'd crept out of the woods and accosted her beside Darlington Lake. *This* was the Lord Darlington who'd called her a liar.

He was a dozen different men in one body, it seemed, each version contradicting the others. Murderer or doting uncle? Cold spouse or loving husband? Kind, generous employer, or haughty arrogant marquess? No sooner would Cecilia begin to suspect he was a cold-blooded killer than he'd do something like rock his niece to sleep, and it would set her wondering.

And now he was dismissing her—*again*—without allowing her to utter a single word in her defense.

It took some moments of private fuming before Cecilia realized she was truly angry. She shouldn't be. She hadn't grown any fonder of Darlington Castle in the day she'd been under its roof. It remained as grim and sinister as it had since she'd first passed under that dreadful portcullis. If she were in her right mind, she'd turn on her heel without another word, run upstairs to pack her case, and demand to be taken away tonight.

So, no one was more surprised than she when she did precisely the opposite, but her temper was roused now, and there was no way she'd end her time at Darlington Castle with another timid *yes, my lord*.

Instead, she remained where she was. "No, my lord."

He gaped at her. "No? What do you mean, *no*?"

Cecilia crossed her arms over her chest. "I realize I wasn't meant to enter the late Lady Darlington's bedchamber, but—"

"That's right, you weren't. I specifically ordered you to stay away from it, and now I've caught you sneaking—"

"I wasn't *sneaking*. I'm trying to tell you what happened. I heard a noise, and—"

"I explained the rules to you, and you broke them," he went on, as if she hadn't spoken. "And I don't think you're being honest with me about how you got into that bedchamber."

"I'm telling you the truth, Lord Darlington." Cecilia's anger was rising with every word out of his mouth. It was the blue ribbons, all over again. "The door wasn't locked."

"The trouble, Cecilia, is I don't believe you." He was toying with the silver letter opener on his desk, moving it between his long fingers, but his gaze remained locked on her face. "I did warn you a foray into my late wife's bedchamber would result in your immediate dismissal. You chose to ignore that warning."

Cecilia bristled. "I did *not* enter Lady Darlington's bedchamber on a whim, my lord. I told you. I was concerned for your niece's safety. I never would have gone into the marchioness's bedchamber otherwise. Given the circumstances, you have no reason to dismiss me."

Lord Darlington gave her an incredulous look. "I'm the Marquess of Darlington, Cecilia. I may do as I choose, for whatever reason I choose."

Cecilia wasn't argumentative in general, preferring to leave such unpleasantness to Georgiana, yet there was her mouth, opening once again. "I'm simply asking you to consider—"

"There's nothing further to consider. I must trust my servants, and I don't trust *you*. That isn't going to change."

Cecilia considered him in silence, her eyes narrowed. Perhaps he hadn't murdered his wife, but he was certainly hiding something. Innocent men didn't require blind loyalty from their servants, nor did they lock empty bedchambers in their castles. He was the most secretive man she'd ever encountered, and there had to be a reason for it.

But whatever he was hiding, she wasn't likely to find it out.

Cecilia thought of Isabella, of the child's wide, sweet smile, and her stomach twisted with worry. If Lord Darlington truly *was* the Murderous Marquess—if he was wicked enough to have murdered his wife—what was to prevent him from hurting his niece?

As much as she might wish to leave Darlington Castle and Lord Darlington behind, she couldn't abandon that lovely little girl to the machinations of a sinister uncle. And what of the marchioness, who by all accounts had been as kind and loving a lady as ever lived? Didn't *she* deserve justice?

Cecilia didn't know if she could find justice for the marchioness, but she was suddenly as desperate to remain at Darlington Castle as she'd been to flee it only moments before. How was she to persuade Lord Darlington to let her stay, though?

Beg his pardon.

Her hands clenched at the thought. She wasn't easily roused to anger, but she had a proud, stubborn streak, and she didn't like to beg pardon when she didn't think she'd done anything wrong.

That is, she knew she *had* done something wrong, but...well, perhaps she didn't like to beg Lord Darlington's pardon for anything at all. But she'd do it, for Isabella and Lady Darlington's sake. She'd beg as prettily as she knew how, then scream her frustration into her pillow later.

Cecilia drew in a deep breath to calm her temper, and forced the words through gritted teeth. "I beg your pardon for disobeying your orders, Lord Darlington. I didn't intend to cause any harm. If you'd give me another chance, I can assure you it won't happen again."

"I don't give second chances." There wasn't a hint of softness in Lord Darlington's face. "There's no point. Once my trust is broken, it can't be regained. It's too late for you to leave tonight, but I want you gone from Darlington Castle tomorrow."

For all that Cecilia wasn't a lady, or an aristocrat, or anything special at all, really, she wasn't accustomed to being spoken to in such an insulting way, as if she were a liar or a thief. It stung, and her hold on her temper disintegrated like wood burned to ashes. "Very well, Lord Darlington. I wish you luck in finding my replacement. I daresay it won't be easy, given the...challenges of the position."

Cecilia didn't enumerate them, but Lord Darlington's black scowl showed he understood her perfectly: a dead marchioness, a marquess suspected of murdering her, and a vengeful ghost haunting his castle and the village of Edenbridge.

He wasn't a bit pleased at the reminder. He tossed the letter opener aside, sprang from his chair and came around the desk. "That will do, Cecilia."

Cecilia leapt to her feet as well. Her knees wobbled, but she resisted the urge to take a step backward. They stood toe-to-toe, facing each other, both of them short of breath. She'd managed to put out of her mind how powerful he was physically, but with him looming over her, his massive chest heaving and his angry heat searing her skin, she was suddenly drowning in the memory of his big hands on her tonight, burning through the thin linen of her night rail, his muscular arms wrapped around her shoulders, holding her still against that hard chest, and the rasp of his voice in her ear.

What do you want? This ends here...

"Tonight, when you grabbed me." She tipped her head back to meet his gaze. "You thought you knew who I was, didn't you?"

His eyes dropped to her arched neck, then skittered away again. His expression hardened. "No. I knew you didn't belong in my wife's bedchamber. That's all."

"No. You said, 'This ends here.'" Cecilia gripped the back of the chair beside her, her wobbly knees now threatening to buckle. "You acted as if you already knew."

Warm fingers cupped her elbow. She glanced down at the place where his big hand cradled her, then back to his face. Oh, he was angry, truly angry, but his touch was gentle as he steadied her. "I just told you I didn't."

"I don't believe you." Without thinking, Cecilia grabbed a handful of his coat. "I think you suspected I was the White Lady." It would explain his extreme reaction, but if he had thought so, didn't that mean he was guilty of murder, and believed his dead wife's ghost was haunting Darlington Castle?

His hand slid from her elbow down her arm. "Do you believe in ghosts, Cecilia?" He laughed softly. "I thought better of you than that." His long fingers curled around her wrist and jerked her hand away from him.

Had he thought she was someone else, then? "If not the White Lady, then who?"

"I will no longer speak on this subject." His voice was soft and controlled, but no less menacing for it. "You will prepare yourself to leave Darlington Castle first thing tomorrow morning. You may take a meal in the kitchen beforehand."

"Did you think one of the villagers had sneaked into the castle?" That had been Cecilia's first thought. Perhaps he didn't have a guilty conscience, and was only concerned for Isabella, as she had been. "Would they go so far as to—"

"Stop it, Cecilia." His voice was harsh, and his eyes had darkened to a stormy black.

She began to shake her head, but to her shock he caught her chin in his hand to still her. She gasped at the press of his fingertips, the heat of his touch. "My lord—"

"No. Listen to me. Tomorrow you will go back to Stoneleigh, or London, or wherever it is you're from."

Cecilia jerked her chin out of his grip. "What were you afraid of tonight, Lord Darlington?"

"Leave me." He nodded once at the door to his study, then turned his back on her and strode to the tall window behind his desk. He didn't speak again, but stood gazing out into the darkness, waiting for her to leave.

The frigid note in his voice chilled Cecilia to her bones. She stared at that stiff, broad back, his big, white-knuckled hands gripping the windowsill, and her shoulders sagged. How could she persuade him to let her stay if he wouldn't even look at her?

Who was she to argue with a marquess?

No one who mattered. No one at all.

That was it, then. She'd been summarily and permanently dismissed.

She turned on her heel without another word and made her way from the study down the hallway and past the row of Lord Darlington's grim ancestors, who seemed to watch her every step. Her feet dragged as she mounted the stairs to her solitary bedchamber on the second floor of the house.

She closed the door behind her and dropped down onto the edge of her bed. How would she explain herself to Lady Clifford, and Sophia, Georgiana, and Emma? They'd been so proud of her, so encouraging. This had been her chance to prove herself worthy of Lady Clifford's faith in her, but here she was, returning to London in disgrace after only a day at Darlington Castle, having learned precisely nothing.

What had ever possessed her to enter the late marchioness's bedchamber when Lord Darlington had expressly forbidden it? Yes, she'd heard a sound, but now she'd experienced the result it seemed a foolish reason to have disobeyed his orders. She'd have been much better off if she'd kept to her *yes, my lord,* and *no, my lord.*

Cecilia smothered a sigh, crawled under the covers of her little cot, and drew the blankets up to her chin, vowing nothing short of a blood-curdling scream would induce her to leave it again.

She squeezed her eyes closed and waited for sleep to take her, but though her body was exhausted, her mind wouldn't allow her to rest. A voice inside her head prodded and poked at her, enumerating all the reasons why she couldn't simply turn her back on Darlington Castle.

Cecilia rolled onto her side, then onto her other side, then tried to silence the voice by burying her head under her pillow, but it was no use. At last she squirmed onto her back with a heavy sigh. Her eyes popped open of their own accord, and she threw her arm over her forehead.

"It's not as if there's a blessed thing I can do it about it," she muttered aloud. "Lord Darlington's dismissed me, and there's rather an end to it."

There must be a way to change his mind, the voice insisted stubbornly. *Why, you hardly even tried.*

"I *did* try. I stood there and argued with an enormous marquess who's quite likely a murderer. What else would you have me do?"

Try again, harder this time.

"Short of simply refusing to leave, I don't see how I can—"

Ah. Now there's an idea.

Cecilia huffed out a breath. The voice was beginning to sound a bit like her friend Sophia, who never gave up on anything, regardless of how hopeless it seemed. She was the bravest person Cecilia knew.

And yet...

"What's to prevent Lord Darlington from simply throwing me out?" Cecilia shivered at the memory of his dark scowl as he'd ordered her from his study. That scowl said more clearly than words he wouldn't hesitate to toss her out the door.

Or drown her in the moat.

Nonsense. He's not going to drown you in the moat.

Cecilia snorted. "You haven't seen him. He's just the sort of man who'd drown his housemaid in a moat."

Don't let him, then.

"How am I meant to stop him? He's the size of a horse." Cecilia let her arm flop down onto the bed beside her. "I'm not brave. I can't...do the things you can."

Cecilia waited, but when that argument seemed to have silenced the voice for good, she forced her eyes to close.

Just as well. She wasn't Sophia, or Georgiana, or Emma.

Not even close.

So, there was an end to it.

She lay in the darkness and drew in calming breaths until a soft scratching sound disturbed the silence of her makeshift bedchamber.

"Oh, *no.*" Cecilia squeezed her eyes as tightly closed as she could, then pulled the covers over her head for good measure, but the faint scratch of claws on wood persisted, growing more frenzied with every moment.

Finally, it ceased.

Silence fell, and Cecilia opened her eyes and peeked over the edge of the coverlet. All was quiet. But before she could release the breath she was holding, the silence gave way to a soft creaking sound.

Cecilia's gaze flew to the connecting door—the door that had caused all the trouble, the door that had been meant to be locked, and certainly should have been locked now, as it creaked open.

Just a crack, then a little more, and a little more...

Cecilia gaped at it with wide eyes. No, it was impossible—

"Ahhh!" Cecilia gasped as something small and light landed on the foot of her bed. She kicked out at it, her fevered imagination conjuring images of tiny ghosts that leapt upon innocent maidens and smothered them with their own pillows. Another yelp left her lips, but the creature on her bed picked its way over her feet, then her legs, padding along until it reached her chest, where it stopped.

Cecilia had ducked back under the covers, but when the tiny ghost sitting on her chest made no move to smother her, she peered cautiously over the edge of the coverlet again.

A pair of green eyes stared back at her.

"Seraphina! I should have known." Cecilia frowned at the black cat, not sure whether she should be relieved or outraged. "Haven't you caused enough trouble for one night?"

The green eyes blinked.

"Where were you when Lord Darlington was shouting at me, hmmm? Nowhere to be found, that's where. You've a lot of cheek coming in here now after abandoning me so scandalously." Despite her irritation, Cecilia reached out to stroke Seraphina's head, chuckling a little as the beast nuzzled into her palm. "You're a shameless creature, aren't you?"

Cecilia tried to nudge Seraphina aside with a gentle sweep of her hand, but the cat remained perched squarely in the center of her chest. She patted the sleek, black head for a moment more, then tried once again to shoo her off the bed. "Go on, then, and leave me to my rest. I've rather a busy day tomorrow, what with being dismissed and having to return to London in disgrace."

Seraphina remained where she was, looking loftily down at Cecilia as if she were the dimmest human imaginable. If cats had eyebrows, Seraphina's would be quirked at her. "All right, then, since you insist on it, you may stay. It isn't as if Lord Darlington can dismiss me a second time, is it?"

Cecilia squirmed into a comfortable position without dislodging Seraphina, and drew the covers over herself. Seraphina settled down on top of her and commenced a low, rumbling purr.

No doubt Lord Darlington wouldn't approve of her having a cat in her bedchamber, but she wouldn't lose sleep over this one last act of rebellion. In a few hours she'd no longer be his servant, and therefore not obliged to explain herself to him ever again.

Until then…well, the less Lord Darlington knew, the better.

Chapter Eight

"You're making a damned foolish mistake, Darlington."

Gideon paused in the doorway of the breakfast parlor, taken aback. Haslemere was seated in his customary place, a cup of steaming tea in front of him, and a glare on his face that would curdle cream.

"What, by coming downstairs to breakfast with you?" Gideon's tone was mild. "I hadn't thought so, but you don't look as if you'll be a pleasant companion this morning. What's the trouble, Haslemere? Has that sour look on your face made the cream go off?"

Haslemere ignored this. "You've no business dismissing your housemaids, no matter what it is you think they've done."

Gideon stopped on his way to his chair, nettled. "For God's sake, Haslemere. I dismissed my housemaid less than eight hours ago. I fail to see how you're even aware of it, unless you've been wandering about the castle pressing your ear to every door."

Haslemere scowled, but he didn't deign to dignify this with a reply. "Your betrothed and her mother will be here in a matter of days, and your castle wants polishing. Look at it!" He waved a hand in the air, as if the breakfast parlor was no better than a cell at Newgate.

"It's not as bad as all that." Even as the protest left his mouth, however, Gideon caught sight of a thick cobweb clinging to one of the heavy beams in the ceiling.

"Bad enough. If you think I'm going to sweep floors and scrub silver, you're sadly mistaken."

"Pity. You'd look so fetching in a white cap and apron." Gideon dropped into his chair and took up his teacup.

"Is that why you dismissed Cecilia? Because she's so fetching?" Haslemere arched a brow. "You did say she was too pretty to be a housemaid. Perhaps she's proved too much of a temptation?"

A temptation.

Warm skin under a thin linen night rail, soft curves pressed against him, her long, thick hair brushing his forearm, and that mouth, so sweet and pink, arguing with him, questioning him, challenges falling from the edge of that clever tongue…Gideon slid a finger under his cravat, which seemed to have gone uncomfortably tight around his throat.

There was no denying he was attracted to Cecilia, but that *wasn't* why he'd dismissed her. He never should have let her remain at Darlington Castle after that first day. He'd suspected her of being a liar even then, and now he'd caught her sneaking about the one room in the entire castle he'd warned her away from.

A cat, she'd said. A cat had lured her into Cassandra's bedchamber.

A *cat*, of all absurd things.

He'd been utterly justified in sending her away. "Not to worry, Haslemere. I'll find another housemaid to sweep and scrub for me."

Haslemere snorted. "Forgive me, Darlington, but you aren't precisely spoiled with choice."

Gideon paused with his teacup halfway to his lips, assessing Haslemere with narrowed eyes. Had Cecilia put him up to this? Because she'd said the same thing to him last night, when she was arguing to keep her place.

How had she put it, again?

Oh, yes. Gideon's brows pulled down into a scowl.

The challenges of the position.

She hadn't listed them, but on this matter, she could afford to be subtle.

Every villager in Edenbridge, and a good portion of the London *ton,* imagined he'd murdered his wife and secreted her bones inside the walls of Darlington Castle. A White Lady was said to haunt his grounds, seeking revenge on him for his sinful deeds, and then there was the new moniker he'd been graced with. That alone had likely put off more than one prospective housemaid.

No one wanted to work for the Murderous Marquess.

Gideon fixed a steady gaze on Haslemere, but the hand resting on his knee had clenched into a fist. "It's nothing less than I expected. Have you forgotten, Haslemere? I'm Edenbridge's own wickeder version of Bluebeard."

Haslemere gave him a pained look, and Gideon's conscience pricked at him. It wasn't fair of him to torment poor Haslemere, but Gideon didn't see any point in mincing words. He'd once been regarded as a gentleman of character, and then in the blink of an eye, he'd become a murderer. What was the sense in pretending otherwise?

"The moniker certainly doesn't help," Haslemere allowed, retrieving his teacup with a resigned sigh. "It took you months to find Cecilia. It will take months more to find her replacement, if you can find one at all, particularly one as qualified as she is."

Gideon frowned. "Yes, about that, Haslemere. Does it strike you as odd Cecilia came to Darlington Castle in the first place? Why should a young woman with such a glowing reference from Lady Dunton wish to work *here*, given the rumors about me?"

And that was to say nothing about the rumors of a vengeful ghost.

That was the crux of the problem, right there. He didn't trust Cecilia—her reference from Lady Dunton was suspect, as was her sudden appearance at Darlington Castle. Every instinct warned Gideon she was a problem in the making, a calamity waiting to happen.

"I can't imagine why Lady Dunton would lie about it," Haslemere replied with a shrug. "But it hardly matters, even if she did. You can't afford to dispense with Cecilia, regardless."

"Why not? She's a dreadful housemaid."

"Yes, so you've said. She's too pretty. Wasn't that your complaint?"

"She dropped the coal scuttle when she was making up my fire yesterday morning. It shocked the life of out of me. I thought the ceiling had collapsed." Gideon stabbed a piece of toast with his knife under the pretense of buttering it. He was a devil for saying it, given it was partly his fault she'd dropped that coal scuttle, but it was the only excuse he could think of for dismissing her.

Haslemere stared at him. "*That's* why you dismissed her? Well, I daresay she looked far too fetching with coal dust smudged on her pert little nose. Very right and proper, Darlington."

Gideon snapped off a bite of toast with his teeth, wincing as the dry crumbs lodged in his throat. He wasn't sure why he didn't simply tell Haslemere he'd dismissed Cecilia because she'd entered Cassandra's bedchamber. Haslemere would understand *that*, but for reasons he couldn't explain even to himself, he held his tongue.

"I don't deny she's pretty, Darlington, but she also happens to be an accomplished nursemaid, from what I hear. Mrs. Briggs and Amy are in raptures over her management of Isabella. It isn't fair to them for you to dismiss her. They need the help."

Gideon set his uneaten toast carefully on his plate, fighting off a pang of guilt. "How is it, Haslemere, you always know so much about what's happening in my house?"

"Ah, now there's a question. I'll leave you to answer it for yourself, but if you won't take my word for it, then ask your housekeeper her opinion on the matter. Mrs. Briggs and Amy say Cecilia has a way with children."

Gideon huffed. Of course she did, because it was too much to ask Cecilia to be impatient and short-tempered with Isabella, and thus easily dispensed with. It would have been a damn sight simpler that way, but no, she had to be pleasant and cheerful and win everyone over after a single day here.

"According to Mrs. Briggs, she's just what one wishes for in a nursemaid." Haslemere dropped another lump of sugar into his teacup, studying Gideon as he stirred. "She has the patience of a saint, and a sincere affection for Isabella."

Gideon pushed his plate away, his appetite deserting him. Nothing was more important to him than Isabella's well-being. If Cecilia made his niece happy, what was left to say?

"You still haven't found a replacement for the last nursemaid, I take it? The thief—what was her name again? Mrs. Vermin, wasn't it?"

"It was Vernon, not—"

"I shudder to think what sort of woman you'll have to settle for if you dismiss Cecilia." Haslemere let out a dramatic sigh.

Gideon shuddered to think what could happen if he *didn't* dismiss her. He grimaced at the memory of the incident last night, of the horror on Cecilia's face, the way she'd frozen with terror when he grabbed her.

But even that paled in comparison to the tension between them in his study afterward. He'd *touched* her. He hadn't meant to, but even now he could recall with perfect clarity the feel of her smooth skin under his fingertips. There was no telling what might happen next, or how he'd react to it. Darlington Castle simply wasn't a safe place for an unpredictable young woman like Cecilia Gilchrist.

He wasn't safe—

"You'll end up with the worst of the lot. Worse than Mrs. Vermin, even, and she was a wretched old thing." Haslemere's tone was dark. "You could settle for Amy, but the girl's as jumpy as a cat with Isabella. Have you tried the scullery maid? Perhaps she'd make a suitable nurse."

Gideon rolled his eyes. "Now you're just being ridiculous."

Haslemere's spoon landed in his saucer with a clatter. "If you're determined to dismiss Cecilia, at least you should send a footman to attend her to the stagecoach, Darlington. It's the proper, gentlemanly thing to do."

Gideon pushed his chair back from the table, a sigh on his lips. He'd spent a good deal of time staring out his study window after Cecilia left last night, cringing as he replayed the events of the evening in his mind. A gentleman didn't manhandle a lady, no matter the circumstances. He'd behaved like a blackguard, and it didn't sit well with him.

He owed Cecilia an apology. Not for dismissing her—she'd more than earned that—but for grabbing her as he'd done last night. "She's meant to leave this morning." Gideon retrieved his watch from his coat pocket and glanced down at it, frowning. Cecilia seemed to have no notion how to follow an order. "I told her to be downstairs by eight o'clock. It seems I'll have to fetch her myself."

He took a last gulp of his tea and rose from the table, but before he could move Haslemere jumped up, nearly toppling his chair behind him. "Perhaps it would be better if I speak to her. If you make a mess of it—"

"It's all right, Haslemere. I promise you I'll be a perfect gentleman." A grim smile twitched at Gideon's lips. Occasionally he could still manage to behave in a manner that befitted a marquess. "Sit down and finish your breakfast."

Gideon made his way from the dining parlor to the entrance hall. There was no sign of Cecilia, but Amy was on her hands and knees at the bottom of the stairs scrubbing the floors, a bucket by her side. "Good morning, Amy."

Amy looked up at the sound of his voice. "Good morning, my lord," she replied, politely enough, but Gideon didn't miss the sour twist to her lips.

Here was one member of his household who wasn't pleased about Cecilia's dismissal. Amy looked as if she was one second away from tossing her cleaning rag in his face. "Did you happen to see Cecilia this morning?"

"Yes, my lord." Amy's voice was chilly. "She ran upstairs to bid Lady Isabella goodbye."

"Thank you." Gideon moved toward the stairs, giving Amy and her bucket a wide berth, aware she was glowering at his back as he passed.

He climbed the stairs and strode down the hallway to his bedchamber, but once he got to the connecting door he paused with his hand on the latch. There was a strange sound coming from Isabella's room. That is, not strange, but not a sound that had been heard much at Darlington Castle these past twelve months or more.

Isabella was *laughing*. Not the muted laugh of an anxious child who'd seen too much loss in her young life, but the carefree, joyful laugh of a child who, if even for only this brief moment, was happy in the way a child should be.

Entirely, unabashedly happy.

Cecilia was singing to her. Gideon pressed an ear to the door, his chest aching at the sound of her low, sweet voice. He couldn't make out her song—something about a pale-faced visage and the darts of death. His lips quirked. Not a lullaby, then, but Isabella didn't seem to mind, because she was *laughing.*

He rested his forehead against the door, gratitude swelling inside him. He hadn't heard Isabella laugh like that since Cassandra died. He'd begun to wonder if she ever *would* laugh like that again, or if the loss had stolen her laughter, and scarred her in ways Gideon didn't yet understand.

"*If Death commands the King to leave his crown, He at my feet must lay his scepter down*—oh, dear." Cecilia interrupted herself with a sigh. "This isn't a proper song for you at all, is it, Isabella? I seemed destined to fail you in that regard."

"What does the king do?" Isabella asked, utterly unconcerned with propriety.

"He hasn't any choice, has he? He turns over his crown and scepter, just as death commands him to do."

"What's a scepter?"

"It's a long stick made especially for a king from gold and jewels, just as a king's crown is."

"It is like Uncle Gideon's walking stick?"

"Not quite the same. A marquess isn't a king, but I imagine your uncle has a very fine walking stick."

Gideon chuckled, then slid the door open as quietly as he could, curious to see this little tableau for himself. He leaned a hip against the door frame, taking in the scene before him.

Cecilia was seated in the rocking chair beside Isabella's bed, her back to Gideon. His niece was enthroned on her lap like a tiny princess, plucking at a fold of her skirts. "I wish I could have a crown."

"Well, of course, you do. Who wouldn't like to have a golden crown? I daresay it would be easy enough to make you one with a bit of gilt paper. Perhaps we could...that is, perhaps Miss Amy could help you make one."

Isabella didn't notice the way Cecilia faltered. She let out a little squeal of glee at the promise of a golden crown, wriggling with delight, her face alight with anticipation.

"Now, shall we see what happens to our king? I believe the fatal wounds and the yielding and dying part are next. Perhaps we should skip those, hmm?" Cecilia caught hold of one of Isabella's hands and pressed a kiss to her palm. "What say you, madam?"

"No!" Isabella's bottom lip poked out. "I want to hear the killing parts."

"You really should only hear songs about spring posies and such. They're much more to a child's taste than songs about death. That's just as it should be, but I'm afraid I don't recall any of those." Cecilia's tone was a little wistful, but Gideon heard a smile in her voice. "There was one about lavender, I think, but—"

"'Lavender's Blue.'" Gideon could have stayed quietly by the door all day watching them, but it felt underhanded to him, as if he were eavesdropping. "'*Lavender's blue, Lavender's green/can we fix the spacing here?When I am king, you shall be queen.*' Don't tell me you've forgotten that one, Cecilia?"

She jumped at the sound of his voice, then glanced over her shoulder. Her smile faded when she saw him. "Lord Darlington."

"Good morning, Cecilia. I expected you to be downstairs by now." Gideon strolled into the room, his lips quirking in a grin when Isabella let out a little cry of welcome. "Hello, Isabella."

"Isabella, go and fetch Amy, won't you? She's downstairs." Cecilia lifted Isabella off her lap and set her down on the floor. "Mrs. Briggs said Cook was making almond cakes today."

"The little cakes with the sugar on top?" Isabella clapped her hands together, then raced to the door and skipped down the hallway, calling Amy's name as she went.

As soon as the door closed behind her, Cecilia rose from the rocking chair and faced Gideon, her brows lowered. "About my departure, my lord. You're making a dreadful mistake, sending me away from Darlington Castle."

Gideon arched an eyebrow. "Is that so?"

"Yes." Cecilia raised her chin. "I've given it a good deal of thought, and I feel obligated to say I think it's remarkably short-sighted of you to dismiss me."

Gideon took in her flashing dark eyes, and all at once he wanted to capture that stubborn chin in his hand and hold her still so he could lose himself in those eyes, even if only for a moment. "I wasn't aware the matter was negotiable," he said instead, clearing his throat.

"No, I didn't suppose you were. I daresay it wasn't negotiable last night, what with you being in such an unreasonable temper, but I had hopes you'd come to your senses by this morning."

Gideon's fingers flexed. The urge to touch her was overwhelming, but he kept his arms at his sides. He'd already decided he couldn't dispense with the services of anyone who made his niece burst into such glorious laughter, but he didn't say so yet. "And if I haven't come to my senses, but instead have come to see you deposited in my carriage and taken away, what then, Cecilia? How will you change my mind?"

He stepped closer, expecting her to step back, but she stayed right where she was, glowering up at him. She was all outraged defiance, but Gideon could see that underneath her bravado, she was nervous. Still, that obstinate chin hitched another notch higher. "As to that, Lord Darlington, I don't suppose I can change your mind, but before I leave, allow me to give you a piece of *mine*."

To Gideon's surprise, a laugh crept to his lips. It was part amusement and part incredulity, but as impressed as he was with her bravery, he couldn't allow his housemaid to lecture him. "There's no need for you to—"

"On the contrary, my lord, there's every need. First of all, you called me a liar last night. Well, I won't permit it. I'm no liar, Lord Darlington, and I won't allow you to call me one, even if you are a marquess."

Gideon blinked. *Had* he called her a liar? "I beg your pardon, but I never called you—"

"Yes, you did. I told you the door connecting my room to Lady Darlington's bedchamber wasn't locked, and you insisted it was. Furthermore, you attacked me last night as if I were a thief invading your castle."

Yes, he *had* done that. To be fair, he'd been convinced she *was* a thief invading his castle, and for good reason. Still, he should have apologized at once when he discovered she wasn't. "I beg your pardon for that," he offered stiffly. "I regret it extremely."

"Well, that's something, anyway," Cecilia allowed, but twin spots of angry color burned in her cheeks, and she muttered something under her breath about arrogant marquesses.

Gideon shifted from one foot to the other, waiting for the rest of what was beginning to feel like a severe dressing down. He couldn't quite believe it was being delivered by one of his housemaids, but perhaps it was just as well to let her have her say, and get it over with.

"There's no reason I can see for you to have reacted with such violence when you found me in the marchioness's bedchamber, despite your having forbidden me to enter it," she said, her dark eyes glinting with temper. "But even that, Lord Darlington, isn't the worst of your crimes."

"It isn't?" Gideon half-expected her to accuse him of murdering his wife and inflicting her ghost on the good citizens of Edenbridge, but she didn't. Instead she pointed a shaking finger at the door through which Isabella had just gone.

"Your niece is fond of me, my lord. After only a few days, she's fonder of me than of any other servant in this house, and yet you'd send me away in spite of it. Who, my lord, will take care of her in my place? Amy does her best, but she isn't experienced with children. Isabella can sense it, and it makes her anxious."

"How I care for my niece is none of your concern, but since you ask, I—"

"But I *am* concerned, my lord. I care for Isabella, too."

"—but since you ask," Gideon went on, speaking over her. "I came up here to see if you'd agree to—"

"I'm aware why you're here, Lord Darlington." She drew herself up to her full height and threw her shoulders back. "You've come to send me away, and I daresay I can't stop you, but I was determined not to leave without unburdening myself first."

He eyed her, a strange exhilaration pounding through him. There was no reason her show of defiance should please him, but it did. That is, no man cared for being scolded as if he were a naughty schoolboy—and by his housemaid, no less—but defiance was far better than having her shrink away from him in horror, or cower in his presence. "Very well. Have you quite finished?"

"I suppose. For now, at any rate. I'm certain I'll think of something more I wished I'd said when I'm in the stagecoach on my way home."

Gideon shook his head, amazed such a delicate, fawn-like young woman could deliver such a blistering scold, but he was beginning to see there was a great deal more to Cecilia Gilchrist than pretty eyes and a sweet singing voice. "No, you won't."

She shot him a resentful look. "Yes, I will. That's always the way with a scold. The best parts never occur to one until it's too late to say them."

Gideon's lips twitched. "No, Cecilia. What I mean is, it won't be necessary for you to leave, after all. I've changed my mind. You may remain at Darlington Castle as Isabella's nursemaid, provided you can promise you'll follow my orders in the future. Do you suppose you can do that?"

For all her lecturing, Cecilia clearly hadn't expected a reprieve. She stared at him for a moment, her mouth open. "Well, I…I can promise to *try*, at any rate."

It wasn't quite what Gideon was hoping for, but since he was no longer willing to dispense with her services, it would have to do. "Very well, then. Have you breakfasted?"

"No. I didn't want to lose what time I had left with Isabella."

"Go on down to the kitchens, then. I'm certain Cook can find something for you." Gideon seated himself in the rocking chair. "I'll tend to Isabella when she returns."

Cecilia hesitated, biting her lip.

He raised an eyebrow at her. "You've no need to worry, Cecilia. I'm perfectly capable of taking care of my niece. This may surprise you, but she's rather fond of *me*, as well."

Chapter Nine

Mrs. Briggs was a true Englishwoman in that she believed a cup of tea could cure every ill. Cecilia used to think so, too, but today had been a long day, and after that dreadful scold she'd dealt Lord Darlington this morning, even the housekeeper's bracing tea couldn't chase away her anxiety.

She'd *scolded* a marquess. Her friends would have been thrilled at her cheek—particularly Georgiana, who delighted in a good scold—but every time she thought about it, Cecilia's knees went weak with alarm.

One didn't scold a marquess, for pity's sake, especially not when one was said marquess's servant, and even more particularly when said marquess wasn't just any marquess, but potentially the Murderous Marquess—

"Will you take another cup of tea, dear? You look a bit peaked." Mrs. Briggs regarded Cecilia with concern. "After the day we've had, I daresay you're fatigued."

Cecilia slid her teacup across the scrubbed kitchen table toward Mrs. Briggs with a grateful smile. "Thank you. I imagine you're tired, too. It was a long day for you, as well."

"I don't mind telling you I don't fancy making up beds." Mrs. Briggs braced one hand in the middle of her back, grimacing. "Hurts my old bones, it does."

Cecilia's bones were young enough, but that didn't stop them creaking in protest with every feeble twitch of her limbs. Yesterday they'd beaten dirt from the carpets until Cecilia thought her arms would fall off. This morning they'd dusted every inch of the downstairs rooms, and spent the afternoon scrubbing bedchambers and making up beds with clean linen.

Every bedchamber, that is, except the late Lady Darlington's.

Miss Honeywell was not, it seemed, to take up residence in the marchioness's apartments. Curious, that. Whatever secret Lord Darlington was hiding behind those closed doors must be a terrible one, indeed. It was on the tip of Cecilia's tongue to ask Mrs. Briggs about it, but she didn't dare pry into that business yet.

She was, however, perfectly willing to pry into other, less sensitive business. "Isabella doesn't look much like Lord Darlington. Does she not resemble her father's side of the family?"

Mrs. Briggs's gaze dropped to her teacup. "No, she looks more like her mother."

"She's an unusually beautiful child, isn't she? Such pretty hazel eyes."

Mrs. Briggs beamed. "Oh my, yes. You can't imagine what an adorable baby she was, with those big eyes of hers, like two bright stars. Fairly hypnotized us all, she did."

"Her mother must be a great beauty." Cecilia took care not to appear too interested, aware she'd have to tread carefully here. Mrs. Briggs had been with the family for years, well before the current Lord Darlington's father inherited the title. She knew more about the mysteries surrounding Darlington Castle than anyone, but she was also the least inclined to gossip.

"Have you not seen Lady Leanora's portrait hanging in the small picture gallery?" Mrs. Briggs asked with surprise.

"What, you mean the gallery outside Lord Darlington's study?" Cecilia did her best not to look at that row of ghoulish faces whenever she was obliged to pass through that hallway, but she was quite certain there wasn't a single beauty amongst them.

"No, no. The small picture gallery is tucked under the eaves on the second-floor landing. Lady Leanora's portrait is there. She is indeed a striking beauty, but then Lord Darlington's elder brother, Nathanial, was as handsome a gentleman as I've ever seen. He and Lady Leanora together were..." Mrs. Briggs paused, as if searching for a word that did them justice. "They were truly magnificent."

Cecilia was stirring her tea, but she paused at the wistful note in Mrs. Briggs's voice. "Indeed?"

"My, yes. They were both darlings of the *ton*, you know, and the toast of London when they were courting. Such a pity their marriage wasn't a happier one, but then that's what comes of a whirlwind courtship, I suppose. They hardly knew each other when they wed."

Cecilia set her spoon aside. "They weren't happy together?"

Mrs. Briggs sighed. "Not after the first year or so, no. Lady Leanora was very young, you understand, and then years passed without a child. It put a strain on their marriage. Nathanial—the late marquess, that is—left Lady Leanora behind in Kent and went off to live with Gideon in London those last few years before he died. He came home now and again, but I doubt he would have returned to the castle to live if Lady Leanora hadn't conceived."

"That is a pity." Cecilia poured more milk into her tea, her gaze on her teacup to hide her expression. "Isabella was only an infant when her father died, wasn't she?"

"Just two months old. Nathanial's death was a terrible tragedy, and a dreadful shock to us all. I've never seen a man more devastated than Gideon—I mean, Lord Darlington—when he returned to Darlington Castle for his brother's funeral. Indeed, he's never been the same."

Cecilia heard a telltale quiver in Mrs. Briggs's voice, and looked up to find the housekeeper's eyes bright with tears. She covered Mrs. Brigg's hand with her own, remorse clawing at her, but she couldn't be silent now. She'd come to Darlington Castle for answers. "He was an affectionate brother, then?"

"Oh, my yes. Gideon—forgive me, Cecilia, for speaking of Lord Darlington so familiarly, but I've been with the family since the two boys were just wee lads, long before their father inherited the title. Gideon fairly worshipped his elder brother, he did. He and Nathanial were as close as two brothers could be."

"How did Nathanial die, Mrs. Briggs?"

"One night he was...oh, Duncan Geary, there you are!" Mrs. Briggs shot up from her chair, wiping a hand across her cheek. "Where have you been all this time, my boy?"

Cecilia's heart sank at the interruption, but she turned around in her chair to offer Duncan Geary, one of Lord Darlington's few remaining footmen a smile.

Duncan was a red-headed Scot from Inverness who was old enough to tower over all the other servants, but young enough not yet to have worked out quite what to do with his long, gangly limbs. Cecilia was fond of him because he was a kind, gentle lad, and because he had the good sense to be sweet on Amy. "Hello, Duncan."

Duncan blushed and ducked his head. "Hello, Miss Cecilia. I've been in the woods again with his lordship and Lord Haslemere, ma'am, chasing that lantern light," he said to Mrs. Briggs.

Mrs. Briggs was bustling about for biscuits and another teacup for Duncan. "I suppose he's got you looking for those poachers, has he? Well, well, sit down and have some tea. You must be frozen half solid."

"What makes Lord Darlington think it's poachers?" Poachers raiding the woods while the household was still awake, in plain sight of the castle, and carrying lanterns? That didn't sound like any poachers Cecilia had ever heard of.

"They're either poachers or pranksters, mayhap, but whoever they are, they've got no business being on castle grounds. But never mind that, Cecilia. It's nearly Isabella's bedtime. You can go straight to her bedchamber. I've had Amy move all your things there."

"My things?" Cecilia asked, puzzled.

"Of course, child. You're to sleep in Isabella's room, now you're to be her nursemaid."

Cecilia stared at Mrs. Briggs in horror. Isabella's room was connected to Lord Darlington's apartments, with only a flimsy door between them. Why, she might as well be sleeping in Lord Darlington's bedchamber with him! "It...didn't occur to me I'd have to change rooms."

"Well, of course you must, dear. Since Amy is taking up your duties, and you're to take charge of Isabella, the two of you will switch places. It makes sense, really. Amy's a good girl, but she doesn't know much about children, does she?" Mrs. Briggs flapped her tea towel at Cecilia to shoo her away. "Go on, then. Isabella likely has poor Amy in fits by now."

"Yes, Mrs. Briggs." Cecilia left the kitchen in a daze. Somehow, she'd overlooked the fact that becoming Isabella's nursemaid meant she was obliged to sleep close to—and within easy reach of—the Marquess of Darlington.

It wasn't a comforting thought. Between the ghosts, secret bedchambers, a haunted cat, and a mysterious, brooding marquess, it would be a miracle if she ever got another wink of sleep again.

The tea she'd had sloshed sickeningly in her stomach as she made her way up the staircase. She hadn't eaten enough today. After beating carpets, dusting up cobwebs, and scrubbing floors, food had been the last thing on her mind, but now her head was bobbling uncertainly on her neck, as if deciding whether to stay attached or topple off and tumble down the stairs into the entrance hall.

She dragged her aching body up one step to the next, then paused at the second-floor landing and glanced around, searching for the portraits Mrs. Briggs had mentioned. The long, narrow hallway to the left didn't lead anywhere, but ended at a large window at the far end.

It might have been another dreary space in a dreary castle but for the intricately carved white plaster ceilings. They were high enough to lend an airiness to the space, and barrel-shaped, with chandeliers set at regular intervals. The candles weren't lit, but Cecilia could see they'd been carefully arranged to emphasize the ceiling's pleasing curve.

It was a lovely place. Rather surprising, really, given the atmosphere in the rest of the castle. She wandered down the hallway toward the first painting, but stopped in her tracks when her gaze landed on a stunningly beautiful face set off to perfection by an extravagant gilded frame.

This wasn't one of Lord Darlington's grim ancestors.

"My goodness," Cecilia breathed. She moved a step closer, drawn by the ravishing vision before her. The lady was dressed in a blue silk gown that had been the height of fashion eight or so years earlier. It flattered the deep blue of her eyes and her thick, rich brown curls. Her eyelashes were as dark as her hair, her lips as red as the deepest red rose petals, and her skin so fine, white, and flawless it didn't look real.

Cecilia had never seen a more magnificent lady in her life, not even Emma, who was an exquisite beauty. Emma's beauty, though, was that of a mere mortal, not a goddess like the lady in the painting. She cocked her head to the side, studying the bewitching features. For all the lady's spectacular beauty, Cecilia found herself unmoved by that face. There was something unnatural about such flawless perfection. She looked as if she'd stepped out of a storybook, a fairy tale.

Yes, that was the trouble, wasn't it? She didn't look *real*.

There could be no doubt who this lady was, but Cecilia ventured another step closer and squinted at the tiny gold plaque underneath the painting to read the inscription.

"Lady Leanora. My late brother's widow, the sixth Marchioness of Darlington."

Cecilia whirled around, her heart rushing into her throat. "Lord Darlington, I didn't—"

"Didn't see me? No, I thought not." He strolled down the hallway and joined her in front of the painting, the thud of his boots on the carpeted floors echoing in the lofty space.

How had she not heard him approach? His heavy steps sounded like gunshots in the narrow hallway. "I beg your pardon, my lord. Mrs. Briggs mentioned there were paintings here. She said I might come see them, but I didn't intend to sneak about." He had, after all, accused her of that very thing last night, and Cecilia didn't fancy a repeat of *that* argument.

Lord Darlington took her meaning at once, and a trace of a smile drifted across his full lips. "Of course, you did. Otherwise you wouldn't be here. Never mind," he added. "I never said you couldn't come here. There isn't a locked door between you and the picture gallery."

It was on the tip of Cecilia's tongue to protest there hadn't been a *locked* door between hers and Lady Darlington's bedchamber, either, but she held her tongue, choosing instead to stroll farther along the hallway, pausing to study the portraits as she passed.

A few Darlington aunts and uncles, all of them handsome, and then...

"Oh, my." She stopped at a painting close to the end of the row, her breath leaving her lungs in a rush.

"That's the usual reaction people have when they see my brother for the first time." Lord Darlington joined her in front of the portrait. "Even if only the painted version of him."

Cecilia felt her cheeks heat, and a soft laugh rumbled from Lord Darlington's chest. His laugh was the same as his voice, deep and dark and rough at the edges, and like his voice, it made an unwelcome shiver dart down Cecilia's spine.

"My brother was a striking man, but he and Leanora together were... well, you can see for yourself. Together, they were...haunting."

Haunting. Cecilia thought it an odd choice of word.

"My elder brother favored our father, as you'll see."

Lord Darlington gestured toward the painting on the other side of his brother's, but Cecilia stayed where she was, studying the handsome face before her, the painted blue eyes holding her gaze. "Isabella doesn't look much like her father, does she? I do see a resemblance to Lady Leanora— all but the hazel eyes."

"She favors her mother." Lord Darlington's tone was curt.

When he didn't offer anything more, Cecilia moved to the next painting, and found another handsome, dark-haired Darlington gentleman gazing down at her from his perch on the wall. It was Lord Darlington's father, the fifth Marquess of Darlington. "You and your elder brother both resemble your father, my lord."

"In some particulars, yes." Lord Darlington's broad shoulders moved in a shrug. "Not as much as we once did."

Cecilia studied the man's features before taking in the portrait of his wife, Lord Darlington's mother, who was fairer than her sons, but with the same bright blue eyes that had caught Cecilia's attention when she got her first close look at Lord Darlington.

"You and your brother have your mother's eyes," she murmured.

"We do, yes," Lord Darlington replied, sounding surprised.

Cecilia turned to him, a slight smile on her lips. "Did you suppose I hadn't noticed the color of your eyes, my lord? They're rather distinctive. You and your brother look very much alike."

Both gentlemen had strong features with prominent cheekbones, angular jaws, and high, proud foreheads. The current Lord Darlington was as handsome as his elder brother had been, but there was nothing of Nathanial's carefree happiness in the man who stood beside her now. Grief had stolen the joy from his face, and painted lines of regret in its place. "Were you and your brother close, my lord?"

Lord Darlington didn't answer right away. He was staring up at the painting still, an expression Cecilia couldn't read on his face. "Yes," he said at last. "We were, particularly when we were boys. Less so once he married, though we spent a good deal of time together in London in the few years before he died."

"Did he...did he fall ill?" Nathanial Rhys's death was none of her concern, and she half-expected Lord Darlington to tell her so, but he answered with a frankness that startled her.

"No. He drowned in Darlington Lake."

Cecilia whirled to face him, a soft gasp on her lips. "I...but how terrible to lose him so tragically. I-I'm truly sorry, my lord."

He drew in a quick, hard breath, but he said only, "I am, too. I can't tell you how sorry."

They were both quiet for a time, staring up at the handsome face, then Lord Darlington moved to the end of the row, and nodded up at the last portrait. "It was taken a decade ago."

Cecilia followed after him, but froze when her gaze locked on the painted version of the man who stood beside her. It was beautifully done, the delicate brushstrokes as exquisite as the face of the young man gazing back at her, but if she hadn't known him to be the current Lord Darlington, she might not have recognized the two to be the same man.

Lord Darlington was about twenty-five in the portrait, a breathtaking young man with a mop of wavy dark hair and a devilish glint in his startlingly bright blue eyes. His posture was easy, relaxed, and though he wasn't smiling, there was a hint of amusement around the corners of his mouth.

Cecilia swallowed the sudden lump in her throat. With Lord Darlington standing so close to his likeness, she could see with stark, heartbreaking clarity the toll grief had taken on him. Whatever had happened in this castle a year ago, Lord Darlington wore the effects of it on his face as surely as he wore his coat or his cravat.

"Amazing, is it not, the ravages unkind years can wreak on a face?" Lord Darlington's voice was light, but there was a note of sadness that made Cecilia's heart clench with pain for him. She turned to look at him, wishing she knew what to say in reply, but he wasn't looking at her.

He was staring at a space on the wall beside his portrait where the portrait of his marchioness should hang. It was empty. Cecilia could see by the pale, rectangular patch in the wood paneling *someone's* portrait had once hung there, and been recently removed. "What of your marchioness, Lord Darlington? Where is her painting?"

It was natural she should wonder, but Cecilia saw at once this was the wrong question to ask. Lord Darlington turned on her, his mouth tight. "I told you once curiosity isn't a desirable trait in a servant, Cecilia. Have you forgotten?"

"Have you ever noticed, Lord Darlington, the more secrets one has, the less desirable curiosity becomes? No, I haven't forgotten what you said. I have quite an accurate memory. Is that also an undesirable trait in a servant?"

His gaze jerked to her face. "You did warn me you had excellent aim," he muttered with grudging admiration.

Cecilia wasn't sure what to make of this cryptic comment, so she said nothing.

"It's nearly my niece's bedtime," Lord Darlington said. "Have you quite finished strolling about the picture gallery?"

"Yes, my lord." A dozen more questions rushed to Cecilia's lips, but Lord Darlington's hard expression made it clear their brief moment of sharing confidences was over.

"Very well." He stepped aside, and waved her toward the stairs.

Cecilia edged around him, but he followed so closely behind her she could feel the heat of him, hear the soft sound of his breaths, and her skin tingled with awareness. "Is there something else you need, my lord?" she asked, when she reached Isabella's door with Lord Darlington right on her heels.

He leaned a hip against the door frame, a smirk on his lips. "I thought I'd bid Isabella goodnight. That is, if you don't object?"

"I—no, of course not, my lord." Cecilia's cheeks heated. What had she thought he was doing? Following *her*?

She opened the door and found Amy seated in the rocking chair with Isabella fussing on her lap. She looked up in relief when Cecilia entered. "Oh, thank goodness you're back, Cecilia. I hope you're ready to sing yourself hoarse, because the poor little thing's been fussing since—"

Amy's words faded to silence when Lord Darlington stepped into the room behind Cecilia. He took one look at Isabella's tear-streaked face, strode over to the rocking chair, and held out his arms. "Give her to me, please, Amy."

"Yes, my lord." Amy rose to her feet and held Isabella out toward her uncle. "Here you are." She bobbed a curtsy and hurried to the door, her wide eyes meeting Cecilia's for a fleeting glance before she went out, leaving Cecilia alone with Lord Darlington.

Cecilia stood awkwardly by the door, but she might as well not have been there at all for all the notice Lord Darlington paid her. All his attention was focused on Isabella. "What's the matter, sweetheart? Why all the tears?"

"I don't want to go to bed," Isabella said, with a pathetic sniffle.

"Well, then. Let's finish our story first. Would you like that?"

Isabella rubbed the tears from her eyes with her little fists. "The story about the snow castle?"

"That very one."

"Yes, please." Isabella's mouth was still trembling, but she snuggled against her uncle's chest.

Lord Darlington tucked the child's head under his chin and began his story, his tone low and soothing. Cecilia couldn't hear what he said—something about building a castle in the snow—but it didn't matter. It was the deep rumble of his voice that caught her attention, the drift of his long fingers through the golden-brown locks of Isabella's hair.

She perched on the edge of her cot, watching the firelight play over Lord Darlington's features, gilding him, blurring his harsh edges. She searched his face for any hint of cruelty, any trace of the brutality of which he'd been accused.

There was nothing.

There was just him. Big, gentle hands, dark hair curling against his neck, his long eyelashes shadowing his cheeks, the curve of his jaw and the vulnerable pulse at this throat, the movement of his full lips as he made his whispered promises to Isabella.

Cecilia couldn't take her eyes off him.

How could such a man as this, a man who touched a child with such care, who spoke to her with such tenderness, be guilty of murdering his wife?

For that one instant, in that one suspended moment, it seemed impossible to Cecilia Lord Darlington could have committed such a crime. If he hadn't, if the malicious gossip was false, and he was innocent, what must his life have been like this past year?

The man in the portrait, that young, handsome man, his face glowing with anticipation and promise, to have had his future stolen from him, his every hope dashed by ugly rumors. The misery, the wretchedness and pain of such a thing made Cecilia's breath catch hard in her throat. She tried to choke back the sound, but Lord Darlington heard it, and his gaze jerked to her face.

They didn't speak. Not a single word passed between them, but even as Cecilia told herself to look away, his dark blue eyes, eyes full of secrets and shadows, held her trapped. The fire crackled, and Isabella sighed in her sleep. Warmth flooded Cecilia's belly and rushed over her skin, and her heartbeat throbbed in her ears.

Still, their gazes held.

Her lips parted. For an instant his eyes dropped to her mouth, and Cecilia felt her tongue creep out to touch her bottom lip. He followed the movement, and a sound tore from his throat, a growl or a gasp.

He rose from the chair and took a step toward her, his eyes darkening to a turbulent blue when she didn't back away from him. "Don't...look at me like that."

Cecilia swallowed, but when she spoke her voice was so breathy, she hardly recognized it as her own. "How...how am I looking at you?"

His heated gaze swept over her, lingering on the curves of her hips and breasts and tracing the lines of her neck. "As if you want—"

But Cecilia never found out how she looked, or what she wanted, because Isabella stirred, mumbling something in her sleep. Lord Darlington blinked, then jerked his gaze from her face to Isabella's.

The tension between them snapped, and the moment was gone.

He turned away from her, settling Isabella in her bed and dropping a kiss on her pink cheek. When he straightened from the bed he stood there awkwardly, as if he wasn't sure what to do. Finally, he gave her a curt nod, avoiding her eyes.

Cecilia rose uncertainly to her feet. "Good night."

He nodded again, and then...then he did something that shouldn't have sent a shiver over her skin, followed by a confusing rush of searing heat.

But it did.

He strode to the door that connected Isabella's cozy room to his own bedchamber, opened it, and closed it again behind him. He was so close she could hear him on the other side, the soft thud of his footsteps moving across the floor.

Cecilia dropped onto her cot, her knees trembling. The only thing separating her sleeping quarters from Lord Darlington's bedchamber was a single, connecting door.

Chapter Ten

Four days later.

Gideon opened one eye as his bedchamber door creaked open, the notes of "The Irish Girl" drifting through his head. Had he dreamed of that song again? Of the sweet, clear voice that sang it, each silvery note falling like soft raindrops against his skin—

His other eye flew open, a grimace twisting his lips. For God's sakes, had he really just compared Cecilia Gilchrist's voice to *silvery raindrops*?

Yes. Yes, he had.

He dragged the pillow over his face with a soft groan. There was no reason *that* song, in *her* voice should still be echoing as clearly in his head as it had since the first notes left her lips. He'd heard dozens of voices sweeter than hers sing dozens of songs much prettier than that one.

Gideon listened to the soft scrape of the brush against the hearth, the chink of coal, then the strike of flint against steel as Amy lay the fire. At least, he assumed it was Amy, as the business was concluded tidily, with no deafening crashes.

Once she'd left him alone in his bedchamber he sat up, plunged a fist into his pillow, and fell back against it with groan. Every night for the past four days, he'd dreamed about Cecilia Gilchrist. If it wasn't her voice, it was her wide, dark eyes. If not that, then it was her affection for Isabella, or her seemingly endless supply of inappropriate ballads.

He was preoccupied with her, and he didn't like it one bit.

Only the worst sort of scoundrel lusted after his servants. He was a man with potent physical urges, but never in his life had he cast a lascivious glance at any of them—not before his wife's death, when there'd been dozens of housemaids roaming about the castle—and not afterward. He'd confined his masculine attentions to his wife, and he'd do the same again when he and Fanny Honeywell were married.

He needed to banish Cecilia from his mind and put his attention where it belonged.

On his *betrothed.*

She'd be here in a matter of days. A week after that she'd become his marchioness, and this strange fixation he had on Cecilia would wither like blighted fruit on the vine.

It *would,* because he wouldn't allow it to be otherwise.

Until then, he'd simply make a point of keeping away from Cecilia. There was no reason for her to remain in Isabella's bedchamber when he spent time with his niece. He was perfectly capable of tending to her on his own. He'd always done so before, and there was no reason to change his habits now, even if his masculine urges reared up in violent protest at the thought.

Especially then.

And reared up they had, damn them.

This morning's protest was more violent than usual, and it took longer than it should have for Gideon to wrestle his body into submission. So long when he crawled from his bed at last, he found the water in the basin had gone freezing cold. He splashed a handful on his face anyway, hoping it would douse the flames in his belly and knock some sense into him, then he donned his riding clothes.

He and Haslemere had agreed to have a ride this morning, and Gideon fancied a good, hard one before the sky released the snow that had been threatening for days, and they all found themselves trapped inside the castle.

Haslemere offered no objection, and so the two of them rode for hours, until Gideon's heart was pounding with exertion, his thighs ached, and sweat poured off him, plastering his shirt to his chest and back. If he hadn't quite managed to silence the lingering notes of "The Irish Girl," it echoed less insistently now, allowing other thoughts to drift into the places Cecilia had seized inside his head.

When he arrived back at the castle, he took the stairs two at a time, stripping off his coat and cravat as he went. He discarded both along with his riding crop and hat, a smile hovering on his lips as he strode toward the connecting door. It was nearly teatime, and there was nothing Isabella adored more than being permitted to have tea in the drawing room with her uncle.

"Good afternoon." Gideon forced a smile as he paused beside the door, ignoring the sinking feeling in his chest when he saw it was Amy, not Cecilia with Isabella. "Do you fancy having tea with me downstairs today, Isabella?"

"Oh yes, Uncle!" Isabella climbed down from Amy's lap, excited at the rare treat. "But we have to wait for Miss Cecilia, so she may come with us, too."

"Where is Cecilia?" Gideon asked, on Isabella's behalf only, of course. It wasn't as if *he* wanted to know where she was.

Amy was sitting in the rocking chair with a storybook open in her lap, but she leapt up, a guilty flush rising in her cheeks. "She, ah, had an errand to run, my lord. I daresay she'll be back soon. May I send her down to the drawing room when—"

"She's in the attics!" Isabella cried, clearly taken with the novelty of anyone venturing into such an exotic place.

"The attics?" What the devil was she doing *there*? Gideon raised an eyebrow at Amy, who was looking more uneasy with every passing moment. "I can't think why. She does know that part of the castle is closed, doesn't she?"

She did, of course. Mrs. Briggs made certain all the servants did. To Gideon's knowledge, none of them had ever ventured up there, but then Cecilia wasn't anything like his other servants, with her talent for poking her nose into places it had no business being.

Amy was biting her lip. "Mrs. Briggs said she might go up to the old schoolroom to search out some storybooks for Isabella, my lord."

"She said she'd look for some pretty paper to make me a crown, and a stick, too!" Isabella jumped up and down with excitement. "A stick with jewels, like a king has."

"Did she? How...resourceful of her." Gideon gave one of Isabella's curls a playful tug, but his eyes narrowed on Amy, who was shifting from one foot to the other, and looking very much as if she'd rather be anywhere but here.

Somehow, he doubted Cecilia was only looking for storybooks and paper. "Please see Isabella is readied for tea in the drawing room, Amy." Gideon turned on his heel and strode to the door. "I'll fetch Cecilia myself."

* * * *

It began innocently enough. Or at least as innocently as anything else at Darlington Castle did, which is to say, not innocently at all.

There was nothing innocent about a murdered marchioness and a missing portrait, and Cecilia would do well to remember that, instead of mooning over how handsome Lord Darlington looked in the firelight. Silly romantic notions were all very well in novels, but despite the crumbling castle and the White Lady, this was no Gothic fiction.

Cecilia was no swooning virgin, and Lord Darlington no brooding hero.

If there'd ever been a time to put sentiment aside in favor of facts and evidence, it was now. So, here she was, in the last place she should be, poking about among centuries of Darlington family secrets. If she didn't quite like it—if being here left a bitter, guilty taste in her mouth—she'd just have to choke it back, wouldn't she?

This was what Lady Clifford had sent her here to do, and she was running out of time to get it done. Each day that passed brought Fanny Honeywell ever closer to Darlington Castle, and marriage to Lord Darlington.

A man who might, or might not, be a murderer.

Cecilia had taken a cursory turn through the schoolroom and found a few books and some sheets of pretty marbled paper that would do for a crown and scepter for Isabella, but she'd come up to the attics in search of something else. Something she hoped she'd find here, buried somewhere among a castle's worth of discarded furnishings, each hulking piece covered with a sheet turned gray from years of accumulated grime.

All but the portraits, that is. Cecilia wasn't certain why they'd escaped without shrouds, unless it was there were simply too many of them. Whatever the reason, the portraits had long since been abandoned to their dusty fates, propped up against the walls and each other, what little light there was glinting off their dulled gilt frames. Dozens upon dozens of past marquesses and their wives and children, one dead Darlington ancestor after another, reaching back generations.

All except one.

Lady Cassandra, the seventh Marchioness of Darlington, was missing.

She wasn't in the small picture gallery, or among the row of unsmiling aristocrats lining the hallway outside Lord Darlington's study. Nor was her portrait hanging in the formal portrait gallery that stretched from one end of the castle to the other, along the east wall on the second floor.

She wasn't…anywhere.

Cecilia leaned the portrait she'd been examining back against the wall, her heart plummeting. She'd thought…she'd hoped she'd find Lady Cassandra here.

It wasn't until Cecilia discovered the portrait appeared to be truly gone that she realized how badly she'd wanted to see Lady Cassandra's face, how desperately she'd wanted her...*not* to be missing. Because surely, surely an absence such as this bespoke a guilty conscience? A husband who couldn't bear to look upon his late wife's likeness, couldn't bear to stare into the eyes of the wife he'd—

"*Mrrar.*"

"God in heaven!" Cecilia jumped back as something scurried under the hem of her skirts. She didn't panic, as she recognized the dark, furry body at once, but she did scold the cat when it darted back out again. "Seraphina, you wicked beast! You nearly frightened the life of out of me! How in the world did you get into the attic?"

Seraphina wasn't ever much inclined to explain herself, and this time was no different. She didn't deign to offer another mew, but padded over to a trunk in a corner of the attic and, with one graceful leap, settled herself on top of it like a queen before turning her expectant green gaze on Cecilia.

"A royal summons, Seraphina? You truly are the haughtiest creature I've ever..." Cecilia frowned, her voice trailing off as she noticed something strange. Pale light peeked through a cracked window shutter, casting an eerie glow over that corner of the room, and it looked as if...

Cecilia drew closer.

Yes, it was.

It was subtle, just the faintest outline of a pathway through the dust. If the light hadn't fallen on the floor just right, she wouldn't have even noticed the bare patch. Cecilia met Seraphina's glowing eyes, and a tremor passed through her. "If I didn't know better, Seraphina, I'd think you came here to lure me to that trunk."

It was impossible. Of course, it was just mere coincidence Seraphina should be here, and have leapt on top of that particular trunk. But as Cecilia drew closer still, she saw something else that made her pause.

The lock on the front of the trunk was broken. It had nothing to do with the trunk's age—the lock wasn't just cracked, or hanging by a rusty hinge. It had been struck with something heavy. The bits of wood and splintered iron scattered on the floor caught in the hem of Cecilia's skirts as she knelt in front of the trunk.

Seraphina hopped down, winding herself around Cecilia as she raised the lid. A length of white sheet had been folded on top to protect the contents, but it had been disturbed, revealing some of what was underneath.

Kid gloves, painted fans, a fashionable blue silk parasol, a comb with a pretty vine pattern etched into the silver handle, a handful of jeweled hairpins, what looked like dozens of pairs of flocked silk stockings, a crystal scent bottle…the items inside were too fashionable and costly to belong to anyone other than a marchioness.

Cecilia lowered the lid again and ran her hands over the top. The Darlington crest had been carved into the wood. The trunk must have belonged to Lady Cassandra, then, but who had been so eager to get inside it they'd broken the lock?

She sat back on her heels, her mind turning over the possibilities. Hadn't Amy said Isabella's previous nursemaid, Mrs. Vernon had been banished from the castle for theft. She might have known where to find Lady Darlington's trunk, seen her chance to fetch a pretty bit of coin, and taken something.

But that had been months ago, hadn't it? Surely the dust would have settled again by now. It looked as if someone had been here more recently than that, but Cecilia couldn't imagine who.

She closed the lid and rose to her feet, but she stood over the trunk for some time, hands braced on her hips, thinking. Amy had said Lord Darlington closed the third floor a year ago, right after Lady Darlington's death. Had Mrs. Briggs been up here since then, searching for something?

Or had it been Lord Darlington? Had he come up here and snatched something from his late wife's trunk? It seemed unlikely a man who couldn't even bear to look at his dead wife's portrait would want her fans and stockings, and in any case, why would he break the lock? Surely, he'd have a key to the trunk—

"This isn't the schoolroom, Cecilia," said a deep voice behind her. "Are you lost again?"

Cecilia whirled around, startled. "I—"

"Wait, let me guess," Lord Darlington drawled. "A cat lured you up here."

She whirled back around again, but Seraphina, who'd been there only moments before had vanished, leaving Cecilia alone to explain herself. Again. "Since you ask, I did in fact follow—" That was as far as she got before she inhaled a cloud of dust kicked up by the swish of her skirts, and fell into a sneezing fit.

"Oh, for God's sakes. Don't expire now, Cecilia, before you've had a chance to peek behind every corner." Lord Darlington strode forward, the thud of his riding boots over the old wooden floorboards sending another cloud of dust into the air, and offered her a handkerchief.

Cecilia took it and pressed it delicately to her nose. "I beg your—"

"Pardon. Yes, you're good at that. Not quite so good at following my orders, however."

Cecilia, who was blinking down at the handkerchief in her hand, said nothing. Dear God, how could one tiny scrap of linen smell so intoxicating? She'd never smelled anything more mouthwatering in her life.

"Well? Let's have it then." Lord Darlington crossed his arms over his chest. "If it wasn't a cat, what was it? Is there some other animal running wild in my attics?"

Cecilia gaped at him with wide eyes, her throat going dry. His white linen shirt hugged his muscular arms and pulled tightly across his chest. He wore no coat, no waistcoat, and no cravat. Just white linen, slightly damp, and beneath it, disturbingly visible, inch after inch of smooth, golden skin. His dark hair, also a bit damp, curled against his neck, and he wore sinfully tight breeches and tall black boots.

He'd been out riding. The handkerchief still clutched in her hand must have been pressed close against his body, absorbing the delicious scent of leather, and clean, masculine sweat. It was still tickling her nose, stealing her breath.

His scent.

Cecilia swallowed. Oh, this was worse than the coal scuttle incident, when she'd been struck speechless by his open shirt. Much, much worse.

Lord Darlington didn't seem to notice she couldn't tear her gaze away from his chest. "Don't keep me in suspense, Cecilia." He beckoned to her with a lazy twitch of his fingers. "What are you doing up here, scurrying around like a curious little mouse?"

"You never said a word about the attics being forbidden." It was a feeble excuse, but it was the best Cecilia could manage with the dark shadow of his nipples peeking out at her as they were. Why, he might as well not be wearing a shirt at all!

"Mrs. Briggs told you the third floor of the castle is closed, didn't she?" He raised one dark, imperious eyebrow at her.

That arrogant eyebrow broke the spell his chest had cast over her, and not a moment too soon. It was a lucky thing he was such a demanding, overbearing tyrant, or she might never have come to her senses. "Yes, Mrs. Briggs told me. You know very well she did."

"Perhaps you didn't understand it's being closed meant you shouldn't come up here?" he asked, with exaggerated patience.

"I understood." Cecilia's eyes were still watering from the dust. His scent was addling her wits, and she tried not to inhale as she dabbed at them with a corner of his handkerchief.

"Yes, I thought you had. Imagine my surprise, then, when Amy said I could find you up here. Four days ago, you were nearly dismissed for sneaking about the castle, yet here you are, where you're not meant to be."

Cecilia's shoulders slumped. "Am I dismissed again?"

"No. Dismissing you wasn't a wise choice the first two times I tried it, and now you've made yourself indispensable to Isabella, it's less of one now. I'll tolerate a good deal of nuisance for my niece's sake."

"Nuisance?" Cecilia's lips pressed together. "Are you calling me a n—"

"You're a housemaid who drops the coal scuttle, a nursemaid who doesn't know a single proper lullaby, and a servant who hasn't the vaguest idea how to follow a simple command." Lord Darlington's lips quirked, as if he'd begun to enjoy himself. "Yes, Cecilia, you're a nuisance."

"When you put it that way, you make me sound awful, indeed, but I hardly think that's an accurate description of—"

"It's entirely accurate." He chuckled at her expression. "You've been a nuisance since the day you arrived, and I found you throwing rocks into Darlington Lake for no better reason than you were *curious*."

Oh, he was enjoying himself, all right. Insufferable man. Cecilia shot him a resentful look. "Forgive me, my lord. I didn't know curiosity was such an unforgivable—"

"Come with me." He wrapped his fingers around her wrist and gave a little tug. "We're wasting time."

"Wasting time? Where are we going?"

"To your bedchamber."

"My *bedchamber*?"

"There's no need for you to look so appalled, Cecilia. Isabella is waiting for us there. The three of us are going to have tea together in the drawing room." He glanced down at her with his lips curved in a mocking smile. "I'm a gentleman, and betrothed to another lady. You have nothing to fear from me."

Her chin hitched up. "I told you before, my lord. I'm not afraid of you."

"No? Well then, you have no reason not to come with me, do you?" Lord Darlington didn't wait for a reply, but led her from the attic, the floor creaking under his boots, his long, warm fingers curled around her wrist.

Later that night, it would occur to Cecilia she'd told him the truth.

She *wasn't* afraid of him.

And she'd lie awake for hours, wondering why.

Chapter Eleven

Gideon gulped in a deep breath of frigid air, then winced as it sliced a raw strip from his lungs. It hurt like the devil, but painful respiration was preferable to unconsciousness.

He couldn't suffocate. Not today. Another cleansing breath, then another... ah, that was much better. He could feel the tension draining from his—

"For God's sakes, Darlington," Haslemere hissed. "She's your betrothed, not your executioner. Smile, will you?"

Smile, yes. That was a good idea. Gideon pasted what he hoped was an engaging smile on his lips as he and Haslemere watched the Honeywells' carriage make its way up the drive. He'd been awaiting his betrothed at Darlington Castle for the past fortnight, yet somehow Miss Honeywell's arrival had taken him unawares.

Rather like an upended glass of wine, or a fall down the stairs—

"Bloody hell. Never mind the smile, Darlington." Haslemere glanced at him and blanched. "You look as if you're about to cast up your accounts. What the devil ails you this morning? Why are you so twitchy? Are you ill?"

Gideon blew out the last of his calming breaths in an irritated huff. "What are you going on about, Haslemere? I'm not twitchy."

But if he *was* twitchy, he knew just who to blame for it. If he hadn't spared much thought for his betrothed since he'd last seen her in London, he could lay his shameful inattention squarely on Cecilia's shoulders.

She was as distracting a nursemaid as she'd been a housemaid. Worse, Isabella adored her and insisted on her constant presence, and so Cecilia seemed to be everywhere he looked, with that playful smile and that musical laugh that filled all the empty spaces inside him. Even when he couldn't see her, he could hear her through the connecting door, singing those improper lullabies, making Isabella laugh—

"Look sharp, Darlington," Haslemere muttered. "They're nearly here. Oh, and do stop looking as if you expect someone to shoot at you at any moment, would you?"

"Don't be absurd. I told you, I'm not twitchy. I'm simply…breathless with anticipation."

Haslemere snorted. "Well, I urge you to fix a more *anticipatory* expression on your face before you frighten Miss Honeywell to death with that black scowl of yours."

"She's made of sterner stuff than that." Still, Gideon did his best to rearrange his features into a more welcoming attitude as the carriage rounded the curve in the drive.

It wasn't that he wasn't delighted to see Miss Honeywell. Of course, he was. Her lovely face would brighten up this grim castle. She was just the sort of mistress it needed with her sunny disposition and pure, uncomplicated beauty.

Not like Cecilia Gilchrist, with her deep, dark eyes and argumentative tongue, and her maddening tendency to appear in the least likely places. He'd never imagined one small woman could wreak such havoc, but he'd hardly had a wink of sleep since she'd arrived. Every time his eyelids grew heavy, he'd imagine her creeping about, sticking her pert little nose into every private corner of his castle. Or worse, he'd recall how she'd looked in her night rail, the filmy white fabric swirling around her bare calves, a breathy cry on her lips—

"Lord Darlington! Hello, Lord Darlington!"

Gideon snapped to attention just in time to stop himself from slapping his hands over his ears. He drew the line at shouting a return greeting across the drive, but he managed a polite nod for the lady fluttering her hand at him from the open carriage window.

"Good Lord, Darlington." Haslemere's smile didn't falter, but he glanced at Gideon from the corner of his eye. "Who the devil is that creature hanging out the carriage window, flapping her arms about and shrieking at you?"

Gideon sighed. Miss Honeywell was an ideal bride, but…well, a man couldn't expect to have everything he wished for in his matrimonial affairs, could he? "That, Haslemere, is Mrs. Priscilla Honeywell. Miss Honeywell's mother."

Haslemere stared at her, speechless with horror.

"*This* is Darlington Castle?" Mrs. Honeywell sniffed, as the carriage rolled to a stop in front of the entrance. "I confess I expected something a bit larger and grander. Something more like Windsor."

Gideon exchanged a glance with Haslemere.

Windsor? Haslemere mouthed, raising an eyebrow.

"But a castle is still a castle, I suppose." Mrs. Honeywell clambered down from the carriage in an avalanche of bright pink silk trimmed with a mountain of white ostrich feathers. "Even if it *is* terribly cramped."

"I don't know that I've ever seen so much pink silk on one lady before, and such an *unusual* shade of pink, too. It's as if the drapes in my mother's bedchamber have come to life. I'm certain to have nightmares," Haslemere whispered to Gideon with a shudder.

"Be quiet," Gideon whispered back through gritted teeth. "She'll hear you."

"Oh, I shouldn't worry if I were you, Darlington. I doubt she can hear anything over the sound of her own chatter."

"For God's sake, Haslemere, will you hush?"

"Miss Honeywell is perfection, Darlington. At least that's some recompense for every second of misery the mother's going to cause you." Haslemere followed Gideon as he stepped forward to hand down the young lady just emerging from the carriage.

"Oh, good day, Lord Darlington!" Mrs. Honeywell bustled forward, her pink skirts dragging across the ground. "Come along, will you, Fanny? His lordship is waiting for you."

"Mrs. Honeywell, and Miss Honeywell. How do you do?" Gideon bowed to Mrs. Honeywell, then took Fanny's hand and drew it through his arm with a smile. "Welcome to Darlington Castle. I hope you had a pleasant journey from London?"

"Certainly not. It was perfectly wretched." Mrs. Honeywell tossed her headful of stiff yellow curls, and the tiny pink hat smothered in pink ribbons perched atop her head wobbled precariously.

Gideon blinked. "Yes, of course. I'm sorry to hear—"

"It's terribly trying to be obliged to hurry off to Kent when all the fashionable people are in London for the season! Why, my poor, dear Fanny will be desolate, moldering away in this dreary old castle! I daresay you might have seen your way to marrying at St. Paul's, my lord, as all the best society people do."

Gideon gave her a tight smile. "Alas, madam, I'm afraid hundreds of years of tradition demand I marry at Darlington Castle. Pity, but there it is."

Mrs. Honeywell had wanted the wedding to take place at St. Paul's Cathedral, with a grand wedding breakfast afterward so she could lord her daughter's good fortune over anyone unwise enough to accept an invitation. She'd been dreadfully disappointed to find the nuptials would have to take place in fusty old Kent, but she'd consoled herself with assembling an extravagant trousseau of silks and laces for her daughter, as befitted a future marchioness.

Miss Honeywell darted a coy look at Gideon as she stepped daintily across the drive. "I think this is a lovely place for a wedding ceremony."

"Well, I suppose it can't be helped, but really, my lord, it's excessively tiresome you should live so far from London. It took ages to get here, and it was so cold I fear poor Fanny has taken a chill. She suffers from a fragile constitution, as you know, Lord Darlington, but then the Honeywell ladies have always been unusually delicate."

This was too much for Haslemere. He was a darling of the *ton*, and thus nearly always behaved as a charming, gallant gentleman should no matter how trying the circumstances, but he was obliged to smother a snort.

Gideon shot him a warning glance over the top of Mrs. Honeywell's head. "Yes, of course. I regret the journey proved so uncomfortable, Mrs. Honeywell. We'll be certain to take extraordinary care with your health and Miss Honeywell's."

Mrs. Honeywell drew herself up with a flounce of her skirts. "Well, I should think so."

Gideon cleared his throat. "May I present my friend, Lord Haslemere?"

"Mrs. Honeywell, and Miss Honeywell. How do you do? Lovely day for February, isn't it?" Haslemere bowed to each lady in turn.

"What, another lord? But how wonderful! How do you do, Lord Haslemere." Mrs. Honeywell batted a pair of bulging blue eyes at Haslemere, then swept into an elaborate curtsy. "The more lords, the merrier, I always say. Are you a marquess as well, Lord Haslemere?"

"Only an earl, I'm afraid." Haslemere bowed over Mrs. Honeywell's hand.

A girlish giggle burst from Mrs. Honeywell's lips. "Well, we're still very pleased to meet you, my lord. Aren't we, Fanny?"

"Indeed, Mama."

Haslemere turned with considerably more enthusiasm to the blushing young lady at her mother's side. "I've heard a great deal about you from Lord Darlington, Miss Honeywell, but even his extravagant compliments don't do you justice."

Miss Honeywell offered her hand, the pretty shade of pink on her cheeks deepening when Haslemere's lips brushed her glove. "How do you do, my—"

"Yes, yes. I'm certain he does very well, Fanny," Mrs. Honeywell interrupted crossly, as if peeved the attention had been diverted from herself. "He *is* a lord, after all. Mightn't we venture inside the castle, Lord Darlington? This wind is making a dreadful mess of my feathers, and I'd welcome a cup of tea."

"Ruffled feathers? How shocking. We can't have that, can we?" Haslemere glanced down at Mrs. Honeywell's hand, which had curled in a proprietary manner around his arm, and arched a brow at Gideon. "Lead the way, Darlington."

Gideon recognized the wicked grin twitching at the corner of Haslemere's lips, and rushed to distract the ladies. "Yes, of course. Forgive me. Come and warm yourselves, and I'll ring for tea."

As he spoke, Gideon led the party through the front door. Miss Honeywell cast a curious glance about her, taking in the entrance hall, but paused on their way toward the drawing room, a surprised exclamation on her lips. "That young woman, Lord Darlington. Is she one of your housemaids? I'm certain I've seen her before."

Gideon knew at once which young woman Miss Honeywell was referring to, before he even followed her gaze. The same young woman who always seemed to be at the center of every disturbance.

Cecilia Gilchrist.

His teeth snapped together. "Which young woman is that, Miss Honeywell?"

"That one, just there, with the dark hair, cleaning the glass lanterns." A thoughtful frown furrowed Miss Honeywell's smooth white brow. "Her face looks familiar."

"I beg your pardon, Miss Honeywell," Haslemere interrupted hastily, "That young woman isn't from London. Now, shall we adjourn to the—"

"Don't be absurd, Fanny. How should you know *her*? You don't keep company with housemaids." Mrs. Honeywell gave a disdainful sniff. "Lord Haslemere is right. You've taken her for someone else."

Miss Honeywell shook her head. "Indeed, you're mistaken, Mama. I *do* know her. I can't quite think how, but I know her from London."

Gideon's gaze narrowed on Cecilia. It was odd, indeed, Miss Honeywell should recognize Cecilia from London, when she'd never ventured beyond Lady Dunton's remote country estate in Warwickshire.

Unless she'd been lying to him since she arrived at Darlington Castle. He'd suspected it, of course, but somehow it rankled more now than it had before. "Cecilia!" Gideon's tone was harsher than he'd meant it to be, and Miss Honeywell jumped beside him.

Haslemere frowned. "Is this really necessary, Darlington?"

"Oh, what nonsense." Mrs. Honeywell clucked impatiently. "I beg you won't trouble yourself with it, Lord Darlington. Fanny is forever mistaking one person for the next."

"It's no trouble, Mrs. Honeywell. Come here, if you would, Cecilia." Gideon struggled to appear casual, but if the tight look on Haslemere's face was any indication, he failed.

Cecilia was at the far end of the hallway, well out of the way of the guests, polishing the glass in one of the lanterns. She hadn't seemed to notice them at all, but at Gideon's command she turned her head toward them.

He was watching her closely, and was likely the only one of the four of them who noticed the slight hesitation in her step when she saw Miss Honeywell. It happened so quickly he'd have missed it himself if he'd happened to blink.

Still, when she reached them, there wasn't the slightest hint of apprehension in her face. She offered them all a calm, graceful curtsy, then turned a distant look on Gideon. "Yes, my lord? How may I help?"

"This young lady here says she knows you, Cecilia, from *London.*" Gideon emphasized the last word, so as to leave Cecilia in no doubt as to the import of his question. If she thought he'd forgotten she was meant to be from Warwickshire, she was very much mistaken. He hadn't forgotten a single word Cecilia had uttered since the first moment she arrived at Darlington Castle.

He studied Cecilia's expression, but she was looking at him as if she'd never laid eyes on him before, nothing but polite enquiry on her smooth, blank face. "Oh, no. I beg your pardon, miss, but I've never been to London. If that's all, my lord?"

"Yes, I think we've kept Miss and Mrs. Honeywell standing about in the hallway long enough, Darlington. Now, shall we have our tea? You may go, Cecilia."

Haslemere waved her back toward the other end of the hallway, but Cecilia hadn't taken more than two steps before Miss Honeywell stopped her. "No, I'm certain it was you. Perhaps I've seen you walking in Hyde Park, or—"

"A *housemaid,* promenading through Hyde Park at the fashionable hour?" Mrs. Honeywell gave her skirts an important twitch as she looked down her nose at Cecilia. "I hardly think so, Fanny."

Cecilia ignored this ill-tempered remark, and smiled at Miss Honeywell. "I imagine there are a great many young women in London who look like me."

"No, there aren't." The words fell out of Gideon's mouth before he realized he was going to say them. Indeed, even before he realized he'd thought them.

Haslemere pinched the bridge of his nose. "Don't be absurd, Darlington. There must be hundreds of young women in London with dark eyes and dark hair."

"There are, indeed," Mrs. Honeywell snapped. "Nothing special in that."

"*No.* Not like Cecilia's, there aren't." Gideon stepped closer to her, with his gaze still locked on her face. There might be thousands of young ladies in London with Cecilia's coloring, but no other young woman in the world could be mistaken for Cecilia.

Her eyes were dark, yes, but it was a warm, velvety, bottomless darkness, unlike any other dark eyes he'd ever seen, and her hair…Gideon's fingers twitched with the sudden need to touch it, run his hands through those rich, mahogany-colored locks. And her mouth, the plump pink curve of it, the hint of vulnerability in that tender bottom lip, the surprising sweetness he hadn't noticed until just now—

"I know!" Miss Honeywell, who seemed utterly oblivious to the sudden tension in the air, let out an excited squeal. "I recall where I've seen you before. You're a friend of Lady Gray, are you not?"

"Lady Gray? What, you mean the *countess*? My dear Fanny, you've gone mad! What in the world would a friend of a *countess* be doing cleaning Lord Darlington's castle? It's absurd."

"But I'm certain I saw you walking with her one day in Hyde Park—"

Miss Honeywell was interrupted by an explosion of shattering glass, followed by a cry of distress from Cecilia. "Oh, no! Oh, Lord Darlington, I'm so terribly sorry."

"Clumsy girl! If you were my servant, I'd have that out of your wages!"

Mrs. Honeywell's face had turned red with outrage, but it wasn't until Cecilia dropped to her knees on the floor that Gideon realized what had happened.

She'd been carrying her polishing cloth and the glass globe from the lantern when she came into the hallway. When Miss Honeywell mentioned Emma Downing's name, Cecilia had dropped the glass, and it now lay in a pool of shards on the flagstones at their feet.

"Oh, dear. I can't bear the sight of blood."

Miss Honeywell turned toward Gideon as if to hide her face in his chest, but he dropped her arm and knelt down next to Cecilia. "No, don't try and pick up the glass. Don't touch it again." He caught her wrist to keep her from gathering up the shards. "Let me see your hand."

He gently turned her hand over, revealing an ugly gash on the fleshy part of her palm. It was deep, with blood already gushing from it. For a moment Gideon stared down at her hand, transfixed by the sight of her pale, tender skin, the dark red blood welling in her palm, and his much larger hand cradling hers.

When he raised his gaze to her face, he found her dark eyes wide with alarm, and her lower lip trembling. "It's all right, Cecilia." Gideon released her hand, but slid his palm under her elbow to help her up. "We'll go find Mrs. Briggs. She'll know how to bind it properly."

"I'll take Cecilia to Mrs. Briggs." Haslemere shot Gideon a warning look before nudging him firmly aside. "Take Mrs. Honeywell and your *betrothed* into the drawing room, Darlington, and have a footman fetch them their tea. I'll join you there soon."

Gideon glanced from Mrs. Honeywell's splotched face to Haslemere's pained one. Mrs. Honeywell was already apoplectic with rage at the suggestion her daughter might be cast aside for a mere housemaid, and poor Haslemere was doing his best to prevent further damage.

Gideon snatched his hand away from Cecilia's arm and let it drop to his side. "Er, yes. Very well. Join us when you're able. Miss Honeywell? Mrs. Honeywell? May I take you into the drawing room?"

Miss Honeywell offered him a gracious nod, but it was going to take more than one lump of sugar and some superior tea cakes to restore Mrs. Honeywell to good humor. He escorted them to the drawing room, but paused after they passed through the door to watch Haslemere lead Cecilia down the staircase to the kitchens below.

She was holding her injured hand in the palm of her other one, and Haslemere still had ahold of her elbow to keep her steady. He towered over her, his shoulders twice the width of hers, and Cecilia looked small and fragile next to him.

Gideon clenched his fists at the sight of them so close together, with Haslemere's auburn head bent protectively toward Cecilia's, murmuring something, as if the two of them were sharing a secret.

Before he had a chance to prod at this startling reaction, he was interrupted by Mrs. Honeywell's voice, lamenting the smallness of the drawing room, the fact that it faced east rather than west, and complaining about the lack of heat emanating from the fire.

Gideon followed the ladies into the room with a smothered sigh. He managed to remain courteous toward Mrs. Honeywell, and he took a tepid sort of pleasure in Miss Honeywell's beauty and good humor, but his mind was elsewhere.

When Haslemere joined them in the drawing room, he quietly reassured Gideon Cecilia's injury had been attended to, but that didn't stop Gideon's mind from drifting toward her again and again throughout the afternoon. As soon as his guests retired to their bedchambers to rest before dinner, he went in search of her.

He told himself he simply wished to enquire after her, just as he would any servant who'd been injured in his house, but the excuse rang hollow, even to his own ears.

* * * *

Cecilia didn't see Lord Darlington again for the rest of the afternoon.

She'd spent most of the day with Isabella, but while the child took her nap she'd scoured floors, polished looking glasses, and helped Amy clean every intricately carved mahogany bedpost in the guest bedchambers, rubbing away the dust from every whorl and curve until they shone. By the time they finished their work and ate a quick meal in the kitchens, she'd convinced herself she didn't care a whit if she never saw him again.

"Miss Honeywell appears to be utterly besotted with Lord Darlington, doesn't she?" Amy placed the silver spoon she'd just finished polishing on the piece of black velvet spread out before them.

They were in the butler's pantry, polishing what looked to Cecilia like enough silver to sink a ship. "Mrs. Honeywell looks a great deal more besotted with him than her daughter does," she snapped. "I've never seen a lady look better pleased with herself." Amy's eyes widened at her tart tone, and Cecilia added, "I didn't pay the least bit of attention to the way Miss Honeywell looks at Lord Darlington."

"It sounds to me as if you did." Amy let out a sly cackle. "But you're right enough. Anyone can see Mrs. Honeywell's not the sort to let a marquess escape her clutches."

Cecilia snorted at that, but said nothing.

"You can't blame Miss Honeywell if she is besotted with him. Lord Darlington *is* very handsome," Amy went on, oblivious to Cecilia's darkening mood. "She seems a nice lady, doesn't she? She'll make a proper mistress for Darlington Castle."

Cecilia snatched up a knife and began a violent assault on it with her polishing cloth, her lips pressed tightly together.

"You're in a bit of a temper this evening, eh?" Amy set aside her cloth with a sigh when Cecilia remained silent. "It's Isabella's bedtime, anyway. Let me just go and fetch the last tray of spoons, then you can go up."

Cecilia set aside the spoon in her hand with a trifle more force than needed, and snatched up another one, but as she attacked the tarnished crest engraved in the handle, her conscience began to prick at her.

Amy wasn't to blame for her vile mood. She'd been on edge since Miss Honeywell mentioned Sophia's name today, and goodness knew her stinging palm and Mrs. Honeywell's poisonous tongue didn't help matters.

"I beg your pardon for my snappishness," she said, when she heard Amy's step behind her. "I'm afraid Mrs. Honeywell's ill humor put me out of temper."

"That's not any way to talk about my future mother-in-law, Cecilia."

Cecilia's hand froze on the spoon.

Lord Darlington's soft, husky laugh brushed across her nerve endings. "Well? Nothing to say for yourself? I don't recall *that* ever happening before."

Cecilia turned, her face on fire. Lord Darlington was standing in the doorway, one hip leaning against the frame and his arms crossed over his chest.

She wished with everything inside her the floor would open up and swallow her whole, but it wouldn't, and so she did the only thing she could do. She raised her chin, and met his gaze. "Surely you didn't come to the butler's pantry to hear my opinion, my lord."

"No. I came to have a look at your injury." He sauntered toward her and held out his hand when he reached her side. "Let me see it."

Cecilia hesitated, her breath catching. It didn't seem a good idea to turn any part of her body over to Lord Darlington just now, not when a delicious shiver chased up her spine every time she thought about his large, warm hand cradling hers earlier today. "I, ah…there's no need, my lord. It's fine."

He raised that commanding eyebrow at her, and she held out her hand, swallowing.

He caught her wrist, his fingertips grazing her knuckles as he unwound the linen cloth Mrs. Briggs had wrapped around her hand to protect the wound. The glass had left a livid red gash across her palm, and the skin around it was swollen. He frowned when he saw it, and raised those blue, blue eyes to hers. "Does it hurt?"

His voice was soft, his tone unbearably gentle, and for a single, blissful instant Cecilia let her eyes drift closed to savor it. "A little."

He traced a finger over the uninjured part of her palm. A soft gasp broke from Cecilia's lips before she could stop it, and his gaze flew to hers. They

THE VIRGIN WHO VINDICATED LORD DARLINGTON 111

stared at each other, one moment after the next ticking by without either of them looking away.

He stepped closer, crowding her against the table at her back, the heat from his big body making Cecilia's head spin with dizzying awareness. "Miss Honeywell seems to be quite certain she knows you, Cecilia. She mentioned it again at tea."

Cecilia's heart began a panicked thrashing against her ribs. "She's mistaken."

"Is she?" He touched her chin, tipping her face up to his. "Or are you lying to me?"

"I-I'm not lying." Dear God, how could he smell so divine? Cool and soft, like a silent snowfall, a faint hint of port on his breath.

He pressed his fingertips more firmly into her chin, titling her head back. "You say so, but I don't know if I believe you, Cecilia. I don't know if I've ever believed you. What will I do with you if I find out you've lied to me?"

It might have been an innocent question, but the wicked edge to his voice turned it dark and sultry, as if he'd already made up his mind what he'd do to her, and was very much looking forward to doing it.

"I-I don't know, my lord." Cecilia fought to keep her eyes from dropping to half-mast as his warm breath drifted over her, stirring the loose hair at her temples. "I suppose you'd have no choice but to order me to leave Darlington Castle."

The corners of his lips curved. "I already tried that. You gave me the scold of a lifetime for my troubles."

"One doesn't scold a marquess, my lord." She meant the words lightly, but the stroke of his fingers against her skin made her breathless, and they fell from her lips as a soft tease.

His gaze dropped to her mouth, his eyes darkening to a hot, stormy blue. He stroked his thumb over her chin, and the tip of it brushed her lower lip.

Cecilia's mouth opened a little in response to the caress, and his own lips parted on a strangled breath. He leaned closer, his mouth drawing nearer to hers, but just when she was certain her heart would leap from her chest, a shadow came over his face.

He cleared his throat, and when he spoke again, the huskiness had bled from his voice. He released her chin and turned away, but paused before vanishing through the door. "The dressing on your hand needs changing. Good night, Cecilia."

Chapter Twelve

Cecilia closed the castle door behind her and descended the stone steps onto the drive, her lips curved in a satisfied smile. She was well pleased with herself this afternoon.

Anyone who happened to catch a glimpse of her wouldn't think she was anything other than a devoted nursemaid taking her adorable charge for a walk in the gardens. That is, she *was* that, but then that was the brilliance of the thing.

It was an inspired idea, disguising herself as...well, *herself.*

But she wasn't only a nursemaid this morning. No, this morning she was part nursemaid, and part investigator. She wasn't quite sure what she was investigating yet today, but one thing was certain. In another six days, Fanny Honeywell would marry Lord Darlington.

She was nearly out of time and the mysteries at Darlington Castle kept piling up, one after the other. She wouldn't get any closer to unraveling them sitting about the castle. After some discreet prodding at breakfast this morning, she'd discovered from Duncan that the White Lady had only ever been seen near the edge of the woods, or wandering through the rose walk before she disappeared again somewhere near the kitchen gardens.

So, Cecilia and Isabella were headed toward the rose walk for a morning's stroll. Cecilia doubted she'd find a ghost there waiting for them, but perhaps something else of interest would turn up. She'd simply have to hope for the best, and trust she'd recognize anything suspicious if she saw it.

"All right, Isabella?" Cecilia glanced down at her charge.

"My nose is cold." Isabella rubbed the offending organ with a mitten-clad hand. "The outside part, and the inside."

"It does look rather pink." It was colder this morning than it had been yesterday, the scent of snow sharp in the air. Cecilia was a firm believer in fresh air for children, but she didn't want Isabella to catch a chill. She'd been tempted to tuck her into a buggy under a thick layer of blankets, but Isabella wouldn't hear of it. She'd insisted on walking, and Cecilia had wrapped her up so thoroughly if it hadn't been for her pink face, she might have been mistaken for a bundle of laundry.

"What about the rest of you? Any frozen bits?" Cecilia asked, dropping a quick kiss on the tip of Isabella's nose.

Isabella squirmed away, and gave Cecilia's hand an impatient tug. "No. I want to walk in the garden. You said we could!"

"We will, but wait just a moment." Cecilia slid a finger under the neckline of Isabella's thick coat, nodding as her fingers landed on warm skin. "Ah, good. Cozy as a kitten, just as you should be."

Isabella was dancing with impatience. "*Please*, Miss Cecilia?"

"All right, then." Cecilia was as anxious to disappear into the grounds as Isabella was, before they ran into someone she'd rather avoid.

Someone like Mrs. Honeywell.

She cast a furtive glance around. She'd heard Mrs. Honeywell in the entrance hall half an hour earlier, her shrill voice easily discernible from the first-floor landing. She'd been complaining about the coldness of the day and fretting about catching a chill.

Lord Darlington must be taking the party for a tour of the grounds. Cecilia might have delayed her own excursion to be certain they'd miss them, but by then she'd already wrapped Isabella up like a small mummy. She couldn't bear to disappoint her, and they could always dart into the kitchen gardens if they needed a quick escape. Lord Darlington wasn't likely to take his guests there—

"Have you noticed, Lord Darlington, how well that particular shade of blue flatters my daughter's complexion?"

Cecilia's eyes widened. Oh, *no*.

There was no mistaking that screech, but which direction were they coming from?

"The Duke of Ashford himself raved about the color of Fanny's eyes. He said they're the same pure blue as a brilliant summer sky."

A male voice—Lord Darlington's, presumably—said something Cecilia couldn't hear in response, but it sounded as if the party was getting closer.

Oh, why must I have such dreadful luck?

"His Grace insisted it's as if the sun himself smiles down upon her, and indeed, I can't but agree with him," Mrs. Honeywell declared, as if not quite satisfied with the homage being paid to her daughter's beauty. "Just look, Lord Darlington, at how even these feeble rays turn Fanny's hair into a halo of gold."

A halo of gold? Cecilia's breath escaped in a frosty huff. Surely, that was doing it a bit brown—

"You look lovely, Miss Honeywell. As dazzling as a summer day." Lord Darlington's deep voice carried clearly through the frigid air, and Cecilia looked up just in time to see him raise Miss Honeywell's dainty hand to his lips. The winter sun toyed with Miss Honeywell's hair, highlighting the gilded curls to great effect, like a...

Halo of gold, blast it.

Cecilia glanced wildly around, but short of leaping into the shrubbery and dragging poor Isabella with her, there was no place to hide.

And then, it was too late.

There was no escape. Lord Darlington's party was upon them, and they were taking up the whole of the pathway. Lord Darlington had Miss Honeywell on his arm, and behind him was Lord Haslemere, escorting Mrs. Honeywell. She was preening as if the entire upper ten thousand was watching her, but Lord Haslemere looked as if he wished himself under the thin layer of ice crusting Darlington Lake.

Mrs. Honeywell was still prattling on about halos and blue skies, oblivious to everything around her, but Lord Haslemere met Cecilia's gaze and, quick as lightning, comically crossed his eyes.

It was so unexpected Cecilia had to bite her lip to smother a laugh. It was wicked of her to laugh at poor Lord Haslemere's predicament, but his droll expression had put her in mind of Georgiana when she was attempting to explain mathematics to the duller pupils at the Clifford School.

"Good afternoon," Lord Darlington called as his party approached. "Is that you under all those layers, Isabella?"

Isabella giggled. "Yes, it is! You're silly, Uncle."

"I hardly recognized you." Lord Darlington chucked Isabella under the chin before turning his attention to Cecilia. "Good afternoon, Cecilia."

Cecilia swallowed. His tone was pleasant enough, his address utterly polite and proper. To look at him now, one would never believe he was the same man who'd teased her last night—who'd taken her hand so carefully in his and stroked her palm with his fingertip, his eyes a hot, dark blue.

The wind was taking liberties with him, tousling the thick, dark locks of his hair and biting color into his cheeks. His snug, buff-colored breeches showed off the long, muscular line of his legs to perfection, and the blue of the coat he wore under his long, dark cloak perfectly matched the color of his eyes.

She'd never seen him look as handsome as he did today. Perhaps he'd taken greater care than usual with his appearance in order to charm Miss Honeywell.

Cecilia squirmed at the thought.

She tore her gaze away from him, shifting her attention to the shrubs, the lake, the half-boots on her feet until Lord Haslemere's quiet cough recalled her attention, and she realized with warming cheeks she hadn't replied to Lord Darlington's greeting.

"Er…good afternoon, my lord." Cecilia dropped into a belated curtsy. "Lord Haslemere, and Mrs. and Miss Honeywell," she added, with a polite nod. "Isabella and I thought we'd have a walk this afternoon while the sun's shining."

Mrs. Honeywell let out a scandalized gasp. Cecilia jerked her head toward the woman, and found Mrs. Honeywell staring at her, outraged. "*Isabella*? Is that how you address the Marquess of Darlington's niece, girl?"

Cecilia blinked. It was a foolish question, really, given that was the child's *name*. "Well, Isabella Olivia Cornelia is rather a mouthful. Too many syllables for such a small little bit of a thing. Isabella suits her better, I think."

"It does, indeed." Lord Haslemere agreed, taking Cecilia's side.

"She's *Lady Isabella* to you, impertinent chit." Mrs. Honeywell shot Cecilia a look colder than the wind. "You may be certain *my* servants don't address the family so familiarly." She settled her ostrich feathers with a violent twitch, but her sneer faded when she noticed Lord Darlington's frown, and she quickly pasted on a bright, false smile. "This is Lady Isabella then, my lord? Let's have a look at her, shall we?"

Cecilia would have preferred to stick her hand in a fire than turn Isabella over to Mrs. Honeywell, but Miss Honeywell, who'd remained silent throughout the whole of this exchange, suddenly spoke up. "Oh, yes! Let us see the dear, sweet little thing."

Lord Darlington could hardly refuse such a request from his betrothed, and thus, Isabella's fate was sealed. Cecilia settled for holding Isabella protectively to her side for an instant before pressing a hand to her back and easing her gently forward. "It's all right, Isabella," she murmured into her ear. "Bid Miss and Mrs. Honeywell a good afternoon. Show them what pretty manners you have, and then you and I will go for our walk in the garden."

Isabella shook her head. "I-I don't want to, Miss Cecilia."

"Don't be silly, child." Mrs. Honeywell tugged Isabella forward impatiently. Cecilia pressed her lips together, nettled beyond measure, but being only the lowly nursemaid, there was nothing she could do except wait for it to be over.

Mrs. Honeywell looked over Isabella with feigned interest, but there wasn't a flicker of warmth in her face as she assessed her. "So, this is your niece, Lord Darlington? Humph. Rather small for her age, isn't she?"

"Not at all, Mrs. Honeywell." Cecilia bit the words out through clenched teeth. "On the contrary, she's rather tall."

"Why, what a lovely face, and such pretty curls!" Miss Honeywell gushed, but she wasn't looking at Isabella. "But then your entire family is handsome, my lord." She darted a flirtatious look at Lord Darlington from under her eyelashes.

Miss Honeywell gushed on for a bit, in raptures over Isabella, but for all her delight, she lost interest in the child rather quickly. She gave Isabella's head an absent pat, then abandoned her in favor of Lord Darlington. "Shall we go and see the rose walk now? I believe you said—"

"It's fortunate your brother didn't have a son, isn't it?" Mrs. Honeywell assessed Isabella with cool eyes. "A son would have been tremendously inconvenient."

Cecilia froze, certain she must have misheard Mrs. Honeywell.

"It's a great deal better for you, Fanny, the child happened to be a girl. She won't be much in your way, thankfully."

A shocked silence fell as Mrs. Honeywell made it abundantly clear she had, in fact, meant just what Cecilia feared she had. Lord Haslemere turned on her indignantly, and Lord Darlington stiffened.

The only one who didn't seem to understand the implication of her mother's words was Miss Honeywell, who regarded her blankly. "Whatever do you mean, Mama? Why, little boys are perfectly charming."

Mrs. Honeywell gave her daughter an impatient look. "My dear child, you've quite missed my point. If Lady Isabella had been a boy, *he'd* be the heir. Since she's a girl, your own son will become the Marquess of Darlington."

Miss Honeywell, who'd caught on at last, glanced uneasily at Lord Darlington. "Mama, I don't think you should say such things."

Mrs. Honeywell ignored her daughter. "Don't be absurd, Fanny. Lord Darlington is no fool. Of course, he wants his own child to inherit the title and fortune."

"I beg your pardon, Mrs. Honeywell. My affection for my late brother's child is absolute, regardless of gender."

Cecilia shuddered at the look on Lord Darlington's face. Never before had she seen a man more coldly furious than he was. He looked as if he'd been carved out of stone.

"I only mean to say, my lord, that it's fortunate it turned out as it did. Lady Isabella seems a rather small, sickly-looking child to me, but it's neither here nor there, no one being much interested in what happens to girls—"

Cecilia turned on Mrs. Honeywell, aghast. A fury unlike anything she'd ever felt before swept through her, and the next thing she knew she'd stepped forward and, without a single word, snatched Isabella away from Mrs. Honeywell.

Mrs. Honeywell gasped. "Why, you impertinent chit! How dare you presume to—"

"She's cold," Cecilia bit out. She whirled around, turning her back on Mrs. Honeywell, and turning Isabella's face into her shoulder. "There we are, dearest. That's better, isn't it?"

"I demand your servant apologize to me this *instant*, Lord Darlington." Mrs. Honeywell's voice could have frozen the remaining water in Darlington Lake. "Once she's begged my pardon, I insist you dismiss her at once."

Cecilia hid her trembling hands under the guise of fussing with Isabella's coat. She, who never lost her temper, suddenly understood what her friends meant when they described being so enraged their skin felt too tight for their body. She was so angry she could hardly think, but at the same time she was aware of a sense of impending doom.

God in heaven, here she was *again*, one word away from being dismissed from Lord Darlington's service. She'd have to return to London and explain to Lady Clifford she'd lost her temper, and insulted one of his lordship's guests.

"Cecilia."

Cecilia went still at the commanding note in Lord Darlington's voice, but she kept her chin high as she turned to face him. Let him send her away, then, because nothing—*nothing*—would make her beg that wretched woman's pardon. She'd sooner jump in the lake than beg Mrs. Honeywell for anything.

"If you still wish to have your walk, you'd better get on with it. It's growing colder, and it looks as if it might snow."

"Lord Darlington!" Mrs. Honeywell was so furious she actually stamped her foot.

Lord Darlington said nothing, but he gave Mrs. Honeywell a look that silenced her at once. "Go on, then." His voice was quiet, but his blue eyes were soft.

She gaped at him, stunned, but he turned away from her to smile down at Miss Honeywell. "Do you still wish to see the rose walk, Miss Honeywell? Or would you prefer a warm fire and a cup of tea?"

Miss Honeywell blossomed under his attention like a flower opening up to the sun. "The rose walk, please, my lord."

"This way, then."

Lord Darlington led Miss Honeywell down the pathway without another glance at Cecilia. It was the most thorough dismissal she'd ever experienced in her life, but it didn't appear to be a *permanent* one. She'd have to content herself with that.

She told herself to turn away, to get on with her walk, not to watch them go, but against her better judgment, she found herself staring after them. Lord Darlington's head was bent toward Miss Honeywell as she said something to him, and the beauty of the two of them caused a pang in Cecilia's chest. They were lovely together, perfectly suited to each other in looks, with Lord Darlington's dark coloring complementing Miss Honeywell's golden fairness.

Not that Lord Darlington's handsomeness made the least bit of difference to Cecilia, who hadn't been sent here to gawk at him like a schoolgirl. His handsomeness was not, after all, any proof he wasn't a murderer. If Cecilia was obliged to remind herself of this more than once as she paced the narrow pathways of the kitchen garden with Isabella…well, no one else had to know about it.

Isabella was subdued for a time after the incident with Mrs. Honeywell. Cecilia kept a close eye on her, being of the opinion that children— particularly bright, thoughtful children like Isabella —were a great deal more sensitive than adults suspected they were.

Isabella soon forgot the incident, however, and skipped between the neat rows of flower beds, pointing out her favorites to Cecilia. They wandered about, with Cecilia pausing now and again to admire a shrub, or try and guess the origin of the plants she didn't recognize.

Which was, admittedly, most of them.

She was fond of flowers, but she hadn't had much opportunity to learn about them, there being only a very small garden at the Clifford School, and all of them too busy to spend much time in it.

The Darlington Castle kitchen garden was a large one, surrounded by a high stone wall to keep any animals from nibbling the vegetation. It was tidy despite its size, and pleasant to wander in, with its gravel pathways and rows of carefully tended plants, though there wasn't much greenery in evidence, everything having been trimmed and tucked away for the winter.

"My mama took me here sometimes." Isabella stopped near the back wall of the garden, near a large patch of lavender in a corner, rather pretty still with its slender gray leaves, though the purple spires had long since bloomed their last.

"Your…mama?"

"Yes. Her name is Leanora, and she's very pretty."

This was the first time Isabella had ever mentioned her mother to Cecilia. She was a bit taken aback, but she said only, "I daresay she is, Isabella. Shall we go and see if this lavender has any scent?"

Isabella gave an eager nod. Cecilia waded into the patch of lavender with Isabella at her side, and leaned over a clump that looked a trifle heartier than the rest. She inhaled, and got a faint hint of the sweet floral scent. "Oh, that's lovely."

"Lovely," Isabella echoed, burying her face in the lavender and taking a deep sniff.

Cecilia smiled, then rose and brushed the dirt from her skirts. "It's time we returned to the house, Isabella." They'd been wandering in the garden for an hour or more, and it was growing colder.

But Isabella was still rooting around in the lavender patch, and after a bit of digging about, she emerged with a peculiar look on her face. "These flowers smell like my Auntie Cassandra."

Cecilia took the stalk Isabella held out to her and gave it a sniff. "It smells like mint." She moved the patch of lavender aside and found a plant she didn't recognize growing against the stone wall. "It looks a little like lavender, but I think it's spearmint."

"It smells like my auntie did, before she died."

"It's a distinctive scent. I'm not surprised you remember it." Cecilia let the stalk drop to the ground, and held out her hand. Isabella took it and scrambled to her feet, and they made their way around the perimeter of the wall. When they reached the tall iron gate, they found Lord Darlington standing there, waiting for them.

"Lord Darlington! I didn't see you there." Cecilia patted her chest to calm the sudden wild thud of her heart. "You, ah…you startled me."

"I beg your pardon. Come here, Isabella." Lord Darlington leaned down, scooped Isabella into his arms and gathered her tightly against his broad chest. "Did you have a nice walk with Miss Cecilia?"

"Yes." Isabella wrapped her arms around her uncle's neck with a contented sigh. "Ever so nice. Miss Cecilia knows all about flowers."

"Does she?" Lord Darlington met Cecilia's gaze over the top of Isabella's head.

"No, not particularly," Cecilia said with a laugh. "I can recognize lavender, roses, and daisies, and…that's pretty much all, really."

Lord Darlington was rubbing Isabella's back, but his gaze remained on Cecilia. "Not so much then, but Miss Cecilia knows a good deal about other things."

He was watching her, a slight tic in his jaw, his gaze uncertain, but also oddly…*tender*?

No, surely not. The shadows were playing tricks on her.

"Things that matter more than flowers," he added, the softness from earlier back in his eyes as he studied Cecilia's face.

Cecilia stared back at him in confusion. She couldn't make sense of his peculiar expression until he tilted his head subtly toward Isabella. Oh. *Oh*. Now she understood. He was pleased with her for shielding Isabella from Mrs. Honeywell earlier.

It wasn't *tenderness*, but gratitude.

The realization caused a strange, sinking sensation in Cecilia's chest, but she forced a smile to her lips. "I'm not dismissed, then?" she murmured, too low for Isabella to hear.

He tilted his head to one side as if considering it, and a crooked grin curved his lips. "Not today, no."

Cecilia's foolish heart fluttered into her throat at that boyish grin, and she was obliged to clear it before she trusted herself to speak. "No promises for tomorrow, though?"

"There's no telling what might happen tomorrow." He held her gaze for a moment longer before pressing a kiss to Isabella's forehead. "Come, it's getting dark."

Dusk was descending, the pale glow of the sky deepening to a slate gray, but it was light enough still to see the whorls of silver frost making patterns on the ground. It was beautiful, in that soft, silent way winter sometimes was, and so still they might have been the only three people here. The thought was…peaceful, Cecilia realized in surprise, as she fell into step beside Lord Darlington.

How strange that it should be peaceful rather than disturbing.

When they reached the entrance hall, they found Lord Haslemere just coming into the hallway, looking harried. "Ah, there you are, Darlington. I wondered where you'd got to." His gaze darted between the two of them, and a slight frown appeared between his brows. "We're waiting for you to join us in the drawing room for tea."

"Yes, of course." Lord Darlington ruffled Isabella's curls, then handed her over to Cecilia. "I'll come to say goodnight later. Be a good girl for

Miss Cecilia, and maybe we can coax her into singing one of her…unusual lullabies for us."

Before Cecilia could reply, Lord Haslemere waved an impatient hand toward the drawing room. "Come on then, Darlington. You don't want to keep your betrothed waiting."

He followed Lord Darlington down the hallway, but before he disappeared into the drawing room, he glanced back at Cecilia over his shoulder with an appraising look that made her cheeks burn.

Chapter Thirteen

"I know what you're doing, Darlington."

Gideon peered over the top of his port glass at Haslemere, who was slouched in a chair near the fire, his legs sprawled out before him and his own glass dangling from his fingers. "I'm pleased one of us does."

He'd woken this morning to the soft murmur of Cecilia crooning to Isabella, her husky voice weaving a spell around him until he'd drifted back to sleep, and dreamed of wide, velvety brown eyes, plump pink lips, and a stubborn, pointed chin. He'd been hard when he woke, his cock twitching insistently against his stomach, his entire body flushed with arousal.

It had been months since he'd felt even a twinge of desire for any woman, much less the dizzying rush of this morning. No, it had been longer than that—more than a year, since Cassandra had become so ill. If his betrothed had been the cause of such an eager erection Gideon might have rejoiced at it, but it wasn't Miss Honeywell who'd inspired him to such unexpected rigidity.

It was Cecilia. Always Cecilia.

Cecilia, with her unpredictable tongue and those unexpected flashes of fire in her eyes. Such a pleasant, agreeable young woman, right up until the moment she *wasn't*. She'd completely forgotten her place yesterday, and acted every inch the impertinent chit Mrs. Honeywell had accused her of being. A wiser man would have dismissed her for her insolence toward his betrothed's mother, yet Gideon had let Cecilia stroll off without a word of reprimand.

And now there was the matter of this wholly inappropriate erection of his. Since its inconvenient appearance this morning, he'd struggled with alternate bouts of irritation, frustration, and yearning until he was half out of his head and couldn't focus on a single thing.

His betrothed, for instance.

Haslemere snorted. "Oh, I think you know well enough what you're about. There's no sense denying it, Darlington. Anyone can see the way you look at Cecilia, and draw the obvious conclusion."

Gideon's face heated. "If you recall, it was *you* who urged me to keep Cecilia on instead of dismissing her."

"I did, yes, but that was before I realized you'd developed a *tendre* for her." Haslemere took a sip of his port. "Your infatuation with her is inconvenient, given you're meant to marry another lady in less than a week's time."

"I'm aware of my obligations to Miss Honeywell, Haslemere."

"Being aware of your obligations and reconciled to them are not, alas, the same thing. Your betrothed doesn't seem to notice it, but I think Mrs. Honeywell has drawn her own conclusions about Cecilia. She's a spiteful, vulgar, ill-mannered woman, but she's not an utter fool."

Gideon didn't bother arguing the point. He'd caught more than one outraged glance from Mrs. Honeywell over the past few days. As for his betrothed, she either didn't care, or didn't notice his preoccupation with Cecilia.

It was difficult to tell with Miss Honeywell.

"I don't know what I'm doing, Haslemere." Gideon let his head fall into his hands. Perhaps he shouldn't have become betrothed again. The business of living what remained of his life had been a great deal easier from behind the walls of Darlington Castle.

Easier, but lonelier, and not really a life at all. Not for him, and not for Isabella. She needed a mother, and hopefully, in time, brothers and sisters.

Haslemere toyed with his glass, his gaze on the swirl of ruby red port. "Tell me, Darlington. Are you in love with Miss Honeywell?"

Gideon's head snapped up. *Love?* No, he wasn't in love with her. He'd chosen Miss Honeywell as his bride for a number of reasons, but not one of them had been because he loved her. He was under no illusions she loved him, either. Theirs was a *ton* marriage in every sense of the word. "She's a decent lady, lovely both in face and temperament, and I believe she'll be an affectionate mother to Isabella."

He needed a wife, and Miss Honeywell wanted a fortune and a title. That was all. Gideon no longer expected anything more from a marriage than that.

"Ah, but that's not what I asked you, Darlington." Haslemere set his port aside and leaned forward, his elbows on his knees. "I asked if you're in love with her."

Gideon ran a weary hand down his face, and wondered when everything had become so confusing. "No, I don't love her, but I don't see what that has to do with anything. This marriage is a matter of practicality, not passion. She's uncomplicated, Haslemere, and her presence brightens up this dreary place."

"I see. You're determined to marry her, then?"

"Of course I am. Do you suppose I'd court and then offer for a lady I wasn't prepared to marry?" A bitter laugh fell from Gideon's lips. "I'm a murderer, Haslemere, remember? Not a scoundrel."

"Damn it, Darlington, will you stop saying that? We both know you're neither. I only ask because I can't imagine anything less than love would induce me to marry a lady with such a mother. But none of that matters. No, the issue here is that Cecilia is distracting you from your betrothed, and it's bound to make a mess of things. I'm amazed it hasn't already."

"Are you suggesting I dismiss her?" Cecilia *did* distract him, more so every day, yet Gideon couldn't bear the idea of letting her go.

"I'm suggesting you find another place for her, yes. I'll take her on, if you like. Oh, she's a bit of a termagant, but I'm rather fond of her all the same. One can't help but admire a lady who puts Mrs. Honeywell in her place."

Haslemere grinned, and for some reason it set Gideon's teeth on edge. "Fond of her, are you? *How* fond? *Improperly* fond?"

It was a bloody unfair question, and one Gideon knew he had no right to ask. Haslemere might be one of London's most dashing rakes, but at his heart he was a gentleman. There were certain lines he wouldn't cross, and trifling with a servant was one of them.

But if Haslemere was offended, he didn't show it. "Fond enough to offer her a place at Haslemere House. I can take her over there myself tomorrow morning, and have her out of Mrs. Honeywell's way before breakfast. You must see you can't keep Cecilia at Darlington Castle after you're wed—"

"No. Cecilia stays here." Gideon was cursing his own foolishness before the words were out of his mouth, but he just...he couldn't let her go.

"*No?*" Haslemere stared at him. "Why the devil not?"

Why, indeed? It was the ideal solution, really, the perfect way to get Cecilia out from underfoot without depriving her of a place, which would be unfair of him. It wasn't her fault she drove him to distraction, heated the blood in his veins, haunted his dreams—

Yet as perfect as it was, Gideon found himself desperately floundering for a believable explanation for why it wouldn't do. "I can't let her go now, Haslemere, not when Isabella's so attached to her." He was half-ashamed of using his niece as an excuse, but then again, it was the truth, wasn't it?

"Ah. Isabella, is it? I suppose there isn't a single servant in all of Darlington Castle aside from Cecilia Isabella can tolerate."

"It's truer than you might think. Cecilia has a way with her. She, ah... she sings to Isabella, and it calms her. Cecilia has a surprisingly sweet singing voice, despite the occasional sharp edge to her tongue."

Haslemere huffed out a breath, but Gideon had hit upon just the right argument. Haslemere, much like everyone else who frequented Darlington Castle, was Isabella's devoted slave, and he wouldn't dream of depriving her of the only servant who could soothe her.

Still, Haslemere cast Gideon an uneasy look. "You realize you're putting Cecilia at risk by keeping her here, don't you, Darlington? Mrs. Honeywell is a low, malicious woman, and she doesn't appreciate her daughter being slighted. If she chooses to take offense—and she likely *will*—it won't be you who catches the razor edge of her ire. It will be Cecilia."

Gideon opened his mouth, but closed it again when he realized Haslemere was right. If Mrs. Honeywell had the opportunity, she'd make Cecilia suffer for his folly. He didn't like the idea of Cecilia suffering—not for his sake, or anyone else's. He didn't like it at all.

"No, she won't." Gideon tossed back the rest of his port. "I'll make certain Cecilia's kept out of Mrs. Honeywell's way. The woman can rage all she likes, but she won't get the chance to harm Cecilia."

* * * *

Mrs. Honeywell *did* choose to take offense, and despite Gideon's best efforts, she found a way to vent her frustrations. Her revenge, when it came, was swift, brutal, and utterly unexpected.

By the time Gideon realized it was coming, it was already too late.

It happened in the drawing room the following evening, while Miss Honeywell was performing on the pianoforte for a small group of neighbors and guests who'd been invited to a lavish supper that evening to celebrate the impending nuptials.

Cecilia shouldn't have been anywhere near the drawing room. Gideon had taken Haslemere's warning to heart, and instructed Mrs. Briggs to keep Cecilia and Amy safely out of the way in the kitchens until the guests had withdrawn to their bedchambers that night.

If he'd known Cecilia was passing through the corridor outside the drawing room, he might have been able to put a stop to it, but Mrs.

Honeywell saw her before Gideon realized Cecilia was there, and before he knew what she was about, her shrill voice rang throughout the drawing room.

"Cecilia! How wonderful you should happen to be passing by just now. We need another young lady aside from my daughter to entertain us, and Lord Darlington has raved about what a *lovely* singing voice you have. Won't you come in and perform for us?"

Gideon's gaze shot to the doorway, and without realizing he did it, he rose to his feet.

The other guests looked at each other in confusion, and Miss Honeywell whirled around at the sound of her mother's voice. She understood at once what her mother had just proposed fell shockingly outside the bounds of proper etiquette, and her pretty mouth fell open, her face going pale.

Miss Honeywell played like an angel, and she looked her best when she played, with flushed cheeks and her long, elegant fingers moving gracefully over the keys. It was expected she'd display her talents for the company.

But Cecilia wasn't a lady. She was a *servant*, and servants didn't perform for aristocratic company. It was unheard of to even suggest it—an insult to both Lord Darlington and his guests.

Miss Honeywell lacked wit, but she wasn't the ruthless viper her mother was, and she knew well enough her mother's spitefulness reflected poorly on *her*. She leapt up from the pianoforte bench in protest. "Indeed, Mama, I'm certain she has no wish to play."

"Hush, will you, Fanny?" Mrs. Honeywell's eyes were glittering with malice. "Why shouldn't the girl wish to show off her fine voice? Come, Cecilia, don't stand there like a half-wit. There's no need for such dramatics. No one here expects a *housemaid's* performance to equal my daughter's."

Miss Honeywell's cheeks flushed with anger and mortification. The rest of the party sat there, speechless with shock, not one of them saying a single word. They looked from Mrs. Honeywell to Lord Darlington to Cecilia in flabbergasted silence.

Cecilia stood frozen beside the door, her face dead white. "I beg you'll excuse me, Mrs. Honeywell, I—"

"No, indeed. Not on any account." Mrs. Honeywell beckoned her forward with an imperious gesture, and jabbed her finger at the pianoforte. "Step aside, Fanny, and give Cecilia your place."

"This is absurd." Haslemere leapt to his feet, his face tight with anger. "Do you make a practice of forcing your housemaids to play for the company at your house, madam? I confess I find your request quite singular."

Mrs. Honeywell gave an ugly laugh. "Not at all, my lord, but my housemaids are simple, *obedient* girls, and they aren't gifted with Cecilia's alleged musical prowess."

Gideon had heard enough. "Cecilia, you are excused." His quiet voice sliced through the thick tension in the room.

Two livid streaks of scarlet painted Cecilia's cheekbones, chasing away her pallor. At first Gideon thought she was flushed with mortification, but then she straightened her spine and lifted her chin in the air. "I'm quite happy to oblige Mrs. Honeywell, with your permission, Lord Darlington."

Her gaze met his, and his eyebrows shot up at the look in her dark eyes. She wasn't mortified. She was *furious.*

"See? The girl's anxious to show herself off. You can hardly deny us the pleasure of hearing her, my lord." Mrs. Honeywell settled her pink ruffles around her with a jerk. "Not when you've gone on at such *length* about her superior skill."

"I've no idea what you mean, madam." Gideon, who could have happily throttled Mrs. Honeywell just then, didn't attempt to hide his anger.

"Why, you couldn't say enough about the girl's sweet singing voice during tea yesterday." Mrs. Honeywell gave him a poisonous smile. "You made me quite long to hear her for myself."

"I said only that my niece enjoys hearing her sing." Gideon's voice was shaking with fury. "I fail to see how you took that as an invitation to demand she perform for the company."

Cecilia stepped away from the doorway and into the drawing room. She was utterly calm, only her tight jaw hinting at her agitation. "I'd be pleased to sing for Mrs. Honeywell, if you don't object, my lord."

Gideon had never before been so tempted to toss a lady out of his home as he was Mrs. Honeywell, but one glance at Cecilia silenced him. He could see she was determined to brazen it out, and he was more than happy to watch her put Mrs. Honeywell in her place. "Very well, Cecilia. If you wish it."

He nodded toward the pianoforte, and took his seat again.

Cecilia made her way toward the instrument, her head high. Mrs. Honeywell smirked as she took her seat on the bench. "What simple little ditty will you play for us, Cecilia? *Sonata Facile,* perhaps?"

A few of the haughtier members of the company tittered behind their hands at this, but most of them were either glaring at Mrs. Honeywell or casting pitying glances at Cecilia.

Cecilia's back stiffened. Gideon half rose from his chair again, but before he could intervene a second time, her fingers began to move over the keys. A moment later her pure, clear voice took up the melody.

Here's a health to the King and a lasting peace
To faction an end, to wealth increase.
Come, let us drink it while we have breath,
For there's no drinking after death.

A gasp rose up from the company, but Gideon's lips curved in a smile.

Cecilia had chosen to sing an old English drinking song. Not just any song, either, but a notoriously bawdy one. By choosing a song so thoroughly out of Miss Honeywell's repertoire, Cecilia had ensured there could be no comparison between them.

Her enthusiasm grew as she progressed through the song, her fingers flying over the keys as she sang with gusto, neatly depriving Mrs. Honeywell of the chance to humiliate her.

Let Bacchus' health round briskly move,
For Bacchus is a friend to Love;
And they that would this health deny,
Down among the dead men let him lie!

When the last ringing notes sounded in the silent drawing room, Cecilia rose from the bench, turned to face a quivering, purple-faced Mrs. Honeywell, and offered her a solemn curtsy.

"Brava, Cecilia!" Haslemere burst into enthusiastic applause, a delighted smile on his lips. "Well done! Your voice is every bit as lovely as Lord Darlington said. Don't you agree, Mrs. Honeywell?"

Mrs. Honeywell *didn't* appear to agree. She was glaring at Cecilia as if she'd like to wring her neck, but for once, she held her tongue.

"Thank you, my lord." Cecilia offered another curtsy to Haslemere, her lips curved in a grin that made Gideon's heart thump wildly in his chest.

Finally, she turned to him, her dark eyes wary. "Lord Darlington."

She looked as if she were expecting him to dismiss her then and there, and toss her out the door of his castle into the freezing night. He gave her a slight smile, his eyes holding hers, but he said only, "Thank you, Cecilia. You are excused."

Chapter Fourteen

Cecilia took care to keep her head high as she left the drawing room, but as soon as she was out of sight of Lord Darlington's guests she fled down the hallway. By the time she reached the staircase, her knees were shaking so badly she wasn't sure she could climb the stairs.

She slapped a hand over her mouth, her other hand tightening on the stair railing as she choked back a sudden flood of saliva. Dear God, she was going to be sick. She was going to be sick all over Lord Darlington's spotless flagstone floors, not a dozen steps away from the drawing room door.

After the scene she'd just made, Lord Darlington's guests might decide they'd had quite enough entertainment for one night, and choose to take their leave. She couldn't bear for any of them to see her in such a state, or worse, for him to see her. No, she'd rather take a tumble down the stairs than face *him* right now.

Cecilia gripped the railing and dragged herself up one stair after the next, her hand still pressed against her mouth. When she reached the first landing, she risked a glance behind her, then sagged against the wall with relief.

No one had followed her, thank goodness.

Of all the songs she might have chosen to sing, why had she chosen "Down Among the Dead"? She hadn't the vaguest idea how it had even entered her head, but once it had, the smug look on Mrs. Honeywell's face had lured it past her lips before she even realized what she was doing. The next thing she knew, she was seated at the pianoforte, singing about celestial joys and the pleasures of the soul and Bacchus being the friend to love, and, and...

Her head fell weakly against the wall behind her, her cheeks bursting into sudden flames as she recalled the last stanza, which she'd sang with particular fervor.

May love and wine their rights maintain,
And their united pleasure reign;
While Bacchus' treasure crowns the board,
We'll sing the joy that both afford.

No, surely that didn't mean…

But of course, it did. It meant precisely what she'd always known it did, and she'd just sang it aloud to a roomful of aristocratic strangers.

With fervor.

She'd just sung a song about…about *copulation* in the middle of Lord Darlington's drawing room. In front of his wedding guests, no less.

Cecilia groaned as she resumed her trek up the staircase. Lord Darlington had been patient with her tonight, kind even, but if none of her other missteps had resulted in her dismissal, *this* one surely would.

They were all likely still sitting in frozen silence in the drawing room, staring at one another in shock. Cecilia's stomach roiled at the thought. She wasn't ashamed of herself—not really, though she probably should be. She wasn't proud, either, but she couldn't deny the little curl of triumph in her chest. It was heady, even as it was tempered by fear, fury, defiance, and yes, a touch of nausea.

In short, her emotions were so tangled she could hardly tell *what* she felt, but without warning, her eyes began to sting with unshed tears.

Tears she wouldn't allow herself to shed. Not yet.

She hurried into the bedchamber she shared with Isabella, closed the door, and sagged against it. Isabella was asleep, and Cecilia took advantage of this rare moment of private, blessed quiet. The knot inside her chest loosened, but as her alarm faded the tears she'd been holding back spilled over her cheeks. She swiped at them with the back of her hand, but they fell faster than she could catch them, and after a fruitless struggle she gave herself up to them, sagging against the door, her breath hitching as quiet sobs wracked her.

I do believe I'm overwrought.

It wasn't a familiar feeling. Indeed, she couldn't recall ever being so overwrought in her life. Sophia and Emma were the ones who became overwrought, and Georgiana the one who fell into tempers. Cecilia had always been the serene one, the only one of the four not prone to bursts of fury or passion. No matter how trying the circumstances, she always remained composed.

How in the world had she ever let herself fall into such a temper tonight? She'd never lost control of herself like that before, but then Mrs. Honeywell was awful enough to shatter the composure of a saint. Cecilia had never before been as vexed as she'd been just now—

She paused, blinking. Now she thought of it, she'd hardly ever been vexed at all before tonight, rarely crossed or challenged. Yet here she was, congratulating herself on her delightful temperament. It was an empty boast, when that temper had never truly been tried.

Of all the things that might have popped into her head just then, Cecilia found herself thinking of Gussie, Lady Clifford's plump pug dog. Gussie spent most of his time splayed out on his back in front of the drawing room fire, his short legs in the air, contented snores gusting from his drooling lips. He was a charming little fellow, but one couldn't deny he was an indolent thing, of very little use to anyone.

Cecilia adored Gussie—they all did. He was a much-beloved member of the Clifford School, and considered by them all to be of a remarkably sweet temper. Every last one of them exclaimed over his affectionate nature, extolled his many virtues, and declared him the loveliest dog ever to grace the canine world. Even Daniel Brixton, who was the sternest man Cecilia had ever known, cosseted, petted, and spoiled Gussie.

Rather like they did with Cecilia herself.

Her eyes opened wide.

Dear God, she was just like Gussie.

Oh, her friends would deny it to their dying breaths. They'd argue she was the dearest, the sweetest, the most tenderhearted of them all. They'd stroke and soothe and murmur consolingly to her, much as they did with Gussie when he had the bellyache from too many treats.

Well, she hadn't been very sweet to Mrs. Honeywell. Not that the woman deserved Cecilia's consideration, cruel, spiteful old thing that she was. Indeed, Cecilia was rather relieved to find she could defend herself when the occasion required it.

No, she couldn't regret her response to Mrs. Honeywell's attack, only…

She wiped away the last of her tears and crossed the room to gaze down at Isabella, who was sleeping like the angel she was, her soft, golden-brown curls a messy halo around her head.

Only she wouldn't be the only one to suffer for her foolishness tonight, would she? Isabella would be hurt, too, if Cecilia was dismissed and sent away from Darlington Castle. A wave of bitter regret rolled over her, drawing fresh tears to her eyes.

Mrs. Honeywell might be haughty and despicable, but Cecilia hadn't acquitted herself well tonight, either. Now, gazing down at Isabella, she wished with all her heart she'd put *her* before her offended pride.

But it was too late for that now. She'd escaped dismissal twice, but after tonight, what choice did Lord Darlington have but to dismiss her? One did *not* sing about drunkenness and copulation in the drawing room. Surely that must be the first and most sacred rule of *ton* etiquette?

A sudden knock on the door interrupted her thoughts, and Cecilia started toward it, thinking it must be Amy, come to commiserate with her. But when the knock sounded again, louder this time, Cecilia realized with dawning horror it wasn't the hallway door that was under assault.

It was the connecting door between her bedchamber and Lord Darlington's.

She raised a shaking hand to her mouth. *Oh, no.* Was he going to dismiss her *tonight*? She'd hardly dared to look at him when she fled the drawing room earlier. He hadn't looked angry, but that knock sounded like a death knell—

There was a third knock, this one louder still, then Lord Darlington's deep voice. "I know you're in there, Cecilia. I'd like to speak with you, but I won't enter your bedchamber under these circumstances without your permission."

He wouldn't? Cecilia was tempted to test the truth of his statement by hiding behind the door all night, but what was the sense in putting it off? She'd have to face him sooner or later.

She crossed the room to the connecting door, drew a deep breath for courage, then opened it to face her fate. Lord Darlington was standing there, one hand on his hip and the other braced on the top of the door frame.

"Er...good evening, Lord Darlington."

He straightened and stepped past her into her bedchamber. "Would you call it good, Cecilia? It's *something*, certainly, but I wouldn't call it *good*."

"I, ah...no, I wouldn't call it good, either." Cecilia thought of the shock on Mrs. Honeywell's face and grimaced. "It's quite the opposite, and I beg your pardon for it, my lord. I shouldn't have...I didn't intend to...there's no excuse for my—"

He took a quick step forward, and to Cecilia's shock he grasped her chin and tilted her face up to his. He studied her in the light from the fire for long, silent moments, the strangest expression on his face, then he asked in a hoarse voice, "Have you been *crying*?"

Cecilia stared up into those bright blue eyes, her throat working. If her humiliation hadn't been complete before, it was *now*. "I-I do believe I'm overwrought, my lord."

He released her chin, but he didn't step back, and to her surprise, the trace of a smile curved his lips. "Yes, I imagine you are, though perhaps less so than Mrs. Honeywell is. Lord Haslemere had to help her from the drawing room to her bedchamber. He wasn't at all pleased about it, either. I daresay he'll take you to task for it tomorrow."

"Oh, dear," Cecilia muttered, worrying at her lower lip. This evening continued to worsen with every moment. Perhaps she should retire to her bed, before she caused further trouble.

But first, she'd get the last, worst bit over with. She cast a guilty look at Lord Darlington. "I'll gather my things together tonight, so I can be gone first thing tomorrow morning."

He went still. "You're...you intend to leave Darlington Castle?"

Cecilia's eyes widened. "I assume you intend to dismiss me."

"Is that why you think I came to speak to you tonight? To dismiss you?"

"Well, yes." What other reason could he have for appearing at her bedchamber door?

He stood quietly before her, his hands braced on his hips and his head down. Then, without a word he crossed the room to his niece's bed. He gazed down at Isabella for some time, then reached in and stroked his big hand gently over her curls.

When he turned toward her again, his face had softened. "I've no intention of dismissing you, Cecilia. I won't say I approve of your musical performance tonight, but I also don't condone Mrs. Honeywell's behavior. The way I see it, you were...unbearably provoked."

Cecilia stared at him, mouth agape.

"You *were* unbearably provoked, weren't you? You don't make a habit of singing bawdy drinking songs to your employer's guests of an evening, do you?"

She peeked up at him from under her lashes. "Bawdy? As to that, I'm sure I don't know what you mean, my lord. It's simply a drinking song, isn't it?"

"I can see by your blush you know perfectly well what I mean. Where would a young woman such as yourself learn such a wicked song?"

"Oh, we used to sing it—" Cecilia broke off, biting her lip. She'd learned that song years ago from the mudlarking boys on the Thames, but it wouldn't do to blurt that particular truth out to Lord Darlington. For pity's sake, one half-hearted smile from him, and she was ready to confess her every secret.

"I, ah...I learned it from one of Lady Dunton's footmen," she finished lamely. "He was a dreadfully wicked young man, I'm afraid."

"I've no doubt."

Neither of them seemed to know what to say after that, so they stood there staring at each other, until the silence became so awkward Cecilia found herself rushing to break it. "He was forever singing wicked songs. I might have done worse than I did, and sang "The Fair Maid of Islington," or the one about Mother Watkin's Ale, or..."

She trailed off, her cheeks burning again. Lord Darlington stared at her for a moment, eyebrow raised, but just as Cecilia braced herself for a stern lecture about the evils of bawdy pub songs and the unspeakable sin of singing one in a drawing room full of company, the unthinkable happened.

He *grinned* at her.

Not his usual joyless twist of the mouth, or the pallid echo of a smile, but a true, unreserved grin that started at his lips and spread over his face, warming his bright blue eyes and revealing a pair of fetching grooves at either side of his lips.

Dimples. Lord Darlington had *dimples.*

Cecilia stared at him, her breath hitching in her throat. "Oh."

Isabella's wide, irresistible grin, that grin Cecilia adored, the one that always coaxed an answering grin from her...it was her *uncle's* smile.

The sweet curve of Isabella's lips, the brightness in her eyes, those fetching dimples at the corners of her mouth...it mirrored the smile now gracing Lord Darlington's lips. Isabella didn't look like him, but she'd learned to imitate his smile.

How could Cecilia not have seen it before now?

Because I've never truly seen him smile.

His smile faded into a look of uncertainty as she continued to stare at him. "Is something wrong?"

"I...no. No, my lord, it's just...well, Isabella's smile is just like yours."

Lord Darlington went quite still, his eyes going as dark as a midnight sky. His fingers flexed at his sides, and for one wild moment she thought he would come to her. Cecilia's breath stopped, every inch of her aching for him.

He didn't, but he didn't turn away, either. Impossibly, his grin widened. "I might even venture a laugh if you sing "The Fair Maid of Islington" to me."

Cecilia stared at him. Was he *teasing* her? "Oh, no. I couldn't. It's terribly improper."

"As opposed to Down Among the Dead," which I've heard sung in drawing rooms all across England."

Oh, he was certainly teasing her. Cecilia had never been teased by a marquess, or by any gentleman, really. She wasn't certain what to do, so she just stood there like a peahen, her cheeks on fire and a foolish grin on her face.

He didn't seem to expect her to do anything more, however. He gazed at her as if her smile was enough to please him, before he straightened and eased away, murmuring, "It's late. Go to sleep, Cecilia."

He crossed the room and went into his own bedchamber, but Cecilia stopped him before he could close the door between them. "My lord?"

"Yes?" His face was half-lost in shadow, but she could just discern the quirk of his lips.

She wanted to say, *I'll sing you any song you like.* She wanted to say, *I believe you're a good, kind man.* She wanted to say, *I wish for you to have more reasons to smile.*

But in the end, she didn't say any of those things. Instead, she drew in a quick breath and said, "Good night."

Chapter Fifteen

It was a day for being overwrought, it seemed.

After those breathless moments with Lord Darlington—moments in which she'd had to fight an overwhelming urge to trace her fingertips over his lips to commit that rare smile to memory—Cecilia knew sleep would elude her for the rest of the night.

After pacing from one end of her bedchamber to the other with the words of the blasted "Fair Maid of Islington" echoing in a wearying loop in her head, she climbed under the coverlet, eyes wide open, and reconciled herself to a sleepless night.

What would Lord Darlington's lips feel like under her fingertips? They looked soft. Were a gentleman's lips soft? They were full, temptingly so, his lower lip a trifle plumper, just the tiniest hint of a pout.

Goodness.

She tucked the coverlet closer as a delicious warmth settled low in her belly. Her eyelids grew heavy, and she was just embarking on a scandalously delightful dream about Lord Darlington's lips when she was startled awake by Seraphina, who suddenly woke from her nap at the foot of Cecilia's bed, let out a growl, and leapt to the floor.

"Seraphina?" Cecilia reached for the cat, but Seraphina darted away before she could get a hand on her. "Whatever is the matter?"

That was when she heard it. It was muffled, so faint she nearly missed it, but it sounded like a—

Scream.

Cecilia shot upright as another scream, this one much louder and edged with panic, shattered the silence of the castle. Seraphina let out another yowl, and scrambled across the floor to the door leading to the hallway, clawing in a frenzy to be let out.

Cecilia vaulted from the bed, tripping over the hem of her night rail in her panic to get to Isabella, but the scream hadn't come from her, nor had it woken her. She was curled up in her bed, sleeping the sound, peaceful sleep of a child.

A door slammed in the hallway. Cecilia whirled around, her breath stopping as a third scream rent the air.

Dear God, it sounded as if someone were being murdered.

Her lungs heaving like a bellows, she snatched up a shawl and flew out her bedchamber door. At the other end of the hallway she could see Lord Darlington, Lord Haslemere, Amy, Duncan, Mrs. Briggs, and Mrs. Honeywell crowded around Miss Honeywell's door. There was no sign of Miss Honeywell, but Cecilia could hear a desperate wail echoing from inside her bedchamber.

"Fanny! Open this door at once!" Mrs. Honeywell was beside herself. She rattled the latch until the door shuddered in its frame, her shrieks drowning out her daughter's howls. Her face was so red she looked as if she were one scream away from a convulsive fit.

Cecilia flew down the hallway, her shawl streaming out behind her, and came to a stumbling halt beside Amy in front of Miss Honeywell's door. "What's happened?"

Amy gave her a stricken look. "I-I've no idea. Mayhap Miss Honeywell had a nightmare?"

"Stand aside, Mrs. Honeywell." Lord Darlington's face was pale, but he was utterly calm as he eased Mrs. Honeywell away from the door. "Some assistance, if you would, Haslemere," he added, gesturing toward the locked bedchamber door.

He and Lord Haslemere made quick work of it, slamming their shoulders against the door until the latch on the other side gave way, and it burst open.

"What the devil?" Lord Haslemere froze on the threshold, his eyes widening, and Cecilia and the others crowded around the door, peeking around him.

Miss Honeywell was in her bed, her eyes squeezed closed, tears streaming down her cheeks, and one deafening shriek after another issuing from her gaping mouth. She was so overwrought, she seemed not to notice a crowd had gathered in her doorway.

Mrs. Honeywell pushed forward, flew across the room, and seized her daughter by the shoulders. "Fanny? Fanny! For pity's sake, child, what's happened?"

Mrs. Honeywell was obliged to shake her daughter until at last Fanny opened her eyes and choked out through breathless sobs, "I-I heard a noise outside, as if someone were moaning. I rose from my bed, and I s-saw... there was a woman, standing under my window!"

"A woman? My dear, it was likely just one of Lord Darlington's servants."

Cecilia and Amy glanced at each other. There was no reason a servant should be wandering around the grounds in the dead of night.

"No, Mama!" Miss Honeywell clutched her mother's arm, her knuckles white. "It wasn't a servant! S-she was a *ghost*!"

A collective gasp rose from the bystanders.

Mrs. Honeywell jerked free, anger replacing the panic on her face. "Goodness, Fanny, all this fuss over a nightmare? Why, you nearly reduced the castle to rubble with your screeching."

"It was no nightmare, Mama! She was dressed in a flowing white gown, and her face..." Miss Honeywell shuddered. "No living, breathing being, no woman of flesh and blood could have such deathly white skin. She looked as if she'd just crept from her grave, and she was staring up at me, and she...she raised her hand and pointed her finger at me! It was a threat, Mama! She wants me gone from this castle."

Another gasp arose from the servants crowding the doorway, and Amy slapped a hand over her mouth. Lord Darlington strode to the window, jerked the drapes open and peered down into the grounds below. "There's no one there now."

Mrs. Honeywell threw her hands up in the air. Servant, nightmare, or ghost, she was having none of it. "How could an apparition threaten you, you silly girl? It was certainly a nightmare. If she were truly there, then where has she gone?"

Miss Honeywell cast a wild look at the window, the coverlet clutched to her chest. "Oh, I don't know! I ran back to my bed, and...and pulled the pillow over my head!"

Amy let out a terrified squeak. Lord Darlington turned at the sound to find all of them standing in the doorway, witnessing the lurid scene, and his face darkened. "Return to your beds at once. As you can see, Miss Honeywell is perfectly safe now."

Lord Haslemere remained where he was, his arms crossed over his chest, but the servants shuffled out and began to make their way back to their bedchambers. Cecilia followed along after them, but she took care to be the last one out the door. She left it open a crack, and lingered in the hallway to listen, with her eye pressed against the narrow gap.

"Safe!" Miss Honeywell rose to her knees in the middle of the bed and pointed one shaking finger at Lord Darlington. "You wicked, wicked man!"

Mrs. Honeywell gasped. "Fanny! How dare you address Lord Darlington in such a way? Beg his pardon at once!"

But Miss Honeywell, who was well beyond rational thought by this point, didn't beg Lord Darlington's pardon. "Darlington Castle is haunted, just as everyone in London says it is! The late Lady Darlington roams the grounds, seeking her revenge on you for her death. You really *are* the Murderous Marquess!"

"Murderer or not, he's still a marquess!" Mrs. Honeywell cried.

"I don't care if he's a *duke*! I'm leaving Darlington Castle tomorrow morning, Mama. I want to go home."

"Leaving! But you're to be married at the end of the week!"

"What, and get murdered, and end up haunting a dreary castle for the rest of my days? No, Mama. I won't do it!"

Mrs. Honeywell, who saw her dream of becoming mother to a marchioness dissolving before her eyes, rushed to the bed and shook her daughter until her teeth rattled in her head. "You'd throw away the chance to become a marchioness over a *ghost*? God in heaven, that I should be cursed with such a fool for a daughter!"

Mrs. Honeywell was now as hysterical as Miss Honeywell, and she might have shaken her daughter into unconsciousness if Lord Darlington hadn't intervened, and dragged her away from the bed. "Release your daughter at once, madam."

"What duke would have you now, you selfish, ungrateful girl!" Mrs. Honeywell had quite lost control of herself, and was spitting and scratching to get free. "You'll be lucky to get a lowly viscount if you jilt a marquess!"

"I don't care! I'll marry a farmer if I have to!" Tears were once again leaking from Miss Honeywell's eyes, and she buried her face in her hands.

Mrs. Honeywell gave up trying to reason with her daughter, and turned to clutch desperately at Lord Darlington. "My daughter is a bit… distraught, my lord, and doesn't know what she's saying. She'll come to her senses by morning—"

"No." Lord Darlington plucked his shirt out of Mrs. Honeywell's grasp.

"No? But my lord, I promise you—"

"Forgive me, Mrs. Honeywell, but I've no wish to marry a lady who doesn't wish to marry *me*, nor do I want a wife who believes I'm a murderer." He turned to offer Miss Honeywell a stiff bow. "I release you from our betrothal, Miss Honeywell."

If any specters still lingered near Darlington Castle, Mrs. Honeywell's deafening shriek would have sent them all scurrying. "I warn you, Lord Darlington, I won't have every malicious tongue in London wagging about my daughter jilting a marquess. Either you marry her, or I'll put it about *you* jilted *her*. It will be your reputation left in tatters, not hers!"

Lord Darlington let out a harsh, bitter laugh. "Do what you will. I don't give a bloody damn."

Mrs. Honeywell gasped at the curse. "How *dare* you?"

"Far more easily than you'd imagine, madam. I trust you and your daughter will be gone from Darlington Castle before breakfast tomorrow."

Silence followed this announcement. It seemed even Mrs. Honeywell thought better of arguing with an enraged marquess who'd just ordered her and her daughter to leave his castle. Sensing this was the end of the discussion, Cecilia whirled around and scurried down the hallway to her own bedchamber before she could be caught eavesdropping.

She closed her own door with a quiet click, but even then, she heard Mrs. Honeywell's shriek of fury, followed by the abrupt slamming of a bedchamber door.

Dear God, that *shriek*.

Miss Honeywell would have done better to take her chances with the ghost, rather than her mother.

Cecilia hovered by the door and waited, her heart pounding, and after a few moments she heard the tread of footsteps coming down the hall. She assumed it was Lord Darlington returning to his bedchamber, but when the steps didn't pass her door, she eased it quietly open and peeked through the gap.

Lord Darlington and Lord Haslemere were standing in the shallow alcove just off the landing, mumbling to each other. Cecilia could see by their earnest expressions that whatever they were saying was of some import, and she edged the door open a bit wider.

It was an evening of eavesdropping, it seemed.

"…didn't believe it until tonight."

It was Lord Darlington speaking. Cecilia would have recognized that deep voice anywhere. His next words were muffled, then he said, "It's possible she's come back, Haslemere."

She? Who'd come back? Who could Lord Darlington mean?

Lord Haslemere murmured something Cecilia didn't catch, then, "… even then, how can she simply disappear as if she's vanished into the air?"

Cecilia pressed her eye to the gap and saw Lord Darlington run a distracted hand through his hair. He said something else, too low for Cecilia to hear, then, "...knows the area better than I do."

Lord Haslemere made a frustrated sound and mumbled a few words in reply.

Cecilia held her breath, her ears straining. Oh, why couldn't they speak clearly?

"...know where to start...grounds too extensive."

Dear God, it was maddening. Cecilia caught her tongue between her teeth to keep herself from shouting at them to speak up.

"...unstable, Haslemere. Miss Honeywell's story...go after her."

Unstable? Cecilia's hands curled in an agony of frustration. Go after *who?*

They were just far enough away she could only catch a word here and there, but she'd caught enough of it to know one thing for certain.

Something was terribly amiss at Darlington Castle.

The two conversed for another minute or so, but aside from a stray word here or there she couldn't make sense of, none of what they said reached Cecilia's ears until Lord Darlington said, "We need to search the grounds."

Cecilia stared at Lord Haslemere's back as he hurried down the corridor toward his own rooms, then she ducked back into her bedchamber and slid her door closed. Lord Darlington's footsteps echoed down the hallway, passed her room, and then she heard him moving about in his bedchamber.

She crept toward the connecting door. She didn't dare open it even a crack, but she could hear rustling on the other side, then the thud of boots across the floor. His bedchamber door creaked open, footsteps strode down the hallway, and then...

Silence.

Cecilia took a stumbling step back from the door, her thoughts in turmoil.

She, they'd said. *She,* over and over again, but the only "she" Cecilia knew of who was in any way involved in this mystery was...

The Marchioness of Darlington.

The *dead* Marchioness of Darlington.

Was this a mystery, a ghost story, or a nightmare? Cecilia no longer knew, and there was only one way to find out the truth.

Follow Lord Darlington and Lord Haslemere. Not tonight—she couldn't leave Isabella alone—but she'd seize her chance when it presented itself. Tomorrow, perhaps, or the night after.

Until then...

She glanced over her shoulder at Isabella, who was still curled up on her side, fast asleep in her bed. Cecilia started toward her, but she paused when her gaze fell on the connecting door between her room and Lady Darlington's forbidden bedchamber.

Her heart took up a dizzying, pounding rhythm inside her chest. She pressed her palms flat against the wall at her back, as if that one small act of retreat might be enough to keep her from moving toward Lady Darlington's door.

What did she think she'd find on the other side of it?

Some mystery Lord Darlington was hiding? Some lie he'd told? A White Lady, or a missing marchioness? A pile of bones secreted away inside the stone walls, or Lady Cassandra, alive and well and tucked under her coverlet as if she'd been there all this time, simply waiting for someone to discover she wasn't dead, after all?

It was madness. Utter madness, and yet...

Even as everything inside her rebelled at it, Cecilia's feet were moving across the floor, every step taking her closer to the bedchamber she hadn't entered since the night Lord Darlington had caught her there.

She'd promised never to enter it again, but it seemed she was every bit the liar he'd accused her of being, because despite that promise she grasped the latch, the cold iron burning an imprint into her hand, and then she was turning it, and pushing the door open, and it was too late to pray it would be locked as it was meant to be, and too late to change her mind, and keep her promise.

She'd already broken it.

Without knowing what she was searching for, without knowing whether she hoped or dreaded she'd find it, she crept forward until she passed over the threshold and into Lady Darlington's bedchamber.

She paused at the door, pulling her shawl tighter around her against the sudden cold, and waiting for her eyes to adjust to the darkness. Once they did, her breath left her lungs in a painful whoosh.

Nothing had been touched. There wasn't a single item out of place.

It looked precisely as it had the last time she'd been in here. The drapes were pulled across the windows, the silk bed hangings arranged against the posts, the coverlet undisturbed by a single wrinkle, and the dressing table with a few jeweled hairpins scattered across the polished surface—

Hairpins? Had those been here the last time? Cecilia didn't remember there being anything on the dressing table.

She crossed the room, plucked up one of the pins and turned it between her fingers. They were a delicate, silver filigree with tiny, winking sapphires at the end. No, she didn't remember these, but she might have overlooked them. The room had been dark, and she'd been distracted by Seraphina at the time.

Seraphina, and then shortly after that, Lord Darlington.

She set the pin down on the dressing table where she'd found it, but as she turned back toward the door, the tip of her bare toe nudged up against something. At first, she thought it was the chair leg, but when she leaned down and peeked under the dressing table she saw a pair of richly embroidered blue satin slippers there, lined up neatly side by side, as if their owner would return at any moment and slip her feet into them.

Their owner being Lady Darlington. The *late* Lady Darlington.

Cecilia snatched her foot back, a sudden chill creeping up her neck as she turned to the dressing room on the other side of the bedchamber. She bit her lip, hesitating. There was no logical explanation why it should be so, but some inexplicable instinct was luring her toward that dressing room, urging her to explore the massive clothes press inside.

This is madness.

No good ever came from poking about in other people's closets, but even as her brain warned against it, Cecilia was already crossing the room, easing the door of the clothes press open, and peeking inside. It was dark, but a flutter of something caught her attention. It looked like...a fold of silk or satin, very much like the skirt of a gown. "No. It's impossible." She reached out a shaking hand, her heart pounding. "It can't be, it can't—"

She broke off on a gasp as her fingertips met a fold of smooth, slippery silk.

No. She couldn't be seeing what she thought she was seeing.

But she was. It was there, as plain as day.

An elegant blue silk ball gown was hanging on its own special hanging rack inside the clothes press. Cecilia stared at it with her feet rooted to the floor. A blue silk ball gown, embroidered slippers, and jeweled hairpins, all appearing in the marchioness's bedchamber as if by magic?

She didn't remember any of these things being here before, but mightn't she have missed them the first time? The hairpins were easily overlooked, and the shadows under the dressing table would have made it impossible to see the slippers from the door.

But a blue silk ball gown? Surely, she would have noticed *that* the first time she'd ventured into Lady Darlington's bedchamber? It seemed too substantial a thing for her to have missed.

Cecilia's mind raced back to that night. She'd heard the strange scratching sound, and found the bedchamber unlocked. She'd followed the sound into the dressing room, and from there to the clothes press. She'd eased the door open, and...

Seraphina had leapt out, frightening the life of out of her, and Cecilia had chased the cat into the bedchamber, without sparing the clothes press another thought. No, she'd never taken a good look inside. She couldn't be certain the gown hadn't been there all along.

Of course, it must have been. It was the only thing that made any sense. The only other explanation—that someone had brought the hairpins and the shoes and the gown into Lady Darlington's bedchamber since the last time Cecilia had been here—made no sense at all.

Unless…

Cecilia swallowed. Perhaps the villagers had been right about one thing—that the Marchioness of Darlington *was* back—but they'd been wrong about another.

Perhaps she *wasn't* a ghost.

Cecilia didn't believe in ghosts, or she *hadn't*, but there were only two explanations for the events of tonight, both of them appalling.

It was either one nightmare, or the other.

Either ghosts truly *did* exist, and the White Lady was haunting Darlington Castle, just as the villagers claimed she was, or…

Or Lady Darlington wasn't dead, after all.

* * * *

She was here.

Gideon couldn't see her face, and he couldn't hear her voice or the echo of her footsteps. He didn't catch her scent floating on the frigid night air, but sight, sound, and scent were no longer of any use to him, now he was chasing a ghost.

Not that they'd ever been much use to him, really. A man's senses could deceive him, with tragic results. If he'd learned nothing else this past year, it was that.

So, he suspended them all in favor of instinct, intuition, reflex. He knew she was here because he could *sense* her nearness, feel her lurking in the darkness of the woods, darting between the bare branches of the trees, waiting. He could feel her cold, ghostly fingertips grazing the back of his neck, leaving a chill in their wake.

"You have servants guarding the castle?" Haslemere's voice was grim.

"Yes. Fraser on the ground floor, Duncan on the second." Both were young, strong Scotsmen, gentle but fiercely protective of the inhabitants of

Darlington Castle. No one, whether ghost or human, would get by either of them without a battle.

Haslemere nodded. "Good. Mrs. Briggs saw the lantern light near the tree line?"

"Past the rose walk, on the south edge of the property." The villagers' rumors about the ghost echoed in Gideon's head as he and Haslemere made their way across the frozen ground.

White gown, white hair, face a deathly white...

He'd never imagined for an instant the rumors could be *true*. He should have known, should have seen it—

"You couldn't have known, Darlington," Haslemere said, as if he'd read Gideon's mind. "Christ, no one could have predicted she'd come back."

"It's been months, Haslemere." Gideon knew he should hate her for it, but underneath the anger, the confusion, all he felt was a cold, distant kind of pity. "Why now?"

"I've thought about that." Haslemere's voice was quiet in the darkness, and Gideon glanced at him as they came around the side of the castle. A muted light shone through the kitchen window, illuminating his friend's unsmiling mouth, his clenched jaw. "There can only be one reason. Your marriage, Darlington. She came to stop it. Nothing else makes sense."

Gideon's steps slowed. "But *why*? She got what she wanted. Why risk it all to return here now?"

Haslemere shook his head. "To punish you? I don't pretend to understand her reasons. I doubt even she understands them. She's not rational, and that makes her dangerous."

Gideon thought of Isabella, and a shudder rolled over him. If all she wanted was to punish *him*, he'd consider himself lucky. A broken betrothal and another scandal were nothing, *nothing* compared to what might have happened. "She's accomplished her goal, then. I'm no longer betrothed."

"Are you sorry for it?"

Gideon glanced at Haslemere. "You're asking if I'm devastated to lose my bride?"

"Yes." Haslemere's voice was guarded. "Are you?"

Was he? Gideon drew in a sharp breath, let the cold air burn his lungs. The horror on Miss Honeywell's face, the ugliness in her voice...

You're a wicked, wicked man.

She truly believed he was a murderer. Perhaps she'd thought so all along.

He'd asked her to marry him. In another four days he would have made her his wife, yet he couldn't muster a trace of regret on her account. By the time a few weeks passed, he wondered if he'd even recall the color of her eyes, the contours of her face. His emotions were a tangled mess, but at least he could reassure Haslemere on this account. "No, I'm not sorry. It's for the best."

Given time, he'd likely be grateful for it.

The lines of tension around Haslemere's mouth eased, and he let out a short laugh. "You're free of her mother, at any rate. Near escape, really."

Yes, he was free of his bride, and free of Mrs. Honeywell, but he wasn't *free*, because another face had taken the place of Miss Honeywell's, another pair of eyes, dark and bottomless, another voice...

Low and sweet, singing.

But he wouldn't think of that now. They were closing in on the tree line. If anyone was wandering in the woods with a lantern, they'd be able to see the light by now. Gideon squinted into the gloom, but not a glimmer brightened the darkness.

He and Haslemere tramped through the woods for some time, bare tree branches tearing at their coats, frigid fingers of wind creeping under their collars, but there were no poachers or pranksters hidden among the trees, no White Lady with a face as pale as death, her white gown trailing along the forest floor.

There was no one.

By the time they turned back toward the castle, their feet and hands were half-frozen, and Gideon's hopes had faded. "Tomorrow, we search again. We've got to find her, Haslemere, before—"

"We'll find her. I promise you that, Darlington."

They didn't speak again as they made their way back to the castle.

In another few hours, the sun would rise. There didn't seem to be much point in retiring now. Gideon knew he wouldn't sleep, but he wasn't sure what else to do, so when he reached his bedchamber, he stripped off his coat, lay down on his bed, and closed his eyes.

Chapter Sixteen

Despite Mrs. Honeywell's frantic promises the night before, Miss Honeywell had *not* come to her senses by the following morning. The two of them descended the stairs dressed in their traveling cloaks before breakfast, Mrs. Honeywell red-faced and breathless, and her daughter pale and determined.

Gideon had been informed of their imminent departure and had dragged a reluctant Haslemere with him into the entrance hall to bid them goodbye.

"My lord." Miss Honeywell swept down the stairs with all the dignity a lady who'd spent the previous night shrieking like a banshee could possibly muster. "I regret our betrothal has come to such a sad pass."

Gideon, who'd spend a good part of the night wondering why he didn't feel even a twinge of regret at the loss of his betrothed, offered her a polite bow. "I'm truly sorry for—"

"Lord Darlington." Mrs. Honeywell grasped Gideon's arm before he could say another word. "*Do* talk some sense into the girl, won't you?"

"Miss Honeywell appears to have made up her mind, madam." Gideon frowned down at the stout fingers twisting his coat sleeve. "I don't know what you'd have me say."

"Why, that you didn't murder your wife, of course, and thus there's no reason for her to haunt Darlington Castle. I'm certain the late Marchioness of Darlington has more sense than to haunt a perfectly innocent gentleman like yourself. It's all a terrible misunderstanding."

"I beg your pardon, madam, but I believe your daughter has made herself quite clear on that matter." Haslemere, who'd had more than enough of Mrs. Honeywell, spoke through clenched teeth. "She believes Lord Darlington to be a murderer. Given the circumstances, I can't think why *he'd* wish to marry *her*, even if she did change her mind."

Miss Honeywell glared at Haslemere, then drew herself up stiffly. "Indeed, Mama, you waste your breath."

Mrs. Honeywell looked between the three stony faces, and threw her hands up in the air. "You're a great fool, Fanny, and you'll be made to realize it soon enough when we return to London, and no one who matters will deign to speak to you. But as you say, I've wasted enough breath on you, and shan't say another word on the matter."

With that, Mrs. Honeywell swept out the front entrance in a dramatic swirl of skirts, marched across the drive, and with her coachman's assistance, heaved herself into the carriage. Fanny followed after her mother without a backward glance. Gideon and Haslemere trailed after them and watched as the coach rounded the curve at the end of the drive and vanished from sight.

"I'd wager my pair of matched bays Mrs. Honeywell will find she has a great deal more to say on this matter, after all." Haslemere turned to Gideon. "What say you, Darlington?"

Gideon shrugged. "Only that I'm glad I'm not Miss Honeywell. Unless she marries a duke, her mother will be berating her for losing a marquess until she's old and gray. Better to marry a murderous marquess than die a spinster."

Haslemere snorted. "I can't say I'm sorry to see them go. Miss Honeywell seems a tolerable enough young lady, but she's rather dim, and God knows my most terrifying nightmare pales in comparison to her mother."

Gideon ran a hand over his jaw, thinking. "We have one fewer thing to worry about now they're gone, but we both know Miss Honeywell didn't imagine that ghost lingering outside her window last night."

"That business with the moaning and pointing is more difficult to credit, especially given Miss Honeywell's hysterical state when we reached her bedchamber. She might have imagined it."

"No." Gideon blew out a breath. "I don't think she did. It's obvious why our White Lady would want to chase off Miss Honeywell."

"Well, she's gone now. Perhaps that will be the end of it."

Haslemere was doing his best to sound hopeful, but he wasn't any more persuaded by this argument than Gideon was. Miss Honeywell's departure wouldn't be the end of this. They both knew it, and Gideon couldn't allow any of his household to be put at risk. "We can't take that chance, Haslemere. Darlington Castle has seen too much tragedy as it is. It ends here."

"Indeed. Well, then, we'll simply have to find your ghost, won't we?"

Gideon glanced up into the pale gray sky. The few rays of feeble sunlight that pierced the thick cloud cover hanging over the castle turned everything a strange, eerie white. Light snowflakes drifted down, the icy pinpricks hitting Gideon's upturned face.

He turned back toward the entrance hall. "I'll ask Mrs. Briggs to gather the servants and tell them there will be no wedding."

Haslemere chuckled. "They likely knew that even before you did, Darlington. Servants always know everything."

Gideon dragged a hand down his face. It was true enough, and he'd wager *one* of his servants knew more than the others. "I don't want anyone wandering into the grounds at night until we've put this matter to rest."

"What do you intend to do?"

"Make a few changes to the sleeping arrangements." And one of his servants wasn't going to like it.

She wasn't going to like it at all.

* * * *

"You've assigned a *guard* to watch my bedchamber door?" Cecilia stared up at Lord Darlington, certain she must have misunderstood him.

"Not a *guard*, Cecilia, a footman, and Duncan will remain in the hallway outside your bedchamber only at night. You may move about the castle as you always do during the day."

Cecilia crossed her arms over her chest. "But I'm to be a prisoner every night, and afforded no more freedom than a criminal at Newgate."

Very well, it was a *bit* of an exaggeration. She didn't believe Lord Darlington was trying to imprison her, exactly, but he was hiding something. A ghost, an undead wife, a misplaced marchioness? He was chasing *someone* throughout the castle grounds.

"How curious you should assume Duncan is there to keep *you* in, Cecilia, rather than everyone else *out*. Though now you ask," he went on, holding up a hand for silence when she would have interrupted, "perhaps it will keep you out of trouble, as well."

Cecilia pinched her lips together. "I don't require Duncan lurking outside my bedchamber door to keep me out of trouble, my lord."

"You wouldn't think so, would you? Yet when left on your own, you turn up in the unlikeliest places. Perhaps Duncan's presence in the hallway will discourage you from wandering about."

Cecilia huffed out a breath. "I have no idea what you mean, my lord."

My, what an accomplished liar she'd become since she arrived at Darlington Castle. There'd been a time when falsehoods hadn't flowed with such ease from her lips, but now not even a hint of a blush stained her cheek at this shameless untruth.

"No? You haven't even the vaguest inkling?" One corner of Lord Darlington's lips quirked in a faint smile. "If you require anything during the night, Duncan will fetch it for you. I prefer for you not to leave this bedchamber once you and Isabella have retired. Isabella must have an attendant at all times, so I can be certain she's—"

Safe.

He bit the word off, but Cecilia took his meaning at once, and she seized on it. "Safe? Does this mean someone really did threaten Miss Honeywell last night? Was it the White Lady? If so, I don't see what use Duncan will be. I've never heard of a ghost who's afraid of a footman."

Lord Darlington crossed his arms over his chest. "I didn't say a word about a ghost. What I was about to say is, where I can be certain Isabella's taken proper care of."

"I *always* take proper care of—"

"Are you *questioning* me, Cecilia? Because I assure you, I'm not in the habit of explaining myself to my servants, and I don't intend to start now."

Cecilia eyed him. His hair was a tousled mess, and purple smudges shadowed the skin under his eyes. Something was amiss at Darlington Castle, and whatever it was, it had caused Lord Darlington a sleepless night. She couldn't blame him for wanting to protect Isabella, and there was no sense in arguing with him about Duncan.

Not when she was certain she could find a way around him.

"Well, of course I'll do just as you say, my lord." She would, too. Right up until the moment it proved inconvenient. Then she'd do what she pleased.

His eyes narrowed suspiciously, but he said only, "Yes, Cecilia, you *will*."

* * * *

Lord Darlington and Lord Haslemere remained closeted in Lord Darlington's study for the rest of the day. Meanwhile, Cecilia was occupied with Isabella, who'd woken in an ill humor, then spent the rest of the day driving Cecilia nearly as mad as her uncle did.

That evening she was obliged to sing to her until her throat was raw. By the time Isabella's big hazel eyes closed at last it was past dark, and Lord Darlington and Lord Haslemere had long since left the castle.

They could be anywhere by now.

Cecilia hurried to the window and peered into the darkness, even as she knew catching a glimpse of them was a futile hope at best. She could only see a small part of the grounds from her window, just the rose walk, part of the kitchen garden, and the edge of the tree line—

There! Cecilia pressed her nose to the glass, a gasp on her lips. Just there, on the other side of the glass, as if she'd conjured it herself from sheer determination, was what she'd been searching for. A light in the darkness, just at the brink of the forest beyond, weaving its way through the trees, bobbing as it would if it were a lantern held in someone's hand.

Cecilia whirled away from the window, snatched up her cloak, and, with one last peek at Isabella, hurried to the door, threw it open, and...

"Oof!" Ran smack into a man's broad back.

She bounced off the wall of muscle. Her hand flew to her nose, which had taken the brunt of the impact, and she would certainly have stumbled to the floor if the man hadn't steadied her with an enormous hand around her shoulder. "Aw right there, Miss Cecilia?"

Cecilia stared up into a fair-skinned, freckled face. A shock of curly ginger hair hung over a wide forehead, and a pair of startled blue eyes gazed down at her. "Beg yer pardon, Miss Cecilia. I didna think ye'd come running out so wild."

Dash it, how could she have forgotten Lord Darlington had assigned a night watchman to her door? Not just any night watchman, either. No, he'd given the job to Duncan, the largest footman at Darlington Castle. Cecilia hadn't a prayer of fighting her way past him.

"It's not the wee lass, is it?" Duncan's brows pulled together in concern.

"No, the wee lass is fine," Cecilia muttered irritably. "It's the big lord who's causing the problem."

Duncan gave her a blank look. "Beg yer pardon?"

"Oh, nothing, nothing. Isabella is perfectly well, sleeping peacefully, and I thought I'd just going down to, er...fetch a book from the library." There, that sounded plausible enough.

"Yer taking your cloak to the library with ye?" Duncan glanced down at the cloak clutched in her hands, then back at her face, his red eyebrows lowered.

"Well, it does get rather chilly in the library at night, so—"

"Nay, Miss Cecilia. His lordship warned me ye'd try to sneak past. He made me promise not to fall prey to any tricks."

"Tricks!" Cecilia's usually mild temper began to burn, and she grew more determined than ever to discover what was happening on the castle grounds. If Lord Darlington would go to such lengths to prevent her from leaving her room, it must be wicked, indeed.

"Aye." Duncan nodded, but he was fighting back a grin. "Tricks. That's what he said, Miss Cecilia."

Cecilia braced her hands on her hips, her mind churning. What might Georgiana do in a similar situation? There was no question of her forcing her way past Duncan, but mightn't she be able to talk her way around him?

For all his imposing size, Duncan was quite a young man, with a sweet, affectionate temperament. He was particularly sweet on Amy, whose presence turned him from a confident, friendly lad into a blushing, stammering schoolboy.

Cecilia would never be so cruel as to mislead Duncan with false hopes, but she happened to know Amy was as sweet on Duncan as he was on her, so what was the harm in it? A little stealth on her part, and all three of them could have what they wanted.

"I don't see what's so awful in wanting a book. I saw a copy of Mrs. Radcliffe's *The Mysteries of Udolpho* on a shelf when I was down there earlier, and I promised Amy we could read a bit of it together tonight, once Isabella fell asleep." Cecilia gave a careless shrug. "Amy will be terribly disappointed, but I suppose it can't be helped."

As Cecilia had expected, Duncan's face flushed as red as his hair at the mention of Amy's name. He bit his lip, struggling between his duty and his affections, then he gave Cecilia a hopeful look. "Just a bit of reading?"

"Yes. Nothing so sinister in that, is there?"

"Mayhap I could go and fetch the book for ye, Miss Cecilia?"

Cecilia thought quickly, then shook her head. "No, you don't know where it is. It will be much quicker if I just nip downstairs and fetch it myself."

Duncan's eyes narrowed. "Ye wouldn't be trying to fool me, would ye?"

"No, of course not." It was awful of her to tell so many lies to poor Duncan, but she had to get out onto the castle grounds. "Here, I'll even leave my cloak behind, if it reassures you."

Duncan let out a sigh, as if he already suspected he was going to regret trusting her, but the lure of the lovely Amy was too much for him, as it so often was with amorous gentlemen, and he stepped away from the door to let Cecilia pass. "Not more'n a few minutes, Miss Cecilia."

"Yes, yes!" Cecilia scurried down the hallway toward the tiny bedchamber where Amy had moved once Cecilia became Isabella's nursemaid, and knocked briskly on the door. Amy threw it open, frowning when she saw Cecilia standing there. "What are you doing running about the hallways? Lord Darlington says we're to remain in our bedchambers tonight."

Cecilia ignored the question. She took Amy's hand and pulled her through the door. "Oh good, you're still dressed. Come with me."

"Where are we going?"

"I was hoping you'd agree to keep an eye on Isabella while I, ah…run downstairs for a bit." Cecilia didn't mention she intended to run downstairs and straight out the front door.

Amy had been following along after her willingly enough, but now she tugged her hand free. "What do you need downstairs at this time of the evening?"

"Just a book from the library, but I don't like to leave Isabella alone."

Cecilia's cheeks heated a little at the lie. Amy noticed it, and gave her a long, searching look, her arms crossed over her chest. "A book."

"Yes. Mrs. Radcliffe's *The Mysteries of Udolpho*. Remember I said we might read it aloud?"

Cecilia had hoped mention of the Gothic romance would distract Amy, but her friend snorted. "Oh, it's Mrs. Radcliffe now, is it?"

"Yes." Cecilia widened her eyes innocently. "What else would it be?"

Amy stared hard at her with her lips pursed. "Don't think I don't know what you're about. You'll catch your death out there in the cold, and if you don't, the ghost will get you."

"Come now, Amy. We both know there's no ghost in those woods—that is, no ghost in the library, I mean." But something, or *someone* was out there, and Cecilia needed to find out who, or *what* it was.

Amy knew Cecilia well enough by now to know there was more to this than a copy of *The Mysteries of Udolpho*. She was quiet as she battled with her better instincts, but at last she sighed and slid the shawl from her shoulders. "All right. Go on, if you must, but take this." She handed the shawl to Cecilia.

"You're a treasure, Amy." Cecilia threw her arms around her friend in an impulsive hug. She turned and dashed toward the stairs, but paused on the landing. "Oh, I nearly forgot. Lord Darlington's set Duncan to guard the door to my bedchamber. He's waiting there for you."

Amy's cheeks turned bright pink. "Duncan Geary?"

"Yes, Duncan Geary. He's the only Duncan in the castle, as far as I know." Cecilia gave Amy a mischievous wink, then scurried down the last flight of stairs, into the entrance hall, and out the door before Amy could change her mind and call her back.

The cold came at her like a blow, and she staggered back a step. She drew Amy's shawl more tightly around her, a quiet exclamation leaving her lips. She didn't dare venture as far as the woods in this cold. She didn't know the grounds well enough, and if she got lost, she could freeze to death. No, as vexing as it was, she'd have to stay near the tree line, in sight of the castle.

The last thing Darlington Castle needed was another suspicious death.

Chapter Seventeen

By the time Gideon and Haslemere gave up searching the grounds and turned their steps back toward the castle, Gideon's fingers had gone numb inside his gloves, and Haslemere's lips were blue.

They'd been out for hours, but the White Lady proved as elusive as ever. They'd explored every corner of the formal grounds, peered behind every tree in the forest, and prodded every hedge and shrub in the gardens, and hadn't spied a fold of a white gown or found a single strand of white hair.

It had been another night wasted, chasing a ghost who vanished at will, and Gideon was weary down to his bones. "It's strange, Haslemere. The White Lady has appeared before half the villagers in Edenbridge, but until Miss Honeywell, not a single person from Darlington Castle has laid eyes on her, despite days of searching."

Haslemere fell into step beside him. "She only appears when she has something to gain by it, and she gains nothing by appearing to *us*."

"What do you mean?" Gideon's brain was so fuzzy with worry and exhaustion, he couldn't make sense of anything anymore.

"Think about it, Darlington. The rumors about the Murderous Marquess began to fade while you were in mourning, but as soon as you returned to society this ghost appears, wandering about your land and haunting your castle. What better way to revive the gossip? Clever trick, really, conjuring your wife back from her grave to start Edenbridge tongues wagging again."

Clever, yes. She'd always been clever when it came to getting what she wanted. "The villagers were right about one thing, then. The White Lady *is* here to wreak her revenge."

Haslemere grunted. "They're wrong about everything else."

Gideon dragged a hand through his hair. "I'm thinking of closing Darlington Castle, Haslemere." There was nothing for him here but loneliness, grief, and a vengeful ghost. "London presents its own challenges, but it can't be worse than—"

"I'll be damned." Haslemere came to a dead stop, his gaze locked on the castle. "Darlington, look. There, on the south side of the castle, near the kitchen garden. I thought I saw something."

Gideon peered into the darkness, the skin on his neck prickling. "What was it?"

Haslemere's gaze met his. "A flash of something white."

Neither of them said another word as they crept from the far end of the rose walk toward the castle. Closer, and closer—

"There." Haslemere's voice was low, urgent. "By the gate. Do you see it?"

Gideon went still, every one of his senses screaming to attention. He squinted into the darkness, waiting, one moment crawling after the next, and then, to one side of the kitchen garden gate, just where Haslemere had said, he caught a glimpse of something white, fluttering in the wind.

He and Haslemere stole forward in silent accord, the frosty grass slippery under their boots, and crept toward the gate.

She was turned away from them, half-hidden in the shadows of the high stone wall surrounding the kitchen garden, invisible but for a blur of white, and strangely still, as if she were…listening for something.

Or someone.

Him.

She must have known he'd come after her, that he'd tear apart the grounds and prowl around every inch of the castle until he found her. It was what she wanted. *He* was what she wanted, and she was about to get her wish.

"Wait, Darlington—"

Gideon dimly registered Haslemere's warning, but it was already too late.

He struck quickly, springing forward, only half-aware he'd moved at all until he caught a handful of her billowing skirts. Her sharp cry pierced the silence, but before she could utter another sound or gather her strength to run, he jerked her back against his chest and covered her mouth with his hand. "Don't bloody move."

Gideon was aware Haslemere was shouting something at him, but he heard nothing, was aware of nothing but the soft press of her lips against his palm, the quivering of her slight body, the brush of her hair against the side of his neck.

Full, trembling lips, soft, silky hair…

Cecilia. Not a ghost, not the White Lady, but Cecilia.

He'd only held her once before, had never inhaled her scent, but somehow, he knew the feel of her in his arms. "It's all right. I'm sorry. I won't hurt you, Cecilia," he murmured, as she trembled against him. He placed a gentle hand on her jaw to still her, and crooned into her ear until his whispered words penetrated her shock, her heaving breaths calmed, and her body went limp against his.

Let her go, let her go before you can't.

He needed to set her away from him, now, before he could no longer think, but even as the warning wound through his head, he was burying his face in her hair, his eyes closing as his lips parted over the soft skin of her neck.

A sound, the crunch of footsteps over frozen ground recalled him back to himself. He opened his eyes, steeling himself to face Haslemere's knowing gaze, but his friend had melted into the darkness.

Gideon allowed himself to breathe her in, to hold her against him for another instant before he took her shoulders in his hands and turned her in his arms. "What are you doing out here? Is it Isabella?"

"No, Isabella's fine." She gazed up at him with huge dark eyes. "I didn't leave her alone. I-I fetched Amy to watch her."

"Then why are you out here, wandering in the dark?" Gideon's fingers tightened on her shoulders as fear gripped him, squeezing his throat. What if the alleged "ghost" had come across Cecilia out here? "Did it even occur to you it isn't safe to be out here alone?"

"I'm not alone. I knew you and Lord Haslemere were out here—"

"But *we* didn't know *you* were!" Relief gave way to a dread that robbed him of his breath. "Damn it, Cecilia. When I saw someone moving in the garden, I thought you were…" Gideon dragged a frantic hand through his hair. "I might have *hurt* you."

"No, you wouldn't. You'd never intentionally hurt—"

"Don't you understand? I'd have done it thinking you were someone else." Gideon covered his eyes with his hand. "I told you to stay in your bedchamber, but you followed us out here onto the grounds even after I'd forbidden it—"

"You never forbade me to—"

"Stop it, Cecilia! You know damn well I don't want you out here. Why do you think I put Duncan on your door? To keep you and Isabella safe! I shouldn't have to tell you not to sneak about the grounds at night, alone, in the dark. Haven't you any sense at all?"

Cecilia's fingers curled into his coat. "I wasn't—"

"But you're not accustomed to following orders, are you? You're no servant." Gideon jerked her into his arms and tugged her against his chest, the last vestiges of his control dissolving like mist in the frigid night air. He was no longer betrothed, and she was in his arms. warm and soft and tempting…

Her scent enveloped him as his lips skimmed her temple, and he couldn't stop himself from burying his face in her hair again. "I knew it the first moment I saw you. I should have sent you away then, but I couldn't… couldn't bear to…"

"What?" She gazed up at him, searching his face. "What couldn't you bear?"

"To let you go." He'd told himself over and over he was betrothed, that it was wrong of him to want Cecilia. That he could never have her. He'd tried to stay away from her, not even to look at her, but with every day that passed, he only wanted her more. "Why did you come to Darlington Castle? What do you want from me?"

She braced her hands on his chest, her eyes dark and wild as she gazed up at him. "I just want the truth, Gideon. I want you to tell me the truth."

His eyes dropped closed at the sound of his name on her lips, and for that one blissful moment, when her body was pressed against his, he wanted to tell her everything.

Everything he knew, everything he suspected, everything he wished he could forget. He wanted to take her to his bed and lose himself in her until her gasps and cries chased the darkness from his mind and he could pretend he was like any other man, if only for a few hours.

But his truths were twisted and ugly, and they his alone to bear. "No, you don't. You don't know what you're asking for. You don't want that darkness in your head."

"What darkness?" She tore free of him then with such suddenness, Gideon was left with his arms still out, clutching at air. "What's happening at Darlington Castle, Gideon? Who did Miss Honeywell see from her bedchamber window? Was it a ghost? The ghost of your dead wife? Or is she not really dead, after all?"

"What?" He stared at her, shocked. "I-I don't understand."

"Is your marchioness truly dead, Gideon, or have you been chasing her all this time?" Cecilia's voice dropped to a whisper. "Is her death a lie, or part of some twisted game? Is it true, what the villagers in Edenbridge whisper about you?"

"Are you asking if I'm a murderer?" Gideon's arms fell to his sides, his body going still. "Do you… do you truly believe that of me, Cecilia?"

"No, I…I don't know! I don't know what to believe anymore, but I know something is terribly wrong at Darlington Castle. The villagers say no one ever saw Lady Darlington's body. They say you murdered your wife and denied her a proper burial. Is she hidden in the walls of Darlington Castle, Gideon, as the villagers claim she is?"

The air seemed to grow darker and colder around Gideon then. A chill rushed over his skin, skeletal fingertips that left a thin layer of ice in their wake. It didn't occur to him Miss Honeywell—his *betrothed*, the woman he'd intended to marry—had accused him of the very same crime a day earlier.

She didn't matter. Miss Honeywell, her mother, his broken betrothal… none of it mattered. The ugliest of the rumors he'd heard whispered in the village, the appalled glances of the *ton* in London, even the nickname the Murderous Marquess—he'd borne them all without a murmur.

But nothing—*nothing*—had ever hurt him as much as Cecilia's words did. They flayed him open like the strike of a whip, tearing through the scars there and opening the raw, bloody flesh beneath. All the ugliness, all the lies and loss of the past year, the grief and the pain and the betrayals came oozing out of the gaping wound, threatening to drown him.

And this time, it *did* matter. Because this time, it was *her*.

So, for the first time since Cassandra's death all those months ago, Gideon clawed his way free of the blackness. With quick, jerky movements he stripped off his coat, draped it around Cecilia's shoulders, then took her hand. "Come with me."

Cecilia's eyes went wide. "What? Where are we going?"

"You said you wanted the truth." Without another word, Gideon led her from the kitchen garden gate into the rose walk.

"Gideon, where are you—" Cecilia broke off with a gasp as she stumbled against him in the darkness. Gideon didn't slow, but he wrapped his arm around her shoulders, leading her farther and farther into the grounds, the grass crunching under their feet, their steps seeming endless to Gideon until at last the rough outlines of Darlington chapel emerged from the darkness, the tall, narrow spire rising into the sky.

They passed under the arch with the enormous cross at its peak, then through the stone gate. Gideon's throat closed as he led Cecilia through the tiny churchyard to the neat row of graves at the back, where centuries of Darlington marquesses and their families had been laid to rest. Each one was marked by a tombstone with the deceased's name and the dates of their births and deaths carved into the white marble.

Here lies…departed this life…in loving memory…

"Read them," Gideon commanded, his voice low and hoarse.

"Nathanial Theophilus Rhys, the fourth Marquess of Darlington." Cecilia turned to him uncertainly, and he nodded at the next gravestone. "Diana Caroline Rhys, the fourth Marchioness of Darlington."

Her voice was so hushed Gideon had to lean closer to hear her. "My aunt and uncle, my father's elder brother and his wife. Who else, Cecilia?"

"Nathanial Theophilus Rhys," Cecilia read, her voice not quite steady. "Fifth Marquess of Darlington, and Frances Isabella Cornelius Rhys, fifth Marchioness of Darlington."

"My mother and father," Gideon said tightly. "All the firstborn males in the family bear the same name. Keep going."

She gazed at him with those dark eyes, eyes that seemed to see all the way down to his soul, before turning back to the gravestones. "Nathanial Theophilus Cornelius Rhys, sixth Marquess of Darlington."

The chasm in Gideon's chest grew wider as he stared down at Nathanial's grave. "My brother," he said quietly. "My father added my mother's maiden name to his." Gideon's lips felt numb, his mouth dry. "The next grave, Cecilia. Whose names are carved onto that headstone?"

Cecilia's gaze followed his, moving over the names carved into the marble, and he knew it, could see in her sudden stiffness and the pained sound that ripped from her throat the moment she saw it, and realized the truth.

"Read the names, Cecilia. Read them aloud."

She gazed down at the headstone, lines of pain and grief etched into her pretty face, and then to Gideon's shock, she knelt down on the frozen ground, heedless of the cold, hard surface abrading her knees, and traced one finger over the names carved into the stone.

He watched, mesmerized, as her dainty fingertip traced his late wife's name. Cassandra's stone was a pure, untouched white still, the carving clean and smooth, her grave so recently dug Gideon could still see the edges where the ground hadn't yet healed.

"Cassandra Elizabeth Belmore Rhys," Cecilia murmured, but she didn't stop there. Unlike with the other names, she read each word carved into the marble in a broken voice that made Gideon's throat close. "Seventh Marchioness of Darlington, beloved wife of Gideon Theophilus Rhys, born November 9, 1769, died October 2, 1793."

Her voice faded, and the finger moving over the words stilled.

Gideon didn't need to hear the rest—the dates of both deaths were forever burned into his heart, into his soul—but they'd come this far, and now they'd finish it. "What else does it say? Read it to the end, Cecilia."

"Nathanial Theophilus Cornelius Rhys, born October 2, 1793, died…" Cecilia let out a shuddering breath and whispered, "Died October 2, 1793."

Her words fell into a silence that might have gone on forever, but after a struggle Gideon found his voice. "I named my own son after my brother—Nathanial Theophilus Cornelius Rhys. He and his mother were laid to rest in a private ceremony, right here, and not inside the walls of Darlington Castle, no matter what the villagers of Edenbridge say."

"The roses?" Cecilia reached out a hand to caress the frozen white petals of one of the dozen roses lying on top of the grave. "You have them placed here for them?"

"Every week since they..." Gideon cleared his throat. The dark green leaves were furred with a light layer of frost. He reached out to touch one, and the thin sheet of sparkling ice melted under his fingertip. "These white roses were her favorite. It's so cold now, they freeze as soon as they're laid here."

"They're beautiful still." Cecilia caressed the ruffled edges of the white blooms with gentle fingers. "Even frozen, they're exquisite."

"Yes." Frozen at the height of their bloom, lovely still, but no less dead for all their beauty. Gideon stared down at the icy petals, and he felt drained, empty. His limbs trembled with exhaustion, threatening to send him to his knees beside the grave that held everything he'd once loved, everything he'd cherished. But the truth was *here*, in this graveyard, buried in the frozen ground, and it had taken him so long to get here, to come this far...

"My wife isn't still alive. She isn't a ghost haunting Darlington Castle seeking revenge for her murder. She became ill, and she and my son died many years before either of them should have. It isn't as thrilling as a murderous marquess and a vengeful White Lady, but the truth never is. This truth, Cassandra's truth, is tragic and...final."

Cecilia was quiet for a long time before she rose to her feet. She faced him, her dark eyes holding his, then she drew in a deep breath and let it out again in a ragged sigh. "Come back to the castle with me, Gideon. It's too cold for you out here."

Gideon blinked, dazed. It was the first time anyone other than Haslemere or his servants had shown the least bit of concern for his welfare. And so, he went with Cecilia without a word of protest, her hand curled around his arm, guiding his steps when he would have stumbled.

When they reached the castle, they met Duncan coming from the direction of the library. His face darkened when he saw Cecilia. "Ye lied to me, Miss Cecilia. Ye promised me ye were only going to the..." Duncan paled when he caught sight of Lord Darlington beside her. "My lord. I beg yer pardon for—"

"It wasn't Duncan's fault. I did lie to him." Cecilia darted an apologetic glance at the footman. "I'm sorry, Duncan."

"Go to your bedchamber, Cecilia." Gideon nodded toward the staircase. "Unless the castle catches fire, I don't expect you to leave it again tonight."

She gave him an uncharacteristically meek look and moved toward the stairs, her hand dropping away from his arm. "Yes, my lord."

"Come with me, Duncan." Gideon beckoned, and Duncan followed him down the corridor to Gideon's study, dragging his feet with every step. It was some time before Gideon could persuade Duncan he wasn't angry. Duncan wrung his hands and begged Gideon's pardon a half-dozen times, but once he understood he wasn't being dismissed, he composed himself and went off to his bedchamber.

By then, Gideon was ready to drop where he stood, but he managed to drag himself to his bedchamber, where he tugged off his boots, stripped off his coat and shirt, and lay down on the bed. It made no sense he could be so exhausted in mind, body, and heart, yet be unable to sleep, but memories and regrets twisted inside him, and his eyes refused to close.

He couldn't have said how long he'd been lying there with his arm over his face before he heard the soft scrape of a latch releasing. He dropped his arm and turned his head at the sound, his heart crowding into his throat.

The door opened slowly, maddeningly so, inch by torturous inch, until she was inside his bedchamber at last. Not a ghost, and not a dream, but real and alive, a woman of warm flesh and flowing blood.

Gideon took in the long, dark curls trailing over her shoulders and down her back as she hovered in the doorway of his bedchamber. She was still clad in her night rail with the thick shawl around her shoulders, which she was clutching to her neck. "What are you doing here, Cecilia?"

"I came to…" Her voice trailed off as her gaze caught on the portrait of the dark-haired lady hanging in a recessed alcove opposite his bed. She drifted closer, just the barest outline of her visible in the darkness as she paused by the window.

"Why did you come?" Gideon asked, his voice hoarse.

Cecilia remained still, staring up at the painted face. "I've been searching for her," she whispered. "I looked through every portrait in the attics, searched in every room but this one." She turned, her face half in shadow, the other half illuminated in the dim stream of moonlight coming through the window.

Gideon swallowed. "You thought I'd taken it. Hidden it, or destroyed it?"

His words seemed to break the spell Cassandra's face had cast over Cecilia. She turned, her dark eyes meeting his, and slowly shook her head. "No. I didn't realize it until I saw her face, but I...I think I knew all along you hadn't."

Gideon's heart leapt with hope at her words, but he said only, "Why did you come to my bedchamber tonight, Cecilia?"

Cecilia's lips parted as he rose from the bed. Her gaze moved from the linen shirt he'd tossed over a chair to trail over his bare abdomen, his chest and his shoulders, until Gideon was forced to swallow back a groan.

Her eyes darkened as she took in the movement of his throat. Her teeth sank into her pink lower lip, worrying the plump flesh there until it turned a deep, distracting red.

"I asked you a question." Gideon couldn't stop himself from moving a step closer to her. "What are you doing in my bedchamber?"

She was so close he could feel the warm drift of her breath over his neck, her scent of soap and clean linen teasing his nose. "I was worried about... Duncan. He didn't do anything wrong. I misled him into thinking—"

"You've no need to worry about Duncan. I'm aware you lied to him. Is that all, then? Or is there some other reason you entered my bedchamber?"

She jerked her gaze away from his body, her eyes finding his, but by then it was too late. He'd seen the flush in her cheeks, the catch of her breath, the way her pulse quickened in her throat. Her dark eyes moved over his skin like a caress, and God forgive him, but he wanted her eyes on him.

He wanted her to look at him, to *see* him.

Wanted her to want him...

"I...I thought I should return your coat." She held up her hand, the coat he'd draped over her shoulders earlier hanging from her fingers. "Just in case you were cold."

He drew closer still, so close she might have touched him, her soft fingertips dragging over his bare skin, and took the coat from her hand. "I don't sleep in my coat, Cecilia."

"No, of course not. Nor your shirt, either." She flushed and backed toward the door, as if preparing to flee if he moved another step closer to her. "I-I shouldn't have come. I'll just...I beg your pardon, Lord Darlington."

She turned away, but Gideon moved quickly, catching her wrist in his hand. "No. Don't go. Please. Tell me the truth, Cecilia. Did you come here for Duncan, or...did you come for me?"

Her slight body was trembling, but she met his gaze bravely, her dark eyes burning. "For you. I came for *you.*"

Desire, passion, the last year of grief and loneliness, the fierce yearning he felt for this fragile, dark-haired woman with her sweet voice and sharp tongue all exploded inside him at once. He drew her against him, his breath catching at the drift of her hair over his skin, her curves against his body.

She settled her hands on his chest, her palms warming his bare skin, and Gideon caught his breath as that warmth flowed over him, through him, touching every part of him, inside and out. He went still, closing his eyes, savoring the feel of her soft hands on his chest, his shoulders, his neck and face—

"Gideon. Look at me."

Gideon's stomach jumped at that sweet voice, a voice he'd come to crave, lower now than when she sang, with a hint of huskiness. He opened his eyes to find she'd risen to her tiptoes, and was gently urging his face down, closer to hers, her dark eyes on his lips…

He caught his breath on a moan when her lips found his. Her kiss was hesitant, shy, as if she'd never kissed a man before and wasn't quite sure how to do it, but the soft, damp drag of her full mouth against his made his lower belly clench with want, and nothing mattered then but getting closer to her.

"Your mouth is so sweet, Cecilia." He wrapped his arms around her waist and lifted her against him so he could take her mouth more deeply. Her shawl fell to the ground, leaving her in just her night rail, and he gathered her closer, a broken groan tearing from his lips.

God, it was maddening, the way her rounded hips fit into his hands and the line of her delicate thighs pressed against his. Did she know what it meant, that he was this hard for her? "Cecilia. Wait, sweetheart."

But Cecilia didn't wait. She pressed a kiss behind his ear, then trailed her lips lower, her teeth grazing his neck before she pressed an oddly chaste kiss to the vulnerable notch of his throat.

Gideon sank his hands into her hair, stilling her as he opened his mouth over hers, his kiss deep and wild and fierce. She gasped when he sucked her plump lower lip into his mouth, and her fingernails dragged over his sensitive flesh as her hands curled against his chest.

"Shhh. Let me…" He dragged his tongue over that pouting mouth once more before he slipped it between her lips. Cecilia gasped, straining to get closer as he devoured her, his hands slipping from her waist down to the firm curve of her bottom.

He didn't realize he'd lifted her against him, his erection cradled snugly against her soft belly until he heard her gasp. He lifted his mouth, dazed, and realized his hips were moving sinuously against hers.

"Cecilia, wait." A despairing groan tore from Gideon's lips at the loss of her, but he took her gently by the shoulders and set her away from him. "We can't...I shouldn't be...you need to go back to your own bedchamber."

She gazed up at him with dark, searching eyes before shifting her hand over his heart. "Aren't you tired of being cold, Gideon? Here." She patted his chest. "Aren't you tired of being cold here?"

He stared down at her, his heart beating a wild rhythm under her palm. How did she know?

He'd been cold for so long, so long, and he was tired. God, he was so tired.

No one had touched him since Cassandra's death—not his body, and not his heart. All that time his heart had been like those icy white roses, frozen inside his chest. Months and months had passed, and all that time, he'd never once been warm.

He didn't need to say so. Cecilia saw the answer in his face.

"Come with me." She took his hand, drew him toward the bed, and eased back the coverlet. "Get into bed, Gideon."

He wanted to. God, he wanted to, but he wouldn't take advantage of the only woman who'd shown him any kindness since the Murderous Marquess was born.

"Just to sleep." She nodded at the bed. "I don't want you to be cold tonight."

Gideon gazed into those sweet, dark eyes and God help him, he couldn't say no. He wanted it too much. Wanted her next to him, her warm body curved against his.

So, he did as she bade him. He climbed into the bed and held his arms out to her. The coverlet rustled, the bed beneath him dipped under her slight weight, and then she was there, curled against him, her head resting on his chest.

"Go to sleep, Gideon."

Gideon closed his eyes, and for the first time since he'd lost his wife and son he slept throughout the night, dreamless and warm.

Chapter Eighteen

Cecilia dreamed of anguished blue eyes and frozen white roses. The dream was disturbing in a way she didn't understand, in a way a dream never had been before, and she woke with a start, her night rail damp and a gasp on her lips.

She lay still for long, uneasy moments, struggling to remember where she was, but then Gideon shifted beside her, and she knew. She hadn't intended to join him in his bed, much less fall asleep beside him. She'd only meant to wait with him until the dreadful cold that had seeped into his body and soul passed, then return to Isabella.

But he'd wrapped his arm around her waist and gathered her against his hard, warm chest. He'd fallen asleep at once, his deep, even breaths brushing against the back of her neck, and she couldn't bear to wake him, this man who'd lost so much, suffered so deeply.

She slid out from under Gideon's arm as quietly as she could, but before she could slip back into her own bedchamber, she found herself pausing, something she couldn't name luring her back, her footsteps silent against the floorboards. It drew her closer, the hem of the blue silk bed hangings brushing over the tops of her bare feet. In a daze, she reached out and rested her fingers on the heavy gilt frame of the portrait.

She hadn't come here for *her.* When she'd entered his bedchamber, she'd thought only of Gideon. It wasn't until she saw the portrait that she realized of course...*of course,* she'd be here. It was, of every other place in Darlington Castle, the only place she belonged.

Lady Cassandra, the seventh Marchioness of Darlington.

Cecilia edged closer, staring up at Lady Cassandra's face. Had she seen it before? There was something familiar about her features, as if Cecilia were looking into the face of a friend, not a stranger.

Cassandra was fair-skinned and blue-eyed, with high cheekbones, a slender nose, and a determined jaw that was just a touch too square to be considered strictly pretty. She hadn't been a beauty like Lady Leanora, who was without dispute a dazzling, glittering diamond of the first water, with a face so perfect it almost hurt to look at her.

Not Cassandra.

The firm jaw, the kindness in those blue eyes...there was nothing about Cassandra's face that could ever hurt a soul. Lady Leanora was a blinding diamond, but Cassandra was softer, subtler, more easily overlooked, perhaps, but her beauty was deeper than her skin, like a ruby with a banked fire at its center.

Cecilia stared up into the blue eyes, speechless. She felt as if she knew her. *As if she'd always known her.*

And Gideon...she turned to look at him, her heart twisting at the vulnerability in his face, his defenselessness. The shadows in his eyes were hidden from her now, the deep lines of pain etched about his mouth relaxed in sleep.

It wasn't the face of a man who'd murdered his wife.

She padded on bare feet back to her own bedchamber, ready to collapse with fatigue, but it wasn't just her body that was exhausted. It was her heart, too. It gave a miserable lurch in her chest when she recalled the look on Gideon's face last night as he stood above the white marble headstone that bore his wife and son's names.

Her heart might not be so heavy now if she'd done what it had urged her to do then—beg his pardon, plead for his forgiveness for her careless words—but she hadn't known what to say, what to do, and now it felt as if the moment were gone.

As if she were too late.

It was still dark outside—not more than an hour or two had passed since she fell asleep. Isabella was still tucked in her bed, her small fingers wrapped around the crown of marbled paper she and Cecilia had made several days earlier.

Cecilia didn't sleep any more, but sat in the rocking chair with Seraphina curled in her lap. She'd banished the troublesome creature to the castle grounds at least a half-dozen times. Once she'd even taken her to the stables, thinking Seraphina could occupy herself by chasing some nice mice and rats, but the cat had returned that night, scratching at the door that connected Cecilia's bedchamber with the late marchioness's until Cecilia gave in and opened it.

It was a mystery how the devious feline kept finding her way back inside the castle. One mystery of many. Why, despite Gideon's insistence, did the door connecting Cecilia's bedchamber to Lady Darlington's never seemed to be locked when Seraphina demanded entrance?

"How are you getting into Lady Darlington's bedchamber? Are you a ghost yourself, Seraphina?" It wasn't the first time Cecilia had demanded answers about Seraphina's mysterious comings and goings. She stroked the cat's sleek, black fur, but Seraphina wasn't any more forthcoming than she'd ever been. One bored green eye opened a slit—just wide enough for Seraphina to hint she found Cecilia very tedious indeed—before it closed again.

When Isabella woke hours later, Cecilia hurried her through their morning tasks. Not because she wished to avoid facing Gideon—certainly *not*, nothing like that—but because Cook had promised to let Isabella help make tartlets this morning. It was also Mrs. Briggs's half day, and after they'd finished the tartlets, the housekeeper was taking Isabella with her to Edenbridge for a visit with her mother, and well…it was just a busy day, that was all.

It hadn't a thing to do with Gideon's having kissed her.

Cecilia raised her hand to stroke her fingers over her lips, shivering at the memory of the press of his full, warm mouth against hers, the hot slide of his tongue between her lips.

Dear God. She'd never been kissed before, but she'd considered herself to be at least somewhat informed on the matter, given how many gothic romances she'd read. But reading about a kiss and being kissed yourself wasn't, as it happened, at all the same thing.

Gideon's kiss hadn't been anything like she'd expected it to be. She hadn't known she'd feel a man's kiss *everywhere*, from her lips all the way down to her curled toes. Just the memory of it tugged an ache into her lower belly and raised delicious goosebumps on her skin.

But none of that meant she was avoiding him, even if she *did* keep an ear open for any sounds of movement from his bedchamber.

"Here you are, then!" Mrs. Briggs said when they entered the kitchen later that morning. "Cook's got the first pan finished already, Isabella."

Isabella clapped her hands. "Will we have any apple tartlets? Apple is my favorite."

"Since cook has a mountain of sliced apples prepared, I think so." Mrs. Briggs gave Isabella a fond pat on the head, then turned to Cecilia with a cheerful grin. "We'll be back after supper. I've sent Amy to the second floor to gather linens and air out the guest bedchambers."

"Yes, of course." Cecilia waved as Mrs. Briggs and Isabella went to join the cook on the opposite side of the kitchen, then turned her attention to the young man sitting at the table. He appeared much less enthusiastic to see her. "Good morning, Duncan."

No response. Duncan was sitting at the kitchen table, a plate of fresh apple tartlets before him. His back was to Cecilia, and he didn't turn around.

Cecilia rounded the table with a sigh and seated herself across from him. "I'm sorry about last night, Duncan. I shouldn't have misled you. Lord Darlington doesn't blame you. I told him it was all my doing."

Duncan reluctantly met her gaze. "It's all right, Miss Cecilia."

It didn't sound as if it was all right. "I truly am sorry, Duncan. What can I do to make amends?"

His face colored, and he glanced up at her from under thick, ginger-colored lashes. "That book ye mentioned last night...it's a romantic book?"

"Mrs. Radcliffe's *The Mysteries of Udolpho*? Oh, yes, it's terribly romantic, and also wonderfully terrifying. Why do you ask?"

Duncan dropped his gaze. "Young lasses like romance, don't they? Do ye suppose Miss Amy might like that book?"

"I daresay she would, yes." Cecilia struggled to hide her smile. "You might even like it yourself, Duncan."

Duncan's cheeks burst into flames. "Ach, well, I only asked on Miss Amy's account, but if ye had a mind to read that book aloud to her, mayhap I could listen, too?"

Cecilia reached across the table and squeezed his hand. "I think that's a wonderful idea, Duncan. You'll be outside my door again tonight?"

"Aye, Miss Cecilia. His lordship said so."

"Very well, then. We'll fetch Amy and read a chapter tonight after Isabella falls asleep, shall we?"

Duncan beamed at her. "Right then, Miss Cecilia. I'll see ye tonight." He stuffed the rest of his tartlet into his mouth, then snatched two more off the plate and shoved them into his pocket before ambling out of the kitchen, whistling under his breath.

Well, that was one problem solved, anyway. Cecilia sat at the kitchen table for a bit, eyeing the plate of tartlets and willing her stomach to cease its uneasy roiling before giving it up for lost, and going in search of Amy.

Amy wasn't upset with her as Duncan had been, but she was nearly expiring with curiosity, which was much worse. "Duncan says Lord Darlington brought you back to the castle himself last night after he caught you creeping about the grounds, and he looked angrier than Duncan had ever seen him. Is it true?"

Cecilia dropped the pile of linens she was carrying on the settee at the end of the bed with a sigh. "I wasn't creeping. I was…" *Sneaking, or prowling, or spying?* "…innocently looking around."

Amy snorted. "Were you, now? Is that what you told Lord Darlington?"

Cecilia hadn't had much time to tell Gideon anything, but she kept her lips stubbornly sealed. The less information Amy had about last night's, er…activities, the better.

Amy took up a sheet from the pile on the settee. "I did warn you not to follow him and Lord Haslemere out there, didn't I? Honestly, Cecilia, I can't think why you'd want to prowl about in the first place. What did he do with you once he caught you?"

Kissed me senseless.

"Brought me back to the castle, just as Duncan said."

Amy snapped the sheet open over the bed with an impatient gesture. "What, that's *all*? There must have been more to it. What did he say? Did he scold, or lecture, or—"

"Threaten to dismiss me? No." Cecilia paused, her hand clutching a corner of the sheet. Now she thought of it, why hadn't he threatened to dismiss her? He'd done so before, and for a far less drastic infraction. Instead he'd taken her to his wife and son's grave. He'd confided in her, and let her comfort him.

Amy cocked her head to the side, considering this. "Lord Darlington's not one for threats. If he was going to dismiss you, you'd be gone by now, and I'd be making these blasted beds all by myself."

Cecilia tried to return Amy's crooked grin, but everything she thought she understood about Gideon had tipped sideways in her head until she could no longer make sense of anything.

"Here, give me that." Amy pulled the end of the sheet from Cecilia's slack hand. "What were Lord Darlington and Lord Haslemere doing when you found them?"

Cecilia shrugged. "Chasing the ghost, I presume."

Amy rolled her eyes. "There is no ghost, for pity's sake. You can't truly believe otherwise."

Cecilia didn't know what she believed anymore. "What about Miss Honeywell's claim a ghost in a white gown with a deathly white face was lurking beneath her window? Do you suppose she invented it?"

"Who knows what she saw? I'll tell you what, that one's pretty head is as empty as a bellows. Like as not she had a bad dream, but whatever it was she thought she saw, it wasn't a *ghost*. Of all the rumors the villagers in Edenbridge have put about, that's one of the most foolish. Not the *most* foolish, mind you, but close."

"Oh? What else do they say?" Cecilia didn't care much what the gossips claimed, but just this once, she welcomed the distraction.

"They say Lord Darlington's the Murderous Marquess. Pure nonsense, put about by that awful Mrs. Vernon. You'd think they'd have more sense than to listen to a wolf in sheep's clothing like *her*, but there's people who always want to believe the worst."

Cecilia couldn't help but agree. The Edenbridge villagers must be more foolish than most, to believe the word of a servant who'd been dismissed for theft.

"You'll hear any number of other wild stories," Amy went on. "The villagers like their gossip, you know, and every rumor is more outlandish than the one before. Like, some say as Lady Darlington's buried in the castle walls, but others claim she's at the bottom of the moat. Then there's that bit of foolishness about Lord Darlington being in love with Lady Leanora."

"In love with Lady Leanora?" Cecilia gripped the edge of the mattress to stop herself from falling face first into the bed. "In love with his brother's wife?"

Amy snorted. "Yes. The way they tell it, Lady Leanora fled the castle when he tried to make her marry him after Lady Cassandra died."

Cecilia gasped. "Marry his *brother's* widow!"

"Hush!" Amy shot a wary glance at the open door. "They say as he always loved her, and after his brother and wife both died, he saw his chance to have her, and he took it."

"If he always loved Lady Leanora, why would he have married Lady Cassandra? Any man scoundrel enough to pursue his dead brother's wife is scoundrel enough to do it before that brother has turned cold in his grave." Lady Leanora was already a widow when Gideon returned to Darlington Castle. If he'd wanted her, he might have chased her. Instead, he'd courted Cassandra.

"Well, it's nonsense, isn't it?" Amy made a disgusted noise. "Mind, these are the same people who think there's a white ghost drifting about in the woods. I don't believe a word of any of it, myself."

Cecilia fell heavily into the chair beside the bed. No, it couldn't be true. She'd seen for herself the grief on Gideon's face as he'd stood by his late wife's grave. That kind of despair couldn't be feigned. Amy was right. These were the same villagers who claimed the late Lady Darlington had been buried inside the castle walls.

No. It was impossible, unthinkable, unbearable. Everything inside her recoiled at the thought, or...was it just her heart that recoiled? She imagined Gideon caressing Lady Leanora's flawless white skin, running his long fingers through her silky, midnight tresses, and gazing into her beautiful blue eyes.

Her stomach churned with nausea, but she choked back the bile crawling into her throat. Lady Clifford had sent her here to discover the truth, but she'd never get to it if she insisted on letting her emotions overrule her logic.

Very well, then. Logic. Logically speaking, it was difficult to imagine any man who'd seen Lady Leanora's face *hadn't* fallen in love with her.

Logically speaking, I never should have kissed Gideon—

"If you ask me, that nonsense about Lord Darlington being in love with Lady Leanora is partly to blame for the rumor he'd murdered his wife. They say he did away with Lady Cassandra so he could be with t'other one, but Mrs. Briggs says it's all nonsense, and I—are you all right, Cecilia? You're whiter than the sheets."

"Yes, I'm...quite well." Cecilia's legs were quivering like a jelly still, but she rose from the chair and gave Amy a weak smile. "Pure nonsense, I'm sure, just as you said. Come on, then. Let's finish up these beds, shall we?"

Much to Cecilia's relief, the topic of Gideon and Lady Leanora didn't come up again, but she couldn't put it out of her mind for the rest of the day. By the time she climbed the stairs to her bedchamber that evening, Amy's words felt as if they'd been carved into her skull.

Cecilia wasn't sure whether to be relieved or ashamed at having avoided Gideon for the entire day, but either way, her luck ran out when she reached the landing on the second floor. He was in the small picture gallery, his body unnaturally still, staring up as if mesmerized at one of the portraits. At first Cecilia thought it must be his brother's, but when she got closer, she saw it was the portrait of Lady Leanora that held all his attention.

He didn't seem to notice Cecilia, not even when she crossed from the stairway to the end of the corridor and paused beside him. She studied his profile, wondering at the strange look on his face as he stared up at the beautiful woman on the canvas. His jaw was so tight it looked as if it would shatter at a touch, but there was despair in his gaze.

Slowly, Cecilia turned her attention to the portrait, stunned once again at Lady Leanora's exquisite face. She'd never seen such pale, perfect skin or such luminous blue eyes, but there was something...unbearable about her beauty.

It wasn't a warm or welcoming face, as Lady Cassandra's had been, but overwhelming. Cecilia dragged her gaze away from it with a shudder, but if Lady Leanora's beauty made her shrink back, it seemed to have a different effect on Gideon, who was still staring up at her as if he couldn't bear to tear his gaze away.

Was it possible the villagers were right, and Gideon truly did have a tendre for his brother's widow? He loved his niece, doted on her, in fact. Wasn't it possible his affection for Isabella arose from a passionate attachment to her absent mother? Perhaps he was lavishing all his frustrated love for Lady Leanora on her daughter. Perhaps he'd refused to let her take Isabella with her when she fled because he'd hoped Isabella's presence would lure her back to Darlington Castle.

Cecilia didn't want to believe it, but the look on Gideon's face, the way his breath seemed to be trapped inside his lungs…she cleared her throat, suddenly desperate to make him look away from that treacherous face. "I've never seen a more remarkable face than hers. I can't help but wonder what it would be like to see her in person. Overwhelming, I imagine."

Gideon startled, as if only now realizing Cecilia was there. "It's a good likeness of her."

Cecilia nodded, but she avoided looking back up at the portrait as she fumbled for something more to say. She wanted to ask if Gideon thought she'd ever return to Darlington Castle—or if he hoped she would—but something made her bite her tongue, something she feared was a desire not to hear his answer.

"It was a good likeness of her, I should say. It was painted a decade ago, when she first came to Darlington Castle after she and Nathanial married. By the time she left again, she looked…quite different."

"Different in what way?"

Gideon laughed, but it was a hard, ugly sound. "One's face is a reflection of one's heart. What's inside your heart makes itself known on your face."

Cecilia swallowed. "What was in Lady Leanora's heart?"

Gideon turned to Cecilia, a bitter twist to his lips. "Ice."

Ice. It seemed a strange word to describe the lady he loved, unless he felt she'd betrayed him. Then it was the perfect word, wasn't it? Just the word a jilted lover would use.

"They were cousins, you know," he added. "Lady Leanora and my wife."

"Cousins?" Cecilia turned to him, surprised. "I-I didn't realize."

"Yes. After my brother's death, Lady Leanora summoned Cassandra to Darlington Castle to act as her companion. I met Cassandra then, and we married six months later. Do you think they look alike?" Gideon's attention had drifted back to Lady Leanora's portrait again, an unreadable expression on his face.

Cecilia followed his gaze, but she flinched away before meeting Lady Leanora's frigid blue eyes. Perhaps there was a similarity in their features, but to Cecilia's eye, no two ladies could look less alike. "No."

That caught Gideon's attention. "Why not?"

One is a diamond, the other a ruby.

That was what Cecilia thought when she'd first seen Cassandra's portrait—that Lady Leanora was like a dazzling, glittering diamond, so bright it hurt to look at her, whereas Cassandra...

"One is fire, and the other ice."

Gideon traced his fingertip down the bridge of her nose, over her parted lips and across her jaw, his gaze following the path of the caress. "Cassandra's heart was written on her face. Her beauty came from here." He lay his palm in the center of Cecilia's chest, over her heart. "Just as yours does."

Cecilia gazed up at him, mesmerized. It seemed like a lifetime ago she'd looked into his eyes and thought them cold. When she looked into them now, she felt she could happily drown in those warm blue depths.

It didn't occur to her they were standing in a place where anyone could pass by and see them. She didn't think of that as Gideon's lips drew closer to hers. She thought of the sweet warmth of his breath against her mouth, his large, gentle hand resting over her wildly beating heart. She never considered refusing him. She simply tilted her head back, and offered her mouth to him.

His lips hovered over hers with a desperate groan, as if he'd waited a lifetime to kiss her, and couldn't wait another moment. But even so, he was slow, gentle, nibbling and teasing and taking tiny sips from her lips as if she were the sweetest wine, and he had all of eternity to taste her.

"Gideon." Cecilia didn't recognize her own voice. It was so husky, a plea hidden just at the edges, subtle, but Gideon heard it, and responded with another hungry groan.

Cecilia slid her fingers into his hair, her fingernails dragging over the back of his neck as she tugged his head down to hers. She opened her lips to him, urging him closer, making no secret of her desire for him.

He gasped against her mouth, cupping her face in his hands. He slid his tongue between her lips, the kiss going on and on until Cecilia was weak-kneed and breathless.

"I want to taste you here, sweetheart. Let me..." Gideon sank his hands into her hair to drop a dozen tiny kisses over her neck, his tongue darting out to taste her skin. She cried out when his mouth, hot and open, pressed into the arch of her throat. "*Gideon.*"

He sucked and nipped at her tender skin, and Cecilia held onto him, overwhelmed with unfamiliar sensations. She wanted to touch him, with her hands and her mouth—his neck, his shoulders, the long, strong line of his back, his firm, rounded—

"Come with me, sweetheart." Gideon tugged gently on her hand, drawing her away from the landing and further down the corridor where the shadows were deeper. "Yes. Here."

She was already reaching for him as he drew her into the alcove. He kissed her again, the demand of his lips and tongue setting her alight until she was clinging to him, gasping for breath.

"Shh." Gideon stroked her hair back from her face, his blue eyes tender as he gazed down at her. "We shouldn't be...I don't want to frighten you."

Her body felt alive, stretched taut, as if tiny flames had burst all over her skin in the wake of his stroking fingertips, and she was one caress away from exploding. Cecilia caught his wrist and dragged his hand down her neck, and then lower, lower, where she needed his touch the most.

Bright color bloomed across his cheekbones as he cupped her breast with a groan. "We can't...we shouldn't be—"

Cecilia pressed her fingers against his lips. "I'm not afraid, Gideon."

She *was* a little afraid, but not of him. Never of him.

She was afraid of herself, of how easy it would be to forget everything— her friends, Lady Clifford and Daniel, the reason she was here—and lose herself in him.

"So beautiful, Cecilia. So soft here." He traced his fingertips over the curves of her breasts, his body going rigid against hers when she whimpered in response. "Does that feel good, sweetheart?"

Cecilia couldn't speak, but another soft cry broke from her lips as he brushed his thumb over a nipple, just the lightest stroke, a tease more than a caress, until he wrung another whimper from her. Then he began to stroke her in earnest, his gaze locked on her face as he caressed both her nipples, circling and pinching the stiff nubs until Cecilia cried out and grasped his forearms to steady herself, her fingernails digging into the expensive fabric of his coat.

"You're so sensitive." His tone was soothing, but his wicked fingers kept up the caress, dragging back and forth over the aching peaks. "Do you want my mouth on you?"

She did, oh, she did, but she was covered in layers of fabric—

"Oh, oh..." Cecilia dragged a trembling hand to her mouth, biting on her fingers to smother her moans as his hot mouth closed over a nipple and drew on her until she was shaking, and the fabric of her dress was clinging maddeningly to the straining peak.

She buried her fingers in his hair, urging him on with soft murmurs and pleas, but all at once he tensed and raised his head from her breast.

"No, Gideon. Don't stop—"

He pressed gentle fingers to her lips, silencing her protest.

That was when Cecilia heard it.

Voices, on the stairwell. "...read you a story until Miss Cecilia comes."

It was Amy, taking Isabella to her bedchamber for the evening.

Cecilia's head fell against his chest as she drew deep, trembling breaths into her lungs. How had it gotten so late? She'd lost track of time, of Isabella ...

Dear God, she'd lost track of *herself.* She'd let Gideon touch and kiss her—no, not *let* him, encouraged him, nearly *begged* him—on the second floor landing, mere steps from the staircase, where anyone might have seen them.

Cecilia braced her hands against Gideon's chest and eased him away from her. "I should...Isabella, I need to—"

"I know. Not a moment too soon." He let his forehead rest against hers before he drew away, an uncertain smile on his lips.

Cecilia was too mortified to return it. She fled, but before she could disappear around the corner, he stopped her with a word. "Cecilia."

She froze, then turned to face him, her cheeks on fire. "Yes?"

"I..." Gideon dragged a hand through his hair. "Never mind. Sweet dreams."

Chapter Nineteen

Cecilia stood outside her bedchamber door for some time after she left Gideon, trying to catch her breath and waiting for the heat in her cheeks to subside.

Amy frowned at her as she stepped over the threshold. "You look a bit flushed, Cecilia. You're not ill, are you?"

Ill, no. Unforgivably foolish and reckless, yes. "No, I'm—"

"Miss Cecilia!" Isabella launched herself across the room toward Cecilia as fast as her little legs would carry her.

Cecilia knelt down to catch her in her arms. "Hello, Isabella. Did you have a nice time with Mrs. Briggs today?"

"Yes. We had apple tartlets for tea." Isabella toyed with a loose lock of Cecilia's hair as she snuggled against her chest. "Mrs. Briggs's mama said they were the best ones she's ever had."

"I'm sure they were." Cecilia cuddled Isabella closer, some of the tension draining from her at the press of the small, warm body against hers.

"She's stuffed to the brim with apple tartlets and nearly asleep on her feet." Amy tugged fondly on one of Isabella's golden-brown curls. The tangles had been brushed from her hair, and she was already wearing her nightdress.

Cecilia gave Amy a grateful look. "Thank you for your help. Go on and go to your bed."

Amy's frown returned as she studied Cecilia's face. "If you're sure? You look as if you're ready to drop."

"I'm sure. A song or two, and Isabella here will be fast asleep."

Amy cast her another worried look. "I think we'll save Mrs. Radcliffe for another night. I'll let Duncan know, shall I?"

"Yes, please. Tomorrow night. I promise it. Now, Isabella." Cecilia turned to her charge as the door closed behind Amy. "What songs shall we have tonight?"

"'Death and the Lady'!" Isabella was still enamored of the golden crown and scepter, and made this same request every night. Tonight, though, the fair lady hardly had a chance to throw her costly robes aside before Isabella was fast asleep.

Cecilia lay her gently in her bed and drew the coverlet snugly around her chin. Then, not sure what to do with herself, she wandered over to the window and wrapped her arms around herself as she stared out into the darkness.

It was a deep, penetrating darkness tonight, the moon shrouded under a thick layer of clouds. There would be snow soon. Cecilia had smelled the crisp, dry scent of it lingering in the cold air when she'd taken her afternoon walk today.

If not tonight, then tomorrow, or the next day, perhaps.

She stood there for long, quiet moments, the only sound in the room the crackle of the fire and the gentle whoosh of Isabella's deep breaths. Cecilia turned from the window at the sound, a smile rising to her lips at the sight of Isabella curled up in her little bed. Her outing today had done her a world of good. She'd drifted off into a peaceful slumber with her small hand cradled in Cecilia's.

But Cecilia's smile faded as she turned back to the window. Isabella was such a lovely little girl. She would never tire of burying her nose in those thick curls and inhaling her fresh, sweet scent. It was a difficult scent to describe, but it reminded Cecilia of clean skin and new milk.

And that was the trouble, wasn't it? She rested her forehead against the cold glass, a sadness that was becoming familiar washing over her. That scent, the silky brush of Isabella's curls against her cheek...

They didn't belong to her. They weren't hers to keep, any more than Gideon was.

Tonight, he'd said one's face was a reflection of their heart. Cecilia had grown to love his face, but there were parts of Gideon's heart that remained a dark mystery to her. How could she bear to delve into the deepest, darkest secrets he hid there, after she'd slept in his arms? How could she ever see him as anything but the man whose kiss weakened her knees, whose smile stole her breath, whose blue eyes made her heart soar in her chest?

If Lady Clifford thinks you're fit for this business, lass, then you're fit.

But she wasn't fit, and she never had been. Lady Clifford should have sent Georgiana in her place, or Emma. Neither of them would have let her emotions run amok as Cecilia had done. Neither of them would have become overwrought, and made such a mess of things.

Neither of them would have fallen in love with him.

But Cecilia had. She was in love with Gideon, and there was no going back from that, no way to change it. No way she could ever look at him and see anyone other than the man she'd come to love.

The way Gideon touched her, so gently, and his expression when he gazed at her, so wary and hopeful at once. The love in his eyes when he looked at Isabella, the grief in his voice when he spoke of his late wife…

How could such a man be a murderer?

He couldn't.

Whoever Gideon was, whatever secrets he held in his heart, nothing would ever persuade Cecilia he could have committed such a violent crime. But while he made her heart flutter madly in her chest, Cecilia couldn't guess as to the state of his heart.

The one thing she did know was he was keeping secrets from her.

Who was he chasing through the castle grounds at night? Cecilia was convinced he knew the identity of the White Lady, but he hadn't confided in her. If he cared for her at all, why was he hiding the truth from her? Or were his kisses and caresses simply a diversion while he hoped and prayed for Lady Leanora's return to Darlington Castle? Perhaps he truly did love Lady Leanora, and had all along. His betrothal to Fanny Honeywell may have been a ruse from the start, a way to lure Lady Leanora away from her betrothed, and back to him. As for Lady Cassandra…

Gideon hadn't murdered his wife. Nothing would ever make Cecilia believe he had, or make her doubt the sincerity of his grief, but she had no way of knowing if he'd loved her or not. Mrs. Briggs had said Gideon worshipped his elder brother. Perhaps he'd hoped his marriage to Cassandra would put an end to his shameful passion for his late brother's widow?

Cecilia's head spun with unanswered questions, but in the end, none of it mattered. Lady Clifford had sent her to prevent Fanny Honeywell from marrying the Murderous Marquess. Miss Honeywell was gone, the betrothal broken, and now there was no longer any reason for Cecilia to remain at Darlington Castle. She'd done what she'd been sent here to do.

She'd hadn't uncovered the whole truth, but if something dark *had* happened at Darlington Castle—if there was a mystery hidden inside these stone walls, if some evil had unfolded here—it hadn't been at the hands of the Murderous Marquess.

Because he didn't exist.

Gideon was no murderer. He was a man who'd suffered unspeakable loss, who'd nearly been broken by grief, and she...she'd *lied* to him. To all of them. Isabella, Amy and Duncan, and Mrs. Briggs. She could never make amends to them for that, but she could leave Darlington Castle, leave Gideon in peace before this wild passion between them went any further. Before Isabella grew more attached to her, only to have Cecilia abandon her in the end.

She'd be returning to London with a wounded spirit and a shattered heart, but no good would come of her staying here any longer. Tomorrow, then. She'd give her notice tomorrow, and be on the stagecoach back to London before—

"Mrrarh."

Cecilia jumped, her heart leaping into her throat. "*Seraphina.* Why must you creep up on me like that, you dreadful thing?"

Seraphina weaved around her legs, then darted over to the door leading into the marchioness's bedchamber and sat, staring at Cecilia with imperious green eyes.

Cecilia pressed a weary hand to her forehead. "Not tonight, Seraphina."

"Mrrarh." Seraphina scratched a black paw on the wooden door, then turned back to Cecilia. "Mrrarh."

"No, Seraphina." Now that Cecilia had seen Cassandra's face, snooping about her bedchamber felt like the worst kind of betrayal. "I promised Gideon I wouldn't enter her room again, and I don't intend to break—"

"*Mrrarh.*" Seraphina scrabbled frantically at the bottom edge of the door with both paws, as if trying to dig her way underneath it.

Cecilia frowned. "You're insistent tonight. I'm certain the door must be locked." She marched across the room and grabbed the latch. "See?"

But as it had every time before, the lock turned easily in her hand, and the door creaked open. Why was this door continually unlocked? It didn't make any sense. "If I didn't know better, I'd think *you* had a key," Cecilia said, watching as Seraphina slipped through the gap in the door and into the marchioness's bedchamber.

Seraphina paused on the other side and waited for Cecilia to follow her. Once she was certain Cecilia was doing her bidding, Seraphina disappeared into the gloom on the opposite side of the room. Cecilia cast an apprehensive glance over her shoulder before creeping after Seraphina, her bottom lip caught between her teeth.

This is a terrible idea.

She half expected Gideon to leap out at her from the shadows, but all remained silent as Cecilia followed her feline guide past Lady Darlington's bed to the dressing room at the back of the bedchamber.

Seraphina stopped when she reached the clothes press, and Cecilia huffed out a breath. "This again, Seraphina? What is your fascination with Lady Darlington's clothes press? One would think you'd be more cautious of it after having been trapped inside."

Seraphina didn't appear to agree with this logic. She was alternately nuzzling the edge of the door and weaving between Cecilia's legs, as if she was urging Cecilia to open the clothes press and peer inside. "Mrrarh."

Cecilia hesitated, but Seraphina wouldn't hear of a refusal. She gazed up at Cecilia with those glowing green eyes until at last Cecilia relented. "Oh, all right, but just a peek. What is it? Have the moths gotten into it, or—"

She went still, the words dying on her lips. The blue silk ball gown, that particular shade of blue…she snatched up a fold of the gown and held it up to the muted light.

She'd seen this gown before. Not the last time she'd peered into the clothes press, but tonight, less than an hour ago. She'd seen it on an exquisitely beautiful dark-haired lady with frigid blue eyes.

This gown didn't belong to Lady Cassandra.

It belonged to Lady Leanora. She was wearing it in the portrait hanging in the small picture gallery, along with the sapphire hairpins Cecilia had found on the dressing table days earlier.

Cecilia fell back against the wall behind her, stunned. How had she not noticed before this was the same gown, and these the same sapphire pins tucked into those thick, dark curls? The embroidered slippers, as well. No doubt those were also Lady Leanora's.

But how did Lady Leanora's gown come to be in Lady Cassandra's bedchamber?

Cecilia stared down at the fold of the gown caught between her fingers. It couldn't be a coincidence the only gown now hanging inside the clothes press was the very gown Lady Leanora had worn in her portrait. It had been chosen purposefully, by someone who understood its significance.

Cecilia tapped her head against the wall at her back in an attempt to knock some sense into it. The most likely explanation was almost certainly the correct one, and the most likely explanation here was Lady Leanora had done it herself.

But when?

Lady Leanora had remained at Darlington Castle for several months after Lady Cassandra died. Perhaps Lady Leanora considered herself the closest thing the Darlington family had to a marchioness, and had decided to seize the marchioness's apartments as her due.

Yes, that had to be it. Nothing else made sense, unless...

The way they tell it, Lord Darlington is madly in love with Lady Leanora.

Was it possible Gideon had put these things here?

It would explain why he insisted Lady Cassandra's bedchamber remained locked at all times. If he was readying the bedchamber in eager anticipation of Lady Leanora's return, he wouldn't want anyone to know of it.

But everyone would know soon enough, because who was the White Lady, if not Lady Leanora? Gideon *must* know it was her. How could he not? Had he been chasing her all these weeks only to see the ghostly rumors laid to rest, or did he have a more tender reason for wanting to find her?

Nausea swelled in the pit of Cecilia's stomach, but before she could give in to the urge to flee this cursed bedchamber, Seraphina darted through the door of the clothes press and disappeared inside. "Seraphina! Come out of there at once!" Cecilia reached inside to snatch the cat out, but instead of soft fur, her knuckles nudged into something hard. Not shoes—it wasn't the right shape, and too heavy. It felt like...a box?

She crouched down, grasped one corner of it and tugged it out from under the flowing skirts of the blue silk ball gown. She drew the object out and stared down at the dusty cover, her chest fluttering with a strange anticipation. It was a book, bound in leather and covered with a thick film of dust.

A diary. The Marchioness of Darlington's personal diary.

Cecilia looked from Seraphina to the diary, which had been tucked into a corner at the back of the clothes press, as if it had been hidden there, waiting for her to find it. "I can't read this. It's a dreadful invasion of the marchioness's privacy."

Seraphina yawned, as if privacy were a matter far beneath her notice.

Cecilia fell back on her heels in front of the clothes press with the heavy book on her lap, hesitating. What good would it do anyone for her to pry into Lady Darlington's secrets? Now she'd made up her mind to leave Darlington Castle, it should be left to someone else to reveal the remaining mysteries, or keep them secret, if they chose.

Yes, yes, that was the only logical, rational response here.

But Cecilia seemed to have abandoned rational thinking, because she snatched up the diary and scrambled to her feet. She glanced down at Seraphina, who was now rubbing against her shins, as if thanking her. "Do you always get your way, you wicked thing?"

A foolish question, really, given that Cecilia was already creeping from Lady Darlington's bedchamber to her own with the diary tucked under her arm. She took care to close the connecting door behind her, then hurried for her bed, and opened the diary to the first page.

Diary of Cassandra Elizabeth Belmore, October 1792.

It began three years ago, just after Nathanial had drowned in Darlington Lake, the year Gideon returned to Darlington Castle to see his brother laid to rest. He must have begun courting Cassandra soon after he arrived, because by February of the following year, Cassandra Belmore became Lady Darlington.

Cecilia ran a finger across the single line, admiring the elegance of Lady Darlington's handwriting—or more properly, Cassandra Belmore's handwriting—but she hesitated before turning the page, an odd foreboding gathering like a dark cloud in her breast.

Once she turned that page, there would be no going back.

She turned it anyway, her gaze searching out the first line at the top.

My dear friend, it began, in the manner of a letter rather than a diary entry.

Entry dated October 1792.

My dear friend,

My heart, my sweet friend, is heavy today. The Marquess of Darlington has been found this morning, drowned at the bottom of Darlington Lake. Such a young, healthy man to have met such a sudden and tragic end. Nathanial's brother has arrived from London, overwhelmed with shock and grief. I've never seen a man more devastated. Lady Leanora has been taken to her bed in hysterics...

Another tragedy at Darlington Castle, another sudden, unexpected death. If Cecilia believed in such things, she would have said the Marquesses of Darlington were cursed.

Then, several months later, in a much different tone:

Entry dated December 1792.

The most wonderful thing has happened! Gideon has asked me to marry him.

Cecilia flipped through until she arrived at a page dated in 1793, the last year of Cassandra Belmore's life. She skimmed through the entries, pausing on one dated in March of that year.

My dearest friend,

Never did I imagine I could be as happy as I am. Gideon has shown me such love, such affection, such tender care in these first months of our marriage, my heart, my body, and my soul are forever his...

Forever his. Cecilia's gaze lingered on the word *forever*, written in Cassandra's elegant, flowing hand, her chest aching for the young lady who'd written that word with such happiness, such hope. In the end, forever had been an unbearably short time for the Marchioness of Darlington.

Six months after writing these words, she was dead.

But oh, how happy she'd been, in the brief time she'd been Gideon's wife! His devotion to her was written into every entry, breathed into every line of those few short months. Every word Cassandra had written, every page of her diary swelled with love and adoration for her husband.

A love and adoration that was generously returned. Gideon had loved his wife. No one who read these pages could ever doubt it. His love for her was right there, page after page of it, in his late wife's own words.

April 1793. My dear friend, such a delightful morning! Gideon has surprised me with a new rose garden on the south lawn. He calls it "Cassandra's Rose Walk," in my honor, he says, and there are ever so many of my favorite white roses planted there...

May 1793. My beloved friend, the most wonderful news! I am with child. My heart is overflowing with gratitude and joy, and Gideon is ecstatic...

June 1793. I woke this morning to Gideon's lips pressed to my belly, a good morning kiss for our child, he says.

July 1793. Isabella's birthday has arrived! She is two years old today. Gideon intends to give her the new foal as a birthday gift. He spoils her dreadfully...

Cecilia couldn't help but smile at the joy in Cassandra's words, the love flowing from her pen, but it wasn't long after this delighted entry that things took a darker turn.

July 1793. Dreadfully ill today. Mrs. Briggs bids me not to fret, and says it means the baby is strong. Gideon ordered me to bed, and stayed with me until I fell asleep.

July 1793. I remain ill. The sickness grows worse with each passing day.

August 1793. I am too weak to leave my bed. My stomach revolts against all food but broth, and a painful red rash has appeared around my mouth and on my hands...

And, only a week before Cassandra's death, this final entry, written in a feeble hand.

September 1793. Gideon weeps, and begs me not to leave him...

Cecilia closed the diary, slid it under the coverlet, and pressed her damp cheek to her pillow. She'd opened it hoping it would soothe her to sleep, but her chest had been aching since she read the first passage.

She rolled onto her back and stared up at the darkened ceiling above, her fist resting on her forehead, tears leaking from the corners of her eyes. Gideon had never been in love with Lady Leanora. That was nothing but another ugly rumor invented by the gossips in Edenbridge. Cecilia was ashamed she'd ever believed it to be true.

What a terrible wrong she would have done him if she hadn't read these pages, not to have read in Cassandra's own words how much Gideon had loved her, only to lose her and their son less than a year into their marriage—

Cecilia went still, Cassandra's written words circling through her head, then she jerked upright in the bed and snatched the diary out from under her pillow. She paged backward to reread the passages written near the time of Cassandra's death, wondering if she'd misread the dates.

May 1793. The most wonderful news! I am with child...

Then, in early July, barely a month after that, *dreadfully ill today...*

And again, later in July, *the sickness grows worse with each passing day...*

Finally, after more than a month of silence, in that shaky hand—

September 1793. Gideon weeps, and begs me not to leave him...

Cecilia let the diary fall into her lap, her head spinning.

She'd read it right the first time. There were only a few weeks between the time Cassandra discovered she was with child and when the first symptoms of her illness began. Then another three months had passed between the start of her illness and her death.

Three months, with the illness growing progressively worse over that time. Certainly, a lady might experience delicate health during a pregnancy, but such an extreme illness as this, that continued to worsen over a prolonged period of time?

It seemed...strange.

Cecilia flipped through the pages once again, searching each entry for a description of symptoms. Cassandra hadn't recorded much aside from nausea, dizziness, and stomach pains. By the end of July, the entries had grown shorter, with many days passing between them, but there'd been one in August.

Painful red rash...

Rash? Cecilia had never heard of a rash being a symptom of pregnancy.

She closed the diary again, her hands shaking as she slid it back under the coverlet, her heart giving a sickening lurch inside her chest as she considered every word, every sentence the late marchioness had written. It was the cruelest twist of fate her life should have been cut so short, her joy in her unborn child stolen from her, and Gideon left alone.

A pregnancy, an illness that lasted for months, a red rash...

Or maybe it *hadn't* been fate, at all. Maybe Cassandra had been sent to her grave by something far more sinister than fate.

Because it didn't sound as if Cassandra had succumbed to a mysterious illness.

It sounded as if she'd been poisoned.

Chapter Twenty

Gideon couldn't determine when it had happened, but sometime between Cecilia Gilchrist's arrival at Darlington Castle and this moment, he'd turned into a drooling, pathetic, lovestruck fool.

Well, he wasn't drooling, thankfully, but it was bad enough, even so. What sort of marquess hovered at the door of his bedchamber, his breath held and his ear pressed to the wood, listening for the sound of a woman's voice?

This was *his* castle, *his* bedchamber, *his* door. He had every right to go through it. Every right in the world, yet his stomach was in nervous knots and his palms damp, as if he were some sort of spellbound adolescent.

He wasn't even going in there to see Cecilia, for God's sake. It was his *niece's* bedchamber. The niece he'd bid a good morning *every day since her birth*. He always saw Isabella before he went about the business of the day, but now he was frozen in place, and for no better reason than Cecilia was on the other side of that door.

He rested his forehead against it with a groan. Their kiss last night, those delirious moments when he'd taken her lips, pressed her curves against him, heard her soft sighs and whimpers in his ear...

Since then, he'd thought of nothing but that kiss. He'd dreamed of it, of *her*, and had woken with a pounding heart and a cock as rigid as an iron spike. This from a man who purported to be a gentleman, and one who heartily disapproved of noblemen who debauched their servants.

The trouble was, it had been weeks since he'd thought of Cecilia as a servant. He wasn't certain he *ever* had, but she was in fact his niece's nursemaid, and now, after a lifetime of restraint, he'd done the unthinkable.

What was he meant to say to her this morning, after such a kiss as that? Worse, what if he lost his wits and swept her into his arms as soon as he laid eyes on her, with Isabella as witness? She'd grow up and fall victim to a rogue, and it would be all Gideon's fault.

But he'd simply have to take the risk. He'd be away from the castle all day with Haslemere, and he didn't like to leave without bidding them goodbye. He could hear them on the other side of the door— Isabella's cheerful chatter, and Cecilia's sweet answering laugh—and knew they'd be leaving their bedchamber in a matter of moments.

Gideon drew in a breath, flexed his fingers, and after a brief knock, opened the connecting door.

"Good morning, Uncle!" Isabella, always delighted to see him, flew across the room and into his waiting arms.

"Good morning, Isabella. You're energetic today." Gideon swept her up with a grin and kissed her cheek. "Good morning, Cecilia," he added, the back of his neck heating as he met her gaze over the top of Isabella's head.

"Good morning, Lord Darlington," she murmured, her own cheeks coloring.

"You, ah…you look pretty this morning."

Dear God. Gideon cringed as soon as the words were out of his mouth, but even as he fumbled to correct his gaffe, Isabella said matter-of-factly, "Miss Cecilia looks pretty every day."

"She does, yes." Gideon's gaze held Cecilia's. She was dressed much as she was every day, in a plain gray gown with a white apron over it, her dark hair pulled severely back from her face, but he could no more tear his gaze from her than he could a miracle unfolding before his eyes.

Gideon cleared his throat. "What will the two of you do today?"

"A long walk in the kitchen garden, I think." Cecilia glanced at the window, tapping her finger against her bottom lip. "I'm certain it's going to snow, and I'd like for Isabella to have some fresh air before it does."

Gideon didn't like to order Cecilia to stay indoors, but both he and Haslemere would be gone from the castle until dark tonight. Duncan and Fraser were here, but he didn't like Cecilia and Isabella wandering the grounds while he was gone, all the same.

But he wouldn't say so in front of Isabella. "Go on and finish your breakfast, Isabella." Gideon set her back on her feet. "I need to have a word with Miss Cecilia."

"All right." Isabella dashed back to her half-eaten plate of tartlets.

Cecilia's cheeks flushed a deeper pink when Gideon took her arm, but she followed him through the connecting door and into his bedchamber. "Lord Haslemere and I ride to Surrey today. I'd rather you and Isabella remain inside the castle until we return."

"Surrey? But why?"

Gideon hesitated. He and Haslemere weren't getting anywhere searching the castle grounds by themselves. It was too much for two men to cover alone, so they were going to fetch a half-dozen of Haslemere's burliest footmen and bring them back to Darlington Castle.

They'd been chasing a phantom long enough. Gideon wanted this thing done, but he didn't want to discuss the White Lady with Cecilia. Not yet. For now, the less Cecilia knew about her, the better. "Lord Haslemere's sister, the Duchess of Kenilworth, and her son arrived at Haslemere House yesterday. They sent word to Lord Haslemere last night, and naturally he wants to see them."

It wasn't a lie, exactly. Her Grace had made frequent and unexpected visits to her brother's estate this winter. Haslemere was uncharacteristically closemouthed about the reasons why, but Gideon had begun to wonder if it had something to do with the duke.

Cecilia searched his face, her dark eyes intent. "Is there some reason it would be unsafe for us to venture outside the castle walls?"

Yes. Something wicked was gliding through the darkness. Not a ghost, but something more sinister. Gideon didn't say so, however. He said only, "It's cold, and threatening to snow. I'd rather you remain indoors today."

Her face fell, and her eyes dropped away. "I see."

It wasn't the answer she'd hoped for. Gideon closed the distance between them and took her hand. Just her hand. He wouldn't risk touching any other part of her while his bed was mere steps away from where they stood. "It's just for today, Cecilia, while Haslemere and I are gone. I'll take you and Isabella for a walk in the kitchen gardens myself tomorrow."

Cecilia nodded. "I suppose we can find some other way to amuse ourselves."

"Thank you." Gideon couldn't resist raising her hand to his lips. Her eyes darkened as his mouth brushed her knuckles, and he had to bite back a moan. "We can spend all of tomorrow afternoon in the kitchen gardens, if you like. I promise it."

"Tomorrow, then." Cecilia's gaze dropped to their entwined fingers, then she gently drew her hand away.

* * * *

All day long, Cecilia had to remind herself she was relieved Gideon was away from Darlington Castle for the day. Each time she recalled he was gone her heart sank in her chest, and she'd have to scold herself back into equanimity again.

It was a long, frustrating day. Instead of the snow she'd expected, the sun struggled through the clouds for the first time in days. Its feeble rays touched the frosted grounds, transforming them into a sparkling garden of diamonds, mocking Cecilia with their beauty.

Isabella soon grew bored and restless, and teased with a child's mercilessness for a visit to the garden. Cecilia was as tempted to venture outdoors as Isabella was, and it wouldn't have been the first time she'd disregarded Gideon's wishes. But she remained firm in her refusal, as it turned out to be much easier to ignore a command from the arrogant Marquess of Darlington than it was a request from Gideon, softly spoken, his blue eyes pleading.

By the time Isabella's bedtime arrived, the poor child had succumbed to a storm of frustrated tears. After she'd cried herself into an exhausted sleep at last Cecilia, who'd forgone her dinner to soothe her fetched Amy, then ventured down to the kitchens to see what tidbit she might forage.

She found Mrs. Briggs at the table, having a nip of sherry. "You look worn to the bones, you do." Mrs. Briggs fetched another glass, poured a measure for Cecilia, and put a plate of bread and cold ham before her. "Isabella was in a bit of a state today. She missed Lord Darlington, I daresay, the poor lamb."

We both did.

Cecilia raised the sherry glass to her lips, considering Mrs. Briggs as she sipped at it. All of Gideon's servants were tight-lipped about the doings at Darlington Castle, particularly anything to do with Lady Cassandra's death.

Mrs. Briggs was the most tight-lipped of the lot, perhaps because of all the servants, she knew the most. She'd known Nathanial and Lady Leanora, had rejoiced in Isabella's birth, and celebrated Lady Cassandra's and Gideon's marriage. She'd mourned Nathanial's tragic death along with the rest of the family, and she'd been here when Cassandra drew her final breath, and she and her stillborn infant were placed in the cold ground.

Mrs. Briggs knew everything. It would be a tricky business to pry it out of her, but while Mrs. Briggs never gossiped, she could be coaxed into reminiscing.

After reading Lady Cassandra's diary, Cecilia felt as if she knew her—almost as if she and the late marchioness had somehow become... friends? No, not that, precisely, but how strange it was, how peculiar that of everyone at Darlington Castle, the key to unraveling the mystery of

Cassandra's death had come from Cassandra herself. It was as if she'd put that diary into Cecilia's hands, whispered her secrets into Cecilia's ear.

Gideon loved me, and he'd never hurt me…

Then the darker, more sinister secret.

Poison.

It was as if Cassandra trusted Cecilia, and only Cecilia, to reveal the truth. Not just for her own sake, but for Gideon's.

Cecilia fortified herself with another sip of sherry, then set her glass aside. "Tell me about Lady Cassandra, Mrs. Briggs. What was she like?"

"You're curious this evening, Cecilia. Why do you want to know?" There was no mistaking the hint of disapproval in Mrs. Briggs's voice.

Cecilia hesitated. It felt like a betrayal of Gideon's confidence, but if she wanted answers, she had no choice. "Lord Darlington took me to Lady Darlington's grave, Mrs. Briggs. Hers, and their son's."

Mrs. Briggs nearly dropped her sherry glass. "He took you…that's…well, my goodness, Cecilia. I've never known him to do that with anyone before."

No, Cecilia didn't suppose he did, but she didn't care to share with Mrs. Briggs the reasons why Gideon had made an exception for *her*. "He said she died of an illness."

"Aye, she did. We thought it was the child at first, of course, the stomach sickness, I mean, but I've seen my share of ladies in the family way, and I never saw anyone as ill as the poor marchioness. It was dreadful to watch her grow weaker with every passing day." Mrs. Briggs shuddered. "One could hardly recognize her by the end, she'd grown so frail."

"She was ill for some time, I believe?"

Mrs. Briggs nodded. "Months, yes. Then the child came too early, and the poor marchioness couldn't…well, that was what ended it."

"Who tended her during her illness? Her cousin, Lady Leonora?"

Mrs. Briggs's mouth turned down at the corners. "No. Lady Leonora wasn't the sort one wanted in a sickroom—too squeamish, that one, and in any case, she and Cassandra grew apart somewhat after Cassandra became the marchioness."

Cecilia struggled to keep her expression neutral. "I see. Did you tend the marchioness, then?"

"No. I tidied her bedchamber and did little tasks for her, but Lord Darlington himself did most of the nursing. He spent every moment he could with her. At the end he wouldn't suffer anyone but himself to enter Cassandra's bedchamber. I think he couldn't bear for anyone to see her that way."

Cecilia paused to draw a deep breath. Her next question would sound strange to Mrs. Briggs, but she had to ask it. "Did she…was she able to eat at all?"

"Not much, no. Lord Darlington brought her a tray of broth every night at dinnertime, but she never took much. I know, because I took that tray down every morning. The only thing she ever touched was the spearmint tea he gave her much later in the evenings to help her sleep." Mrs. Briggs shook her head, a sad smile twisting her lips. "It was heartbreaking to see how hard he tried."

Cecilia gave a sympathetic nod, but her mind was racing to make sense of this new information. Gideon was the only one permitted to enter Cassandra's bedchamber, and Gideon the one who brought her broth every night.

It led to only one logical conclusion. If Cassandra had been poisoned—and Cecilia was more certain than ever she had been—then Gideon must have been the one who'd poisoned her. It was a tale worthy of Bluebeard himself. A wicked marquess poisons his young wife and their unborn child so he can seduce his brother's widow.

But…*no.*

She simply wouldn't—couldn't—believe that. Everything inside her, her every instinct screamed the most logical conclusion was, in this case, the wrong one.

The man Cassandra described in her diary would never have hurt her. He'd never have harmed a single hair on her head. Gideon might no longer be the cheerful, openly affectionate man Cassandra had known—he was much more reserved and secretive now, even distant. Grief had wrought these changes in him, made him darker, and thus an easy target for the gossips.

But he wasn't wicked, and Bluebeards only existed in the grimmest of fairy tales.

Gideon was innocent.

Cecilia knew it in the same way she knew she could always trust Lady Clifford, in the same way she knew Sophia and Georgiana and Emma loved her; in the same way she knew Daniel Brixton would always protect her.

She knew it down to her very soul.

Since she'd arrived at Darlington Castle, she'd told herself time and again she needed to use her wits, as Georgiana did, to rely on her talents, as Emma did, and to be strong and brave, as Sophia was. She'd told herself her heart was untrustworthy, too prone to sentimentality to be relied upon. Too soft, too apt to romanticize a man like Gideon who, for all his darkness, was lost and grieving, and beautiful in his vulnerability.

She'd told herself she couldn't trust her heart to lead her to the truth, but all this time, she'd been wrong. Her heart whispered Gideon was innocent, and, at last, she would allow herself to listen to it.

Someone had poisoned Lady Cassandra, but it hadn't been Gideon. Whoever *had* done it had escaped justice thus far, but they wouldn't escape forever. Cecilia would make certain of it.

"I'm off to bed. Mind you eat the rest of your dinner." Mrs. Briggs nodded at Cecilia's plate, then pushed her chair back from the table. "Good night, Cecilia."

"Good night, Mrs. Briggs."

Cecilia sat in the darkened kitchen for a long time after Mrs. Briggs left, trying to fit the puzzle together from the pieces Mrs. Briggs had given her.

Never seen anyone so ill...frail and weak... broth and spearmint tea...

Cecilia's brow furrowed, her mind lingering over that last thing. Spearmint tea. The plant she and Isabella had found in the kitchen garden, the one she'd thought was some variety of lavender. It smelled strongly of spearmint.

Ill for months...poison...spearmint tea...

Perhaps the plant wasn't lavender, after all, but something far more sinister. Could Cassandra have been poisoned by a plant growing in the kitchen garden? One with leaves that could be brewed into a tea?

She rose from her chair and passed through the arched doorway of the kitchen and down the corridor into the entrance hall. It was silent, without a soul wandering about, and the door leading into the courtyard and the kitchen garden beyond it beckoned to her.

Once she got a few sprigs of the plant, she could look it up in *Culpeper's Complete Herbal*. She'd seen a copy of it on a library shelf when she'd gone in to fetch *The Mysteries of Udolpho* to read to Duncan and Amy the other night. It would take some searching through the illustrations to find the plant, but find it she would.

But first, she needed to make a trip to the kitchen garden.

Except she'd told Gideon she'd stay inside the castle today. If one chose to quibble over words, it wasn't *daytime* any longer, darkness having fallen while she and Mrs. Briggs were talking, but that was splitting hairs, indeed. Whatever Gideon had thought was a threat during the day surely became much more so at night. That was always the way with threatening things. They thrived in darkness.

Was the White Lady truly a threat, though? Gideon must think so, or else he wouldn't have warned her to stay inside the castle, but despite having pretended to be a ghost and frightening Edenbridge out of their feeble wits, The White Lady hadn't *hurt* anyone.

Still, it was a risk.

Cecilia bit her lip. She could put off the task until tomorrow, but it was already snowing. The plants she needed could be buried by morning. Even if she did manage to get to them, they might look entirely different after languishing under a heavy snow, and she'd no longer be able to recognize them in *Culpeper's Complete Herbal.*

It was the work of a few moments only. It would be the quickest thing in the world for her to dash out the door and through the courtyard to the corner of the kitchen garden, snatch up a few stalks of the spearmint-scented plant, and dash back inside again.

Cecilia straightened her shoulders, her mind made up. She'd known there'd be risk before she'd agreed to come to Darlington Castle. She wasn't without her own resources, nor was she as easy a target as she appeared to be.

Only the dim light from the entrance hall lamps followed Cecilia out the door and into the courtyard beyond. Dear God, it was cold, and the sharp, dry scent of snow tickled Cecilia's nose. Thick clouds scudded across the sky, obscuring the moon, and Cecilia sent up a quick prayer of thanks that she and Isabella had spent so much time in this garden, or she might have found herself wandering around in search of that plant until she froze to death.

As it was, she knew just where to find it.

She hurried through the gate and down the gravel pathway toward the opposite corner of the garden, wincing as the icy ground penetrated the thin soles of her shoes. By the time she reached the lavender patch her toes were half-frozen and her fingers clumsy with cold, but she pushed as much of the woody stalks of lavender aside as she could and searched with both her eyes and hands until she found…yes, there it was, growing up against the high stone wall behind it.

Cecilia was just reaching down into the clump when a strange noise made her go still. It sounded like the crunch of footsteps running over the gravel pathway, but when she turned and peered into the gloom behind her, there was nothing.

She shook her head, grimacing. All this talk of ghosts was frazzling her nerves.

Still, the sooner she was back inside, the better. She reached down again, took ahold of the plant as close to the root as she could, and plucked up a few stalks, the scent of spearmint thick in her nose as she shoved them into the pocket of her apron.

She turned back toward the garden gate, but before she could take a step, she heard the sound again. Footsteps on gravel, running faster this time, what sounded like the muted creak of an iron gate opening, and then—

Cecilia froze where she stood, the crash of the gate slamming shut echoing throughout the garden.

There was no time to stop it, no time even to cry out. By the time Cecilia realized what was happening and ran for the gate, it was already closed. She grabbed the latch and shook it desperately, but it didn't move, and a quick glance at it confirmed the sick suspicion twisting in her stomach.

Whoever had slammed the gate closed had latched it from the outside. Of all the doors in this blasted castle that were meant to be secure, this had to be the only one that actually *was*.

Cecilia whirled around and ran to the opposite end of the garden where there was a high wooden door set into the stone wall, but it was locked, just as she'd known it would be, and so was the door leading from the garden into the stillroom.

She turned back to face the garden, her gaze darting this way and that in the darkness, searching for an escape, but it was no use. The wall had been built to keep animals out. It towered over her, as did the arched gate at the front, which had been set into the stone wall.

As she stood there shivering, the snow falling from the sky quickened, and the downy flakes grew heavier. She didn't have a coat, or boots, and the wind was sneaking up her skirts and down the back of her neck, turning her flesh to ice.

No one knew she was out here. Amy would miss her when she didn't return to Isabella's bedchamber, but the kitchen garden was the last place they'd look for her. It could be hours before anyone found her.

Cecilia pressed her body close against the castle wall and huddled there to shield herself as best she could from the raw, bitter wind biting through the thin layers of her clothing.

Someone would come after her. When she didn't return to Isabella's bedchamber, Amy would send Duncan out to look for her. He'd find her out here, sooner or later.

All she could do now was pray it would be sooner, rather than later.

Chapter Twenty-one

It looks like a nightmare.

Gideon stopped in front of the iron-studded oak portcullis, and Haslemere and the half-dozen men they'd brought back to Darlington Castle with them drew their horses to a halt behind him.

Had it only been three weeks ago he'd stood in front of the castle that had once been his home, and cursed it as a living nightmare, the withered heart at the center of all his shattered dreams?

It looked as grim now as it had then, but when he gazed up at it, his chest no longer tightened with bitterness. No shudders of revulsion rolled down his spine. His stomach wasn't clenched with anger, and he wasn't choking on grief.

Everything had changed, and there was only one way to account for it.

A smile drifted over his lips as he recalled his first glimpse of Cecilia, wrapped from head to toe in a dark traveling cloak, tossing pebbles into Darlington Lake.

I wanted to know how deep it is.

Perhaps he should have realized even then she'd tilt everything sideways, turn it upside down then right side up again, but forever changed. Perhaps he should have known she'd do the same thing to his heart. Such a small woman, to cause such an upheaval. Such a quiet coup. She'd conquered him before he realized he was under siege.

As they'd plodded toward the castle through the darkness this evening, he'd sworn a hundred oaths he'd wait until tomorrow to see her—that it was too dark, too late, terribly improper to bother her tonight.

What a fool he was. What a blind, arrogant fool. He could no more resist her than he could refuse to draw his next breath—

"Well, Darlington? Do you intend to enter the castle at some point this evening, or are we all to sleep on the drawbridge tonight?"

Gideon turned in the saddle. Haslemere was watching him, a sly grin on his lips. How long had he been lingering here, staring up at the castle, lost in dreams of Cecilia? Long enough to put a knowing smirk on Haslemere's face, at least.

"Careful, Haslemere, or I'll put you in the moat," Gideon replied mildly as he urged his horse into a walk and led the party forward.

"You're distracted tonight, Darlington. Why is that, I wonder? Ah well, it's not my concern." Haslemere leapt down from his horse, gathered his reins, then held out his hand for Gideon's. "Well, go on then, give them here. I'll take him in. He deserves better than to have a distracted marquess pawing at him."

Gideon dismounted and handed his reins over, his lips quirking. "You're a diligent horseman, Haslemere, and a good friend."

"I am, indeed, both of those things." Haslemere shrugged, but he looked pleased. "Come on, men. The stables are this way."

Gideon forced himself to wait until the men had rounded the side of the castle before he hurried over the footbridge. He was a marquess, after all, and it wouldn't do to sacrifice all his dignity by scrambling about like an overeager puppy. But as soon as they were out of sight he darted through the courtyard and into the entrance hall.

He took the stairs two at a time. He didn't pause to remove his coat or boots when he reached his bedchamber, but rushed through the connecting door, his heart soaring with desire and love and anticipation.

Only to crash again when he entered Isabella's bedchamber. His niece was sound asleep in her bed, but it wasn't Cecilia dozing in the rocking chair by her side.

It was Amy.

The thud of his boots echoed in his ears as he hurried across the room. He crouched in front of the rocking chair so he wouldn't frighten Amy by looming over her, then nudged her gently awake. "Amy? Where's Cecilia?"

Amy blinked groggily, frowning at Gideon as if she'd never seen him before. "Who?"

"Cecilia, Amy. It's late. Where is she?" Gideon was making a great effort not to shake Amy into full consciousness and interrogate her as if she were a criminal.

"Lord Darlington?" Amy rubbed her bleary eyes and blinked again before focusing on him. "Oh, I beg your pardon, my lord. I must have dozed off." She sat up straighter in the chair. "Isabella—"

"Isabella is fine. She's fast asleep. Where is Cecilia?" Gideon repeated with growing urgency. There was no reason to be alarmed, as Amy often watched Isabella when Cecilia left the room, but a knot of foreboding was gathering at the base of his spine.

Amy stared at him in confusion for another moment, but then understanding dawned, and she shot up from the chair so quickly she nearly knocked Gideon backward. "Oh, my goodness. What time is it?"

"It's late, Amy. Past midnight."

"Oh, dear." Amy wrung her hands, her face turning pale. "That's not… she should have been back ages ago."

Gideon didn't like the panicked look on Amy's face, but he wasn't yet ready to alarm the whole castle. He took a deep breath, and forced himself to speak calmly. "Back from where? Where did she go?"

"Down to the kitchens, to have a bite of dinner. Cecilia stayed with Isabella until she fell asleep, as she always does, but Isabella was fussy, and Cecilia missed her meal. But that was hours ago, Lord Darlington!"

An icy chill rushed over Gideon, followed by a dark, nameless dread. "How long, Amy? One hour? Two? When did you last see her?"

"Eight o'clock or so, I think? She said she'd come right back up, but I fell asleep, and didn't realize how much time had passed."

Hours. Four at least, maybe more, and no sign of her? It seemed an eternity. Gideon fought back the fear clawing at his throat. "The last you knew, then, she was going to the kitchens?" Perhaps Mrs. Briggs had seen her.

"Yes, she…you don't suppose she ventured out onto the grounds alone again?" Amy looked panicked. "She wouldn't be so foolish as that, would she?"

"No," Gideon said, with more conviction than he felt. Cecilia had promised him she wouldn't leave the castle today, but she had a mind of her own. She wouldn't hesitate to disregard her promise if she felt it necessary. She'd never risk Isabella's safety, but God knew she wasn't nearly as careful of her own.

"I don't like this." Amy began pacing in front of the fireplace, her fingers twisted in her apron. "Where could she have got to?"

"It's all right, Amy. I'll find her." If Cecilia had turned up in the kitchens, Mrs. Briggs must have seen her. He'd have to wake his housekeeper, but there was no help for it. "Stay here with Isabella until I return."

Gideon didn't wait for Amy's reply, but strode from the bedchamber into the corridor, every instinct urging him to rush outside and have Haslemere order his men to search the grounds while he and Gideon tore the castle apart, stone by stone, until they found Cecilia.

Four hours. Good Lord, anything could have happened to her in that time. He pounded down the stairs, his head spinning as he examined and then discarded one possible explanation after the next. Had she been trapped in some remote part of the castle? The attics, perhaps? Or had she fallen, and was lying in some out-of-the-way place, unconscious and bleeding? By the time he reached the last stair he'd conjured a dozen nightmare scenarios in his head, all of which included Cecilia's broken body at the bottom of a flight of stairs.

He ran straight toward the entrance hall, bypassing Mrs. Briggs's apartments. There was no time to speak to his housekeeper now. No, he'd go to the stables first, and fetch Haslemere. They had ten good, strong men, including Duncan and Fraser. He'd put a half-dozen of them on the grounds—three mounted, and three on foot, while he, Haslemere, Duncan, and Fraser searched the castle.

Surely between them all, they'd make quick work of finding one small woman? She couldn't have gotten far. Damn it, where was she? Where—

Just as he reached the door, he stopped with his hand on the latch, a noise making him freeze in his tracks. It sounded like...a moan, or gasping breaths? He turned in a circle, his body tensed, but he wasn't sure where it was coming from.

He waited, ears straining and every muscle twitching until at last he heard it again, a cry so faint he might have believed he'd imagined it. Not a moan this time, but a plea for help coming from the direction of the drive. Gideon sprang forward, throwing the front door open with a crash, but what he found on the other side made him stumble backward in horror.

It was Cecilia—thank *God*, it was her—but even in this dim light he could see how deathly pale she was, her strange clumsiness and the slow, heavy steps with which she crept up the drive. She was limping, and her arms were thrust out at her sides as if she thought she'd topple over at any moment.

"Cecilia." Her name left his lips on a strangled breath. "*Cecilia.*"

Her gaze had been fixed on the gravel beneath her feet as she made her painstaking way up the drive, but at the sound of his voice her head came up, and when she saw him there, her face just...crumpled. "Gideon."

She swayed where she stood, but Gideon leapt for her, catching her before her knees gave way and she collapsed onto the gravel drive. "Shhh, love. I've got you." He wrapped his arms around her trembling body and swept her up, gathering her tightly against his chest.

"I...I'm sorry. I didn't think I was doing anything dangerous. I broke my promise—"

"Hush, it's all right." Gideon stroked her hair back from her damp forehead. "You're all right."

But she *wasn't* all right, because his hand came away wet with blood.

Gideon was shaking badly, but he managed to turn her head toward him with a gentle nudge of her chin, and that was when he saw it. Blood, livid against her pale skin, running from her temple down her neck. Her dark hair was matted with it, her white apron stained with it, as if she'd used it to try and staunch the flow. Her hands were scraped bloody as well, her palms torn to shreds, and the hem of her gray skirt was ripped.

She was clutching at his shirt, mumbling something about the kitchen garden and footsteps and a locked door, but Gideon hardly heard a word of it. He just kept murmuring to her, his voice low and soothing as he carried her into the castle.

As it happened, Haslemere and his men entered behind him, having finished in the stables. "Darlington, what are you..." Haslemere began, but he trailed off with a curse when he caught sight of Cecilia, limp and bleeding in Gideon's arms. "Jesus, what happened? Is she—"

"She'll be all right." She *would* be, because Gideon wouldn't hear of anything else. "But I need to get her upstairs and into bed. Summon Mrs. Briggs for me, will you, Haslemere? Have her find Duncan and Fraser, as well. I want everyone accounted for."

Haslemere nodded. "Of course."

"Good man." Gideon didn't wait, but turned and hurried up the stairs with Cecilia in his arms. She was shaking like a leaf, her eyes glassy. She didn't seem to quite understand what was happening, but she let her head fall against his chest with a grateful little sigh.

That sigh went straight to Gideon's heart. She trusted him. Him, the man half of England feared, and every soul in Edenbridge would swear had killed his wife.

Him, the Murderous Marquess.

She *trusted* him.

Behind him, he could hear Haslemere speaking to his men. "Search out Darlington's men, then meet me on the second floor for further instructions. Look sharp, boys. We don't want anyone else getting hurt."

"Aye, my lord." It was Fletcher, Haslemere's top man. "Ye heard his lordship, lads. Off we go."

In the end, there was no need for Haslemere to wake Mrs. Briggs. The sound of half a dozen men mounting her staircase was enough to bring her running. She came to an abrupt halt when she saw what was taking place, eyes wide and fingers clutching at the neckline of her robe. "Heavens above, Lord Haslemere. Where did all these men come from? What's happened?"

"Cecilia's been injured. I'm not sure of the details, but I believe Lord Darlington would appreciate your presence, Mrs. Briggs."

"Injured? Oh, my goodness. Yes, of course." Mrs. Briggs didn't wait to ask any further questions, but scurried up the stairs, her robe flapping against her ankles.

Amy was pacing and muttering to herself when Gideon returned to Isabella's bedchamber with Cecilia. When she saw her friend pale and bleeding in Gideon's arms she gasped and covered her mouth with her hand. "Oh, *no*. What's happened?"

"Something to do with the kitchen garden, footsteps, and a locked door. That's all I know." Gideon carried Cecilia across the room and lay her gently in her bed.

"Cold." Cecilia scrabbled for the blankets, her hands shaking. "So cold."

Amy made a strangled noise and started toward Cecilia, but she hadn't gotten a step before Mrs. Briggs swept into the room, instructions already on her lips. "Amy, dear, will you fetch some hot water from the kitchen, and a few rags from the scrap pile, too."

Amy ran to do Mrs. Briggs's bidding, but she jerked to a halt when she reached the bedchamber door. Haslemere and his men had joined the party by now, with Duncan and Fraser in tow. The entire castle was gathered outside Isabella's bedchamber, shuffling their booted feet and whispering among themselves.

Amy fell back with a gasp. "There's a crowd of men in the hallway!"

"Yes, I know, dear. Those are Lord Haslemere's men, and I daresay they're harmless enough. Go on now, there's a good girl."

Amy skirted around the men, eyes as big as saucers, and fled down the stairs.

"Now then, Cecilia. No, no, don't close your eyes, dear. We can't let you sleep quite yet." Mrs. Briggs inspected the wound at Cecilia's temple, prodding gently with her fingers. "It's quite a gash, my lord. Deep, but not dangerous."

"Are you certain?" Gideon was hovering over the bed. He'd seen his share of bloody wounds, including a gentleman whose shoulder had been run through with a sword in a duel, but nothing had ever disturbed him as much as the blood smeared across Cecilia's pale skin.

"There. It's all right. I'm all done," Mrs. Briggs soothed when Cecilia flinched. She patted Cecilia's hand before turning to Gideon. "Quite certain, yes. As you know, my lord, I've seen my share of cuts and scratches."

"But how can you tell anything with so much blood?" Mrs. Briggs had tended to his injuries when he was a child, and Gideon didn't doubt her nursing skills, but he wasn't taking any chances with Cecilia.

"Yes, head injuries do tend to bleed, I'm afraid," Mrs. Briggs replied cheerfully. "It's a bit alarming, I know, my lord, but blood doesn't necessarily mean there's a serious injury. I'll be able to tell more once we've cleaned her up, but I shouldn't worry. Cecilia's sturdier than she looks."

"She doesn't look that sturdy to me," Gideon muttered. To his anxious eye, she looked like a crumpled rag doll tossed aside by a careless child. "Her hands are torn up, as well, and she was limping up the drive."

"Oh, dear, your hands are a bit of a mess, aren't they?" Mrs. Briggs tutted as she inspected Cecilia's palms. "I imagine those cuts hurt, don't they, Cecilia?"

"Not too much, really." Cecilia's dark gaze was fixed on Gideon's face over Mrs. Briggs's shoulder. "They sting a little."

Mrs. Briggs chuckled. "Well, you're not the complaining sort. I knew that from the first moment I met you."

They heard Amy's voice in the hallway then, shooing the men away from the door. A moment later she appeared with the basin and cloths, which she brought to Mrs. Briggs.

"Thank you, Amy. Now, take Isabella back to your bedchamber with you for the night, dear. She'll be better off there, where it's quiet."

Incredibly, Isabella had slept through the chaos. She murmured sleepily when Amy scooped her up, but she didn't wake. Gideon followed Amy out the door, and motioned Haslemere aside.

"What happened?" Haslemere's voice was grim.

"I'm not sure yet. Cecilia's a little incoherent, but it sounds as if she may have gotten locked inside the kitchen garden. I'll find out more when Mrs. Briggs is finished with her."

"Locked outside, in this cold?" Haslemere's mouth fell open. "Jesus, Darlington. She might have frozen to death."

"I think that was the idea, Haslemere." Gideon looked steadily into his friend's eyes, so there'd be no mistaking his meaning.

Haslemere nodded, then turned to address his men. "Fletcher, I want you, Hobbes, and Thompson on horseback. The others can go on foot—"

"No. There's no use in chasing after her tonight, Haslemere. You can be sure she's long gone by now. But let's keep two men on each bedchamber door, just to be safe. Duncan and Fraser can keep watch over Amy and Isabella, and two of your men on Mrs. Briggs's door. The others can keep watch at the doors leading outside, and in a few hours we'll switch off."

"What of Cecilia? Who will watch over her?"

"Me," Gideon said, in a tone that discouraged argument.

But Haslemere, being Haslemere, *did* argue. "That's not a good idea, Darlington. Why not let Mrs. Briggs stay with her?"

"*No.* I'll stay with her."

"Darlington, be reasonable. Her reputation—"

"Do you truly think I'll let Cecilia out of my sight after what happened to her tonight, Haslemere? I won't risk her safety." As for Cecilia's reputation, no one here would carry tales into the village, but even if they did, it wouldn't matter.

She was *his*, and he wasn't giving her up.

Ever.

Haslemere held up his hands in surrender. "All right then, if you insist. I don't envy you the wrangle you'll have with Mrs. Briggs over it. She's far more alarming than I am."

Alarming? Gideon had once seen Mrs. Briggs take a broom to a footman who'd tried to steal a kiss from one of her housemaids. She wasn't *alarming*, she was downright terrifying, and never more so than when a scoundrel tried to trifle with one of her girls.

But to Gideon's surprise, she only gazed hard at him for a moment when he returned to the bedchamber and seated himself in the rocking chair with the air of a man who intended to stay there.

"Very well, my lord," she said, with a small smile. "Stay if you must, but mind you keep to that rocking chair."

With that she was gone, and Gideon and Cecilia were left alone.

Chapter Twenty-two

Cecilia lay in the middle of her bed, her arms wrapped around herself, shivering with cold, and…something else. Anxiety, or anticipation? She couldn't have said which in that moment, only that her entire attention was focused on the man now seated in the chair beside her.

She waited, her belly leaping with nerves, for him to say something, *do* something.

But he didn't speak, didn't reach for her, didn't even sigh. He simply sat there, his body tensed, gazing at her.

She'd broken her promise to him. She'd sworn she wouldn't venture outside the castle, then she'd done it anyway. Worse, she'd done it at night, and alone, utterly careless of her own safety.

Anything might have happened to her. It almost *had* happened.

"Gideon, I…I'm sorry I—"

Cecilia broke off with a gasp as he shot to his feet. She gazed up at him when he stopped beside her bed, her lower lip caught between her teeth. "I know I promised I wouldn't—"

She broke off again, this time with a faint cry as he leaned down, and without any warning or so much as a by your leave, scooped her up into his arms, coverlet and all.

"Gideon!" She clutched at his coat to steady herself, the fine wool wet to the touch, damp all the way through to the silk lining and his heated skin beneath. "What are you doing?"

He didn't answer. He strode across the room to the door that connected their bedchambers without a single word, and passed through it with her still in his arms. He didn't stop until he reached his bed, then he lay her down and tugged his thick coverlet over her. "My bedchamber is warmer than yours. You're staying here until you stop shaking with cold."

Half-formed warnings, arguments, a protest that she shouldn't be in his bedchamber, much less his bed, all rushed to Cecilia's lips, but each of them died a withering death before she spoke them.

This was where she wanted to be, where she needed to be. Not because his bedchamber was warmer than hers, but because Gideon was here, and he was the warmest thing she'd ever known. Even if it was only for tonight, this was where she belonged. "Gideon, I—"

"Shhh." He stirred the banked fire until it was blazing again, then turned back to her. "Are you warm enough?"

Cecilia nodded, eyes widening as he drew closer. His voice was gentle, but his lips were pressed into a stern line.

"You broke your promise to me, Cecilia. Why?" Gideon stopped halfway between the fireplace and the bed, waiting for her answer.

"I did, yes. I, ah…realized I'd left my sketchbook in the kitchen garden when I was out with Isabella the other day." Cecilia swallowed. "I—it began to snow. I didn't want it to be ruined, so I just nipped out to fetch it."

"Your sketchbook," Gideon repeated, searching her face.

"Yes. I'm sorry, Gideon. I should have waited until morning." She *was* sorry, so sorry to lie to him, but there were so many unanswered questions still, so many mysteries as yet unsolved…

Cecilia peeked up at him from under her lashes, hesitating. She'd prodded and poked into every corner of this castle, searched his attics and quizzed his servants, but the one thing she hadn't done was simply *ask* Gideon for the truth. "Gideon, why have you insisted Lady Cassandra's bedchamber remain locked all these months?"

He blinked, surprised at the question. "Because of Isabella."

"Isabella?" What did Isabella have to do with Lady Cassandra's bedchamber?

Gideon blew out a breath. "A week after Cassandra died, Isabella woke in the night and crept into Cassandra's bedchamber, searching for her. I found her there the next morning, huddled in Cassandra's bed, shivering, with dried tears on her cheeks. It was…" He dragged a hand through his hair, his face pained. "Unbearable. After it happened a second time, I had the bedchamber doors locked."

Cecilia gazed up at him, her throat working, and wondered why she hadn't known it at once, when everything he was, everything he did, was for Isabella's sake. "I…yes, I see." She wanted to say more, to tell him everything then—her real reasons for venturing into the garden tonight, what she'd read in Cassandra's diary, her suspicions about Cassandra's death, but she bit her lip before any of these truths could spill out.

Because they weren't truths. Not yet. They were suspicions only. She had no evidence, just her instincts and a half-dozen of the purple-tipped stalks she'd picked in the garden tonight, hidden in her apron pocket. There were too many uncertainties still, too many questions she had no answers to. She wouldn't turn Gideon's world upside down until she knew beyond a doubt that she was right.

"I asked you to remain inside the castle because I was concerned for your safety." Gideon drew closer and pressed gentle fingers to her lips, hushing her when she tried to speak. "The Darlington Castle ghost, Cecilia. The White Lady. She's my brother's widow, Lady Leanora."

Cecilia stared at him, stunned. Until this moment she hadn't realized how badly she'd needed to hear him tell her the truth, and how uncertain she'd been he ever would. "H-how long have you known? Since she first appeared?"

He shook his head. "No. Until a few days ago I thought the White Lady was just another rumor invented by the Edenbridge gossips. I still don't know what she's doing here—she's meant to be marrying the Marquess of Aviemore in a few months. I foolishly allowed myself to believe we were safe from her until Miss Honeywell saw her. Then I realized there really was a White Lady. I knew then it must be Leanora."

It made sense. Fanny Honeywell had no reason to lie about it, and every reason not to, given how determined her mother was for her to become Marchioness of Darlington.

"I believe she's come back to take Isabella. She's…not well, Cecilia. I didn't want you to venture out because I can't be certain what she'll do, or how far she'll go. Until tonight, I never believed she'd hurt anyone, but it must have been her who locked you in the kitchen garden." Gideon met her gaze, his eyes bleak. "You might have frozen out there."

"But I didn't, Gideon. I'm perfectly well, as you can see. I climbed up the limbs of an espaliered apple tree to get out. That's how I cut myself." Cecilia tried a smile. "I did tell you I'm much heartier than I look, didn't I?"

Gideon's lips twisted into something that wasn't quite a smile, but it was close. "You did, yes. I should have listened to you."

"Certainly, you should have." Cecilia settled against the pillows at her back with a huff. "Let that be a lesson to you, Lord Darlington."

"It's not the first lesson you've taught me. Not the last either, I imagine." Gideon's lips quirked in a smile, a real one this time.

"No, likely not." Cecilia grinned at him, nestling further into his bed. It was warm and soft, the fire crackling in the grate, and Gideon…he was here, with her, so close she could touch him. "Your bedchamber is much warmer than mine. May I stay here with you tonight?"

He laughed softly. His eyes, such a deep blue tonight, drifted over her, and a smile of pure masculine satisfaction crossed his lips. "Did you think I'd let you go? I like seeing you in my bed."

Cecilia shivered at the low rumble of his voice, the heat in those deep blue eyes that seemed to stroke every inch of her skin until the last vestiges of cold and fear still lingering in her body turned to pulsing warmth.

He watched every shift in her expression, every breath she took as he stripped off his cloak and tossed it onto a chair near the bed. His riding coat followed, and then he set to work on his cravat, his long fingers working the knot until the length of white linen unraveled. He slid it free from his neck and wound it around his hand, his gaze still holding hers.

Cecilia's breath caught as he tossed the cravat aside and moved his hands to his waist. He tugged his shirt free of his breeches, but paused, his fingers toying with the hem as he waited to see if she'd object.

She didn't. Her teeth sank into her lower lip, her breath quickening as she watched him.

The white cotton clung damply to his skin as he dragged it up his torso and over his head, and then the muscular chest that had so fascinated her that first morning at Darlington Castle emerged, bare, sleek skin pulled over taut muscles, that smattering of dark hair, thicker in the center of his chest and around his navel before vanishing in a tempting line into the waist of his breeches.

Cecilia waited for him to come to her, to join her in the bed, to stretch out beside her and press his body to hers. Her fingertips ached to stroke his bare skin, but he paused beside the bed to take her chin gently between his fingers, and raise her face to his.

"Look at me, Cecilia." His deep blue gaze flickered over her features, lingering on her parted lips, the flush on her cheeks, the madly beating pulse at the hollow of her throat.

She wrapped her fingers around his wrist. "Come to bed, Gideon. Come keep me warm."

His eyes slid closed, and he drew in a long, shaky breath. Cecilia understood then he'd been waiting for her invitation, for her to welcome him. Her heart squeezed in her chest, a wrench both painful and sweet, and then she was in his arms, her cheek pressed to his warm skin, his steady heartbeat a rhythmic thump in her ear.

They were quiet for a time. Gideon ran his fingers through her hair in long, sensuous strokes, raising goosebumps over every inch of her skin. Finally, she lifted her head to glance up at him. "You—you're not angry with me?"

"Not at the moment, no. I make no promises for tomorrow." He nuzzled her neck, the rough stubble on his face scraping her sensitive skin.

Cecilia dragged her fingertips down his chest to his stomach, a small smile rising to her lips as his muscles tensed under the caress. Her skin felt as if it were about to burst into flames everywhere their bodies touched. She closed her eyes to savor the slow movement of Gideon's hand in her hair. She listened to the crackle of the fire, and, just for now, she let herself float in his warmth, his touch, the crisp, masculine scent of his skin.

She should have fallen asleep, but even as the languorous warmth stole over her and her limbs melted against his, she remained awake, every inch of her alive and clamoring for his touch, a strange, hot knot pulled tight inside her lower belly.

"When I arrived home tonight and Amy said you were missing, I think I…went a little mad." Gideon curled his big hand around her hip and pulled her tighter against him. "I was afraid for you. I…I can't lose you. I'm in love with you, Cecilia."

His voice was quiet, but his body was shaking against hers. Gideon, the strongest man she'd ever known, was *shaking* at the thought of losing her. Cecilia could feel his love for her in the way he held her, the break in his voice, the pounding of his heart against her ear.

Tears sprang to her eyes at the sweetness of him, this man who'd lost so much, yet could still feel so deeply, love so fiercely. She thought, fleetingly, of the Gothic romances she'd read, the lovers she'd found between the pages of her books, and wondered how she hadn't realized, the moment she set foot in Darlington Castle, that Gideon wasn't the villain, but the hero.

This was love. Love for a real, flesh-and-blood man who'd suffered unspeakable loss and grief, a man who had every reason to be bitter and angry, but still had the courage and strength to love again. "I love you too, Gideon." She pressed a fervent kiss to the center of his chest. "I'm in love with you."

Gideon's breath caught, then his chest moved underneath her cheek in a sigh, as if he'd waited an eternity for those words. "Sweetheart," he whispered, dropping a soft kiss on her temple.

Cecilia clung to him, joy and love and despair gathering like a storm inside her, both beautiful and heartbreaking at once. This love was more than anything she ever imagined love could be. She wanted to give him everything. All she carried inside her, everything she had, and everything she was, was his.

But it wouldn't matter, in the end. He *would* lose her, or maybe it made more sense to say she'd lose him. They'd lose each other, because she'd lied to him about who she was, and her reasons for coming to Darlington Castle. Even if there hadn't been lies between them, they came from two different worlds.

But now, tonight—just for this one night—she could make it matter. She raised her head from his chest and propped it on her hand. "Gideon, I…"

She fell silent, her tongue suddenly shy. What was she meant to say? She'd never been with a man before. Before Gideon, she'd never even kissed a man. She hadn't any idea how to tell him she wanted him.

But perhaps he already knew. Cecilia's lips curved. She was in his bed, clad in nothing but her night rail. Perhaps she didn't need to say anything more.

"That's an intriguing little smile." Gideon's gaze dropped to her mouth. He traced his thumb over her lower lip, but he made no move to kiss her.

So she reached for him, curling her hand around his jaw before dragging it slowly over his neck, and down his throat to his chest, the springy hairs tickling her palm. He watched her, his eyelids growing heavy as she eased her hands down his chest to his abdomen.

She trailed a finger over the skin just above the waistband of his breeches, but he caught her hand, stilling her. "Do you know what you're doing, love?"

"Well, no." She laughed softly, her hand still caressing his skin. "I was rather hoping *you* did."

He dragged his knuckles down her cheek. He gazed at her for a long time without speaking, his blue eyes filled with heat and shadows. "I know this. If you stay here with me in my bed tonight, I won't let you go until I've made you mine."

His.

She'd never wanted anything more, and she told him so, in the best way she knew how—by gently pulling his hand from her face and placing a sweet, gentle kiss in the center of his palm.

Gideon went still for an instant, his body tensing, and then with a low growl he took her face in his hands, sank his fingers into her hair, and brought his mouth down on hers.

He kissed her like a drowning man gulps air into his lungs. Roughly, desperately at first, and then softer, tender, his mouth clinging to hers as he prodded delicately at the seam of her lips with the tip of his tongue, seeking entrance.

Cecilia didn't hesitate. She twined her arms around his neck, pulled him closer, and opened her mouth under his.

He groaned in response and gathered her closer, nibbling and teasing at her lips until she went limp against him, boneless and breathless and *stunned*, that anything could feel as good as his mouth on hers, the angles of his warm, hard body pressing so perfectly into her soft curves there was no space left between them.

He kissed her again and again, until everything—the bedchamber around them, the crackle of the fire, his past, and their doomed future—faded from existence, and all she knew was the warmth of him, the hot, slick slide of his tongue, his sharp intake of breath when she let her fingernails graze the bare skin of his back.

"Ah God, sweetheart, you're so..."

Cecilia never found out what she was, but it didn't matter, because he was easing her back against the bed, his legs tangling with hers, one thick, hard thigh settling between hers as he moved over her, so close, but careful not to crush her with his weight.

"You need to be kissed everywhere. Every inch of you. Here." He dropped a tiny kiss at one corner of her mouth, then the other. "Here," he went on, raining sweet, open-mouthed kisses on her eyelids and cheeks, the pulse point at her throat. "And here," he whispered, scraping his teeth lightly over her neck.

"*Gideon.*" Cecilia squirmed when his teeth closed over her earlobe, but her surprised gasp turned to a moan as he tugged gently, his warm breath in her ear as he toyed and played with her sensitive flesh. She sank her hands into his hair, wringing a hungry groan from his lips with each tug on the thick, dark strands.

When she couldn't stand his teasing any longer, Cecilia guided his head gently down, down, down until his cheek was resting over her heart. "Kiss me here, Gideon," she whispered, bringing his hand to the curve of her breast.

He let out a soft groan before cupping her breast in his palm. "You're so pretty here, love, so perfect," he murmured as he teased her nipple with his thumb, dragging it back and forth across the tender nub until it hardened and darkened to a deep pink, the blushing tip easily visible under the thin covering of her night rail. He pulled back to gaze down at her, his breath ragged, seemingly mesmerized by her breasts, by her nipple straining for his caresses. "Oh, yes, you need to be kissed here." He licked his lips, hovering for a long, teasing moment over her before he leaned down and drew her nipple into his mouth.

Cecilia gasped and sank her trembling fingers into his hair to hold him against her. Dear God, his mouth was so hot, so insistent as he sucked and licked at her. He dallied there for long, breathless moments, wetting the fabric of her night rail before drawing back to gaze at her with hot blue eyes. He hung over her, a red flush across his cheekbones. "God, look at you, love, so hard, straining for me. Do you like my mouth on you?"

"*Yes*. Please." She urged him back down to her breasts, crying out when he took her deep into the heated cavern of his mouth again, suckling and drawing mercilessly on one nipple while he stroked the other with his thumb. This exquisite torture went on and on until both her nipples were flushed and peaked for him, and Cecilia was squirming against the bed, unable to contain her breathless cries and whimpers.

She might have blushed at her wantonness if Gideon hadn't been as wild as she was. By the time he relinquished her breasts with one last lingering stroke with his tongue, he was moving against her, thrusting subtly. His chest was covered with a fine sheen of sweat, and his breaths sawed in and out of his chest. He didn't appear aware he was doing it, his hips moving in mindless, desperate arousal until she reached down between them and, with one careful flick of her fingers, slipped open the buttons on his breeches.

He froze then, swallowing. "Cecilia, are you sure you're…is this what you want?"

She smiled and reached up to tug gently on a disheveled lock of his dark hair. He looked so young and boyish with it falling into his eyes, and it was so soft, she wanted to play with it forever, to wake up with her fingers buried in those thick waves. "Yes. I want *you*, Gideon." She didn't hesitate, but took his hand and dragged it down her thigh to the hem of her night rail, and closed his fingers around it.

He paused just long enough to draw in a deep breath before he caught a handful of the fragile linen and drew it up her legs, the fluttering cloth tickling her belly and dragging across her tender nipples before he drew it over her head and tossed it over the side of the bed.

Cecilia fell back against the pillows with a shy smile as Gideon gazed down at her, his breath not quite steady as he took her in with feverish blue eyes. "Is that a blush, sweetheart?" A soft smile crossed his lips as he touched gentle fingers to her cheek. "Here, and here, too." He followed the sweep of pink from her face down her neck, his smile fading as it swept over her breasts and lower, lower…

"Such perfect skin," he murmured as he splayed his big hand over her lower belly. "So soft and white, but for that sweet blush."

Cecilia couldn't speak, couldn't move, could only gaze up at him, mesmerized by his murmurs and the gentle stroke of his hands over her skin. He couldn't seem to get enough of her, touching her everywhere— her neck and shoulders, the tender skin under her breasts, the soft swell of her belly, until at last his hands settled on the inside of her thighs and he eased them gently apart.

He caught his breath as he looked at her center, his big, strong hands holding her open for his gaze. Cecilia felt her blush deepen, but it never occurred to her to try and cover herself, or push him away. She *wanted* him to look at her, *wanted* to see the desire in his eyes as he gazed down at her.

"God, look at you, so pink and beautiful here." He toyed with the dark curls between her thighs, his blue eyes hot, and then, before Cecilia realized what he meant to do, he brushed his thumb over her damp center.

"Ah!" She arched underneath him as heat pooled in her belly.

Gideon's gaze darted to her face, and a small smile rose to his lips. "Yes, that's right. No, don't do that, sweetheart." Cecilia had pressed the back of her hand against her mouth to smother her cries, but he reached up and tugged it gently away. "I want to hear you cry out for me."

Cecilia's blush seared her skin. She didn't know whether it was embarrassment or arousal, but when Gideon took both her wrists in his hand and drew them over her head, she kept them there, and soon enough whatever embarrassment she felt gave way to a desire unlike anything she'd ever known before.

Gideon dragged his thumb through her folds again, then again, watching her face and crooning to her as he slowly drove her mad.

His touch was light at first, soft—just the tip of his thumb brushing against the tender bud at her center, but as her soft moans grew desperate, he touched her with more deliberation, circling the straining nub over and over again, teasing and stroking it, his touch still maddeningly light, but faster now. "You look so beautiful like this, Cecilia. So wet for me."

Small, helpless cries tore from Cecilia's lips as he increased the pressure, his slippery fingers working her, gliding over her center. Her hips began to move in the same rhythm as his hands, chasing his touch until a low growl rumbled in his chest.

Cecilia cried out in protest when he withdrew his hand, leaving her open and throbbing for his touch. "No!" She tried to grab his wrist, but he was already lying flat on his stomach on the bed. She felt his hot breath drift over her aching core, and his palms against the insides of her thighs. "Open wider for me, sweetheart," he demanded, his voice harsh and tight. "Yes, like that. That's what I want."

A fleeting thought flew through Cecilia's head—that she would have given him anything he asked for at that moment, anything he wanted, but it was gone again in an instant when she felt something fluttering against her...*there*...a soft tickle, the flick of the tip of his tongue, quickly, once, then again, and then...God, over and over again, teasing and stroking and making her wild for him, her hips arching to get closer to his teasing mouth.

She whimpered and moaned and cried out for him, and Gideon gave her what she wanted, what she needed, and more—all the things she didn't know she wanted, didn't know she needed. His hot, panting breaths, his tongue and lips, kissing and nibbling and sucking at her, his low, crooning voice telling her how beautiful and perfect she was, and urging her to take what she needed, take her pleasure...

Then she was falling, tumbling over the edge into a bliss she'd never known before, sharp and sweet at once, and Gideon stayed with her, his hands holding her hips to the bed as he took her through the delirium, his mouth gentling and slowing as the peak passed and the knot inside her unraveled, slow and so sweet, until she was lying boneless against the bed, half dazed, Gideon's head resting on her belly, and her hands in his hair.

It was some time before Cecilia came back to herself, but at last her breathing calmed, and she was able to raise her head. Gideon looked up when he felt her shift, and a satisfied smile curved his lips when he saw her face. "Are you...was that all right?"

An incredulous laugh left Cecilia's lips, and she gave his hair a playful tug. "Was it all right? It was a good deal better than all right, although I may never move again."

Gideon's smile widened, as if he was pleased to find he'd rendered her comatose. He lifted his head from her belly as she held out her arms to him, and he shimmied up the bed to gather her close. He pressed a kiss on her forehead, then eased her head against his chest. "Go to sleep, sweetheart."

Sleep? But surely, that wasn't...all?

No, at one time she might have thought so, but she *did* live in London, and she was one of Lady Clifford's pupils. She'd seen a number of things another young woman might not have, and heard even more. Whatever few mysteries remained had been dispelled by Sophia, after her marriage to Lord Gray.

Cecilia knew very well the long, hard length Gideon was trying to keep from prodding into her hip meant he hadn't taken his pleasure, and that he was certainly suffering now because of it. She also knew he was attempting to be decent and noble, the ridiculous man.

Well, she wouldn't have it. The bedroom was no place for decency and nobility.

Cecilia raised her head from Gideon's chest, and before he knew what she was about she'd scrambled to her knees. Her expression must have given her away, because Gideon's eyes widened as his gaze met hers. "Cecilia, what are you—"

"I'm not ready to sleep yet." She braced her hands on his chest, and with one quick move settled herself on top of him, her thighs straddling his hips. Her gaze moved hungrily over his bare chest and flat stomach. "I'm not tired," she murmured, teasing her fingers through the line of dark hair that disappeared into his breeches.

His mouth opened, but he struggled to get any words past his lips as his heated gaze moved slowly over her bare, flushed skin, lingering on the curves of her breasts. "I-I don't think we should…"

He trailed off to watch, mesmerized, as she played with that trail of springy hair on his belly, her fingernails scraping lightly against his bare skin, until she slipped her hand under the waistband of his breeches and drew him out, hard and aching, from the crumpled folds of his falls. "*Cecilia…*" he swallowed, his gaze meeting hers.

"I'm awake, Gideon." Cecilia hesitated, shyness overtaking her, but his long, hard length was throbbing against her palm, and the need in his eyes, the ragged edge to his breath decided her. "I've never been wider awake in my life," she murmured, as she began to caress him.

"Cecilia, I…*ah*." Gideon broke off with a gasp as she dragged her hand up and then down again, her eyes opening in wonder at the slide of that thin, silky skin over the heated length beneath. She bit her lip as she met his gaze. "Is this right?"

Gideon stared up at her, his eyelids falling to half-mast and his lips parting as she kept stroking him. "Yes," he choked out on a low groan. He shifted underneath her, spreading his thighs wider as if he couldn't stop himself. "It's so good, sweetheart."

He didn't need to say anything more. His body—his broken moans, his strangled breaths—told her everything she needed to know. Cecilia tightened her grip around him and watched, transfixed, as he began to meet her every stroke with a subtle thrust of his hips. Cecilia slid her thumb up to circle his tip, her tongue darting out to touch her bottom lip when his hips jerked. "I could watch you like this all—*oh!*"

A groan tore from his lips, and the next thing Cecilia knew she was on her back with a large, aroused marquess on top of her, nudging her legs apart with his hips. "Do you want me, Cecilia?" He slipped his hand between her thighs and parted her swollen flesh with gentle fingers to stroke her. "Do you want me here?"

"Yes." Cecilia sighed, twining her arms around his neck. "I want all of you."

Gideon's body was taut with leashed desire, but he held back, his lips in her hair and on her neck and breasts, circling and rubbing her eager nub, tearing whimpers from her throat. He waited until she was thrashing against the bed before he slipped one long finger inside her.

Cecilia's mouth sought his as she arched into his touch. "Gideon, please."

"Shh. I've got you." He pressed a tender kiss to her lips, but still he took his time, reducing her to quivering flesh until at last…dear God, *yes*, at last…with a guttural groan he eased the tip of his hard length inside her. He paused when he met resistance, his every muscle tensing with the effort to remain still. "Don't want to hurt you."

"No, don't stop." Cecilia arched against him, clawing at his sweat-slick back. Gideon groaned again, then with a quick shift of his hips, thrust inside. Cecilia gasped at the sharp burst of pain, but Gideon crooned to her through his panting breaths until the pain faded, and her body eased around him.

He pulled back to gaze down into her face, his beautiful blue eyes dark with concern. He started to speak, but Cecilia touched her fingers to his lips, hushing him. "I need you, Gideon."

His eyes slid closed for an instant, and then…then he began to move. Slow, careful nudges until his gentle thrusts weren't enough, and Cecilia wrapped her legs around his hips to urge him on. "More."

A desperate groan tore from Gideon's lips as he surged forward. Cecilia sank her fingernails into his shoulders, a needy cry on her lips. His heated length seemed to swell inside her then, pushing her closer toward that mindless pleasure with each thrust. "Oh, oh…oh, please." She clung to him, that delicious heat pulling tighter until with a fierce thrust of Gideon's hips, it exploded inside her.

"That's it, Cecilia. Come for me, sweetheart—" Gideon broke off with a gasp and buried his face in her neck as the tight, hot grip of her body hurled him into his own release. He clutched her against him until their bodies stopped trembling, then he raised himself up and drew back to look into her face. "Now are you ready to go to sleep?" he asked, his lips quirked.

Cecilia's body was flushed, languid, her limbs so heavy with satisfaction she wondered if her bones had melted, but she returned Gideon's smile with a sleepy one of her own. "Yes, my lord."

He chuckled, and brushed the damp hair back from her forehead. "Ah, dutiful at last."

He took her lips in a kiss so sweet it made Cecilia's eyes sting, then gathered her against his chest and wrapped his arms around her. She fell asleep to his hand drifting through her hair, and his heartbeat in her ear.

Chapter Twenty-three

Gideon didn't sleep that night, but for the first time since Cassandra's death, it wasn't because worry and grief kept him awake, or tumbled him in and out of nightmares.

It was because he didn't want to miss a moment of holding Cecilia in his arms.

He tucked her close, her head nestled against his shoulder and her dark hair spread in wild disarray across his chest. He stroked her back, his fingers learning the smooth, soft texture of her skin, the way her thick eyelashes fluttered against her cheeks as she slept.

She woke before dawn, her eyelids lifting over sleepy dark eyes.

"You're in my bedchamber, and…my bed," Gideon murmured as soon as she focused her drowsy gaze on him. He'd half expected her to wake in a panic, unsure where she was, but she looked far from panicking as her lips curved into a soft smile.

"I know." Her warm breath drifted over his skin, and she trailed her soft hand down his chest, tugging gently on the whorls of dark hair there. "I remember." Her smile turned teasing. "Did you think I could forget last night, my lord?"

That teasing smile, her heavy-lidded eyes and flushed skin, the nimble fingers stroking his chest—Gideon took a long, slow breath and prayed for strength. She wasn't his countess yet. As far as anyone at Darlington Castle was concerned, Cecilia was still Isabella's nursemaid, and Gideon wasn't a gentleman who debauched his servants.

At least, he didn't do it *twice.*

Cecilia, however, had other ideas. "This is very nice, right here." She squirmed closer, her fingers playing over his chest.

Gideon caught her hand in his to still it. "What, my chest hair? You do seem fascinated with it."

"I am. It's softer than I would have thought. But it's not just that." She tugged her hand free and resumed stroking, a slow, maddening slide over his chest and down his body, her curious fingers sifting through the trail of hair under his navel. "It's all of you. All muscle and long, elegant bones." She traced her fingertips over his collarbones. "Every inch of you is lean and hard."

And growing harder by the minute.

Gideon tried to hold still, but his body grew more impatient with her every slow, sweeping stroke over his eager skin. It had been so long since he'd been touched, so long since he'd held a woman's body next to his own.

So long since he'd given up on love...

He moaned when her fingertips grazed his nipple. "Cecilia—"

She did it again, a gentle tweak that made his eyes roll back in his head. "Oh. You like that, too. I've never...no man has ever touched me there before."

An instinctive growl rumbled in Gideon's chest at the mere thought of another man touching her. "No other man ever will."

Cecilia's hand stilled, and she peeked up at him from under her lashes. "Is that so, Lord Darlington?"

"It is." Gideon reached for her hand and pressed a kiss to her palm.

"Are you this possessive with all your servants?" She leaned over him and pressed a kiss to the center of his chest.

"No," Gideon bit out, gritting his teeth against the pleasure of her warm lips exploring his flesh. "But it's been some time since I regarded you as my servant, if I ever did."

"Hmmm." Cecilia didn't appear to be listening to him. She nipped at his chest, pressed an experimental kiss to his nipple, then drew back to study the effect. "Oh." Her eyes widened when it hardened, then her lips curved with an impish smile. She kissed him there again, lingering this time, then drew back and ran her thumb over the damp peak.

"Ah, God." Gideon's breath left his lungs in a rush, blood pooling between his legs, fierce desire unfurling in his belly. He was doing his best not to writhe under her touch, but his cock was hardening, twitching insistently against the coverlet.

Cecilia watched in fascination as the touch of her fingers and lips made it jerk and strain for her. She licked delicately at his nipple, like a cat licking up cream, tearing one low groan after another from his throat.

When she lifted her head at last, his nipple was hard and aching, and his entire body was flushed with arousal. She gazed at him with heavy-lidded eyes, as if she were contemplating what to do with him next.

Gideon let out a broken moan as she slid her hand down his belly and under the edge of the coverlet, and took his straining length into her small hand. His hips gave a helpless thrust, all thought of restraint dissolving as he pushed his cock into her fist.

She sank her teeth into her lip. "May I stroke you?"

Gideon's battle with his conscience was a brief one. He simply wanted her too much to resist. "Please." His voice was hoarse.

Her lips parted as she began a slow, languid stroking.

Gideon arched into the caress, which was somehow both too much and not enough at once. "Harder, love, like this." He closed his hand over hers and showed her how he liked to be touched. "Yes," he hissed, his hand falling away as her fingers tightened around him, giving him the firm, fast strokes he needed. "Run your thumb over the head," he begged in a choked whisper.

Cecilia circled the slippery head with a dainty thumb, her cheeks flushed with arousal as she watched him jerk and moan beneath her. "Tell me what you want, Gideon. I want to see you...I love watching you like this."

Gideon arched his neck, tipping his head back against the pillow as her caresses grew bolder, her firm, slow strokes enough to drive him mad, but not enough to satisfy. It went on for what seemed an eternity to Gideon, one tormenting stroke after another until his chest was sheened with sweat and he was thrashing against the bed, incoherent pleas falling from his lips.

"Come here, love. Yes, like that." Unable to stand it any longer, Gideon grasped her hips and eased her down on top of him. "Closer, sweetheart, so you're...ah, God, yes. Yes, Cecilia," he moaned when she was straddling him, her damp core nudging against his straining cock. "Let me just..."

Cecilia braced her hands on his chest, her breath coming in short gasps as he slid his fingers through her silky folds. "Gideon," she moaned when his thumb brushed against the aching nub at her center. "Gideon, please," she panted as he circled and plucked at the sensitive bud.

"So wet, Cecilia. You're so wet for me." He rubbed and stroked her until her hips began moving in an insistent rhythm, then he held her steady and positioned her over his throbbing cock. "Come down on me, Cecilia... slowly, sweetheart. Take your time."

Gideon gritted his teeth as she lowered herself onto him, fighting the urge to thrust into her seductive heat. But he held back, his hands shaking as she took him inside, her mouth opening in wonder as he slid deeper, one torturous inch at a time.

They both sighed when he was seated all the way inside her at last.

Gideon moved his hips in a restrained, shallow thrust, his gaze fixed on her face as he did, gauging her reaction. Her lips parted on a gasp, her body tightening instinctively around him. He thrust upward again, his eyes closing at the hot grip of her body around his cock. "Is it good? I'm not hurting you, am I?"

She shook her head, her eyes dazed as she gazed down at him. "No, I need…do it again."

Gideon groaned as he thrust into her damp heat, setting an easy rhythm. "Move with me," he whispered, his hands on her hips guiding her, showing her how to meet his thrusts. "Yes. So perfect, Cecilia."

Her fingers curled into the slick skin of his chest as she quickened their pace. Gideon surged into her, his climax coiling in the base of his spine, but he held off, fighting against the pleasure that threatened to rush over him. "Take your pleasure, love," he begged, working his hips against hers.

"Gideon, please, please…" Cecilia let out a cry and closed her eyes, throwing her head back as her release swept over her. Her body clenched around him, the sweet pressure tearing a guttural moan from his lips as his climax pounded through him. He held her tightly against him as they rode out their release.

When Cecilia went limp, sagging against him, Gideon gathered her into his arms and eased her onto her side. He buried his face in the damp hair at the back of her neck and draped a possessive hand around her soft belly. They fell asleep curled around each other, Gideon's lips pressed to her nape.

They dozed for a bit—not long, perhaps an hour or so. When Gideon woke again it was dark still, but he could hear the faint stirring of the servants as they woke and began their work for the day.

Cecilia was awake, her hands folded on his stomach and her chin resting on her hands. "I should return to my bedchamber before someone appears to lay a fire for you."

"Soon." He reached for her and gathered her close, burying his face in her hair. "Not yet."

She sighed, but nestled into his arms and let him hold her until they heard the sound of doors opening and closing, and Mrs. Briggs's voice in the downstairs hallway.

"Gideon." Cecilia gently disentangled herself from his arms and slipped out of the bed, draping the coverlet over herself as she reached down and snatched her night rail from the floor. "I can't be here when Amy comes in."

"No." Gideon didn't argue, though he wanted to weep with frustration as all the smooth, pale skin he'd caressed disappeared under her night rail. "Wait, Cecilia. Promise me you'll remain in your bedchamber today."

"My *bedchamber*?" Cecilia had crept across the room to the connecting door, but she turned back, a frown on her face. "Gideon, that's absurd. I have work to—"

"No, you don't. Not today. You nearly froze last night. You need to rest today."

Cecilia braced her hands on her hips. "I take back what I said that first day about you not looking like a marquess, Gideon. You look quite lordly when you're ordering people about."

"Then you won't dare to disobey me, will you?" When Cecilia didn't answer, his eyes narrowed. "Cecilia. Promise me—"

"I promise I won't leave the castle. Can you make do with that?"

Gideon was about to refuse, but she gave him a winning smile, and he shook his head, a return smile rising to his lips in spite of himself. "You promise it? Not one toe over the threshold?"

"Not a single toe. I swear it."

Gideon didn't like it, but he gave a reluctant nod. She'd be safe as long as she didn't wander the grounds. "All right. Haslemere and I have business to attend to that will keep us out all day. We'll return for dinner, and when we do, I intend to find you and ask if you've kept your promise."

"Yes, my lord. As you wish, my lord." She gave him a mischievous smile, but he must have looked as forlorn as he felt because her eyes softened, and she darted across his bedchamber, hopped onto the bed, and pressed a quick kiss to his lips before darting away again.

"It's fortunate you're so quick. If I'd caught you, I wouldn't let you go again." He gave her what he knew to be a ridiculously foolish, infatuated smile, and waved his hand toward the door. "Go on then, before I change my mind."

* * * *

Cecilia did *not* break her promise to Gideon. Not this time.

She might have done so easily enough. By the time she pulled her gray work dress over her head, donned her apron, and bid Amy and Isabella a good morning, Gideon and Lord Haslemere were gone. Mrs. Briggs insisted she rest after her ordeal the night before, and chased her out of the kitchen after breakfast, so by mid-morning Cecilia found herself with a rare empty day on her hands.

It couldn't have come at a better time.

Darlington Castle's library was an impressive one. The bookshelves towered over Cecilia, stretching from the floor all the way to the ceiling. If she hadn't had the great good luck to spy *Culpeper's Complete Herbal* when she went searching for Mrs. Radcliffe the other night, she likely never would have found it among the thousands of exquisitely bound books.

But it was right where she'd last seen it, lying on its side on the end of one of the lower shelves. She sat at the table with the thick tome, and rummaged around in her apron pockets for the plants she'd picked in the kitchen garden last night. They were wilted and shrunken, much as she'd expected them to be, but she was certain she'd recognize a picture of them when she saw it. The trouble was, she had no idea what the plants were called, so she'd have to go through the entirety of *Culpeper's Complete Herbal* until she spotted them.

All four hundred and eleven pages of it.

Each entry included a detailed illustration of the herb, but it might take hours for her to find the illustration she needed. So, she settled in, her wilted stalks on the table beside her as she flipped through one page after the next, searching for the spiky purple plant.

In the end, it didn't take hours. Just when she was certain she'd go cross-eyed if she had to study another illustration, she found what she was looking for. Green stalks, spear-shaped leaves, topped by a spiky purple flower like a fuzzy starburst.

Pennyroyal.

She leaned over the book to read the page. The entry was brief, as all the entries were, but by the time she came to the end of the short series of paragraphs, her blood had turned to ice in her veins.

...it provokes women's courses, and expels the dead child and after-birth.

Cecilia read it again, then again to be sure she hadn't confused the words, or somehow misunderstood.

Being boiled and drank, it provokes women's courses, and expels the dead child...

The tea Mrs. Briggs had mentioned hadn't been spearmint at all, but pennyroyal. Cecilia slapped a hand over her mouth as a horrible, sick feeling twisted in her stomach. An herb such as this, that brought on bleeding...

What might it do to a lady carrying a healthy child? What might it do to the *child*?

She blinked blindly down at the page, tears blurring her eyes, because she knew…she already knew. Cassandra and Gideon's child, their son…someone had seen to it he'd never draw breath, and they'd taken Cassandra away too, ensuring she'd be laid in the cold ground before she ever conceived another child.

Cecilia pressed her hand tighter against her lips as bile flooded her throat, gagging her. Dear God, she was going to be sick. She gripped the edge of the table, and sat for a long time, the library swimming around her, until at last she gained control of herself. She stared down at the book open on the table before her, not seeing it, her mind working to untangle the interwoven threads of the mystery of Cassandra's death.

Ugly questions, and even uglier answers, but in the end, there was only one question that mattered. Who at Darlington Castle stood to gain the most if the Marchioness of Darlington died before she could give birth to her child?

Not Gideon, and not any of the servants.

No one else had been at the castle during Cassandra's illness and death but Lady Leanora.

But why would she want to hurt Cassandra or her child? From what Mrs. Briggs had said, Lady Leanora hadn't even been permitted in the sick room during Cassandra's illness. It didn't make sense, unless…

They grew apart somewhat after Cassandra became the marchioness.

Cecilia tapped her palm against her forehead, trying to think. There was nothing so sinister in Lady Leanora's being jealous of Cassandra once she was elevated to marchioness, but could she have been so jealous she'd have poisoned her own cousin?

No, surely not, but then…

There was one odd thing that had struck Cecilia about Cassandra's diary. She'd hardly said a single word about Lady Leanora.

Cassandra had mentioned Isabella hundreds of times, and Gideon twice as many as that. She could hardly put pen to paper without saying how grateful she was for them both. She wrote constantly of the people she loved, including Mrs. Briggs and the other servants.

The one person whose name rarely came up in those pages was Lady Leanora's.

Cecilia thought of Lady Leanora's portrait in the small picture gallery—of her haughty expression, the petulant curve of her lip—and wondered how such a lady would have reacted to her cousin's sudden elevation in rank. Cassandra had come to Darlington Castle as Lady Leanora's lowly companion, and six months later she'd supplanted her as its mistress.

Still, jealousy was one thing, and murder quite another. In any case, Cecilia strongly suspected it was the pennyroyal tea that had killed Cassandra, and according to Mrs. Briggs, it had been Gideon who brought Cassandra's broth and tea on her dinner tray every night, so how—

But no, that *wasn't* what she'd said, was it? A chill rushed over Cecilia's skin as she recalled precisely what Mrs. Briggs had told her.

Lord Darlington brought her a tray of broth every night at dinnertime... only thing she ever touched was the spearmint tea he gave her much later in the evening, to help her sleep.

The way Mrs. Briggs had described it, the tea hadn't been on the dinner tray with the broth. Had anyone actually *seen* Gideon give Cassandra that tea? Mrs. Briggs had only mentioned seeing the teacup with the dregs of the tea when she'd taken the dishes down the next morning.

Could it be Gideon had only given Cassandra the broth, and someone else had given her the tea? Someone like Lady Leanora, for instance?

But *why*? Why would Lady Leanora go to such lengths to poison her cousin, and when would she have had the opportunity? Gideon was the only one permitted in Cassandra's bedchamber. Lady Leanora could have crept past him and the staff, of course. But there'd been a great many people in the castle back then, and whoever had administered the poison would have had to sneak into Cassandra's bedchamber every night for months. Surely, someone would have seen her?

Lady Leanora as the evil villainess didn't quite fall into place, yet Cecilia's brain had seized on it with a familiar dogged determination born of instinct. She couldn't let it go. Her hands were shaking as she rose from her chair and replaced the book on the shelf. She hurried down the deserted corridor, surprised to find she'd been in the library for hours, and the afternoon was waning.

The stillroom was through an arched door off the back of the kitchen and down a narrow stone hallway that let out onto the kitchen garden. Cecilia had never ventured inside it. Given the shortage of servants, no one seemed to make much use of it anymore, but Lady Leanora would have been mistress of it in the years she'd been the lady of the castle.

It was much like every other stillroom Cecilia had ever seen, but bigger and grander, with a large stone fireplace at one end, and a huge cabinet made up of neat little drawers and topped with a counter that ran the entire length of one wall. Beside the counter was a long table with a dusty wooden top, likely put there for mixing herbs.

There was no window, but the beamed ceilings were high, to help disperse any smoke from the kitchens, and dried herbs were hung from the beams. Cecilia reached up to pinch a few leaves from one of the bundles. She crumbled the leaves between her fingers, raised them to her nose, and inhaled the woody scent of rosemary.

She wandered to the cabinet, opened a few of the drawers, and peered inside. Fennel, sage, comfrey—the usual herbs one would expect to find in a stillroom. Another drawer held bunches of lavender wrapped in silk and tied with string, sachets for scenting drawers or closets, and a few bottles lined up on the counter held lavender oil, the scent faded now.

There was nothing unusual or sinister in any of it. Even if she did find pennyroyal, it wouldn't prove anything. According to Culpeper, it had a number of perfectly innocent medicinal uses, and many households favored an herb with such a strong scent of spearmint for use in soap.

Cecilia turned in a circle, rubbing her hands up and down her arms. The stillroom fire hadn't been lit in months, but for a room right off the kitchen it was colder than it should be.

The draft was coming from this side of the room. The temperature here was at least a degree or two colder than the side closest to the kitchen. Not so surprising, perhaps, given all the cooking that took place there, yet Cassandra's bedchamber was cold in this same drafty way, as if a window or door had been left open. But where? There was no window in this room, and only the one door—

She crossed to the door that led out into the kitchen garden, thinking the draft must be coming from there, but a quick inspection revealed it to be locked and tightly sealed. Well, perhaps it wasn't all that mysterious. Castles were drafty places. She turned from the door with a sigh and made her way back across the stillroom toward the kitchen.

That was when she saw it. Hidden in a shallow alcove in the darkest and coldest part of the room was a stack of wooden boxes containing messy piles of glass jars, and behind it...

Behind it was the edge of a door. Only the merest sliver of it was visible—if she'd blinked, she would have missed it. She approached the stack of wooden crates, her heart pounding. They looked heavy, much too heavy for her to move them, but just as she was trying to make up her mind whether to fetch Duncan or not, she noticed the dust pattern on the floor.

Grime had accumulated over every surface in the abandoned stillroom, and the floor was no exception, but there was a wide space just in front of the boxes that was clear of dust and dirt, as if someone had shoved the crates out of the way of the door, leaving a length of bare floor.

Cecilia nudged her toe against the corner of one of the crates, and to her surprise, it shifted easily out of her way. A quick rummage through them soon revealed why. The jars had been carefully arranged along the tops of the crates, but underneath they were filled with sawdust and hay.

Cecilia pushed them aside just enough to slip behind them. There was a bolt lock on this side of the door, but it wasn't bolted. Just as she went to open it, she noticed a smear of something white on the iron latch. She touched it, then rubbed the substance between her fingers and thumb. It was thick and white, and a bit sticky, rather like…

White face paint. The sort of paint ladies and gentlemen used to achieve the perfectly white skin considered fashionable some years earlier. No one had much use for it anymore, now that a more natural look had taken precedence.

Unless…

Cecilia stared down at her white fingertips, her heart rushing into her throat. Unless one was a white ghost, and then it might prove very useful, indeed.

But she didn't have time to consider it now. She turned her attention back to the secret door. A quick twist of her wrist revealed it to be, as she'd hoped, unlocked. It creaked open, but beyond was a darkness so thick Cecilia couldn't see a thing. It was cold, too, terribly cold, with walls of damp stone.

It was a passageway. Cecilia's heart pounded with dread at the thought of being trapped inside it, but she wasn't going to turn coward now. It was so narrow and so low she was forced to duck to pass through. It seemed to her as though she crept along it for miles, but it likely wasn't more than ten minutes before a thin line of weak light appeared ahead.

A few dozen steps more, and she came to a steep stone staircase, and embedded in the stone ceiling above them was a wooden plank fitted with an iron ring that served as a makeshift handle. A thin strip of light peeked around the edges, and as she drew nearer, Cecilia saw it was open just a crack, and a branch stuck into the gap to keep it from slamming shut again.

Cecilia heaved it up the rest of the way, and with a little cry threw one arm up to shade her eyes. She knew at once it led outside, because the snow was still falling. The cold drops landed on the bare skin of her hands and neck, and the wind whipped her hair around her head.

It wasn't terribly bright, the sky being dark with snow, but after the tunnel it took a few moments for Cecilia's eyes to adjust. Once they did, she knew where she was at first glance.

She'd come out just beyond the wall that surrounded the kitchen garden. From here one could easily disappear into the rose walk without being seen, and from there to the edge of the tree line and into the woods beyond. She fell back a bit, stumbling on the step as the pieces of the puzzle clicked suddenly into place.

Of course. The mysterious lantern light weaving among the trees in the wood, the White Lady with her filmy gown, scarlet lips, and pale face, who always appeared near the tree line, and then seemed to disappear as if into thin air when she neared the kitchen garden. The Darlington Castle ghost, the specter all of Edenbridge believed to float on air and vanish at will, was making use of a secret passageway leading from the edge of the rose walk into the castle.

A secret passageway only a person who'd spent a great deal of time at Darlington Castle could possibly know about. Not Gideon, who'd only come to live here after his brother's death.

No, someone else. Someone who knew every inch of Darlington Castle, and every hidden door leading into and out of it. Someone who was in a position to have a key to those doors, and might unlock them at will, just as she pleased.

Someone like Lady Leanora.

Cecilia swept her gaze over her surroundings again, and noticed something else.

Footprints in the snow.

Not just human footprints, but neat little paw prints, of the sort that might belong to a dainty, fastidious feline who'd found a secret way into Darlington Castle that led from the kitchen garden, past the stillroom, and straight to...

Cassandra's bedchamber.

There was a hidden door that led from the secret passageway into Cassandra's bedchamber—there had to be. That was why it was always so cold in there. It must be in the dressing room. Perhaps behind the clothes press?

Cecilia's shaking fingers clenched into fists as everything fell into place at once. Lady Leanora had brought the blue ball gown, the embroidered shoes and the sapphire hairpins into Cassandra's bedchamber. They *hadn't* been there all along, as Cecilia had thought, and Gideon hadn't put them there.

Lady Leanora had had the run of the castle from the very start.

It was the only explanation, and it explained everything. Seraphina's mysterious comings and goings , for one, but it was more than that.

The secret passageway was the means by which someone had accessed Cassandra's sick room without anyone else in the castle knowing she was there.

Gideon wasn't the only person who'd brought Cassandra refreshment in those last months before she died. He was simply the only one who'd been *seen* doing so. All the while, someone else—someone who wished to see Cassandra and her unborn child harmed—had also had access to her.

It would have been the easiest thing in the world for that person to bring Cassandra a cup of pennyroyal tea every night, and stay with her while she drank it down. A person Cassandra believed would never hurt her, despite the resentment between them.

A person she trusted, like her cousin, Lady Leanora.

The last person in the world she should have trusted.

Lady Leanora was far more dangerous than Gideon suspected. She was a murderer, and all the time they'd thought themselves safe, she'd been roaming about the castle. Why, she might have snatched Isabella at any time, carried her off while they slept—

She might have, but she hadn't. Fear clawed at Cecilia's throat as the full force of this truth slammed into her. If Lady Leanora hadn't returned to Darlington Castle to take Isabella, why *had* she returned? Who did she intend to hurt this time?

There was no time to consider it now. She had to find Gideon. Cecilia snatched at the iron ring to close the door, but she stopped it from slamming shut at the last minute.

Something else caught her eye, something…strange.

She'd been staring at the footprints in the snow all this time, but she hadn't made sense of what she was seeing until now. Seraphina's tidy little paw prints were marching in a neat line *away* from the castle. They pointed toward the wood, but the corresponding human prints in the snow pointed in the other direction.

Into the castle.

Lady Leanora must have entered the castle last night, after the snow had accumulated enough to make her footprints visible. But unless she truly *was* a ghost, and had found a way to walk in the snow without leaving any prints, then she hadn't come back out this way again.

Which meant…Lady Leanora was *inside* the castle.

Inside with Duncan, Isabella, Amy, and Mrs. Briggs, and they had no idea she was there.

Dear God. She had to get them out at once, while at the same time doing all she could to keep Lady Leanora *in*, just long enough for Gideon to be found. Lady Leanora would try and escape through the passageway, but if it were sealed, and she became trapped…

It would put an end to the White Lady haunting Darlington Castle.

Cecilia turned and fled back down the passageway, her footsteps echoing on the stone floor. She was breathless by the time she burst back through the door into the stillroom and ran into the kitchen. In a stroke of good luck, Duncan was sitting at the kitchen table, stuffing a piece of buttered bread into his mouth.

"Duncan, thank goodness!" Cecilia fell against the table, panting.

"Miss Cecilia, ye near scared the life out of me!" Duncan shot to his feet, his eyes going wide. "What's wrong? Ye look peculiar, like ye seen a ghost."

"Not yet, but perhaps soon, with any luck. Come with me." Cecilia took him by the arm and dragged him to the back of the stillroom, where the crates were stacked near the open door. "Listen to me carefully, Duncan. There's a passageway on the other side of this door. Follow it to the end, and you'll find a door set into the ceiling. It's held open with a branch. Go through that door, and see to it it's sealed from the outside. Once you've done that, go and find Gid—that is, Lord Darlington, and bring him back to the castle at once. Tell him it's urgent."

Duncan gaped at her with his mouth open. "But—"

"Quickly, Duncan."

Whatever Duncan saw on her face made him snap his mouth closed. He turned without a word and disappeared into the passageway at a run. Cecilia bolted the door behind him, cutting off access to the stillroom, then ran for the stairs.

Isabella and Amy were likely in Isabella's bedchamber, readying for her nap, and Mrs. Briggs...she hadn't the vaguest idea where Mrs. Briggs was. She could be anywhere in this enormous castle. If she was alone, and Lady Leanora caught her unawares...

Cecilia sucked in a ragged breath, panic threatening, but she shoved it down, and forced herself to focus on one thing at a time. First, she'd find Isabella and Amy. Once she did, Amy could help her push the clothes press in Cassandra's dressing room flush against the wall to block that escape into the secret passageway. Then they'd find Mrs. Briggs and leave the castle together. With any luck, Duncan would return with Gideon soon afterward, and all would be well.

She rushed up the stairs to the second-floor landing, but stopped there, a strange feeling sweeping over her. Later, she wouldn't be able to say if she'd simply sensed something was amiss, or if she'd heard something, nor would she recall making her way down the corridor to Cassandra's bedchamber.

But she *would* remember the sickening drop of her stomach when she opened the door.

The White Lady was hovering in the archway that led to Cassandra's dressing room, the candle in her hand casting a pool of light around her, lending an unearthly glow to her painted face. She wore the white gown the villagers had described, her dark hair hidden beneath a silvery-white wig.

But it wasn't her gown or her wig or even her ghostly white face that caught Cecilia's attention. It was her blue eyes, as cold as ice, and glittering with madness.

A blinding diamond, so bright it hurt to look at her—

"Good evening, Cecilia. It's kind of you to come, rather than making me search for you." Lady Leanora's scarlet lips split into an arrogant smile. "Then again, you are a *servant*, after all."

Cecilia couldn't have said why, but instinct urged her to drop into a respectful curtsy. "Good evening, Lady Leanora."

Lady Leanora's blue eyes flashed. "I'm the sixth Marchioness of Darlington, and mother to the future heir, while *you*...you're nothing but Gideon's whore."

Cecilia's head snapped back at the ugly words. Lady Leanora *knew* Gideon had taken Cecilia to his bed? Oh God, had she seen them together? Had she *watched?*

"Did you think I didn't know?" Lady Leanora's red lips curled in a sneer. "I confess I was fooled at first. I didn't realize Gideon wasn't in love with that foolish Honeywell creature until after I chased her off. It's been you all along, hasn't it?"

Cecilia opened her mouth to reply, but no words came out.

"The trouble with you, Cecilia, is you won't *leave*," Leanora went on, edging closer to Cassandra's bed as she spoke. "I thought a night spent freezing in the kitchen garden would do it, but you're cleverer than that Honeywell chit, and you found a way out. You understand, then, that I have to find another way to get rid of you."

With that, Leanora lowered her arm, and casually, as if she were buckling her shoes, she touched the candle flame to Cassandra's coverlet.

"*No!*" Cecilia screamed, but before she could move, before she even had a chance to draw a breath, the heavy silk coverlet caught fire.

"Oh, yes, I'm afraid so." Leanora turned to the windows, and brought the candle within inches of the drapes.

"Wait!" Cecilia thrust her hands out in front of her. "I'll leave Darlington Castle, just as you want."

"No, I don't think so. I don't believe you will, and in any case, it's too late for—" Lady Leanora broke off, her gaze darting to the door.

Cecilia dimly registered the sound of feet pounding in the hallway. The lock on Cassandra's door rattled, and in the next moment someone threw the door open. "Cecilia! What in the world—"

"Don't come any closer, Amy." Cecilia never took her eyes off Lady Leanora, but she held out her hand behind her, a warning to Amy to stay back. "Fetch Isabella and Mrs. Briggs, and leave the castle."

"No! I can't...I won't leave you—"

"Listen to me, Amy." Cecilia heard the thread of hysteria in Amy's voice, and struggled to keep her own voice calm. "You and Mrs. Briggs must take Isabella out of the castle *at once*. Do you understand me? I'll be right behind you."

Amy was sobbing now, but after a pause in which Cecilia prayed harder than she'd ever prayed before, she heard Amy's retreating footsteps, and a door being thrown open at the other end of the hallway.

"See? Clever, just as I said." Lady Leanora's smile was strangely benevolent, but her eyes were pure, blue ice as she hovered the lit end of the taper inches away from the silk drapes. "I think it's best if we keep this business between us."

Chapter Twenty-four

"What will you do with yourself, once we've caught your ghost, Darlington?" Haslemere blew on his gloved hands to warm them, releasing a cloud of frosty breath. "Kent will be dull enough without a haunting to keep you busy."

They'd ridden out early to the northernmost edge of the grounds in search of the ghost. Gideon didn't expect they'd find her so far from the castle, but this morning they'd sent Haslemere's men out in pairs to search the western, eastern, and southern borders of the property nonetheless, with orders to reconvene at the edge of the forest this afternoon.

By the time the sun set this evening, not a single acre of Darlington earth would remain unturned. If the White Lady was on his grounds, they'd find her. Gideon released a breath, some of the tension in his shoulders easing as they neared the tree line leading to the formal grounds. The closer he remained to the castle and its inhabitants, the easier he was.

He turned to Haslemere with a shrug. "I've had enough excitement these past few months." A ghost, a haunted castle, a broken engagement, and a heart full of love, beating once again. "The duller Kent is, the better."

"Oh, I imagine you'll find *some* way to pass the time." Haslemere darted a sly glance at Gideon. "Tell me, how does Cecilia do this morning, Darlington? She's recovered from last night's ordeal, I hope?"

More than recovered, judging by her, ah…enthusiasm this morning. Gideon's cock ached every time he thought of her soft lips and the brush of her hair against his skin. So he did his best not to think of her, as he didn't choose to spend a day in the saddle battling a persistent erection. "She seemed well enough. I only saw her for a moment."

Haslemere snorted. "A memorable moment, by the looks of you today."

"I have no idea what you mean," Gideon replied, pinching his lips together. There were times when Haslemere's acute powers of perception were a great nuisance.

"Not a thing." Haslemere gave an innocent shrug. "Unless it's that you're a damned fool if you don't declare your love for her, make her your marchioness, and be done with it, that's all."

A half-hearted protest rose to Gideon's lips. Not because he didn't intend to make Cecilia his marchioness, but because *she* should be the first person to hear him say it, not Haslemere. "I wasn't going to—"

"Of course, you were. For God's sake, Darlington. Do you think I don't recognize that absurd, besotted expression on your face?" Haslemere laughed. "We've known each other since Eton."

"You're a bloody menace, Haslemere. You do know that?"

"I'm aware, yes. It's good fun, being a menace."

Gideon's lips twitched. "Your talents are wasted in Kent. London must miss their most dashing rake by now. I thought I'd take Cecilia there, after we're married." He was looking forward to exploring the city with her. He used to love London, before he became the Murderous Marquess. Perhaps if he saw it through Cecilia's eyes, he could learn to love it again. "She's never been."

Haslemere shot him an uneasy look. "Yes, er…about that, Darlington."

Gideon frowned. "What is it?"

"Well, the thing is…damn it, this is deuced awkward, Darlington, but Cecilia is…that is, she isn't *quite* who you imagined she—"

"Lord Darlington!"

Gideon was staring at Haslemere, but now he snapped his head around, his brow furrowing. That had sounded like Duncan's voice, but he'd given explicit orders for Duncan to remain at Darlington Castle today—

"Lord Darlington," the voice called again. "My lord, wait!"

Gideon caught a glimpse of red hair, and alarm rose in his chest. It *was* Duncan, in the last place he should be, galloping toward them from the direction of the castle, waving his hat over his head to catch Gideon's attention. "Something's wrong, Haslemere."

"Miss Cecilia sent me," Duncan panted, leaning over his horse's neck and struggling to catch his breath. "She bid me to fetch you at once, my lord. There's something amiss up at the castle, and—"

"Christ, Darlington. Look."

Gideon turned at the cold dread in Haslemere's voice, and found his friend staring at the castle in horror. "What? I don't see—" But in the next breath he *did* see, and his heart gave a sickening lurch in his chest. Smoke was issuing in a thin, black stream from one of the second floor windows.

Cassandra's bedchamber window. Her apartments—the apartments attached to Cecilia and Isabella's bedchamber—were on fire. For a frozen moment Gideon could only gape at that ominous thread of smoke, his throat working. "Where is everyone, Duncan? Are they—"

"They've all gotten out, my lord. I looked back when I rode off to fetch ye, and I saw them all gathered on the drive."

Gideon snatched up Duncan's reins, jerking his horse closer so he could look directly into Duncan's eyes. "*All of them*? Are you absolutely certain of it, Duncan?"

Duncan swallowed. "I didna get a close look, but I-I think so, my lord."

"Fetch the rest of your men, Haslemere, and bring them back to the castle to help us fight the blaze."

Haslemere shot off in the direction of the woods, snow and bits of torn ground flying from his horse's hooves. Gideon took off toward the castle at a flat run, Duncan right behind him, but the castle seemed to recede into the distance with his horse's every stride. His gaze was locked on the window, his lips moving in a prayer to a God who'd taken his wife and son from him—a God Gideon believed had long ago forsaken him.

Please. Please don't take them, too.

As they drew closer, he began counting heads, the frantic prayers still pouring from his lips. Mrs. Briggs, and Amy, with Isabella clutched in her arms, and Fraser beside her, yes, they were there, four of them were there, but—

Cecilia. She was missing.

Gideon leapt from his horse before he'd brought him to a stop. "Cecilia? Where is she?"

Amy whirled around at the sound of his voice. She was sobbing as if her heart were torn apart, tears streaming down her cheeks. "The White Lady! S-she's got Cecilia trapped with her in Lady Cassandra's bedchamber! I didn't want to leave her there, my lord, b-but she begged me to get Isabella and Mrs. Briggs out—"

Gideon didn't wait to hear more, but burst through the doorway and into the entrance hall. The fire hadn't spread to the ground floor, and there wasn't much smoke yet. Wild hope flared in his chest. There was still time to get Cecilia out.

The White Lady's got Cecilia trapped...

But there was no White Lady. She was an illusion, a ghost born from a rumor, the rumor born from lies, lies told by those who didn't understand the truth could be far uglier than the worst thing their imaginations could conjure.

He'd known Leanora would come back, despite her promises to stay away. From the moment she first set foot in Darlington Castle she'd been unpredictable, selfish, and vindictive, and she'd only grown more bitter and resentful with each year that passed. He'd known she'd stay away only as long as it suited her to do so, and not a moment longer.

How had she found her way into the castle? Had she been wandering his hallways all this time? All these nights he and Haslemere had spent searching the grounds, hour upon hour roaming the darkness—had it been a fool's errand?

Gideon raised a shaking hand to his face, trying not to think about the damage Leanora could have done while he'd been out chasing her ghost.

He slowed his steps to a crawl when he reached the second floor landing and crept silently down the corridor. The stench of burning—of a life going up in flames grew stronger as he neared Cassandra's bedchamber. Wisps of smoke were drifting from the narrow crack under the door, and he heard female voices.

One was Cecilia's. The other...

It had been months since Gideon had heard it, but he knew that chilly voice, the sharp edges of it that cut like broken glass. Leanora had ruined Nathanial with that voice—chased him from Kent back to London. Even then he hadn't truly escaped her, and now...

Now she'd turned it on Cecilia.

Gideon's hands fisted with the effort it took not to crash through the door and throw himself between Cecilia and Leanora, but he had no idea what was happening inside that bedchamber. If he startled Leanora, it might lead to disaster. So, instead he crept to his own bedchamber, then through the connecting door into Isabella and Cecilia's room.

The haze of smoke was thicker here, and there was an ominous crackling sound coming from the other side of the door, as if flames were licking up the drapes or burning through the carpet.

And above it, Cecilia's voice, threaded with panic.

The door between the two rooms should have been locked, but the latch turned easily in Gideon's hand. He eased it open, just a crack at first, then wider, wide enough for him to slip through, and...

He froze on the threshold, panic swelling in his chest.

The coverlet spread over the bed was on fire, and the heavy silk window drapes were smoldering. If the walls hadn't been made of stone, the bits of charred silk and the showers of sparks raining down would have set them ablaze already, and there would have been nothing left of the bedchamber. Even now, if a stray spark should catch the bed hangings, it would only be a matter of time before the carved wooden posts went up in flames.

In the middle of this nightmare stood Cecilia, the hems of her work dress scorched and ragged, as if she'd been stomping down flames. Facing her, dressed in a white gown and wig, her face painted a ghastly white stood Leonora, waving a candle in her hand threateningly, as if she were about to hurl it onto the bed.

Both women noticed him at the same time.

"Gideon." Cecilia took a quick step toward him.

He'd never seen her so pale, and her fear tore at his heart, but he turned all his attention on Leonora, circling her warily. "Back so soon, Leonora? I'm surprised to see you here again."

Leonora threw her head back in a laugh. "Come now, Gideon. We're old friends, aren't we? You knew I'd return to Darlington Castle to take back what's mine. Why pretend otherwise?"

"What's *yours*? I don't know what you mean." Gideon edged closer, one cautious step at a time, his body tensed to spring. "Don't you remember, Leonora? You gave Isabella up to me in exchange for thousands of pounds and your freedom. She's no longer yours. If you think you're going to claim her now, you're very much mistaken."

"*Isabella*?" Leonora waved a hand, as if Isabella were an insect she was swatting away. "Isabella is of no use to me. A daughter does me no good, and we both know she isn't Nathanial's child."   ‘

Cecilia choked on a gasp, but Gideon kept his gaze on Leonora, fury and fear burning through him. "You don't deserve Isabella, Leonora. You never did."

"No, I deserve a great deal *better* than her! I was the belle of my season. Not a single young lady in London could compare to me. I should have had *everything*, but instead I was cursed with a husband who couldn't father an heir! Nathanial was never going to give me a son, but you can make up for your brother's shortcomings."

"Is this a seduction, then?" Gideon let out a mocking laugh, his gaze darting between Leonora's face and the candle in her hand. "I can't say I'm much tempted. What's become of the Marquess of Aviemore, Leonora? Does he approve of his betrothed attempting to seduce her brother-in-law?"

Leonora paled at mention of Aviemore. "Aviemore hasn't anything to do with it. *My* son will be the future heir of the Darlington title and fortunes.

Mine. not Cassandra's, not Fanny Honeywell's, and not your housemaid's, no matter if you are fool enough to marry her."

Gideon slowly shook his head. "It's too late, Leanora. Nathanial is gone, and you're no longer the Marchioness of Darlington."

Leanora laughed again, a high-pitched, feral shriek. "Oh, but I will be again. You and I will wed, and *our* son will inherit the title and fortunes. Yours, and mine."

"*Wed*?" Gideon stared at her in shock. Leanora's sanity had always been tenuous, and now her last shred of reason had fled. "You and I will *never* marry, Leanora. It would be blasphemy for you to wed your late husband's brother."

Leanora's blue eyes, still so beautiful, burned with madness. "I deserve a husband who can give me a son. I don't care which Darlington brother fathers the heir, as long as he's *my* son."

An incredulous laugh tore from Gideon's lips. "You have a strange idea of courtship. Dressing up in a white gown and wig and play acting at being a ghost?"

"I didn't invent the White Lady." Leanora's fingers tightened around the candle. "The gossips in Edenbridge are responsible for *her*. Some fool saw me in the woods and started the rumor. I simply turned it to account by dressing the part. I don't deny she served me well. She frightened off your bride, didn't she?"

"That's why you came back, then. To get rid of Miss Honeywell." Gideon had suspected Leanora wanted to put an end to his betrothal, but to find she'd done so because she believed he'd marry *her* was unbearable, as if he'd been sucked into a nightmare.

"I didn't expect to have to return at all. I never thought you'd find another bride after I turned you into the Murderous Marquess." A hysterical laugh spilled from Leanora's scarlet lips. "I should have known there'd be some witless girl eager enough to marry a wealthy nobleman, even if he's rumored to be a monster."

Cecilia gasped. "*You!* You started those rumors? You turned your brother-in-law into a murderer, and your own cousin into a ghost?"

Leanora shot her a look of malicious glee. "Well, I couldn't let him marry Miss Honeywell, could I? You're going to marry *me*, Gideon. It's the only way to ensure my son becomes the heir."

"Marry you?" Gideon's laugh was bitter. "I can't stand to look at you. Go back to Aviemore, Leanora. Become his marchioness, and give him a son and heir. You'll get nowhere with me."

Underneath the thick layer of white paint, Leanora's cheeks burned. "I'm afraid that's impossible. Aviemore's gone."

"Gone?" Gideon stared at her. "Jesus, Leanora. What have you done?"

"I've done only what I had to do." A strange look crossed Leanora's face. "And you see, I did the right thing. If I'd permitted Cassandra to give birth, *her* son would have become the Marquess of Darlington."

Gideon went cold at her words, so cold and numb he couldn't breathe. *If I'd permitted Cassandra to give birth...*

He sifted frantically through his memories of the months of Cassandra's illness, but his brain was sluggish with shock. All he could recall were flickering visions, each one more heartbreaking than the last. Cassandra, too ill to eat, growing weaker by the day, and his son, his eyes forever closed, laying on his dead mother's breast, and blood...

Blood everywhere.

Gideon lifted his gaze to Leanora's stark face, her fevered blue eyes, her livid lips. If Leanora's madness had driven her to hurt Cassandra, there was nothing she wouldn't risk, nothing she wouldn't do.

"Go, Cecilia," he choked out, smoke searing his lungs. The drapes were engulfed in flames now, and they were devouring everything in their path. Cassandra's mahogany dressing table would be next, and soon the carpet would catch. "Out the hallway door, now."

Cecilia was gasping for air, but she didn't move. "*No.* I won't go without you."

"Cecilia, please." Gideon glanced away from Leanora for an instant. "I'm begging you."

But Cecilia didn't meet his gaze. She was watching Leanora over his shoulder. "You can't escape down the passageway, my lady. I've had it blocked at the other end."

Gideon jerked around and saw Leanora was skirting the edge of the bed, moving toward Cassandra's dressing room at the far corner of the bedchamber. Her arm was raised, as if she were prepared at any moment to light the bed hangings on fire.

"You're risking your own safety as well as ours." Cecilia was tracking the movement of the candle in Leanora's hand. "I'm telling you the truth, my lady. There's no longer a way out that way."

"The truth?" Leanora spat. "Do you suppose I'd believe a whore?" She pointed a shaking finger at Cecilia. "I know you were in his bed last night. I *saw* you."

The color drained from Cecilia's face, but she held her hand out to Leanora. "Neither Lord Darlington nor I want to see you get hurt, my lady. There's still time for us all to get out the hallway door. Give his lordship the candle."

Soon it would no longer matter whether Leanora lit the bed hangings on fire or not. The bedchamber was almost entirely engulfed in flames, the smoke growing thicker by the moment. Gideon held out his hand to Leanora, beckoning with his fingers. "Give me the candle, Leanora."

Leanora backed away from him. Gideon tensed, about to leap on her and tackle her to the floor when Leanora let out an inhuman shriek that made the hair on his neck stand on end, and touched the lit end of the candle to the fragile silk bed hangings. They caught at once, and within seconds the flames were crawling up the carved wooden bed posts to the canopy above.

"No!" Gideon made another grab for Leanora, but it was too late. The candle fell to the floor behind the bed. Gideon prayed the flame was snuffed out before it dropped, but a second later the thick carpet under their feet caught fire.

Leanora whirled around and… somehow vanished into the clouds of smoke billowing toward the ceiling, as if she truly were a ghost.

Gideon stared with his brain frozen in shock. He took a step toward the empty place where she'd been moments before, but Cecilia grabbed his arm. She was shouting something at him, but Gideon couldn't hear what she said over the roar of the fire. Something about a blocked passageway, and getting trapped inside the castle.

"Gideon!" Cecilia clawed at his arm. "Listen to me!"

He jerked his attention back to her, dazed, but as he stared into her dark eyes, the fog dissolved, and his brain snapped back into focus.

Cecilia. The only thing that mattered now was Cecilia.

Without a word, he swept Cecilia into his arms, but just as he turned toward the door leading into the hallway, the beam above exploded in a shower of sparks, then collapsed to the floor with a thundering crash.

Their only hope now was to flee through Cecilia's bedchamber. The connecting door itself was on fire, the hungry flames devouring the wood, but for the moment, the beam was still sound. Gideon rushed toward it, and with Cecilia still in his arms, kicked the burning door open and flew through it.

"Isabella!" Cecilia screamed. She struggled to get free as they ran through her bedchamber, but Gideon held her fast. "She's safe."

The flames hadn't reached this room yet, but the smoke was so thick Gideon could hardly make out the door. He staggered in that direction, his head going dizzy as his lungs burned for air, but just as he was certain he couldn't take another step—that he'd fall to his knees—he was through the door and into the hallway, Cecilia clutched in his arms.

They were both choking and gagging on the smoke, but Gideon kept running, the fire at his back and a desperate prayer on his lips. He ran down the stairs and through the entrance hall, sucking in breath after greedy breath as they left the worst of the smoke behind them.

His eyes were burning and stinging, but as he stumbled through the entrance hall, he could see Mrs. Briggs, Amy, and Isabella on the other side of the door. Duncan and Fraser stood behind them, and Haslemere and his men were just thundering up the drive, Haslemere's face as white as death.

Gideon burst through the door, and a shout went up when they staggered onto the drive. He fell to his knees, still clasping Cecilia against his chest. A second shout went up—Haslemere and the men—and then everyone was rushing upon them at once.

Gideon didn't know how long they sat there in the drive with everyone crowding around them. All he knew was he had Cecilia in his arms, and she was holding him tightly against her, as if nothing in the world could ever make her let him go.

Chapter Twenty-five

Lady Leanora, the sixth Marchioness of Darlington and Edenbridge's notorious White Lady, died in the fire at Darlington Castle, overcome by the smoke billowing into the secret passageway.

Alerted by the smoke pouring into the sky, a group of men from Edenbridge arrived at the castle soon after Cecilia and Gideon escaped, and worked alongside Gideon, Haslemere, and their men to battle the fire. By dawn the following morning the flames were out, but the entire eastern wing of the castle where Cassandra's bedchamber had been had collapsed into rubble.

Cecilia, Amy, and Mrs. Briggs were sent to the Dower house with Isabella, who, after a warm bath and much petting and soothing, had at last been coaxed into bed. Amy took a bed in the same room so she could comfort her if she woke.

Mrs. Briggs made up beds for herself and Cecilia on the same floor, but neither of them retired. Cecilia had been standing at the window in the front parlor since they arrived at the Dower house, gripping the windowsill with white knuckles.

"Go to bed, Cecilia." Mrs. Briggs stood behind her, wringing her hands. "You need to rest, child."

Rest. There'd be no rest for her until the truth was known. Not just the truth about Lady Leanora, but the wicked, ugly truths behind all of Darlington Castle's secrets. Lady Leanora's perfidy, Cassandra's death, Gideon's innocence, and the truth about Cecilia herself.

The truth about the lies she'd told.

She wanted to blurt it all out to Mrs. Briggs, to unburden herself with a confession and weep on that motherly shoulder, but Gideon had to be the first to hear those truths.

Cecilia pasted a trembling smile on her lips and turned to face Mrs. Briggs. "You go ahead, Mrs. Briggs. I, ah…I need to have a word with Lord Darlington before I retire." Gideon would come to her. Sooner or later, he'd come, and when he did, she'd tell him everything. Until then, there was nothing for her to do but wait.

Mrs. Briggs studied Cecilia in silence before taking both her hands. "A fire is a terrible thing. I used to live in fear Darlington Castle would burn one day, but now the worst has happened, I see it as a chance to start anew."

"A chance for who, Mrs. Briggs? Not Lady Cassandra, and not her infant son." Cecilia wanted with all her heart to believe hope could rise from the ashes, but the frightened, defeated part of her wondered how one could overcome such devastation, such loss.

"For Lord Darlington, Cecilia." Mrs. Briggs squeezed her hands. "He's a young man, one I hope will have years of happiness ahead of him. He never deserved to suffer as he has."

"No, he didn't." Angry tears flooded Cecilia's eyes. An innocent man who'd borne unimaginable loss, then been victimized a second time by his own sister-in-law, someone he should have been able to trust.

The Murderous Marquess. Whatever else happened between her and Gideon, Cecilia would see to it that malicious slur was consigned to the flames. If nothing else, she could do that for him.

"Oh, my dear." Mrs. Briggs patted Cecilia's cheek. "It will be all right in the end. You'll see. Now, promise me you'll rest after you've spoken to Lord Darlington."

Cecilia swiped the tears from her cheeks. "I will."

"Good girl." Mrs. Briggs didn't say any more, but left Cecilia alone by the window, waiting.

By the time Gideon appeared hours later, the haze of smoke rising from the charred remains of Darlington Castle had turned the sky above a steely gray. Underneath the ashes and soot, his face was pale and lined with exhaustion.

He paused in the parlor doorway when he saw her. "Is everyone all right?"

"Yes. Isabella is sleeping. Amy is with her, and Mrs. Briggs in a nearby bedchamber. Duncan and Fraser, and Lord Haslemere and his men—"

"Ready to collapse, but otherwise well enough. Duncan and Fraser will stay in the gamekeeper's cottage until the castle is habitable again." He gave a short laugh. "If it ever is. Perhaps I'll leave it in ruins."

Cecilia flinched at the bitterness in his voice. "Gideon—"

"Haslemere and his men are returning to Surrey later this afternoon. There's no reason for them to stay, now our ghost is gone. No place for them, either."

The mystery of the White Lady had been laid to rest, yes, but what of the other secrets, the nightmares hidden inside the stone walls of Darlington Castle? Only Cecilia knew the truth of what Lady Leanora had done. How could she tell Gideon his beloved wife and child had been sent to early graves by his brother's mad wife?

As gently as I can, one word at a time.

Cecilia drew in a deep breath. "You knew about Isabella all along? That she wasn't your brother's daughter?"

Gideon dragged a hand through his hair. "Yes. Isabella doesn't look a thing like my brother, but she does bear a striking resemblance to Darlington Castle's former steward."

The hazel eyes.

"If Isabella had been a boy, I've no doubt Leanora would have tried to pass him off as the heir. Nathanial knew everything, of course. He was hardly at Darlington Castle at all in the month Isabella was conceived. It didn't matter to him—he loved her with all his heart—but all the love in the world won't save Isabella from scandal if the truth of her birth is revealed."

Cecilia thought of Isabella's bright eyes, her lively mind, and sunny smile, and her heart sank in her chest. It broke her heart such a beautiful, loving child as Isabella should suffer for her heartless mother's sins.

"Why didn't you tell me?" Cecilia asked quietly, trying to hide her hurt.

"I've never revealed Isabella's secrets to anyone, Cecilia. Only Haslemere knows the truth. Isabella will bear the brunt of Leanora's betrayal of my brother, and now she'll be made to bear the shame of her mother's madness. I thought only of protecting her."

"From me, Gideon? You thought you had to protect Isabella from *me*?"

Gideon flinched at the question, but he met her gaze. "I know you'd never hurt Isabella, but I also know you're keeping secrets from me, Cecilia. You're no housemaid, are you? You didn't come to Darlington Castle to polish silver and scrub floors. Even so, I still trusted you with my own secrets. But I couldn't trust you with Isabella's when I don't know who you really are."

His words tore into Cecilia, claws raking across her heart, but what could she say in reply? Weeks ago, when she'd first arrived at Darlington Castle, Gideon had called her a liar, and he was right. As much as she'd grown to love Isabella, she had no claim on her secrets.

When she didn't answer, Gideon turned toward the window, away from her. "Leanora has always been selfish and unpredictable. She was a spoiled belle when she and Nathanial first married, and over the years she's grown more unstable, and more volatile. I knew she was unbalanced, but this...I never imagined she'd go this far."

"But you did suspect she'd come back someday." Cecilia pushed the words through numb lips. "That's why you turned the sitting room into Isabella's bedchamber, and put Amy in there with her. To protect Isabella from Lady Leanora."

"I thought Leanora would try and take Isabella away from me, yes. Not because she wanted her. Isabella has never been more than a means to an end for Leanora. She would have ruined her if given the chance."

The thought of Lady Leanora having control over Isabella chilled Cecilia to her bones. "Is that why you sent her away from Darlington Castle? To protect Isabella?"

"I never sent her away. A few weeks after Cassandra's death, Leanora came to me demanding money so she could escape Darlington Castle for a new life as a merry widow. I agreed to give her the funds she demanded, but only if she left Isabella behind with me. A few months later, she was betrothed to Aviemore, and I hoped we'd seen the last of her. God only knows what's happened to him." Gideon's blue eyes were bleak. "Leanora didn't put up much of a fight over leaving Isabella."

"She didn't come back for Isabella. She's been roaming freely through the castle since she returned to Edenbridge. If she'd wanted Isabella, she could have taken her at any time." Cecilia swallowed. "She came for *you*."

"As if I could *ever*...she was my brother's *wife*, and Leanora expected me to..." Gideon's hands clenched into fists. "Leanora never gave her daughter a second thought. Her *own child*. All those months I lived in fear she'd take her from me, but she never wanted Isabella."

A half-sob tore from Cecilia's throat at the despair in his voice. She reached for him to caress his cheek with her fingertips, but he flinched away from her. "Tell me about the secret passageway."

Lady Leanora's body had been found outside the locked stillroom door, her fingernails torn and bloody from clawing to get out. "One end of it lets out into the dressing room in Cassandra's bedchamber. From there, she could get anywhere inside the castle. I kept wondering why the door between Isabella's and Cassandra's rooms were always unlocked, despite your orders. Leanora must have had a key."

Gideon braced his arms against the windowsill, his head dropping down between his shoulders. "This would have broken Nathanial's heart."

"All those vicious rumors, all those lies about the Murderous Marquess." Cecilia knew Leanora was responsible—she'd said so herself—but even so she could hardly believe anyone could be so hateful. "How *could* she have done such a thing?"

"Far more easily than you'd ever imagine." Gideon turned to face her, a bitter laugh on his lips. "I know what Leanora is. I've always known. As soon as I knew she was the White Lady, I should have realized what she was capable of. God knows what she might have done, who else she might have hurt—"

"You tried to stop her, Gideon. You and Lord Haslemere spent every night for weeks searching the grounds for her. This isn't your fault." Unable to stop herself, Cecilia rushed to him and took his face in her hands. "Leanora's madness, the things she did…how could anyone imagine she'd go so far?"

"How far did she go, Cecilia?" Gideon took Cecilia's wrists in his hands and jerked them away from his face. "Her madness may have ended with the fire, but it didn't begin there, did it?"

Cecilia choked back the sob that rose in her throat. She didn't want to tell him, didn't want to be the one to put this ugliness in his head, but Gideon deserved to know the truth. "No."

"Cassandra, and my son. Did she…did she hurt them?"

Cecilia pressed her face against his chest, inhaling the scent of smoke, ash, and burnt wood that clung to him. "Yes."

He went still, not speaking, hardly seeming to breathe, but then he took her shoulders in his hands and eased her away from him so he could look into her eyes. "Tell me all of it."

Cecilia gazed up into his wounded blue eyes, and knew she was about to break both their hearts. His, because he'd blame himself for Cassandra's death, and hers, because she'd broken his. But she hadn't any choice. "Isabella pointed out some flowers to me, growing against a back wall in the kitchen garden. She said they smelled like her Aunt Cassandra. I thought it was lavender, but it had a strong scent of spearmint. At the time, I didn't think anything of it."

Gideon nodded, but his face was white. "Go on."

"The night I got locked in the kitchen garden—I didn't go out there to fetch my sketchbook. I went because of a conversation I had with Mrs. Briggs. She told me Cassandra couldn't eat during her illness, that she could only take a little broth and some spearmint tea."

"Spearmint tea? No. I gave her broth, but I never brought her spearmint tea."

"No, you didn't." Cecilia pressed her palm to his face to make him look at her. "Lady Leanora did."

Gideon shook his head. "That doesn't make any sense. Leanora detests sickrooms. She never went near Cassandra during her illness."

"She did, Gideon, but no one in the castle knew it because she entered Cassandra's bedchamber through the hidden passageway."

"Spearmint tea, stolen keys, and secret passageways?" Gideon tried to pull away from her. "It sounds absurd, like something you'd read in a Gothic horror novel."

Cecilia held him fast. "Listen to me, Gideon. Until today, you didn't know the secret passageway was there, did you?"

He closed his eyes and blew out a breath. "No."

"No. No one did, not even Mrs. Briggs. There was no reason you should have known unless you'd grown up at Darlington Castle. Then you might have discovered it. But Leanora was mistress of the castle for eight years, and occupied the marchioness's apartments. No doubt she stumbled across it then."

Gideon stared down at her, and his face twisted with pain. "Why would Leanora sneak through a secret passageway to give Cassandra spearmint tea?"

He knew the answer already, but he was fighting so desperately against it his entire body was shaking. He didn't want to know this secret, didn't want to have this knowledge in his head, or his heart. But ignorance wouldn't lead him to happiness or forgiveness, only more darkness.

"It wasn't spearmint tea, Gideon," Cecilia whispered. "The plant I thought was lavender wasn't lavender at all. It was pennyroyal."

"Pennyroyal?" He laughed, but it was a desperate, pleading sound. "You mean the herb Mrs. Briggs uses in the salve that soothes insect bites? Well, what of it? It's harmless enough."

"Not to ladies who are with child, Gideon. It brings on bleeding, and can be used to…" Cecilia swallowed, wishing with everything inside her she didn't have to say it. "To expel a child from the womb. I-I believe Leanora was brewing it into a tea, and giving it to Cassandra."

He stared down at her in horror, then jerked away with such violence Cecilia stumbled forward a few steps. "You can't know this for sure, Cecilia. That day in the kitchen garden with Isabella, you told me you didn't know anything about flowers and plants."

"After Mrs. Briggs mentioned the spearmint tea, I went into the kitchen garden and picked the pennyroyal," Cecilia said, struggling to stay calm. "The next day, after we…after you left the castle, I searched through a copy of *Culpeper's Complete Herbal* in your library until I found the illustration that matched the plants I'd picked."

Gideon said nothing, but he backed away from her as if afraid she'd try and touch him again. Cecilia followed him, unable to choke back the truth any longer. "I already suspected Cassandra had been poisoned, even before Mrs. Briggs mentioned the spearmint tea."

His shoulders stiffened. "How could you?"

"I found Cassandra's diary on the bottom shelf of her clothes press." It occurred to Cecilia to tell him about Seraphina, and the unusual way in which she'd led Cecilia to the diary, but strangely enough, it felt private, as if she'd be betraying Seraphina if she did.

Or perhaps not Seraphina so much as...*Cassandra.*

"You read my wife's private diary?"

The shard of ice in his voice pierced Cecilia's chest and lodged in her heart, but she and Gideon were long past denials now. "Yes. Her description of her illness seemed strange to me. I became convinced she'd been poisoned, and once I found the secret passageway, I realized Lady Leanora must have done it."

Gideon's face was as blank as a stone, and the blue eyes that had looked at her with such heat just hours before had turned as cold as ice. "Who are you? You're no ordinary housemaid, that's certain. Is your name even Cecilia Gilchrist?"

Cecilia twisted her hands in her soot-stained skirts. This was the moment she'd been dreading, but there was nothing for her to do now but face it. "My name is Cecilia Gilchrist, but I'm not a housemaid, and I didn't come here from Stoneleigh. I live in London, at the Clifford School, with Lady Amanda Clifford. Lady Clifford is—"

"I know who Lady Clifford is, and I know what she does." Gideon's voice was hard, flat. "She sent you to Darlington Castle to prove I'm the Murderous Marquess all of London believes me to be."

It hadn't been as simple as that, but Cecilia didn't try and explain herself. "She sent me to find out how Lady Cassandra died. My task was to uncover the truth before your marriage to Miss Honeywell could take place."

If anything, his eyes grew even colder. "So, I was right about you that first day we met. You *are* a liar."

Cecilia's eyes dropped closed, pain pressing down on her, stealing her breath. She knew the worst of his anger and bitterness wasn't truly directed at her. He was in shock, exhausted and devastated by the fire, and heartbroken over his wife's death all over again. He felt as if he'd failed Cassandra and his son, and was blaming himself for their deaths.

She knew it, but that didn't make it hurt any less.

But she'd told him everything now, just as she'd promised she would. There was no longer any reason for her to remain at Darlington Castle, unless…unless Gideon wanted her here. "The next stagecoach leaves for London in an hour. I'll gather my things together."

She waited, every part of her aching for him to stop her from leaving, to tell her he wanted her to stay with him. To tell her he wanted her at all.

"No. No stagecoach."

Her heart gave a cautious leap, but her hopes were dashed to bits when he added, "My coachman will take you."

Cecilia nodded, her eyes stinging. "Yes, I…all right. Thank you."

He didn't spare her another word or glance, but left the house, closing the door behind him with a finality that echoed in every chamber of Cecilia's empty heart. Within the hour a coach with the Darlington crest pulled up in front of the Dower house. Cecilia just had time to say goodbye to Mrs. Briggs and Amy, and kiss Isabella's forehead, before she found herself huddled in a corner of it and on her way back to London.

Gideon didn't come to bid her goodbye. She didn't see him again.

It was dark when the coach arrived at No. 26 Maddox Street in London's West End. By then Cecilia felt as if she'd been dragged halfway across England. Every part of her ached—her legs, her shoulders, her head—and she was exhausted in a way she never had been before.

In her body, her mind, her heart, and her soul.

She staggered up the stairs of the Clifford School, opened the door, and slipped inside. Perhaps she could sneak upstairs without a word to anyone, pull the coverlet over her head, and fall into a dream where there was no grief, no loss, no fire, and no death.

No icy blue eyes staring down at her as if they'd never seen her before.

But it was not to be. Lady Clifford herself happened to be coming down the hallway from the drawing room just as Cecilia paused in the entryway. "Cecilia? Is that you? My goodness, child! Why didn't you send word? Daniel would have come for you, and…Cecilia? Why, whatever's the matter, dearest?"

Lady Clifford moved closer and took Cecilia's hand, bringing her into the light. When she saw Cecilia's face, her own face fell. "Oh, my dear girl."

She said no more, just opened her arms.

Cecilia dove into them, the tears she'd been holding back since Gideon walked into the Dower house running down her cheeks, slowly at first, like a trickle of water from a cracked dam, then bursting forth with a fury as the dam gave way. Her chest heaved with sobs, because Gideon despised her now, and nothing would ever be right again.

Chapter Twenty-six

Haslemere House, Surrey
One week later

"How long do you intend to keep up this nonsense, Darlington?"

Gideon raised his head in surprise. He'd been staring into the fire, and he hadn't noticed Haslemere enter the library. "I don't know what you mean. What nonsense?"

Haslemere threw himself into the chair opposite Gideon's with an irritable sigh. "This ridiculous pouting over Cecilia Gilchrist. For God's sake, man. Saddle a horse, ride to London, and claim your lady."

"She's not my lady, and I never pout." He brooded occasionally—he'd own to that. Even moped now and again, but pouting was just pathetic, especially over a woman. No matter how soft her skin might be, or how sweet her dark eyes, how intoxicating her kiss—

"Oh, no? You forget how well I know you, Darlington. Remember when you were nineteen, and fancied yourself in love with Caroline Ivy? There was a good deal of besotted mooning then, if I recall. Thankfully it was short-lived, but then you weren't madly in love with *her*."

Gideon let his tumbler drop onto the table beside him, then turned a glower on Haslemere. "Are you implying I'm madly in love with Cecilia, Haslemere?" Just because he couldn't stop thinking of Cecilia, dreaming of her, that didn't mean—

"Implying it?" Haslemere lifted an eyebrow. "I'm not *implying* a bloody thing. I'm declaring it to be so, and asking you what the devil you intend to do about it aside from languishing in my library, brooding like some romantic hero and abusing my crystal."

Gideon set the tumbler upright again with a sigh. "Have I been as bad as all that?"

Haslemere had never been one to indulge a sulk, and he didn't do so now. "No, you've been worse. We both know you're not going to let her go, so why not get her now, and put us both out of our misery?"

"She lied to me, Haslemere."

Haslemere rolled his eyes. "Yes, yes. She lied to you, entered your home under false pretenses, and pretended to be someone she wasn't. What of it? I lied to you, too, and it hasn't stopped you from drinking all my port."

That caught Gideon's attention. "*You* lied to me? When?"

Haslemere dropped his booted feet onto the leather ottoman in front of his chair. "I told you I didn't know who Cecilia Gilchrist was, and I did. The moment I heard her name that first morning, I knew she was one of Lady Clifford's girls."

Gideon gave him an incredulous look. "You *knew*? Why the devil didn't you tell me who she was, then?"

"Because I didn't want you to send her away. Lady Clifford sent Cecilia to find out the truth about Cassandra's death. I knew you didn't murder your wife, so I decided to let Cecilia go about her business and prove you innocent."

"You put a remarkable amount of faith in the Clifford School," Gideon grumbled.

"I had a bit of a tangle with one of Lady Clifford's girls myself—impertinent little chit named Georgiana Harley. Dreadful nuisance of a girl with a tongue that smarts like a whip, but not lacking in wit. She despises me," Haslemere added, an oddly satisfied grin crossing his lips. "In any case, I was right about Cecilia. No one in Edenbridge is calling you the Murderous Marquess anymore, are they?"

It was true. The villagers who'd helped contain the fire had seen Leanora in her white gown and wig when her lifeless body was removed from the castle. The rumors of the notorious White Lady had come to an end after that, and with it the worst of the gossip about the Murderous Marquess.

There would always be people who believed he was guilty—nothing would change that—but there were more of them who believed him innocent now, and they were willing to shame those who continued to spread the rumors.

Cecilia had done that for him, had fought to prove his innocence. She'd kept prodding, kept digging until she got to the truth, so far buried beneath the rubble Gideon had long since despaired of it ever coming to light.

Everything had changed when Cecilia came to Darlington Castle.

It would have been the easiest thing in the world for her to simply declare him guilty and be done with it. Everyone else in England had, and when she arrived at Darlington Castle, she'd had every reason to believe he was a murderer.

But she hadn't. She'd believed in *him*. How many times had he dismissed her from his service? Twice, three times? Yet she'd hung on, and somehow, between dropping the coal scuttle and singing those dreadful lullabies, she'd made everyone love her.

Isabella, Amy and Mrs. Briggs, Duncan and Fraser, and…

Him. She'd made him love her.

Haslemere gave him a reproving look. "In case you've forgotten, Cecilia did just as she was sent to Darlington Castle to do. She uncovered the truth."

Gideon squirmed under the rebuke. He *hadn't* forgotten. How could he? Cecilia had set him free from the vicious rumors that had plagued him since Cassandra's death. The lies she'd told him were nothing against all she'd done for him.

He was in love with her—madly, deeply so. There was only one reason he'd let the woman he adored walk out of his life, and it had nothing to do with a few meaningless lies.

"Let's have it out, shall we, Darlington?" Haslemere's voice was quieter now, and, for all that he disliked coddling the tenderer emotions, gentle. "I told you, you forget how well I know you. You didn't send Cecilia away because she lied to you. Why don't you tell me the real reason?"

Haslemere already knew, of course. He knew Gideon well enough to have guessed it. He'd simply been waiting for Gideon to say it aloud. "Leonora murdered my wife and son, Haslemere. Poisoned them in *our* home, right under my nose."

Haslemere nodded. "Yes."

"I knew who Leonora was, *what* she was. I should have seen what was happening and put a stop to it, but somehow, I didn't. I let my wife and son die."

Haslemere was quiet for a moment, then he said, "Look at me, Darlington."

Gideon looked, half afraid of what he'd see, but Haslemere's face was full of compassion. "You *didn't* know who Leonora was. You knew she was selfish and erratic, even devious, yes, but you didn't know she was mad. You didn't know she was a *murderer*. How could you?"

Gideon wanted it to be true, wanted it more than anything, but he wasn't sure he could ever make himself believe it. "I failed Cassandra, Haslemere. I failed both her and my son. I didn't take care of them. What if...what if I fail Cecilia, too?"

Haslemere let out a deep sigh. "You didn't fail anyone, Darlington. What happened was a tragedy, but it wasn't your fault. Do you think Cassandra would want you to spend the rest of your life alone, punishing yourself for her death?"

"No." After Cecilia left Darlington Castle, Gideon had found what remained of Cassandra's diary buried in the rubble. Most of it had burned in the fire, but he'd read enough of the few singed pages that remained to remind him Cassandra had loved him as much as he'd loved her. His happiness had been as important to her as her own.

Somehow, in all the chaos of her illness and death, he'd forgotten that.

"No. She'd want you to be happy, and for you, Cecilia is happiness. So, I'll ask you again, Darlington. When are you going to put an end to this nonsense?"

Gideon closed his eyes, ready to search inside his heart for the answer, but it was right there already, waiting for him. It had been, all along. Now he'd given himself permission to seize this second chance at happiness he was desperate to get to Cecilia, and couldn't bear to wait another moment. "It ends here, Haslemere. Here, and now."

"You know what, Darlington? I'll join you." Haslemere rubbed his hands together, a sly smile curling his lips. "I've a notion to pay a call on Georgiana Harley. I wouldn't want her to forget about me, now would I?"

* * * *

"If ye didn't think Miss Cecilia was fit to take on Darlington, ye wouldn't have sent her there in the first place." Daniel Brixton folded his massive frame into the seat on the other side of Lady Clifford's desk. "If ye thought her fit, then she's fit."

"Perhaps I miscalculated."

Lady Clifford tapped a finger against her lips, considering it. She'd realized any number of scenarios could play out in this case, including the Marquess of Darlington chasing Cecilia from his castle and right back to London the day she arrived, but she hadn't anticipated *this*. "What does Lord Darlington mean, sending Cecilia back to me with a broken heart?"

Daniel grimaced at that. He didn't believe in broken hearts. "She'll be all right. That lass is as strong as any of the others."

"Yes, she is. Not in the same way, of course. She's always been the tenderest of my girls." It was the very reason Amanda had sent Cecilia to Darlington Castle in the first place. Even now she couldn't regret it, as Cecilia had done just what Amanda hoped she would. Yet she couldn't deny her plan appeared to have gone awry in one respect. "I didn't foresee any romantic entanglements."

Daniel, who also didn't believe in romantic entanglements, let out an irritable grunt. "Aye. Never thought of Darlington as a scoundrel, but I'm not surprised. Marquesses are shifty. Only thing worse than a marquess is a duke."

"To be fair, Daniel, we don't know Lord Darlington *is* a scoundrel. If you recall, most of London thought him a murderer, and he's never been that. Perhaps we should give him the benefit of the doubt."

"Don't see why." Daniel didn't believe in giving anyone the benefit of the doubt, especially a man who dared trifle with one of *his* girls.

Lady Clifford pushed back her chair with a sigh. "Well, at the very least, I think I should have a word with Cecilia. Will you call her down to the drawing room, Daniel? Emma and Georgiana, too. They may as well hear what Cecilia has to say. Perhaps then they'll stop fretting over her."

"Aye, my lady." Daniel did as she asked, then vanished once they were all settled together in the drawing room. Lady Clifford let him go. One of the girls was sure to start weeping, and he couldn't bear it when they wept.

"Ah, here you are, girls. Cecilia, come sit with me, dearest." Lady Clifford held out a hand to Cecilia, who took it gratefully, and settled beside her on the settee. "It's been a week since you returned from Kent. I think it's time we discuss what happened at Darlington Castle."

"What happened?" Georgiana threw her hands up in the air. "We *know* what happened! Cecilia went to Kent, proved Lord Darlington innocent of murder, and he thanked her by breaking her heart, the villain."

Cecilia turned red-rimmed eyes to Georgiana. "That's not what—"

"Now everyone in London is prattling on about how ill-used poor Lord Darlington's been." Georgiana rolled her eyes. "Mind you, these are the same people who spread the rumors in the first place, and called him the Murderous Marquess behind his back."

"They should all beg his pardon." Cecilia's face flushed with anger. "It's a horrible thing to—"

"He may not be the Murderous Marquess, but he's certainly a cold-hearted rake, and that's not much better," Emma declared, sprawling in the chair beside the settee.

Cecilia shook her head. "He's not a rake, Emma. He's—"

"Of course, he's a rake, just like his friend, Lord Haslemere. Dear God, what a pair they are." Georgiana shuddered. "I hope they both stay in Kent, or Surrey, or wherever it is, and we never lay eyes on either of them again."

"Girls, if I could have a word?" Lady Clifford held up a hand, and everyone went silent. "Thank you. Now, I didn't bring you downstairs to discuss Lord Darlington."

Emma sat up. "You didn't?"

"No. As far as Lord Darlington himself is concerned, the matter is closed. You'll have your wish, Georgiana. There's no reason for us to see him, or Lord Haslemere ever again."

"*Never* again?" Georgiana deflated. "Are you certain that's the best...er, what I mean is, I'm vastly relieved to hear it, my lady. *I* certainly haven't got any use for either of them."

Lady Clifford's lips twitched. "Yes, well, our concern is Cecilia, not Lord Darlington or his friend. Cecilia, dearest, do you know why I sent *you* to Darlington Castle, rather than Georgiana or Emma?"

"Yes. Because Georgiana and Emma are both busy with other tasks. Otherwise I'm certain you would rather have sent either of them."

"Indeed, you're wrong. Even if I'd had Georgiana or Emma at my disposal, I still would have sent you."

Cecilia blinked. "*Me?* But why?"

Lady Clifford smiled. "For the same reason I always choose to send any one of you over the others. Because you were the best suited to this particular task."

"But I'm the worst one of all of us! I mean...well, you know what I mean, my lady. I'm too soft-hearted, too romantic, too apt to try and find reasons to excuse someone rather than think the worst of them."

Lady Clifford sighed. "My dear child, you're not 'too' anything. You're just as you should be. You rely on your emotional intelligence to make decisions about what's true and what's not. You were the same as a child, you know. It never ceases to amaze me, how well you can read people. Your instincts are unparalleled."

"Yes, that's true." Georgiana gave Cecilia's hand a fond squeeze. "You're the shrewdest of all of us that way. I've often remarked it."

Emma was nodding. "You are. It's quite unusual, I think, for a person to be as empathetic as you are, Cecilia. You have a gift for putting yourself in another's place."

Cecilia looked around at them, horrified. "But…but that's horrible!"

"Horrible?" Lady Clifford raised an eyebrow. "My dear girl, why should that be horrible?"

"Because I'm supposed to be clever and logical like Georgiana, and…" Cecilia waved her hands about, searching for words. "Brave and shrewd like Sophia, and wily and cunning like Emma. I'm not supposed to be…*me*."

Both Emma and Georgiana stared at her, flabbergasted. "But that's nonsense!" Georgiana managed at last. "Why, you should be just who you are."

"Of course, you should," Emma exclaimed. "You're perfect just as you are, Cecilia."

"It's rare for a person, especially one as young as you, to read others so accurately, Cecilia," Lady Clifford said. "I don't mean to say you're illogical, or discard evidence and facts. I only mean you're apt to give your instincts equal weight. You're right to rely on them as you do."

"But I still don't understand why you sent *me* to Darlington Castle, my lady. I let my emotions overrule my better judgment when it came to Lord Darlington. If he'd been guilty—"

"But he *isn't* guilty. If he had been, you would have found him so."

Tears gathered in Cecilia's eyes. "You don't understand. All the evidence pointed to his guilt, yet I kept refusing to accept it."

"Precisely." Lady Clifford smiled at Cecilia's expression. "You only prove my point, dearest. Remember, Lord Darlington is *innocent*. He has been all along. Your instincts told you that, and so you kept prodding, even when the evidence pointed to his guilt. That's how you discovered the truth. I never believed Lord Darlington was guilty. That man's no murderer. Indeed, I sent you there to prove him innocent, and that's just what you did."

Cecilia glanced from one beaming face to the next, and a watery smile curved her lips. "I *did* make a terrible nuisance of myself. Gideon—that is, Lord Darlington dismissed me three times."

Lady Clifford laughed. "Did he, indeed?"

"He did. I managed to talk him out of it each time."

"Well done. But I'm afraid he's broken your heart, Cecilia, and I *am* sorry for that." Lady Clifford's smile faded. "I didn't anticipate that would happen. Perhaps I should have."

Cecilia lay her head on Lady Clifford's shoulder. "I'll be all right."

But tears started to her eyes again, and Emma, seeing them, leapt up from her chair and squeezed onto the settee on Cecilia's other side. "Don't cry, Cecilia."

Georgiana rose as well, but before she could squeeze in next to them, there was a loud knock on the entryway door. "What spectacularly bad timing." She glanced at the mantelpiece clock with a frown. "Who's calling at this hour? I'll go, and send them away."

* * * *

Gideon tensed as the echo of footsteps marching down the corridor met his ears. He'd spent the carriage ride from Surrey to London imagining Cecilia would turn him away at the door. Now the moment had come, he was caught in a purgatory of hope and dread.

But it wasn't Cecilia who flung open the door. It was a tall, cross-looking young lady, her mouth already open as if she were ready to launch into a lecture, but she snapped it shut again when she saw Gideon and Haslemere standing there.

Whoever she'd been expecting to find on her doorstep, it wasn't *them*.

"Miss Harley. What a tremendous pleasure it is to see you again." Haslemere swept his hat off his head and offered her a bow too extravagant to be anything other than mocking. "I hardly recognized you with your mouth closed. Last time I saw you, you were shouting at me."

Miss Harley recovered quickly from her shock. "Indeed. Well, Lord Haslemere, I'd be pleased to shout at you again, if you like. I'm certain you've done *something* to deserve it."

"Likely as not." Haslemere gave her a devilish grin. "Not that it matters much. You were perfectly willing to shout at me the last time we met, and I hadn't done anything wicked."

Miss Harley snorted. "Don't be so modest, my lord. You might not have done the thing I thought you had, but I'm certain you'd committed a number of other sins unworthy of a gentleman that day. Choose one of those."

Haslemere chuckled. "You bring out my ungentlemanly side." He braced an arm against the door and leaned in, which put him much closer to Miss Harley than was proper. "I wonder why that is?"

She drew in a breath, as if preparing to deal Haslemere the set-down he deserved, but before she could say a word, Gideon cleared his throat. "I beg your pardon, Miss Harley, but may we come inside? I'd like very much to have a word with Cec...Miss Gilchrist."

She turned to him in surprise, as if she hadn't even noticed he was there. "Lord Darlington." Her gaze was cool as she considered him, but he must have looked as miserable as he felt, because she sighed. "Oh, very well, if you must. I'll ask Cecilia if she'll see you." She stepped away from the door so they could enter, but cast a dark look at Haslemere. "Wait here."

"Good Lord, Haslemere," Gideon muttered, when she was out of sight. "What did you do to make her so cross with you?"

Haslemere's eyes were glinting with humor. "Nothing much, I assure you. She's just remarkably bad-tempered. I like her immensely."

Gideon didn't get a chance to answer, because Miss Harley was coming back down the hallway toward them, and behind her...

His heart leapt, hope and love and anxiety all tangling together in his chest. "Cecilia." He removed his hat, clutching it in his hands as he took a step toward her. "I...I beg your pardon for calling at such an hour. I miss... that is, Isabella misses you."

Haslemere snorted, and Miss Harley turned a quelling eye on him. "Despite my strenuous objections, Lord Haslemere, Lady Clifford says I must bring you to the drawing room for refreshments. Cecilia, go along with Lord Darlington to Lady Clifford's parlor."

She gave Cecilia an encouraging smile, then turned to Haslemere with a grimace. "Come on then, my lord, and do try your best not to behave like an utter savage, won't you?"

Cecilia waited until Georgiana and Haslemere were gone, then she glanced up at Gideon from under dark eyelashes. "This way, Lord Darlington."

He followed her down to a cozy parlor tucked at the back of the house overlooking a small, neat garden. He closed the door behind him, then stood there awkwardly, staring at her. "Is it Lord Darlington now, Cecilia? Not Gideon any longer?"

Her cheeks flushed scarlet. "I didn't mean to cause offense, Lord Darlington. I wasn't sure—"

"I know you're not sure, and I'm so sorry for that, sweetheart." Gideon drew closer, close enough so he could see the faint light from the hallway shining in her dark eyes.

God, he loved those eyes, loved every part of her.

He took her hand in his. "There are so many things I want to say to you, but first, I want to thank you for what you did for me. I never thanked you, that last day at Darlington Castle, and it was unforgivable of me. It's haunted me ever since."

"You don't have to thank me, Gideon. I only did what Lady Clifford asked me to do. You don't owe me anything, no matter what we..." She dropped her gaze. "You don't owe me anything. So, if that's why you're here—"

He touched a fingertip to her lips to quiet her. "It's not why I'm here. I'm here because I love you, Cecilia. I'm madly in love with you."

She was quiet for a moment before raising her gaze to his. "You...you still love me?"

"I never stopped loving you, Cecilia, and it's not because you saved me, or proved my innocence." Gideon took her hand and pressed a dozen tiny, ardent kisses on her palm. "I've loved you since the first day I met you, when you scolded me for being ungentlemanly, and told me I didn't look fashionable enough to be a marquess."

Her lips parted in surprise. "You fell in love with me because I was rude and impertinent and refused to leave when you dismissed me?"

Gideon laughed softly. "No, sweetheart. I fell in love with you because you told me the truth, and reminded me I'd once been a better man than the man I'd become. I fell in love with you because you dropped the coal scuttle in my bedchamber and shook me awake, and I've been awake ever since, and because you sing bawdy songs to Isabella, and because you love and protect her. I fell in love with you because you believed in me, Cecilia. Do you still believe in me?"

"Yes," she whispered. "I've always believed in you, Gideon."

He tipped her chin up and gazed into her eyes. "Can you forgive me for letting you go, and for hurting you? I never should have said those things to you. I was cruel, and worse, I was a coward."

"You weren't a coward." Her dark eyes turned fierce. "You were afraid, Gideon. It's not the same."

"I was afraid, yes. Afraid I wasn't worthy of you, or that I'd fail you somehow, but I'm not afraid of anything anymore, except losing you, Cecilia. I can't lose you, sweetheart."

"You haven't lost me, Gideon," Cecilia whispered, laying her hand on his chest. "I'm right here."

Love and gratitude swelled inside Gideon, nearly bringing him to his knees. He leaned closer, hovering his lips over hers. "May I kiss you?"

"Yes." She gave him a shy smile. "I really think you must."

It started as a sweet, chaste kiss, but her scent and the taste of her soft mouth soon had him wild. He swept his tongue between her parted lips with a groan, and she returned his kisses with a passion that set his blood on fire. "You told me you loved me once, Cecilia," he murmured. "Do you love me still?"

"Yes," she choked out on a sob. "So much, Gideon."

He slid his lips down her throat, groaning when she arched her neck in offering. "Marry me, Cecilia. Become my marchioness. Come back to Darlington Castle with me, and help Isabella and me make it a home again."

"Yes." She pressed closer, stroking the skin at the back of his neck until he eased away from her, afraid her teasing caresses would drive him so mad he'd forget himself.

"Does Isabella truly miss me?" Cecilia asked, when he drew away.

Gideon traced his thumb over her lower lip. "Very much, yes. Every day she demands to know when you're coming back, and every night she becomes cross with me because I don't know all the words to 'The Fair Maid of Islington.'"

Cecilia laughed. "Oh, dear. I'll teach it to you, if you like."

"I would," he whispered, touching his forehead to hers. "I'd like it more than anything."

Epilogue

Darlington Castle, Edenbridge
Three months later

The sunrise peeked through the canopy of trees, dappling the patch of ground with its gentle rays. Cecilia sat with her knees drawn up and her head resting on top of them, enjoying the warmth on her back and the stillness surrounding her.

"It's different here," she said at last, her quiet voice breaking the lingering silence. She closed her eyes and inhaled the scent of freshly thawed earth and tender new grass, and a wry smile drifted over her lips. "If you'd told me I'd grow to love this place one day, I'd have said you were mad, but it's like another world here in the spring."

She'd taken this same walk every morning for the past week, since she and Gideon had returned to Darlington Castle. They'd intended to remain in London until next year, or at least until the repairs on the eastern wing of the castle were completed, but...well, it was strange the way one grew to love a place—to long for it, even when the joyful memories were inextricably tied to the tragic ones.

"But it's never too late, is it?" Cecilia turned her head, pillowing her cheek on her knees, and opened her eyes. "Never too late to make more happy memories."

A soft breeze caught her words and carried them into the trees above, waking the birds dozing on the branches, who began a startled warbling.

"He's happy again." Cecilia raised the bouquet of white roses in her hand to her nose, breathed in their sweet scent, then nestled them at the base of the white marble headstone beside her. "Not in the same way he was when he was yours, but happy still. You gave that chance to him…to *us*. Neither of us will ever forget that, Cassandra. We won't ever forget you."

Cecilia remained where she was for a while longer, then rose to her feet and dusted the dirt from the back of her dress, anxious to return to Gideon. She'd left him sleeping peacefully in their bed, and she already missed him. If he woke and found her gone, he'd come in search of her, and she'd miss the chance to wrap herself around him and lose herself in his warm, sleepy body.

"Until tomorrow then, Cassandra." Cecilia paused for an instant to run her palm over the cool, smooth marble before she turned back toward the Dower House. She and Gideon were staying there until Darlington Castle was repaired, along with Isabella and Mrs. Briggs. Duncan and Amy, who'd married in the early spring were nearby in the gamekeeper's cottage.

Cecilia paused, a smile curving her lips, because she knew what she'd find before she even turned around. Or, not so much *what*, as *who*. "Ah, here you are again. I did wonder when you'd turn up." She retraced her steps and knelt down in front of Cassandra's headstone. "I don't suppose it would do me any good to ask how you manage to always appear out of nowhere, would it?"

Seraphina wasn't any more forthcoming than she'd ever been, but she presented her glossy head to Cecilia and allowed herself to be petted and admired before curling into a tidy ball beside Cassandra's grave and commencing a loud, contented purring.

"As mysterious as ever," Cecilia murmured, scratching behind Seraphina's ears. "But then perhaps it's just as well if you keep your secrets."

It was still early when Cecilia arrived back at the Dower House. She entered quietly, pausing to listen, but there wasn't a sound to be heard yet—not the patter of Isabella's running footsteps, or the low voices of Amy and Mrs. Briggs, chatting amiably as they lit the fire in the kitchen.

The morning was still hers and Gideon's, just as she'd hoped.

Cecilia was careful to remain as silent as possible as she made her way up the stairs and crept down the hallway to the bedchamber she shared with her husband, her heart leaping with the joy she always felt when he was near.

It was a joy that belonged only to Gideon. It was his alone.

He was asleep still, his dark hair tousled against his pillow, the sheet low around his hips, his bare chest rising and falling in deep, even breaths. Cecilia tiptoed across the room, making quick work of shedding her dress and chemise as she went. She lifted the coverlet and slid into bed beside

Gideon, who turned instinctively toward her and gathered her into his arms before his eyes were even open.

"Mmmm." He nuzzled his face into her neck and smiled against her skin. "You smell like sunshine."

He smelled like everything she loved—sleep, and warm masculine skin, and *Gideon*, but Cecilia didn't say so. Instead she wrapped her arms around his neck, dropped a kiss onto his disheveled head, and murmured, "Shhh. Go back to sleep."

A growl left his chest, but if Cecilia thought it was a growl of agreement, she soon found out otherwise when Gideon opened his mouth against her neck, and his hand slid up her body to cup her breast. "I'm not tired," he whispered, stroking her nipple with his thumb, teasing it to hardness.

Cecilia closed her eyes on a gasp, her head arching back against the pillow. "I am. You kept me up half the night, if you recall."

"Is that a complaint, love?" Gideon nibbled his way from her neck to her throat, pausing to press a kiss to the hollow there before raising his head, a playful smile on his lips. "Because I can stop."

"Can you?" Cecilia gave a lock of his hair a gentle tug. "That's not the impression I had last night."

"Mmmm. It's your own fault, Lady Darlington." He stroked a fingertip down her cheek, his gaze holding hers. "Even if I kept you in my bed forever, I'd never have enough of you."

"Forever is a long time, my lord," Cecilia teased, but she took his hand and pressed a kiss to his fingertip, tenderness for him swelling in her heart.

Gideon leaned forward and took her lips in a kiss so perfect Cecilia's eyes stung with the sweetness of it. "Not long enough, my lady. Never long enough."

Author's Notes

The term "mudlarks" refers to the impoverished children who scavenged in the mud of the River Thames during low tide, searching for items to sell.

Hever Castle, Anne Boleyn's childhood home in Edenbridge, Kent, features a double portcullis and moat, and is the inspiration for Darlington Castle. https://www.hevercastle.co.uk/.

John Rann, a highwayman in the mid-eighteenth century, was renowned for his charm and gentlemanly demeanor. He was executed in London in 1774. Debra Kelly. "10 Highwaymen Who Gallantly Terrorized Britain." June 21, 2014. https://listverse.com/2014/03/23/10-highwaymen-who-gallantly-terrorized-britain/.

"Death and the Lady." Printed on a broadside by J. Deacon between 1683 and 1700 as *The Great Messenger of Mortality, or a Dialogue betwixt Death and a Lady. The Penguin Book of English Folk Songs.* Edited by Ralph Vaughan Williams and A.L. Lloyd. Baltimore: Penguin Books, 1968. Originally published 1959. Lyrics and the music available at http://www.contemplator.com/england/death.html.

Marriage to one's in-laws was not technically illegal in England until the Marriage Act of 1835. Regina Jeffers. "A Voidable Marriage in History: Marrying the Sister of One's Late Wife or the Brother of One's Late Husband." February 26, 2018.

Mozart's Piano Sonata No. 16 in C is a beginner's piece sometimes known as *Sonata Facile* or *Sonata Semplice.* https://en.wikipedia.org/wiki/Piano_Sonata_No._16_(Mozart).

"Down Among the Dead' is an English drinking song first published in 1728 in *The Dancing Master,* but it may be older in origin. The song's blatant references to sexual activity and drunkenness make it singularly inappropriate for drawing-room entertainment. https://en.wikipedia.org/wiki/Down_Among_the_Dead_Men_(song).

For information on the symptoms and effects of pennyroyal poisoning, see https://www.cardiosmart.org/Healthwise/d044/79/d04479.

Nicholas Culpeper's herbal compendium was first published by Peter Cole in Cornhill in 1652 as *The English Physitian*, then republished the following year as *The Complete Herbal and English Physician.*

Lady Leanora would not have been known as the Dowager Marchioness of Darlington, because the new peer is her husband's younger brother, and not her husband's descendent: "A widow of a peer may be called dowager only if (a) her husband bore the title and (b) the current peer is a direct descendant of her deceased husband." In other words, "**A dowager peeress is the mother, stepmother, or grandmother of the reigning peer, and the widow of a preceding one. In no other case is she a dowager.**" *Titles and Forms of Address: A Guide to their Correct Use.* London: A. & C. Black Ltd., Third Edition, 1932. Accessed via Chinet.com. https://www.chinet.com/~laura/html/titles09.html.

Printed in the United States
by Baker & Taylor Publisher Services